D1564030

THE

UNFORGIVEN

KING

L. M. AFFROSSMAN

To Jim, Margaret, Aileen and my beloved Panda,
who still believe in the beauty of words.

It is probable that, if Josephus had another written account at his disposal in addition to the writings of Nicolas, it was hostile to Herod: this would help to explain the contradictory assessments of Herod's character and motives scattered throughout the narrative.

The Life of Herod

Translation from the Greek ©John Gregory 1998

Introduction and other critical material J. M Dent 1998

Hasmonaean Family tree, 67 BCE – 29 BCE

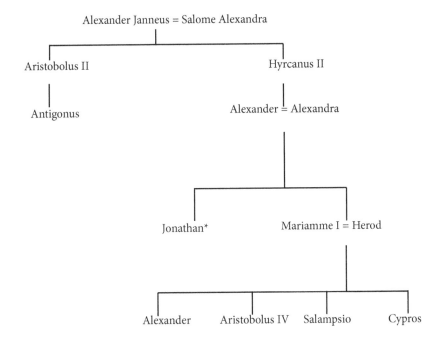

Herod Family tree (two generations only)

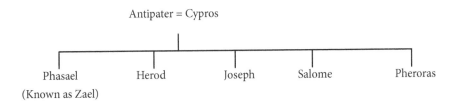

* Jonathan was allegedly the Hebrew name of Mariamme's brother, Aristobolus III. It is used throughtout the book to avoid confusion between characters with identical or similar names.

Contents

Part III- The Queen of Heaven

Part I

The Woman In The Shadows

1

In which some things are revealed and others not

I SEE YOU! *No, don't be afraid. After all, this is not a virtuous house, and you hardly imagine that you're my first. Yes indeed, there have been others. Some coming nervously, their guilty hands shaking, their lips tingling with the taste of forbidden fruit. Others, filled with savage desire, like Pharaoh in the days of our bondage, consumed by the age-old lust to possess, tearing me open, spreading me wide.*

Always they come. And, like you, their eyes are too bright, their breath, hot and rapid, quivering in the dry air, moist with expectation. O, I feel the hungry looks you cast upon me. But you need not worry. I don't flatter myself that I am the object of your interest. Not yet.

And, after all, this is not my story, at least not to begin with. Certainly, I have my part to play, but, initially, I will be your guide. I will lead you through this world, so very different to yours it might be from a book of myths. But this is no morality tale; don't expect the good and the pure to be there taking a bow in the final act. Many innocents will die before this story is over. Though they won't be the ones you are expecting. And the son of God has less to fear in this world than the sons of man. But why waste time? We both know why you are here. You want to see the monster.

Quickly now. Only a little further. He's lying there, just beyond the curtains. So still. He might be a statue set there by a pagan devotee. His ears are dead to the chanting of the priests. He does not rise, save for the dry rattle that shakes his lungs.

What's this, hesitation? How can you bear to have come so close yet not take that final step? Come. Don't be afraid. I've felt it too, that tingling in the breast, the lips suddenly dry, a pricking of the thumbs. Draw closer. That sound? It's the beating of your heart. The beast lies there, only inches away. He is near death, choking on the fumes of myrrh that thicken the air. And there, weeping at the foot of the bed, is scheming Salome.

You recognise the name? But you are wrong. This is not the woman immortalized by a thousand artists, their members growing stiffer than their brushes, as they try to capture the moment when a young girl swaps her virtue for a prophet's head. This woman is far from being a maid; she has danced before no royal personage. Yet there's blood on her hands. She is the ancestor of the lascivious girl, who sways in your imagination. And the only king of the Jews she knows is her dying brother.

Ah, I can see I am making you uncomfortable. You did not expect to be addressed directly. O, I know you'll pretend this isn't real, that we cannot possibly be conversing. Yet I am older, wiser. I know there is more than one way to commune with the dead.

But now it's time to make your choice. Stay with me forever or cast me aside. Which will it be? I can promise you that my road is not an easy one. Before we reach the end two dynasties will fall, their heads rolling, like the great stone heads of idols toppled by the followers of a jealous god. And all along the way, the bleached bones of kings and queens will litter our path. QUI PETIT ALTA NIMIS, RETRO LAPSUS PONITUR IMIS. *So the ineluctable pride of kings comes before a fall.*

But you're intrigued I can tell. In your mind's eye you see diadems of silver and gold glinting beneath the fierce sun of the East. Strain your ears and the thunder of hooves and shouts of battle can be heard in the distance. **Slaughter and blood and the choking groans of men.** *It is a piercing sound. So much death. The crows fly in great swooping circles across this story.*

And always there is that yearning at passion hinted darkly, that strange communion between the sexes, which cannot be contained by the fragile temple of a ribcage, but explodes in violent constellations of stars, raining down fire, consuming worlds. You want to see it, to be a part of it, if only from behind the shield of my skirts. Well, grasp them tightly. You wouldn't last a minute left out here on your own. Now close your eyes and take a breath. It's time to go. But first the warning, given too late. Don't expect to leave unscathed.

You don't know me at all, but I can read you like an open book.

JERUSALEM 47BCE

Open your eyes. Take a moment to blink and shake off the dust of decades. You understand that you are somewhere new? Gone is the thick, choking smoke, the chanting priests with their stink of death, the dying king with his belly full of worms. This room is opulent, the fat Doric columns painted cinnabar to their midpoint, then finished in a glaze of malachite green. At their tops the echinae and astragals are noted in gold leaf to match the gold threadwork on the drapes. But despite all the conspicuous pomp, it is not a king's room. And the man, who sits behind the marble-topped desk, his veined hands drumming on the veined surface of the stone, is not a king, but he does have the king's ear.

It is fear of losing that ear that clouds his face now.

A pause. The room grows hotter. Pools of golden light shimmer on the mosaic floor. And just when you feel your attention slipping, it comes. The knock. Knuckles rapping insistently against wood. A slave opens the door then quickly pulls back to allow the entry of a young man. And the story begins…

His legs were long, and it took him only three paces to reach the desk, to face his father. It was not his place to speak first, but he let his defiance be known in the firm placing of his feet, the tension in the hands clasped behind his back.

He was not obviously or immediately this man's son. The clean-shaven planes of his face, the restrained cut of his tunic and a dozen other subtle clues, set him out as a citizen of Rome. He would not have looked out of place on the streets of Capua or Apollonia or marching along the Via Appia in the great capital itself. But he was not a Roman, and the clues of his features were as subtle and manifold as those of his garb. The sloping cheekbones and the aquiline nose belonged to a desert people, gifts from his Nabataean mother, while the man, staring up at him across the desk was clearly the source of the black hair and tapering brows, the long limbs, which had scrambled up the mountainous regions of Idumaea. Of his eyes, they were his own —or of some distantly forgotten, singular ancestor—dark eyes, intense with the fires of intelligence and ambition burning intensely and misleadingly, black coals hot to the touch.

The man behind the desk got to his feet and leaned forwards on his palms. 'Hordos, what have you done?'

That name? It means nothing to you. Haven't you guessed yet? We're back near the beginning. But you have only known of this man from scholars of the Greek tongue, who named him, Herodes. And later yet, Christian bishops, with their Latinizing habit of dropping the terminating 's', so that he became Herod in the minds of one and all. Very well then. A little magic. We will begin again.

The man behind the desk got to his feet and leaned forwards on his palms. 'Herod, what have you done?'

'What was asked, father.'

'Was it asked that you execute Ezekias and his men?

Herod leaned back on his heels and raised his chin a little. 'I was asked to put down banditry. I put down banditry.'

'You were not asked to take the Law into your own hands.' A forceful stab at a stack of unravelled scrolls. 'The reports. Have you read them? They speak of unrivalled violence, of men cut down as they offered up their swords, of Ezikias' sons begging on their knees— '

He broke off, not recognising this man before him as his son, and recognising it as the moment when he did not recognise his son. 'You acted without the authority of the Sanhedrin.'

'I acted with the authority of Judea's procurator.'

The older man sighed. 'My authority does not exceed that of the Sanhedrin. They will make trouble for us if they can.'

'Then a show of strength will be in our favour.' Herod lent forward, lowering his gaze to meet his father's. 'If you had heard them. All along the Syrian border they celebrated me as the man who brought peace.'

It was an attempt at reconciliation, but it failed. A tightness appeared on the older man's face, features drawn back against the arrogance of that singular remark, ... they celebrated *me*. But this man had not beaten every rival to the procuratorship because he lacked self-control. He reached for a brass goblet and, eyes still on his son, held it at arm's length. 'Boy!'

Here's our cue. Time to enter the action. What is it? What's wrong? Ah, you took me for a woman. Well, there's no mistake. That will come. But for this scene I play the boy, hair cropped, the concave chest of a seven year old. The other slaves know; we're all in on the joke. Batia's daughter who went out one day and came back with a tail between her legs, or at least pretended to. And when my mother saw me she wept because she knew the price a woman must pay for refusing to pay the price of being a woman.

But quickly now, we are called and, in this palace, a member of the Herodian family must be obeyed more quickly even than a king.

His goblet filled, Herod's father sat back down, a firm gesture, a calculating gesture. He took a sip and savoured it, as though the wine told him things his son could not. 'You are to appear before the Grand Sanhedrin.' Herod smiled, and it was the smile he always gave when he felt least like smiling. 'Then I will appear before them.'

'I am glad you feel so at ease.'

'Should I take that as a warning?'

Herod's father closed his eyes for a moment, and when he opened them again his expression was gentler than before. 'My son, these men are dangerous. Do not underestimate them because a few Syrian goat herders cheered you. They trace their ancestry to the time of the patriarchs and they are jealous of their power.'

'Yet their king's family barely traces itself back five generations.'

'That is different. Those men are true Jews.'

'And we? What are we, father?'

Ah, that is the question. The older man pushed his chair back, took another sip of his wine and did not answer.

2

The principal players are introduced

KEEP UP! KEEP UP! *This Herod is young and vital and full of life. The legs that take him down the long, cool corridors, with their whorled mosaics and smoky lights, are long and lean, and it's hard to keep pace with a seven year old's stubby limbs. But he barely notices me. And, of you, nothing at all. You are a* RUAH, *a ghost, a shade.*

He is unsettled by the thought of facing the Grand Sanhedrin, the most prestigious council in the land. Its powerful members have ruled in Judea for centuries, and they do not like Herod's family. Tales of his violence, little enough exaggerated he knows, have given them the bait to lure him in. A slight falter in his step, the beginnings of self-doubt. But he is not used to the sensation, and it hits him with the force of an open assault, as though some blade of special malice has been thrust into his side. He is under attack. He will fight back. But not before he has seen the one person in the world who can never betray him …

Herod slammed through the door so violently it shook in its surround, and this was a door of cedar-wood, thick as a man's wrist and placed there by the king's grandfather. He almost cut in half a small slave boy, who scurried in at his heels, and so greatly startled the young woman, sitting embroidering on a couch near an open window, that she dropped her needlework.

It was a beautiful apartment, although perhaps a trifle old-fashioned in its décor. A few of the embroidered cushions could only be displayed facing a certain way and some of the furniture showed small marks of mishandling. Again, not a king's apartment, but generous enough for the family of the procurator.

Herod's violence took him half way across the room with the undaunted steps of a raiding party commander before he brought himself up short.

'Where is she?'

'Who?'

'Don't play the fool, Salome.' His voice struggled to sound as though he was jesting, and in this he failed so miserably that the girl got up from her couch and ran towards him.

'What is it? What has happened?'

'I am to appear before the Grand Sanhedrin.'

Salome's hand flew to her chest, a plump chest, straining slightly against the restraint of a silk tunic. She lacked the litheness of her brother, taking rather after her small, sturdy paternal grandmother, but for now she was still dewy with youth and unaware how small was her allotted portion of beauty. She reached a hand for her brother's arm. 'What does father say?'

Herod shook her off impatiently. 'What does he ever say?'

'It's hard for him.'

'Hard because he imagines he can get them to like us. You know what they call him behind his back.' Brother and sister looked at each other, but neither voiced what was common knowledge in the corridors and courtyards of the palace. *Idumaean upstart. Kos-worshipping bastard, and worse.* Salome drew back, as though there was disloyalty even in their thoughts then her face brightened. 'Surely the king will help you?'

Herod's bark of laughter sent shivers down the spine. 'Don't be stupid. Hyrcanus is an old man and afraid. His fear of the Sanhedrin is why he brought in an Idumaean, like father, to redress the balance in the first place. But he's starting to realize how much he relies on us, so he fears us now too.'

Salome opened her mouth, as though something was just occurring to her, then closed it again, but Herod had seen it.

'What? What is it?'

'Nothing.'

'No.' His voice dropped and suddenly he was dangerous. 'Not nothing.'

She backed away, but he grasped her wrist. 'Tell me.'

'You're hurting me.'

'Answer me.'

'Only … you are right.' She turned moist, frightened eyes towards him. 'This morning Gedaliah —you know the one, the son of Avram, the Hero of Alexandrium—, always strutting about, as though the palace belonged to him, he muttered 'Idumaean whore' as I walked past. I called him out, and he would not repeat it. But he stood there, smirking at me. O, Herod, the Sanhedrin know that the king is not on our side.'

Something like a shudder went through Herod. He dropped Salome's wrist and pressed the heel of his hand against his eyes. 'This cannot be the end. It cannot end like this.'

'What is this? When does youth talk of endings?' The voice interrupting them was low and harmonious, the Aramaic strangely interspersed with the hiss of exotic sibilants. Herod raised his eyes, but did not speak, and it was left to Salome to say, 'He is to appear before the grand Sanhedrin, mother.'

If Cypros was disturbed by the news she showed no sign. A Nabatean married to an Idumaean living in Judea. She was twice the foreigner in a foreign land, and had long ago learned that there was nothing to be gained in life by revealing too quickly what one was thinking. She sank down on an Aegyptian-style chair —two crescents fastened back to back so that she sat within the convex edge, like the goddess Hathor taking her ease in the dip of the new moon—, and gestured for Herod to join her. He did so, falling to his knees before her, and laying his head on her lap, a gesture never quite shaken from childhood when he would crawl into this same lap to escape some injury or imagined hurt.

Cypros held his face and stroked his brow, and there was something possessive in the way her long fingers caught and held his hair. 'There now. We will think of something.'

She raised her eyes to Salome, who was ostentatiously rubbing her wrist —the redness clearly visible— and mother and daughter shared a look. For an instant Salome was defiant then something seemed to give way. She crumpled, then, pouting, fled the room.

Cypros waited for the door to shut before she spoke again. 'We have reached a dangerous point. I have been expecting this.'

Something in her voice made Herod shift position to look up into the narrow, vulpine face. Still, he spoke despairingly. 'Gedaliah, the Hero of Alexandrium's son, openly insulted Salome. It is obvious that the Sanhedrin feel strong enough to attack father. And I am to be their weapon—' He broke off. 'You know something.'

Cypros glanced at the door then lowered her voice. 'Not a word beyond this chamber.'

Quickly. Into the shadows. In this world you can be invisible if you are a slave, or a ghost, or a woman.

Cypros sighed and did not speak for several moments. Her hands tightened on her son then, suddenly, she let go and sat back. 'Your father is a good man,' she said. 'A brave man, a wise man. Think how he brought us from the obscurity of Idumaea. What were we there? Citizens of a country forced to Judaism by this king's grandfather. Now your father sits second only to Hyrcanus himself.'

At this Herod made a restless gesture. 'I need no lesson in loyalty.'

Swiftly, Cypros reached out and took his chin in a pinching grasp. 'Then it is well that it is not my intention to give one.'

Mother and son stared at each other, but, unlike his sister, there was no bending, no moment of uncertainty that led to inner collapse. Cypros smiled and sat back once more. 'Your father, as I said, is a good and wise man.' Her voice dropped, became harsh and low—wind blowing over sand. 'But he will never, in this life or the one to come, be considered a great man. Your father has chosen to worship only one god, and that god is diplomacy. A weak deity, and one that will forever hold him in second place.' She leaned forward. 'Do you understand my meaning?'

Listening, Herod's expression became tense. There was in him the knowledge that this was the moment when he must choose between being the son of his father or becoming the man that was himself. And also came the knowledge that made the blood drain from his face and his heart pound in his chest, that whatever he chose here, it was the choice between obscurity and destiny, and all must be gambled on a single throw of the dice. He blinked up at his mother. The streaming light from the high, narrow window fell on her skin so that she was suffused with a strange golden glow, almost as though she was embalmed in honey. In the tension of the moment her almond-shaped eyes had fixed on his face, and he knew she was waiting for an answer. His lips parted—

What? What now? Do you imagine you can interrupt when you please? Am I Rahab or Rizpah, Oholah or Oholibah or any one of those named and unnamed, so willing to open up for the right price? And still you persist. How is it possible that I know what Herod is thinking or how he behaved as a child? You want to know what is 'real'. Now there's a question fit for philosophers or children. How Pheroras would have enjoyed it. But no, I will not think of him yet. Though it was he who taught me the mimetic method.

O, must I explain everything? Do you imagine that Homer knew the thoughts of Odysseus or Agamemnon or Penelope? Do you read the blood-soaked words of King Medes, and think that Herodotus sat, pen in hand, in a corner recording infanticide?

No, the biographer cleaves lips and moves tongues because he knows the characters of his work better than they know themselves. A look can tell a writer far more than an ocean of words. We are masters of divination, able to slide beneath the skin of our subject and look out at the world through their eyes. What have I not seen? Words exchanging their meaning in a single glance. A fleeting brush of fingers betraying the bitterest enemies as lovers. Love most warmly protested, veiling a heart filled with the cold desire for vengeance.

I see everything. I am behind the twitching curtain; I am the eye at the keyhole; I am the shadow that never leaves your side.

'He's coming.' *Salome was kneeling on a cushioned bench, and leaning so far out of the window that there was little to see of her, beyond her well-attired rump and the soles of her small, plump feet. (Yes, we have moved on. That is the price of interrupting.)*

'Who is coming?' Pheroras put down the scroll he had been reading and looked towards his sister's backside. Immediately Salome's head shot back into the room. 'Have you no heart? Herod. Herod is coming.'

This made Pheroras blush. The youngest of the brothers, he was in awe of his elder siblings, their ambition, their ruthlessness.

Of the five children, Cypros had jealously guarded along the deadly path of childhood he was most like her in looks —olive-skinned and finely, almost delicately made— yet the least like her in temperament. He lacked the molten core that burned so vividly and irrepressibly in the others, and which they carried, like Cain, as their mark. He was considered, even by himself, as the weakling of the family. And none saw beneath the gentle, scholarly façade to the place where a desperate need for recognition was growing, year on year, in hard nacreous layers, like some ominous pearl. —*Not even I, who saw more than most.*— But, for now, he was eager to placate his sister.

'He is dressed in purple.' Pheroras breathed, awe-struck. 'Like a king.'

16

'You may thank our mother for that. She counselled him to enter the trial with a show of force.'

'He took his men?'

Salome stared at her brother. 'Truly you are a marvel. A fantastic animal with neither eyes to see nor ears to hear. What would have been your fate at the time of the Flood, I wonder? Your head in a book while all the other creatures of the world fled to safety?'

Pheroras' expression became sulky. 'I only thought that when our brother has a hand in something it is usually in the form of a fist.'

Salome arched a brow. (She had recently begun to practice coquetry.) 'Prettily put,' she conceded. 'But no, he took with him only a bodyguard of ten. It would have been unwise to provoke a fight in the presence of so many powerful men.'

'Even so Herod will not easily forgive the insult.'

Herod's voice came out of nothingness behind them. 'Nor will I.'

Startled as cats, Pheroras and Salome turned. Of their brother's approach they had heard nothing. He had come upon them as a miracle, a sudden and powerful presence robed in Tyrian purple, his face already beginning to show the hard, uncompromising lines that the hot winds of Judea uncovered in a certain type of man.

Neither Salome or Pheroras spoke. All their eager questions were held in their widely open eyes, their parted lips. And the sight of them made Herod break into one of his rare shouts of laughter.

'Why the doomed looks? I haven't murdered the Grand Sanhedrin.' (These are words to remember.)

Salome was the first to react. She ran to his arms and embraced him. 'We were afraid for you.'

'Then you can have had little faith in my ability.' The words were playful, but, for those with ears to hear, there was just a hint of displeasure in with the mix. He turned to the small slave hovering near a sideboard covered with plate. 'Here!' And threw his cloak. 'Take it to my chamber.'

You don't want to go. Not when things are just getting interesting. But you are powerless in this world. Did you imagine that, in becoming a slave, there would be a certain erotic thrill? Down on your knees trembling before your master. Delicious little frissons of fear slithering down your spine. What will he do with you?

But you have failed to understand. This world is too far removed from your experience. There is no you. He does not see a person standing meekly before him, eyes downcast. He sees an implement, a tool, an extension of his will. In this world you are only an empty vessel waiting to be filled. When you crack he will throw you away...

But all this talk is indulgence. Set down the cloak and let us return quickly to the action. Before we miss too much.

3

Vengeance is taken

H EROD'S FATHER WAS A MAN of middle height, who often appeared taller than he was. At this moment, pacing across the room, hands clasped behind his back and shoulders hunched, he seemed smaller than usual. As he paced he was watched by his wife, who was reclining on a padded couch, one arm acting as an elegant pedestal to balance her small skull. She gave the impression of being at ease. But a closer inspection revealed a certain tightness at the corners of her mouth, something restless about the eyes, a lioness hunched down, waiting to spring.

'Really, my dear. You worry too much.'

Herod's father stopped pacing and looked squarely at his wife. 'He went to the Sanhedrin dressed as a member of the royal household.'

'He is a member of the royal household.'

'Not a blood relative. He went as someone with an eye to the throne.'

Cypros gave a little shrug, as if to say, Is that really such a bad idea? But Herod's father was in no mood for games. 'You encourage these wild notions. Don't think me blind. Herod and Zael' —*Herod's elder brother was given the name, Phasael. But in the family he is still known by the moniker a lisping two year old Herod bestowed upon him. Besides Cypros likes it. She claims it means strength.*— 'Herod and Zael no longer consider governorships good enough reward for their time in the campaign to free Caesar.'

'Is it wrong for a mother to tell her sons to aim high?'

Herod's father frowned. 'And what do you imagine they can aim for? Do you think the Hasmonaeans will sit by while you advance your children? And what would be the outcome should you win? Can they both sit on the throne? Or perhaps you want to set them at each other's throats, as the king was with his brother.'

Cypros' eyes flicked towards a small slave boy, waiting dutifully nearby a tray laden with jug and goblets in the Etruscan style, then flicked away again as if he were no more than an insect. She lifted a delicate little ivory fan from the table at her side and wafted it to and fro before her throat.

'Really, my dear, you should not give so much credit to court gossip. As you say, our king, Hyrcanus, has both a brother and a grandson to succeed him. The Almighty would work in mysterious ways indeed if he were to set Zael or Herod over the Jews.'

'Yet Herod deliberately provoked them. The mystery is why the king sat there saying nothing, while that Pharisee, Samaias, spoke out on his behalf.' Herod's father wound a finger into the curls of his beard. 'It is said that Samaias not only sided with Herod, but spoke with great passion, telling the Sanhedrin that they should think twice before attacking one whose star was still on the rise, and that the day would come when he would mercilessly punish those who had stood against him.'

'Mysterious indeed.'

Look closely now. Here is a moment when you can catch truth fluttering beneath the skin of the lie. Cypros' fan conceals her mouth, her coolly amused smile. It is no mystery to her why Samaias spoke on Herod's behalf. She knows him to be the follower of Pollio. Pollio is a well-known doctor of the Law, whose disciples come from the most exalted families. They say that his teaching offers such marvellous insights that his disciples cannot help but love and respect him. Trouble is, sometimes he loves them back a little too much. There have been indiscretions, families paid off with coin from Cypros' purse. She did not send her son, dressed in the purple of kings, to face the grand Sanhedrin without knowing that she had first purchased friends to defend him.

Herod's father stares down at his wife, sensing there are things beyond his ken, but he sees only the reclining woman, the clear, steady eyes above the fan. He shrugs. And, as he cannot ascribe duplicity to such fragile flesh, he credits his god with ways too mysterious to comprehend.

As soon as Herod's father left the room Cypros put down her fan. Her thoughts were restless and this made her body grow very still. She lay on her couch with the faraway look of a dreamer or a diviner of strange augers.

One of her women entered and bowed before her mistress. 'Lady, your son has returned.'

Animation sprang back into Cypros' face. 'Bring him. Bring him at once.'

Herod came, his hair perfumed, still wearing the robe of a king. At the sight of him, her eyes glittered, but she said nothing, waiting while he crossed the room and sank to his knees beside her. 'Mother.' He pressed her small hand to his lips. And his touch was enough to make her shiver and stretch her spine, like a satisfied feline.

'My son. My good boy.'

He lifted his eyes, and mother and son shared a look. Cannier than his father, Herod recognised power when he saw it.

'You were with me in the chamber. I felt your presence.'

She stroked his face. 'But the trial is not over?'

'No. Hyrcanus received a letter from the governor of Syria urging him to release me from the charges.'

Cypros smiled. 'Sextus was ever our friend.'

And Herod knew his mother had had a hand in this also.

A sharp knock at the door made mother and son spring apart, guilty as lovers. An elderly slave, a trusted man of the king, entered carrying a letter. This he gave to Cypros and waited silently as she broke the seal and scanned its contents. As she did so the light in her face dimmed, and she glanced up once or twice at the slave, as though trying to determine if the contents of the letter were known to him. Herod leaned forward.

'Mother, what is it?'

But Cypros ignored her son. She folded the letter crisply in two and addressed the slave. 'There is no reply. That will be all.'

Even after the man had gone she remained staring after him. Herod touched her arm. 'Mother?'

She spoke without looking at him. 'Our noble king, Hyrcanus warns you to leave Jerusalem. He fears that he cannot control the Sanhedrin a second time.' Her hand made an angry fist, and she turned to her son brandishing the crumpled letter, as though she was Judith holding up the severed head of Holofernes. 'The spineless old fool has listened to their poisonous talk. But he's afraid to show his hand too readily now that Sextus has waded into the fray.'

Herod was on his feet, heading for the door, before knowing it. 'I'll deal with this.' But his mother's cool voice wrapped itself around him, held him back.

'You'll do no such thing. You will take his advice and flee.'

'Like a whipped dog?'

'Like the clever *strategos*, Samaias, was at pains to paint you. Or have I chosen the wrong son? Should Samaias have diverted them by heaping praise on Zael instead?' She addressed these words to her son's back. And just as well because she could not see the terrible fury that broke across his face, like night opening on to deeper blacker night. 'You prefer Zael?'

The question so quietly spoken, but Cypros too was canny at recognising when the delicate scales of power began to shift. She sprang to her feet and came up softly behind him. 'I prefer you alive.' She put her hand on his shoulder and felt how taut his muscles had become. Then she was close against him that dry desert voice whispering in his ear. 'The Almighty alone knows the trouble we have gone to, trying to win over the nobility. They hated us from the start. And it is only strength that has kept them at bay. They will never accept us. And while your father may choose to bury his head in the sand, you cannot.'

Herod turned, a sharp, swift motion that was the indicator that his anger had gone from fire to ice. 'What would you have me do?'

'Go to Sextus.'

'And put my trust in Romans?'

'Better that, than hope to change the Jews.'

A strange procession of emotions crossed Herod's face, like the sun appearing and disappearing between clouds then, with a strange formality —as though he stood before a resplendent Cleopatra— he bowed, kissed her hand and was gone.

His leaving left something in the room. Cypros sensed it, and it made her restless. For the stretch of an hour, she could not sit down, but paced round the spot where he had stood, knuckles pressed against her lips, casting furtive glances towards his absent form, as though it was ill luck to catch the ghost of the living.

A sudden crash somewhere beyond the door, followed by shouts and the sound of running footsteps. Cypros started then raced out into the corridor. Men's voices, and the high, frightened keening of a terrified woman, rose up one of the four marble stairwells that led down to the shady colonnaded walkways.

In fewer steps than her small frame might have credited, Cypros was at the head of the stairs.

'What is it? What has happened?'

A youth, his face so bruised that it took a moment to recognise him as Gedaliah, the Hero of Alexandrium's son, was lying, head cradled in his mother's lap. The mother, a sharp-faced daughter of an old aristocratic lineage met Cypros' eyes with bright hatred.

'My son has been attacked.'

'No, mother.' He reached weakly for her arm, pushing the rest of what he had to say with difficulty through lips already swelling. 'A fall. Only a fall.'

But she did not believe him, and her eyes held those of the mother of Herod, and demanded, 'Where is he?'

Cypros' face betrayed none of her thoughts. She glanced at the small crowd gathered about the scene —the shocked, excited faces, the whispers behind hands, the knowing looks— and asked, 'Who does she mean?'

'Your son?' Gedaliah's mother hissed. 'Where is your son?'

'Zael has gone with the visitation to Nabatea. And surely you do not mean Joseph or Pheroras.'

At this the face of Gedaliah's mother grew livid. 'Herod. Where is Herod?'

'Herod is not here.'

'Lies!'

Cypros took a single step closer, head tilted as if in concern. 'My dear, it is only natural that grief and shock should perplex you. But Herod has returned to Galilee. I surely need not remind you, that as governor, he is zealous in the pursuit of his duties. We must not forget that it is thanks to him that there is no fear of banditry now in the northern provinces.' With one hand she lifted the hem of her skirt and turned to leave.

'Stay!' Gedaliah's mother was on her feet, pointing a finger at Cypros' back. 'My father is Chief of the Court, and I will have justice. No one will leave until Herod is found.'

Look now. You cannot see her face, but observe how Cypros' grip on the balustrade tightens, the knuckles bleaching to marmoreal whiteness.

Cypros turned, her expression a study of the utmost compassion. 'Of course. We must do everything we can to put this matter to rest. Find Herod at once.'

But the heat of the sun began to cool and the shadows lengthened across the stairs before two slaves, sent to discover the truth, returned with trailing steps and downcast faces. Of Herod no trace was to be found. And several grooms swore that he had ridden with his men bound for Galilee hours ago.

'A trick,' screamed Gedaliah's mother. 'He might have hidden, might have doubled back and lain in wait.' But the whispers at her back began, fluttering round the room, heads were shaken, pitying glances cast.

'Well,' Cypros clapped her hands together lightly. 'Now that you are reassured I am certain you will see no further reason to detain the wife of the Procurator.' She did not look at Gedaliah's mother, but at the faces of the crowd, and her smile was one of gentle patience. 'We will pray for your son's speedy recovery.' Then she turned and walked away, her gaze set firmly ahead. It was clear that the procurator's wife had more important issues to attend.

With the last rustle of her skirts the crowd began to melt away until there was no-one left but the wounded boy and his mother, and a small slave who watched from a corner as the mother put a hand to her temple and began to sway. She seemed to be experiencing the vertiginous sensation of falling, which is how understanding comes that the world is changing. Then even the slave scampered away and they were left quite alone.

Salome's head was bent over her embroidery when Cypros entered the room. There was a sense of preoccupation about her, and she did not look up, but her hands tightened on the embroidery and the stitches pulled too close. Cypros stopped and stared at her daughter, and under that burning gaze Salome slowly dared to raise her eyes.

'Mother, I did not hear—' She faltered, the lie dying away on her lips. Cypros' eyes narrowed.

'It seems you need have no further fear of slights upon your honour. Gedaliah, the Hero of Alexandrium's son, lies gravely wounded at the foot of the south stairwell.'

Salome dropped her needlework and jumped to her feet. Her colour had drained, but her eyes were hot. 'Then Herod, he—'

'Your brother left for Galilee hours ago,' Cypros said sharply. 'He can have had nothing to do with this.'

'I will pray for him.' Salome lowered her head. And this attitude of humiliation she kept, even after Cypros had left the room, so that only a very small slave could see the triumph in her eyes or remember the eager, fond looks she had previously bestowed on Gedaliah or how he had spurned them for the greater beauties of the court.

4

We learn the manner of a king's dying and discover a thing or two

INTERLUDE, 4BCE

*E*NTER NOW, IF YOU DARE, *into the valley of the shadow of death. But, first, cover your nose and mouth. There is a stench here that will cling to you long after you have fled this place, and not even a ghost can leave entirely unscathed.*

There, at the foot of the bed paces Salome, back and forth, casting hateful glances at the physicians. Yesterday she screamed they were quacks and charlatans, and sent them away with threats of having them whipped out of Judea. But during the night the monster's condition worsened, and she called them back, the Jews, the Greeks and even the little Aegyptian. And now they stand, choking in the thick, stale clouds of incense that cannot cover the stench of rotting, pulling on their beards and shaking their heads.

A frightened glance at Salome then one leans forward and inhales the monster's foetid breath, breathing deeply as though it were the sweetest perfume. He nods thoughtfully and confers with his fellows, while another prods the monster's abdomen, unleashing such an unholy, inhuman howl that all jump back in terror, and the Aegyptian cries, 'Seal the windows. Pull the drapes tight.' But they are too late. Now in the room is Abaddon, the dark angel of the Lord, who presides over all endings. He waits, breath cold, wings folded. The monster's earthly sufferings are not over yet.

Don't shy away! This is what you came to see. In your wildest imaginings did you conceive what a monstrous thing it is to witness the death of a king, to discover beneath the glamour that he is, after all, just a man filled with piss and blood and shit, like the lowest common beggar?

Salome ceases pacing. She glances nervously about, as though sensing the presence of others, besides herself and the physicians, about the monster's bed. But she cannot see what cannot be seen in this world, the angel, the ghost, the widow. She demands of the medics,

'What can be done? What causes such affliction?'

A dozen ailments are cited. They point to his dropsical limbs, his swollen abdomen. One suggests morbidi metallica, another worm fever. They make extravagant promises and stake their reputations. But Salome knows what they are thinking, no one can help him; this is the just punishment of the Lord.

You are puzzled. Are we near the story's conclusion already? No, this is not the end. You must learn a little patience. I have brought you to see the manner of a king's dying, not his death. Not yet. Look, the monster's lips are moving. One of the Greeks bends close then

24

straightens, frowning.

'Well?' *asks Salome.*

'He is asking about the prisoner.'

46 BCE

Letters

The Procurator of Judea and entrusted servant of the Ethnarch and High Priest, Hyrcanus II, to his son Herod, Governor of Galilee.

Under no circumstances are you to march on Jerusalem with the army raised by Sextus Caesar. You cannot ignore the singular fact that your rise to power has been at the behest of the very man you march against. My son, do not forget that it is Hyrcanus, our king, who acquitted you in the face of the Sanhedrin. If you make threats against him now, he will have no choice but to turn to them as his protectors.

Jerusalem is a seething mass of conflicting loyalties. My spies tell me that the king's own nephew, Antigonus, is scheming against him. (There are worrying reports that he believes the Parthians would see it to their advantage to have him on the throne.) The Sadducees and Pharisees mistrust each other as only old and new blood can. Yet even amongst themselves they cannot agree. There is talk of a Pharisee, who goes by the name, Hillel, who has openly announced, "That which is hateful to you, do not do to your fellow. That is the whole Torah; the rest is commentary." Extraordinary. As you can imagine he has made himself almost as many enemies as you.

My son, do not despair. Trust in the Lord to provide. There is indeed a solution to our current predicament. While pondering the root of our troubles, the Almighty moved me to consider that it stems from the fear in which we are held. I have thus made it my business to encourage Hyrcanus in promoting Malchus, whom you may remember is a distant cousin of your mother's. We may thus count on his loyalty, while giving the impression that there is a counterweight to our ambitions.

Take heed from this lesson, Herod. With force a man must expose all of himself, but diplomacy offers a more subtle route to success. I hold you in my thoughts and heart, and pray to the Almighty that he might keep you safe in the North.

Zael, governor of Jerusalem to my brother Herod in second year of the reign of Julius Caesar, Dictator.

My brother, I greet you and pray for your good health. It has come to my certain knowledge that Sextus has made you governor of Coele-Syria. I well believe that Rome has rewarded you out of respect for your skill as a commander of men and with no thought to the hundred talents of silver our mother sent. By all accounts you are living a life of indolent luxury attending dinner parties in the Greek fashion given by Sextus. I fear you are in danger of returning to us a philosopher with no taste for war.

But now I must come to the true purpose of my message. Brother, you must come home, and do it speedily. Unrest swells here, like the angry tides the Lord once used to drown the world. This is not news to you, but at the centre of the storm sits Malchus. Although younger than father, he is of the old school that to be a Jew is to drive the foreigner from the land, as did the Maccabees in the days of old. He has already defied Rome when it came to the collection of taxes, and if father had not spoken out on his behalf —I counselled him strongly against the move— then he would certainly have lost his life. Afterwards he made many fawning gestures to father, whom he proclaimed his saviour, but I could see the look of hatred that burned in his eyes.

He is Hyrcanus' man. Not that the doddering old fool can see it, of course. They say he spends all his waking hours in prayer, and not a single moment on policy. Truly it is said that crowns weigh heavily on the heads of saints.

Malchus strikes me as the kind of man with little talent for politicking, but finds glory in attaching himself to powerful men and championing their cause. He cannot deny the good that has come about through father's administration, but I fear he means to drip his poison with the intension of doing you and I some harm.

Salome to her brother, Herod. A desperate entreaty.

First off, I greet you and console you on the loss of your friend Sextus Caesar. The reports say it was a supporter of Pompey who carried out the deed. When we heard the news father expressed his shock, exclaiming that he could not believe that Pompey knew of it, for he is a man of honour, who refused to loot the Temple treasures when he invaded in the early years of the strife between the king and his brother. But after he had gone I heard mother say, 'Did father imagine treachery to be an exclusively Jewish disease?' Pheroras was in the room, (it is hard to credit our baby brother is almost eighteen from the way he acts) looking up from his book —bewildered as one of those blind beggars who hang around the Sheep's Gate pool hoping for a cure— with no idea who she was talking about or what had happened.

But this is not why I write to you, dear brother. The most calamitous event has occurred. I can neither eat nor sleep for thinking on it, and my eyes are quite hollowed out from weeping. Mother has announced that I am to marry. That I am a goodly age for the marriage bed I do not dispute, but never in my thoughts and prayers did I imagine—

But I run on too fast. It happened like this. Mother sent a slave, one of those little boys who swarm the palace carrying messages, which they are too young and guileless to understand, to fetch me. And when I reached her, father was there too, and his face was grave. For an instant my heart became a stone because I feared some ill news of you had reached us. But, seeing my expression, father's face lightened, though it seemed a forced kind of lightness, and he said that he had good news. And when he said this, he glanced at our mother, and she nodded, and said the time had come for me to be a woman. Then my heart, which had been stone, dissolved into a score of birds' wings, all flapping frantically to free themselves from my breast. My voice was almost lost in the noise, but I asked, 'And who is to be my husband?'

'Your father's brother, Joseph,' they replied. O, Herod. They are marrying me to our uncle, a man nearly father's age, an old man. Mother says he is a figure of maturity and standing, and that it will strengthen our family to pull the thread of blood ties closer.

But I cannot bear it. He is not like father. He is a fat man. And the thought of his hands upon me, as a husband, fills me with a deep, abiding horror. I am like Jephtha's daughter, sacrificed for political gain. I entreat you to come home. Surely you can move mother against this.

Also you should know mother has chosen you a wife.

A LESSON IN HISTORY

Consider Plato, (yes, yes, I am versed in the Greeks) who claimed that the punishment for cowardly men is that they be reborn as women. In his work, De Insomniis, Aristotle announces that **whenever a woman, who is menstruating gazes into a mirror,** *the glass ends up covered with blood. This is because we are filthy creatures, malformed males forever in the shadow of our superior masters.*

Nor are we Jews, who are known for our contrariness to the customs adopted by gentiles, immune to this point of view. What male does not include in his prayers his gratitude that the Almighty saw fit not to make him a woman? And in our rite, known as Passover, the Law states that the sacrificial lamb must be male because the male is more perfect than the female.

Few are the places in the world allotted to women, first comes the disappointment of being born a daughter (in Ben Sira we read that, "the birth of a daughter is a loss."). Then, as wives we are never allowed to forget our lowly place. (One no less than Sophocles tells us in the words of Ajax, "Wife, women are beautiful only when they keep their mouths shut."). And then we are widows, made unclean by our submission to masculinity so that injunctions are

27

needed to remind men not to mistreat us. And, as the emphatic voice of Leviticus tells us, the High Priest may not marry us. O yes, the purest of those virile creatures made in the image of the Almighty may not be joined to the widow in marriage lest his purity be tainted with the reek of feminine flesh.

A woman must be protected as a sacred bud of fruit, who, if allowed out in the sun will ripen and rot from the branch. And what of the woman, who is not the daughter of a virtuous house, safeguarded from her fallen status as seductive Eve, by fathers, brothers, uncles, sons? Why she is a whore. And who should know it better than I who am both daughter and sister to whores.

5

In which there are two marriages, many deaths and the birth of a child

*T*HE WORLD IS MADE UP *of walls. Jericho's walls fell when Joshua's army blew on their trumpets. Jerusalem's walls were torn down by Pompey during the war between the king and his brother, but now they are rebuilt. Strong, thick walls, reflected over and over within the boundaries of the city, every house repeating the pattern in miniature.*

The palace of the Hasmonaeans is built along these lines. From the outside it is blank, featureless, a citadel, hidden from the dusty fury of Jerusalem, forever turning introspectively on its own secrets. Inside? Well, look for yourself…

The walkway that Herod chose to take was one of the most magnificent in the palace. Indeed, it was said that it was one of the most magnificent in the world, rivalling even the gorgeous interiors of the palaces belonging to the Julii family in Rome. The murals were painted by the best artists of the time, and the pigments, glowing, like dull jewels in the strong sunlight, were a costly mixture of leadwhite, hematite, azurite, cinnabar saffron, lapis, limonite and cobalt blue.

Possessing an eye for beauty, Herod had stood in awe of them the first time he had been brought to the palace. Now he strode past unmoved, as only one who takes opulence as his right can be unmoved, and while a little part of him was awed by this new coldness in his perceptions, for the most part, his mind was occupied with the business that lay ahead.

'Herod!' A figure in vivid rose silks, which did not entirely suit, threw itself across the enclosed garden at the head of the walkway. 'You did not come for so long. I am quite withered away with misery.'

Herod held his sister at arm's length and noted that, if anything, she was plumper than before.

'Indeed, I was not quick to recognise such frailty.'

Salome's eyes narrowed, but the sulkiness of her mouth dissolved into a smile of genuine sweetness. She linked her arm through his. 'How colourless life is when you are not here. Zael is always busy, and Pheroras has his head buried in a book all day long. There is nothing for me to do but to think on my impending— ' She broke off and tightened her grip on his arm. 'You will talk to mother, won't you? Of all people she will listen to you. I cannot marry uncle Joseph. I would *die.*' This last was said with such intensity of feeling that she did not realize, at first, that there was some subtle alteration in her brother's posture, some pulling away, though he remained perfectly still. Her mouth and eyes grew round and she turned to follow his gaze to an archway at the opposite end of the garden where Cypros now stood.

Cypros said nothing, but the gaze of mother and son locked on one another, as though some unseen lines of magnetism drew these two inscrutable objects together. Salome's hand dropped away. She looked hesitantly at her brother then, after a moment, slipped quietly from the garden, unnoticed.

Mother and son went up to the family apartments where Cypros called for wine. But when it came she took the jug from the young boy and filled Herod's goblet herself. Bending over it she said, 'I have found you a wife.'

'Yes.'

At once Cypros' eyes flicked up, though the wine still flowed from the jug. 'You knew this?'

Herod nodded.

'And you did not come to me?'

Herod made a gesture, as if to suggest, I am here now. Cypros laid the jug down and studied her son's face. 'Have you no curiosity then about your bride?'

A shrug. Herod sat back and looked at his mother over the rim of his goblet. 'She is chosen by you.'

A look that was not a smile, but more a luminous acknowledgement brightened the bronze cast of Cypros' complexion. 'Well, it is said that a son is a blessing from the Almighty. Yet a daughter is often a bitter fruit.'

'Do not be too harsh on Salome,' Herod interrupted. 'How can she be otherwise at the thought of marrying Uncle Joseph?'

Cypros' face hardened. 'Your uncle is a man of means.'

'But Salome is young.'

'Have young girls never married before?'

'Surely another family— '

Cypros got to her feet and crossed the room to look out of one of the high narrow windows, deliberately averting her face to show she was displeased. 'Can you think that there is another subject between your father and I? Long into the night, who will it be, who will Salome marry? And approaches were made.' She turned suddenly, her expression sorrowful, and all the more terrible because this was sorrow on the face of Cypros. 'Not one of the great Sadduccean houses would offer their sons. We even considered an alliance with the Pharisees.' Seeing a frown on her son's face, she held up a hand to forestall him. 'Do not underestimate them. For all their talk of being of the people there are those who count themselves amongst the wealthiest citizens in Jerusalem. Even then they offered us only scraps. Would you have your sister humiliated as a second or third wife?'

In three paces Herod was at his mother's side, feeling the trembling in her shoulders beneath his lean hands more used to the feel of a sword hilt than a woman. 'They hate us still.'

Cypros, looking up into his face, saw her own face mirrored, if only the Almighty had blessed her with both the body and freedom of a man. 'Your father believes he has made peace by promoting Malchus, but better to make alliances with serpents.' Her voice became low and urgent. 'We have no choice but to secure our house. When the time comes we must be ready.'

Come. Surely you want to meet the bride. Not Salome, no. We will pass over her marriage. What is there to say of someone who blubs and snivels and drips snot all over the priceless Aegean silk of her long-sleeved KUTTONETH? *Look at her lift the* SIMLAH, *draped so delicately over her shoulders, intricate silver threadwork glimmering in the light, like captured drops of precious rain. And what does this daughter of the palace do with such a marvel, only wipes her nose with it.*

No, this is not to be borne. Her blubbing. Her cries of, O pity me!

Yes, yes. Pity one who goes to her wedding feast having never felt hunger, who will lie on her marriage bed never knowing weariness, who has never suffered the rub of fabric so rough it left your flesh red and itching by the end of the day. Yes, pity the one dressed in wonders, while rubbing your own raw knuckles, earned for having dared to take hold of a corner of those glorious threads.

Come, time to make our departure; it would not do for Salome's blushing cheeks to be the result of a sound slap.

But out in the streets of Jerusalem it is a different story. Everyone is eager and smiling. Herod will take his Idumaean bride today and the spectacle will be worth the wait. Stay close. It is easy to get lost in the press of bodies, the narrow winding streets that lead everywhere and nowhere. And the heat. You have never experienced such bright, searing heat. In this temperature you feel your nakedness beneath your clothes. Already sweat is pouring in rivulets down your body, running over you, like long curious fingers searching out your most intimate parts. You are uncomfortable, panting beneath this unwelcome touch, pressed up against the anonymous bodies of strangers. Don't think to hide; there are no shadows. The earth has sucked them all away.

Now you must ask yourself this, as all beings must ask who live in the scalding regions of the earth, can you accustom yourself to this strange hot clime? You must be prepared to find a way if you intend to stay to the bitter end. And the end will be bitter I promise you that. How then are you to stay? In the great Aegyptus heat is a god, before whose great round face the populace fall in worship. But we Jews know better. To us heat is memory. It reminds us how we toiled under the yoke of the sun, where the air is white-hot and it burns even to take a breath. At Qurna and Giza, at Abu Simbel and Thebes we laboured until we were freed by an Aegyptian prince, born of our people, who led us across the blazing desert so that we might not be slaves.

I asked once of one of the old rabbis, who hang round the palace preaching, with an eye to being fed, why if this were so, there were still Jewish slaves in the land of Judea? He replied that the Jews are unique in the world in that they will not allow their own to be slaves more than seven years, and compel owners to release them without fail on the sabbatical year.

Then I asked why, this being true, the law did not apply to women, who can only be freed by coin or master's whim, and received a heavy cuff about the head for my impudence. I was still rubbing the tender spot behind my ear when another rabbi, kinder than his companion, explained that it is because the Almighty made men first, and so his laws speak first to them. 'Is it not true that after the birth of a boy a woman is unclean for seven days? But the Lord has decreed that the number of days of uncleaness will be twice that after the birth of a girl. In matters of inheritance it is laid down that the son will receive before the daughter. And in the Temple, a man may draw closer to the Holy of Holies than a woman who must wait without.'

He smiled at me then, as though that was the matter settled, and I thought to say that if the Lord made woman second might it not be the case that he saved the best of his works till last? But my ear had begun to ache and I feared a second blow.

Ah, you hear that, the wedding hymns? The bride is approaching. Was it not worth suffering the piercing rays of the sun for a view such as this? Behold! There is the litter held aloft, not by slaves, but by her kinsmen. See, they are proud lads, dark and spare, their shoulders knotted and powerful from heavy labour, for few Idumaeans can avoid putting their backs into the land, even amongst their most exalted.

And the bride, do you see her, robed in splendour, her veil glittering with pearls and diamonds. Herod's family has been generous with the dowry, and it would appear that her kinsmen have spent most of it on outfitting the bride. They want this marriage to work, to find themselves invited to dine with the procurator, or perhaps —dare they dream it— the king himself, to become part of that privileged set who walk without wonder through the wonders of the Hasmonaean palace.

Herod was a charming bridegroom. He was courteous and attentive to his guests, treating the *garum* exporters from Galilee —who smelled faintly of fish, despite their perfumed beards, and who stood legs planted firmly apart in their striped robes, openly appraising the other guests as though they had been invited to a market to assess stock— with the same civility he bestowed upon the bejewelled sons and daughters of Jerusalem's most ancient aristocratic families.

But, for all his gallantry, there was a coolness about him that was noted by his guests. He went from group to group, but did not make merry or laugh. And when he lifted his bride's veil they saw that he smiled, but it was the same smile with which he greeted the exporters of fish-oil, though it was noted that Doris —for that was the name his wife went by— was comely enough. Yet those, who knew what to look for, saw that she was not so comely as Cypros.

A good girl. A pious girl. The whispers were approving. Such bowed shoulders! Surely her dedication to her prayers must be great indeed. Though some thought that they were bowed more by the weight of expectations laid upon her by her family. Whispers, whispers. They blew, like little coloured birds across the wedding party, but Doris kept her head modestly down, fanning herself with her blue/green fan of peacock feathers, looking at nothing but her perfumed feet and the tiny black and white tiles of the mosaic beneath them. Which was just as well because she did not see how her bridegroom barely glanced in her direction.

Forward now. Quickly through three years. The sleeping years Herod will think them. But the stage is being set. Changes are afoot. Turn west, and there is Julius Caesar, DICTATOR PERPETUO, bleeding out his life at the foot of Pompey's statue. And here come the wolves creeping towards him ready to tear over his corpse. When they are finished their greedy eyes shift eastwards. Cassius is first, demanding taxes and yet more taxes. He has a war to fight against Mark Antony, the man who stood at Caesar's shoulder through Alesia and Pharsalus, and also against that strange youth, with the hard glittering eyes, who is Caesar's adopted son and named heir. Cassius needs money, and the Jews are a bottomless purse in his hand. He squeezes, and when he does, far away in Jerusalem words come spurting out of Malchus' mouth.

Malchus is making a name for himself. Come, the Temple's the place to hear him. There he is, standing on the broad, white steps that lead up to the pillared entrance, where anyone might listen, beggars, gentiles, women. He has dressed for the occasion, all in white, like one of the monastic Essenes who live by Lake Asphaltitus or a hermit prophet back from fasting in the desert. He has come to be heard. And what a speaker he is. Do you see the crowd? — Fishermen from Galilee, merchants from Phoenicia, peasant farmers making a pilgrimage from the countryside, scholars from Alexandria, doctors of the Law, Jerusalemites who trace their ancestry all the way back to the days of King David— all willing to stand under the sun's furious gaze to hear what he has to say.

The words he chooses. AUOLTSANEA. B'KHASHEA. What can they mean to you? He is talking of oppression, of the suffering of the people (though if we followed him we would see him step over beggars in the street). He is reminding anyone who will listen that the king is the direct descendant of the never-to-be-forgotten Judah Maccabaeus, who banished the successors of Alexander the Great from Judea. 'Did we rid ourselves of the Greek only to become the servants of Rome?' he asks. 'Or are we not the servants of the Almighty, who alone dispenses justice to mankind?' The crowd roars.

And when he talks of those who persecute the flame of freedom, these fishermen and merchants, these scholars and aristocrats know he speaks not only of Rome, but of the procurator of Judea and his two sons. For Herod's family understand the Roman virtues of POLITIKOS and INGÉNII. They recognise that a Roman is not like a Greek. Horace might argue that "GREECE, THE CAPTIVE, MADE HER SAVAGE VICTOR CAPTIVE.", but at heart the Greek is still a philosopher, a son of Socrates, Antisthenes, Chrysippus, Epicurus. Crack the surface of a Roman, and you will find Mars, a soldier raw from the battlefield, single-minded, ruthless, governed only by the MOS MAJORAM.

Herod's family understand the nature of the Roman. When they think they are alone they speak the unspeakable. Not God, but the Jews swept the Greek from Judea. When a Jew fights a Greek he is essentially fighting himself for the Greeks are a people of individuals, like the spheres in the heavens, connected yet separate, held together by invisible bonds of history and ideal. When you fight a Greek you are fighting a man. But a Roman is a creature of a different order. He does not fight for Rome. He is Rome. In the way that a single drop is indistinguishably part of some greater body of water so the Roman can lose himself in the vastness of belonging. Cut a Jew or a Greek and he will bleed. Cut a Roman and a thousand more will appear to take his place.

So Malchus rails while Herod appeases, and the world grows ever more dangerous. Cassius and Brutus face Mark Antony and Octavian, like gladiatorial pairs across the battlefield of the world. On the streets they talk of ruined Lycia and sacked Rhodes, of the voice of a god heard in thunder, of twisted bodies covered in pelts of black, tarry blood, strewn across the battlefields as far as the eye can see. Death, death and more death. And in the midst of it all, listen. Do you hear that? The sound of an infant's whimpering. Doris has given birth.

It happens in Coele Syria, where Herod is governor. See, here comes the messenger, a lanky Syrian Jew with scrub instead of a beard, bowing before Cypros with all the grace of a newborn calf.

"Yes lady, a boy. A fighter like his father. Surely they heard his screams all the way to Jerusalem. Indeed, lady. Herod is delighted; he has given his wife jewels. He rejoices." (Though not enough to come with the news himself.)

And what is Cypros thinking, a long forefinger tapping on her lips. There is a silence. Her face is unreadable. Then she smiles.

A baby. In all the turmoil that has descended upon the world such a small event. His arrival hardly makes a ripple. A dinner party will be thrown. Hyrcanus will attend and bless the child in its absence. Herod's father will distribute coins to all his slaves and servants, and even I will receive a small bronze as. In court circles and kitchens a little gossip will flare. They have named the boy Antipater after his grandfather. Antipater. A Greek name meaning, "like the father". A common enough choice. Though there is another meaning, a meaning that no one considers at the time. Antipater can also mean "against the father", his enemy, his adversary.

But, for now, the messenger fidgets and Cypros smiles, a cool smile, registering this small victory in the midst of a disordered universe. All around great men are rising and falling, like inconstant mountain ranges, and the birth of a child seems a commonplace miracle in a world where the fantastic no longer raises a brow. So Cypros smiles, and far away in Coele Syria Herod goes about his business, while his wife prays for him to remember her existence, and I pour wine and fetch and carry as I am bid whenever someone calls, "boy!". And, in the west, Brutus draws his sword and Mark Antony is lured into the Aegyptian queen's serpentine grasp. And of all our destinies it is the baby, the baby who will connect us all. But we don't know it yet, not even I.

6

The death of a good man

M
Y MOTHER AND SISTER ARE whores, *as I've said. Not in the sense that the prophet Ezekiel likened Israel to a whore, accusing her of prostitution and lusting after Aegptians whose genitals he compared to those of donkeys with their seminal emission as strong as that of stallions.*[1] *No, there is nothing metaphorical about the term; my mother and sister are whores in the ordinary way of things.*

—Ah, you are curious now. You have recalled that I am not the anonymous voice who guides you through other tales. I have a narrative of my own. Very well then, I will tell you a little—

My mother grew up in the palace of the Hasmonaeans, a slave, the daughter of a slave, and my sister the daughter of the daughter of a slave. See them now, down on their knees, feet bare, hair wrapped in rags, scrubbing at the kitchen steps. Sometimes, when she is not scrubbing, my mother claims that her family came from a village called Chasalous, which lies in the shadow of Mount Tabor. 'We come from the tribe of Ephraim, as did the prophetess Deborah,' she would suddenly announce, breaking off from her scrubbing to stare into the ripples of dirty water in the bucket. Then equally on another day, 'Surely we are Isaccharites, amongst those who light the beacons on the high places to mark the holy days and the kalends of each month.' And though my sister and I roll our eyes to hear her, it is hard not to be a little affected by the thought of a shared history that does not revolve round fetching and carrying and the cleaning of pots and pans.

Of course, my sister has a history all of her own. And she often carries herself with the poise of a daughter born to better things, which she is, at least on her father's side. The name of her father is known, though may not be spoken. He comes from one of the best families, closely connected with our priestly king, Hyrcanus, himself. And, once long ago, when visiting the kitchens, he found my mother in the first bud of youth and lay with her as a husband.

Now it is written that a man shall not uncover his daughter-in-law's nakedness or that of his neighbour's wife or of the wife of his brother. But a maidservant cannot be legally married for she is the property of her master and therefore exempt from the

encompassing reach of the Law. So my mother's belly grew round and she was labelled a whore and her child was also a whore being as she was the daughter of a whore.

My mother often spoke with pride of her first born. Gomer was the name suggested by

---

1   EZEKIEL 23:19–20

her father. A cruel name in my opinion, for who is Gomer in the holy texts except the harlot of all harlots selling herself freely to any man who will have her. Nonetheless, my mother displayed that peculiar quirk of the desperate, the habit of reading hope where only tragedy is written.

'Did the Lord not instruct Hosea to buy Gomer from slavery?' she would quote, her eyes bright as the beacons on Mount Tabor. 'Did he not make a free and respectable woman out of her?' From this she deduced that my sister's father had made her a promise to free his eldest child. And no argument of mine could ever shake her from this belief.

Of my own history I know nothing at all. By the time I came along there had been so many men my mother had lost interest. 'He was a merchant,' she says sometimes. 'From Gaul or was it Noricum? He traded in scents and gold.' And on another day. 'A merchant? No. When did I say that? He was a scholar from a place called Ynys Môn. Or perhaps that was the name of his tribe. I don't recall. He knew many stories though, all of them strange. Of a tree where a god slept and of a lady bound forever to the shores of a lake. All his stories had something marvellous about them. Or perhaps it was just in his way of telling them. But sometimes— ' She looks away blushing. 'Sometimes I let him pay me in words.'

Whoever my father was he is from a cold place, the North lands I think. Traces of ice were left on me in the blue green of my eyes and the light streaks in my hair. And in other ways too I am very much my father's daughter, lacking all the full, sensuous beauty of my mother and sister. I have nothing of their warm curves or large, accepting eyes. But there was one particular thing left me by my father. And on this matter alone was my mother constant. "He was a clever man," she would say. 'Yes, a man with a clever mind. Never still. Like you, always asking questions. Always in need of an answer no-one could give.' And she would stare off into the distance and bite her full bottom lip. 'He was a scholar, you know.' Or 'A travelling actor and versifier. Yes, that was his trade. Well, it might have been. I don't recall.'

One other thing he left me, and that was a name. Although he was long gone before the smallest signs of my presence were noticed, he had a feel for such things. He left my mother two words, one for a girl and one for a boy. Sometimes, when I beg and plead, she tries to recall what he said. 'VAH-nah,' she says, screwing up her face, as though she is about to give birth to a malformed child. 'KHUN tchorn ghal a.' She cannot say the word; she is simply twisting her tongue round syllables so alien that they sound to her ears like nothing more than the meaningless babble of birdsong or babies.

Yet, for all this, my mother has an ill-defined sense of loyalty to the men who gave her children. And for this reason, when she was asked what name she had given her newborn, she would always answer, 'No name. No name.' The hope being that one day the Almighty would bestow upon her the gift of memory and resolve this peculiar predicament. And thus, with the passing of time, was the matter settled. I became No-name, Loshema in our tongue, until even my mother barely recalled the irony.

But I do not mind. I have watched the noble men and women strutting around the palace corridors crowing their credentials. A Sadducee will sneer at a Pharisee's claim to know the name of his great, great grandfather when he, the Sadducee, can rhyme off an ancestry that goes back to the time of Aaron. An ambassador from Athens will ask the legate from Rome about his family merely for the pleasure of shaking his head and saying, "Never heard of them." And a Samaritan envoy once dared to repeat Herod's name with a kind of insolent wonder, before saying, "Of course, not a Jewish name."

So proud they are, these Kohains and Solomons, these Ptolemys and Cassii. They call me 'boy', quirking their nostrils in disgust, as though I was dirt upon their shoes, and not one amongst them would raise an eyebrow at my anonymous state because upon one thing they are agreed, a slave possesses nothing, not even their name.

Well, let them think what they like. I do not care. In this world names can be dangerous. In years to come I will see a name pull a boy under the water, the weight of it dragging him down, down into the bottomless depths. I have seen a woman, —eyes bulging, tongue protruding— tearing at her throat, while her name tightened around her neck. Better to be Loshema, weightless, invisible, watching from the shadows.

Besides, I am twelve now and I have learned, to my cost, that there is no more safety to be found in the skin of a man than there is in the flimsy garb of a woman. My change of heart happened thus:

This morning a merchant, visiting from one of the cities of the Decapolis, from Pella or Gadara or Damascus or some such, here to sample the exoticism of an oriental court, grabbed me and forced me into a cellar. It was dry and earthy inside, the walls lined with tall amphorae, pointed bases buried deep in the sandy floor, and from them rose a distinct smell of spices, sharp laurel and sweet, peppery saffron. They keep wine here. Sweet Galilean wine, red as blood.

The merchant kept his hand pressed against my mouth as he forced me down and loosened his robe. In the dark I sensed his member, pale against the dimness, its head, a blind serpent's head, twitching towards me. And this was the moment that a free child might have screamed or an animal would have torn with its teeth. But this is not so with a slave. A slave is a creature from which all the will has been hollowed out. A slave is a dry gourd or a lump of dead clay to be formed by another's fingers.

I lay there, a black horror, creeping over me, like manacles around my limbs, while his hands took hold of the ragged hem of my tunic, lifting it with slow exacted delight. 'Easy. Easy now. I won't hurt you.' His hand was no longer round my mouth, and inside my head I was screaming and cursing both him and his progeny unto the tenth generation, but I made no sound. Not even when I felt his fleshy hands on my backside, parting my buttocks in the Greek fashion. I held my breath. Then—

'What's this?' The merchant leapt back as though scorched. He pulled me upright by the scruff, and pushed his face savagely into mine, raining down a wave of invective that called down the wrath of every capricious god inhabiting his heathen universe. He seemed to want

38

an explanation of how I had cheated him out of his meal of boy flesh. And when I offered none, he spun me about, kicking me with such force that I went sprawling, face-down, onto the dusty floor. I lay there, while he stood over me in silence for some moments then he kicked me once more in the ribs, before turning tail and stalking from the room, rage and injury echoing, like thunderclaps, from his heavy footsteps.

No. Don't look at me that way. I don't want your pity. There's worse goes on in a palace, believe me. I thank the Almighty that our merchant friend proved such a disciple of Rome, aping their squeamish horror at the secret places of women.

O, but they do. And don't quote Ovid at me. A loving line does not negate endless poetry to comely youths with their inviting anuses or contradict the satire of Plautus, Martial, Juvenal and all those who find female genitalia loose, filthy, likened to a ditch or a grave. Let us not forget the horror of Horace. HIETQUE TURPIS INTER ARIDAS NATIS PODEX VELUT CRUDAE BOVIS. *The lovely image of a woman's backside running with cow dung.*

What happened next? Here, let me show you. There I am, a miserable bundle huddled facedown in the cellar.

Time passed for the child on the floor as ages pass bringing changes too deep for the eye to follow. Then, at a certain moment, the child pushed itself up to a kneeling position and wiped hot tears from her face. She was not certain why she was crying. She had lost something in that room, though what it was she could not precisely have explained.

Once on her feet she made a slow, limping lunge at the door, and halted there, breathless from a throbbing in her kidneys. The kick had been a harsh one and she would piss blood for a week. The door she opened only a crack and waited, knowing the merchant had gone, yet needing to be certain. And while she waited she lifted her fingertips to the top of her head and stroked the cropped bristle, until memory recalled that it had proved no amulet against rape, and she let her hand fall.

Outside the air was fresher and a square of light was reflected from the beyond the staircase that led up to the garden and the better levels of the palace. In the distance came the faint murmur of voices. Then, amongst them, a voice was raised in song and another joined it in harmony. A kitchen slave hurried past without a glance. Everything was as it should be. And nothing particularly strange had taken place in the cellar, except for the fact that it was a young boy who had been dragged inside, yet it was a girl who came back out.

Her first desire was to hide, to find the smallest, darkest corner of the palace and to climb inside. But, Shlomi, the steward, caught her and thrust an amphora of oil into her hands with orders to take it to the royal chambers.

And so here I come across the garden, past the little alcove that shelters the stone bench with the lion's feet, head down, feet dragging, not even noticing the chafing rub of the amphora through the sad weight of my thoughts when—

A madwoman stumbles into my path. We spring apart, caught in the immediate paralysis of shock then recognition comes and all thoughts in my head evaporate on a single gasp of clarity. Here is Cypros, whose poise is that of a marble statue, broken, eyes reddened with weeping, tearing at her hair and clothes. The amphora slips from my hands. And the sound of its destruction on the tessellated path brings Cypros to life so that she springs forward with the sudden darting movement of a cobra, pressing her face close to mine. There is the smell of sour wine on her breath and her whisper is the harsh, lost voice of a desert wind,

'He is dead. My husband. Murdered. By that snake, Malchus.'

7

In which a lesson is learned on the value of property

THE FUNERAL OF HEROD'S FATHER took place on a strange day, clouded and sombre with only a faint wind moving across the air from time to time, like a chill breath of displeasure. It made the crowds that lined the road uneasy and superstitious.

Herod's father passed them on his final journey, laid out on a bier of gold, his right hand curled round a staff of office, his body carried aloft through the winding streets of Jerusalem by his four sons, with Zael and Herod in the lead and Pheroras and his second youngest Joseph, —Yes, he has been scarcely mentioned. He has nothing to add to this story except the manner of his death. Of that more later— back from his travels in the Decapolis, at the rear.

Behind them came his guard, stern-faced men from the furthest reaches of the empire, Germans and Thracians, Gauls and Nubians. And behind them, members of his household, slaves and freedmen followed, waving in their hands sweet spices, myrrh and aloes-wood. Their eyes streamed tears, and they kept up a perpetual agonised moaning, a wordless dirge to sorrow and the end of all things.

Before the bier went Cypros and Salome and Doris, and the various other women of the household, their position a mark of their kinship with Eve, who first brought death into this world. Cypros moved like a statue, her movements strangely un-lifelike and aloof. But Salome's pain was clear for all to see. When Doris tore at her clothes there was something hot about it, a religious fervour that flushed the cheeks of her modestly lowered head. But Salome's grief was raw and ugly and very real. The dust she poured on her head was the dust of the grave.

Those that saw her were awed by the power of her grief, and there were many amongst them who began to recall the times of unrest before Herod's father arrived in the city and the times of peace that followed. They saw Hyrcanus, their king and High Priest, leading the procession bare-headed and barefoot, his head lowered with sorrow, and they began to sense that something good and irreplaceable had been taken away from them.

Ah, you want a closer look. Come then. Down to the Kidron valley, where a marble tomb already contains the body of Herod's father. Hyrcanus has finished his reading of scripture and the last prayers are dying on his trembling old lips.

'... May he step with the feet of the righteous in Gan Eden, for that is the place of the upright, where the Almighty will guard the feet of his pious ones. Blessed are You,

41

who gives great mercies and multitudinous compassion to the deceased of His people Israel. Amen. May it be Your will.'

And here comes Malchus, red-eyed, smeared in dust, protesting his dismay at the calamity which has befallen the procurator's house. Zael's greeting is warm enough. But all eyes are fixed on Herod. We, of his household, have witnessed the scene between the widow and her elder sons. Her spies all point to Malchus. He's much too clever to be implicated directly. A bribe to Hyrcanus' cupbearer was all that was needed, and an invitation to Herod's father to accept the poisoned chalice.

When Cypros describes finding her husband's corpse, his face twisted into an agonized scowl, eyes staring fixedly on understanding come too late, Zael listens stony-faced. But Herod's anger is legion, a blind, white thing he cannot control. Fists are slammed, wild threats shouted, a delicate faience vase smashed next to my head in a thousand tinkling shards.

So now it is not only the spruce trees that shiver as Malchus approaches Herod. All Jerusalem is waiting, breathless. Malchus lowers his head, extends his arms. 'In sorrow we are brothers.'

Herod looks at the extended arms. He looks at Malchus. Nothing happens. Everyone is frozen not daring to make the smallest movement for fear of admitting that the moment has passed. A breath of wind lifts hairs, rustles clothes and still no-one twitches. Then, just as I am learning the pain of eternity, Herod breaks the spell. He leans down. He grasps Malchus' hands and kisses him on the lips. 'Indeed, now we are brothers.'

A sigh goes through the crowd, a collective slumping in relief. A few even start to clap before remembering that they are standing before a tomb not yet closed. And, amidst the suppressed jubilation, Zael exchanges a secret glance with Cypros. He is his father's son. And he still believes that patience will win the day.

But in the days that follow Malchus seems set to try the patience of the most saintly disposition. Cypros' spies are red-faced and sweating with the number of times they are forced to run to their mistress with news of Malchus' scheming.

'He breaks bread with the king and they toast the fall of our house.'

'He has made overtures to the king's nephew, Antigonus. Some say he means to use Antigonus to overthrow Hyrcanus and seize power for himself.'

Cypros listens, expressionless. But when Zael asks, —Shall Herod know of this? — she shakes her head.

—Not yet. —

Yes, Malchus spreads his homemade wings of feathers and wax and flies up towards the sun. But whatever his transgressions he is judged less harshly than my sister whose sin is far greater in the eyes of men than merely plotting the death of kings. While all eyes have been on Herod, Gomer has had the impudence to fall in love.

Not that it is easy to spot love on the face of a whore. A woman who must pretend gratitude for the unwelcome attentions of men grows used to hiding her innermost feelings, and who can read the strange beatings of a veiled heart?

The dusty month of Tammuz brought everyone indoors on the slightest excuse. And so it was for the skinny girl who slipped into the kitchens hoping for a pitcher of cool water. Her newfound femininity precluded her from the more stimulating roles young boys might aspire to in the upper apartments, messenger, cupbearer, apprentice. And, with the exception of the ladies' maids, the duty of a woman was to be neither seen nor heard. Such affectations did not come easily to her and she banged the door and strutted across the rough slab floor, with an assurance unbecoming to her sex.

Batia, her mother, looked up from the cooking pot she was stirring, and frowned. 'Loshema, where is your sister?'

A blank stare, a shrug of a bony shoulder. Batia put down her wooden spoon and came towards her daughter. She put out a hand and ruffled the ragged spikes of her hair. 'What's this?' she asked, fondling a length almost two inches long. 'Are you becoming a woman?'

Loshema pushed her mother's hand aside and took a wary step back. She had told no-one about the cellar or the noble with his Greek manners or his Roman disgust. But, late at night, a creeping horror would rouse her from the dark refuge of sleep, forcing her upright with violent self-loathing. Femininity was a refuge she had fled into blindly, and the clothing of womanhood, as she perceived it, sat loosely and uncomfortably about her.

Batia had taken a step back and was examining her daughter critically. 'Still flat as a boy.' Her voice was a tender mixture of relief and curiosity. 'You may see it as a sign that the Almighty is keeping you safe.'

So many were the angry, bitter retorts crowding Loshema's lips that she kept silent, and Batia nodded, as though a deep understanding had been shared. She was looking thin and worn, and though Loshema acknowledged these facts with her eyes, they did not penetrate deeply into a psyche too wrapped up in the folds of its own dissatisfaction.

'And you saw Gomer?'

A sigh, an irritated shrug. Gomer, always Gomer. 'She's hiding in the formal gardens, staring at her reflection in the fish pond. Where else?'

A lie, but a plausible one, and if Gomer was to find herself in a little hot water she had no-one to blame but herself. An unreadable look crossed Batia's face. She opened her mouth, as though on the point of confessing something, then gave herself a little shake and turned back to her cooking pot. A prickling sense of pique washed over Loshema, who felt her own air of unhappiness merited further enquiry. Still, the deception pleased her, and she left the kitchen, after gulping down a ladle of cool water, humming tunelessly under her breath.

She meant to go straight back to the chamber of wool, where she had been set to sorting aside the best skeins for the ladies of the palace, yet the day was such a rage of heat that she found herself taking the long way round, through the warren of corridors that only a child born to the palace could possibly have navigated. Even then she skipped up a narrow staircase of roughly hewn stone and found herself in unfamiliar territory. A dusty tapestry, threadbare and eaten through in places by moths blocked the way. Illumination came from small apertures set high in the walls, which let in only a thin wan light not up to the task of dispelling the shadows gathered on the floor.

Nonplussed, Loshema consulted the map inside her head and came to the conclusion that here was a back way into the apartment of some noble, perhaps even the chamber of a royal personage, for who but a king must be ready to flee his bed at a moment's notice? No matter, for it clearly did not lead to the chamber of wool. She turned to go, and then she heard it, a voice. Not words, but laughter and quite distinctive. It was Gomer.

Loshema stood with her ears pricking up. This was something outwith her experience. Kitchen whores were not brought to the chambers of the nobility. There were plenty of nooks and crannies, disused storerooms and corners of cellars that provided a place to throw up a woman's skirts. And whores did not laugh, at least not in their real voices. There were words, whispers too low to hear then more laughter. And it came to Loshema in a way that made her stomach sicken and her cheeks flush that what she was hearing was a worse profanation than sex; this was love.

For an instant she stood, like an animal caught between fight or flight, torn by the urge to throw the tapestry back to expose the sacrilege within and the desire to unmake the knowledge that caused her earlobes to burn and her throat to dry up. But a sense of shame that was more and deeper than shame, brought her slowly back down the stairs one trailing step at a time.

And later she told herself that it was because her head had been filled with the swamping confliction of her thoughts that she had begun to run as soon as she reached the great supporting pillars that led in a line from the bottom of the staircase. Head down, fleeing the terrifying possibility of her own sexuality until she collided with a soft, yet strangely unyielding force which reached out hard pincers into the soft flesh of her upper arm, and asked in Salome's imperious voice, 'What are you running from?'

The question, so penetrating and fierce, made salty tears spring from Loshema's eyes. She bit her lip then, and without quite conscious acknowledgment that she was breaking the great slave rule of silence, she turned her head and looked over her shoulder back the way she had come. Salome's head followed, and her eyes traced the corridor and stopped at the foot of the steps. For a moment she looked puzzled then she frowned, and in that frown was something of premonition. Her mouth fell open and her fingers loosened, and Loshema seized the moment, struggling free, running for all she was worth in the opposite direction, through the low arch at the head of the corridor and out into the searing noonday light.

For two days nothing happened. Unable to eat or sleep Loshema hovered in the background, watching for signs of divine retribution with the fervour of a royal astrologer. Were Gomer's cheeks too pink? Had she always sung when she scrubbed the floors? Once or twice she thought of confiding her fears in her mother, but Batia always seemed to be praying or lamenting that the great Temple accepted the offerings of pagans, but not those a woman earned while on her back. And so it went on until the tightness in Loshema's chest began to subside and she felt safe enough to bicker with Gomer again and to sulk out of the room wordlessly when Batia asked what was troubling her. But, on the third day, punishment fell from the sky as Loshema had known it must.

Into the kitchens she came, dragging a basket of soiled linens. It was now one of her duties to collect them, and it was a wearisome, thankless task that inspired in her no great sense of diligence. Shlomi, the steward was leaning against a worktop, chatting to one of the cooks. He took one glance at her then straightened up and left the room. Surprised he should miss the opportunity to tell her she was shit beneath his boots, Loshema watched him go.

'Who fed Shlomi bitter herbs?'

The cook did not answer. She had her back to the girl, and was stirring a pot of vegetables, rather violently Loshema thought.

'Tell my mother that is all for now. But there is more to come. The wife of ben Avrim says she has sheets stained during her monthly *niddah* and she wishes me to bring fresh ones.' She waited for an angry reprimand at her failure to refer to the *noble* ben Avrim, but the cook was strangely preoccupied. Loshema stretched her aching spine and wiped sweat from her brow. The kitchen was hot, the air moist from the steaming pots and filled with the aromas of warm baking bread and the cooking herbs used to season the meats. They were good smells, homely smells. Her mother was nowhere to be seen, but that was not so strange. Batia was just as often busy elsewhere, selecting fruits or mending a sheet or lying beneath every noble in the household in possession of a stiff member and the need of a place to stick it.

And knowing this was a comfort, and caused Loshema to prattle, 'And tell my mother that I have not finished the mending she set me, nor have I cleaned the pots as she asked, but she must not worry for it will all be done before she gets back, and—'

She got no further. The cook interrupted. 'She's not coming back. Nor your sister.'

There were more words. Surely they were words, though they chirped and rumbled, like the meaningless syllables of the name left her by her father. She stood there, in the centre of the kitchen, while everything receded further and further away, as though creation was unmaking itself. Yet she did not faint or cry out, and to the figures who entered from time to time, their heads filled with the day's business, she was just a small slave with clenched fists and bowed head, who has failed to understand what happens to property when it loses its value.

8

To be a king

*T*HERE IS A STINK IN *the air. Do you smell it? Today corruption burst from the monster's belly and worms crawled out. See, the physicians huddled round him, shaking their heads. They talk of moving him into the Temple, hoping for a miracle. This is the method favoured by the Greeks, but he is too sick. And now it is the turn of one of the Pharisees. He has consulted the medical remedies of Asaph the Astronomer and recommends apples of Mandragora, but these have been tried before, as has the laying on of hands, favoured by the physician from Galilee.*

A little apart, the Aegyptian is hiding in the folds of his sleeves an onyx amulet of Heka, his god of magic and medicine. From time to time he rubs it between his fingers, but it is not clear if he does this for the monster's sake or his own. There by the door, Salome is cowering, a hand pressed over her mouth and nose. Her husband is also there, come to lend his support, but he looks greener than she.

A knock. Don't jump. Do you think the Almighty announces himself with lowborn custom? Salome answers it, and lets in ben Boethus the High Priest. He does not come in his sacred vestments, but there is gold thread in his robe and glittering jewels twinkle behind each thick knuckle. It is as if he thinks Abbadon, the angel of Death, a gentleman who will be intimidated by a show of wealth.

He enters the room with a pomander of orange blossom and cinnamon pressed to his nose, and dispenses blessings from a distance, until Salome silences him with a look. She points at the rotting body of the monster, which for all its putrefaction will not open wide enough to allow his spirit to escape.

'Worms,' she says.

Everything about the High Priest's face grows wide, and he uses a jewelled fist to stopper his mouth. 'May the Almighty in his mercy— ' he begins then breaks off. What mercy can there be here?

But, what's this? Shaking your head, pursing your lips. You don't believe me. The backs of the physicians obscure the view, and you think I exaggerate to colour the drama. —This is Thucydides' account of the Athenian plague, you argue, or surely we are hearing an echo of the rotting death of the Greek dictator, Antiochus Epiphanes, perhaps it is even that ancient king, Jehoram, whom the Lord punished with disease until his bowels fell out. It is a metaphor only, an allegory for wickedness brought low —

46

What a sophisticate you are, why you could walk the streets of Athens philosophizing cynicism along with Crates of Thebes himself. Of course there is a flaw in your argument as there was with poor Crates. In his case he gave away a king's ransom only to find that rejecting everything didn't make him any happier. And the flaw in yours is to think that some things are too vile to be true. O yes, the worms are real. Won't you come a little closer to see for yourself …

No? I didn't think so.

43 BCE

Yes, we are back in the sad days that follow the disappearance of my mother and sister. Sold, at the demand of the noble Sohemus for harlotry and the teaching of harlotry, by which read at the demand of Sohemus' wife, who has it from Salome that her husband has been lying, not with whores, —that might be forgiven— but with a particular strumpet, whom he favours above all others, most especially over a wife who lies in the marriage bed, stiff as a board, eyes rolled heavenwards, lips intoning prayers throughout the very act for which they were conjoined.

And so it came about, in a strange reversal whereby the sins of the child are visited upon the parent, that my mother is held responsible as my sister's pedagogue. Sohemus' wife, full of spiteful piety, was there to see them off, calling my sister and mother 'MERETRIX' to their faces, the lowest way to say whore using the gutter Latin of soldiers and street hawkers. My sister wept and made promises no-one believed, while my mother fell on her knees and begged the Almighty to take pity on them. But mercy is a rarity among humankind and the divine heart, which knows no sorrow, shows it not at all. Within an hour they were gone.

Some said it was kindness that I was spared a harrowing goodbye, others that it was a further punishment heaped upon my mother's head. Yet it was neither. Only slaves believe that their masters care about the feelings of slaves. I was not there when they came for my family and no-one thought to fetch me. Is the lamb told when the sheep is taken for slaughter? Does the seed know when the wheat falls before the scythe? Perhaps the only kindness came from my mother, who did not remind the Almighty of my existence during her lamentations. FELIX, QUI NUMQUAM EXPERTA EST VINDICTA DEI, as Sophocles would have it. Indeed, happy are those who have never known the vengeance of God.

And that is the strange thing about calamity. The storm that sweeps away a single world is unfelt by the hearts and minds around it. O, not that there weren't a few sympathetic glances, a little extra food pushed my way (which I could not eat), a passing ruffle of my hair. But the waters have receded, the ripples scarcely noticed now. Besides, bigger waves have come crashing down. Herod has killed Malchus.

The palace is buzzing with gossip. Some say that Malchus received word that his son was being held hostage in Tyre, and that it was Herod's hand behind the letters. Certainly Herod is in thick with Rome. Not that Cassius can openly sanction an act of vengeance, such pillars of the Law are these Romans. But sufficient coin dulls the sharpness of his eyes, and he looks elsewhere when Malchus enters the city.

They nearly miss their mark, wily old fox that Malchus is. He is drawn by the lure of his son, but his nose is wrinkled with the stench of treachery, and he has plans of his own. The spies bring Herod news that Malchus is waiting for the moment when Cassius is preoccupied with attacking Antony then he will stir up revolt and seize power for himself. His fatal mistake is to allow paternal love to overwhelm his judgement, a character flaw Herod will not make the mistake of repeating.

At sunset they surround him, Herod and the Roman tribunes bribed by Herod, a dozen blades, glinting wickedly as the smile that reveals Herod's fine white teeth. It is a quick death, —though legend already begins to fill Herod's mouth with fine speeches— Herod is already walking away, his arms around the shoulders of the two handsomest tribunes. Behind him the crumpled body of Malchus lies bleeding dark blood across the pale sand of ancient Tyre. In the light of the setting sun the blood has a purple hue, like the twilight-coloured dye so prized on this coastline.

But all of this is talk, and what is it to me, who must find a way to go on living in the world? Yet I do not. I do not go on living. I am a shade, an insubstantial thing hovering near the bright warmth of the living, seeing no colours, feeling no warmth, dreaming no dreams. And every-where I look the world is a place of horror and death. In faraway Phillipi Cassius is killed by lies. Clever Octavian sent him false messages of Brutus' defeat, and, in despair, Cassius persuaded his freedman to run him through with a sword. They say it will not be long before Brutus, too, falls before the new order.

Only Herod walks through the blood and chaos, unscathed. He grows taller on a back-ground of exquisite treachery, as though his natural setting is that strange underworld de-scribed by the Greeks and he is kin to their dolorous overlord. Herod is made new by violence, and he is not yet aware of a growing fondness for the cup of vengeance, nor how he must drink deeper each time to experience its dark thrill. He walks through the lamp-lit corridors of the palace, his back straight, his mind like an arrow. He has settled his account with Malchus; now it is time for Hyrcanus.

It is true to say that when Herod, flanked by his German bodyguard, entered the grand court of Hyrcanus there was a reaction. But it was not the stuff of legend nor of history, nor even gossip. It was a reaction that was no reaction at all. Conversations did not stop. The dour doctor of the Law did not break off his lecture on the eighteen articles of Shammai. The aristocrats standing in a group near the king's presence, laughing behind their hands at the vulgarity of a Cappadocian merchant gaudily bejewelled in his merchandise, were not sobered by Herod's entrance.

Yet their indifference was noisome. Like children, who fear the wrath of a parent, their gestures rang false; the head thrown back in laughter had eyes that watched the door; the fingers that stroked a scented beard were taut with anticipation. Already it was becoming clear that to encounter Herod was to draw in breath.

He walked straight towards Hyrcanus, turning his head neither left nor right, acknowledging no-one, and the crowd parted before him, like the walls of the Red sea bowing to a prophet's will. Hyrcanus had leapt to his feet, and some thought he might turn and run. —It was rumoured that he had fainted dead away on hearing news of Malchus' demise, and when revived had clutched at the neck of his linen robe, mumbling brokenly, —*All is lost. Judgement has fallen upon the house of Hasmonaea*— But he stood his ground and descended the steps that led to his throne and embraced Herod, like a long lost son, asking earnestly after his health and that of his men.

Herod stood stiff and unyielding within the king's embrace. He was aware that a few hot-headed youngbloods were glancing askance at the German guard, but he had no fear of them. Together they might overpower the two blond giants and extinguish the Idumaean threat with a swift upward thrust of the dagger, but intelligence rather than might was the Jewish weapon. They looked at Herod and understood that this was no subject here to abase himself, but a representative of the *nova progenies,* the heir of a new lineage, with all Rome's might at his back. No Sadducee drew his blade, no Pharisee raised his voice in condemnation. And Hyrcanus, his withered arms around a man, who scarcely seemed like a man, but more like a pagan deity made of stone, suddenly felt alone.

Hyrcanus cleared his throat. He let his arms fall from Herod and took a step back. And in that gesture some of the deviousness of the Hasmonaeans was revealed. The door of the antechamber opened, as if in response to some unseen signal, and there stood his granddaughter, Mariamme, flanked by her mother and younger brother.

But wait. Let the scene freeze. The frenetic gestures calcify half completed. A silver ZUZ, *tossed carelessly at a page, hangs winking in the air just beyond his immobile outstretched fingers. Mariamme is still in the doorway. Hyrcanus' wrinkled gaze is still on Herod. And Herod? Herod looks like a man emerging from a cave of shadows, who has just seen the light.*

Stand with him then. Take a moment to feast your eyes on this Jewish princess, daughter of the proud house of Hasmonaea. Her great grandfather converted Herod's ancestors to the faith of the One True God. And after his death, his wife ruled over an unruly land, while she raised her sons, one for kingship, one for war. All the weight of history bears down on Mariamme's head, and she wears it like a golden crown.

As a rule, history is kind to women of royal blood. Only consider the busts of Cleopatra or Olympias to see how their features have been softened by biographers who were all too willing to dip their pens into the twin wells of artifice and invention. Surely that blunt-featured face cannot be the one that seduced the two most powerful men on earth? Or that matronly-looking woman? Where did she get the gall to claim her son was sired through union with a god?

Yet this cannot be said of Mariamme. She possesses the kind of beauty that comes along once in a century, or perhaps even a century of centuries. A beauty that seems not quite human. It hurts to look at her. And this is not so strange a notion. Because to behold beauty so immaculate, so flawless that it seems touched with the divine, is at once to be struck in the heart with an inescapable sense of longing and loss.

If only this tableau could be eternal, a prince of the new blood enchanted by a princess of an ancient line. But time cannot stand still forever. Animation returns. Conversation hiccoughs back to life. The coin drops to the floor. And led by her mother across the marble floor of the court comes Mariamme, like a cool breath of wind, touching everyone yet touched by none. Only when she is gone does Herod turn back to Hyrcanus. No words are exchanged. Not yet. But a contract is drawn up between them. Hyrcanus has purchased an extension to his old age by selling youth that is not his own.

'Open it.' Alexandra's voice was at once imperious and eager. She took a pace towards her daughter, as though she might actually shake the limpness from the girl's shoulders, but, finding her as unapproachable as a stranger, pulled herself up short and stood shaking her head in exasperation.

In truth, the two women did not seem related. There was a heaviness about Alexandra's features, as though the marks of her illustrious ancestry were too weighty for her face. In less polite circles the word 'inbreeding' was whispered. But her daughter, as has been said, was painted with a finer brush. Where nobility made Alexandra gravid, there was a lightness about Mariamme, and this despite her tenebrous features. Alexandra, too, was dark, but she was the dark of solidly-built corridors or low-lit halls, whereas Mariamme embodied the living night filled with numberless stars.

Slowly, so slowly that the small slave folding linens in a corner did not notice at first, Mariamme's hands uncurled and she lifted the lid on a handsomely-carved box of tamarisk wood. She stared at its contents quite expressionlessly until Alexandra became incensed.

'Well?'

As though lifting a soiled rag, Mariamme held up a golden collar between her pinched thumb and forefinger. The slave folding linens in the corner, who was no longer folding them but merely making the motions as though engrossed in the task, saw that its shape was that of two golden peacocks, their necks entwined, their eyes and feather-tails, enamelled and winking with precious stones.

Mariamme held the collar higher, into a slanting shaft of light so that it flared and the precious stones caught fire. The slave, whose hair was too long to belong to a boy and too short to belong to a girl, was entranced. She had lived long enough in the palace to recognise when something was truly exquisite, and she gazed at it with such longing her hands forgot to make useless folds in the linen, and lay limp and forgotten at her sides.

Alexandra made an irritated motion. 'Well, don't just sit there. Try it on.'

Mariamme obeyed, but there was something lifeless about her hands as she fumbled with the catch behind her neck, trying and failing several times before it caught. And once fastened the gold collar proved too heavy for her slender neck; dragging her chin down towards her chest.

Alexandra shrugged. 'A pretty enough piece. A tad gaudy perhaps. Still he wants us to know he means business. I shall tell your grandfather we are ready to discuss the marriage contract.'

At the thought of her wedding contract Mariamme's head snapped up. 'Is there not— Surely there must be— .'

But her words trailed off and the pleading expression in her eyes sank back beneath blankness, as Alexandra walked away, hands raised in exasperation. She stopped before the window and stood looking out. 'Think of your brother.'

The phrase was enchantment. Mariamme lifted her head and her cheeks flushed pink.

Still facing the window Alexandra went on, 'You know well the danger we are in. Any thought of our own happiness must be put aside for now. Look to the Almighty to be witness that no daughter holds her father more dearly than I. But we must face facts. My father is no Matthias Maccabeus, and no match for a crude assault of power.' She glanced over her shoulder, not at her daughter, but pointedly at the peacock collar. 'And Herod is warning us that he is the favoured son of Rome. To oppose him now would be to slit our own throats.'

'Instead you would hand him a kingdom?'

'Never that.' The light from the window washed Alexandra in a pitiless radiance that made her features shrink back so that only the black of her eyes and the red of her lips stood out. 'Your brother will be king.'

'How so when you let Herod show the world that he is to be eternally joined to the house of Hasmonaea? Already they are saying that he is king in all but name.'

Alexandra drew in a breath that made her bosom swell then let it slowly out. 'Herod is a half Jew. Not even Rome can change that. Can Herod be High Priest? Who will accept a king who cannot even enter the Temple's inner sanctuary?' She turned back to the window and spoke musingly, as though her words were forming with her thoughts. 'No, Herod means to use Rome against us. But we will use Herod as a shield against Rome.'

Mariamme shook her head and flashes of gold showed through her black curls. Alexandra sniffed, but she went on,

'You know what Judea is. Sadducee opposes Pharisee. Hillel versus Shammai. My father against his brother —at least until someone had the wit to poison the fool—. Every political faction against the other. But there is one thing Jews agree on, and that is that their king must be chosen by the Almighty. An Idumaean upstart pushing for the throne will unite every Jew in the land.' She paused and laid a hand on her breast, as though suddenly aware of the beating of her heart. When she began to speak again her voice was lower and more controlled. 'Herod is an ambitious man. But a Hasmonaean princess is no small prize. He will be satisfied for a while.' She gave Mariamme a sidelong glance. 'You will make sure he is satisfied. And if the Lord wills it, your brother will be able to reach maturity in peace.'

'And then?'

'And then … ' Alexandra hesitated, her eyes opaque. 'Then we will see.' Saying nothing more, she turned and left the room, closing the door behind her.

Pheroras it was who told me the legend of Tantalus, that wicked Phrygian king who dared to snatch at godhood by dipping his tongue into a bowl of nectar. Odysseus met him later in hell, where he found him reaching perpetually for a morsel of sustenance forever dangled beyond his grasp. So it is for Herod in the months that follow his betrothal to Mariamme. He has reached his hand where it does not belong, towards kingship, and repeatedly it has been snatched from him, like the curling branches hanging above Tantalus' head.

In the chamber Zael now claims as his own, the brothers sat facing each other. Without warning, Herod got to his feet and began to move rather wildly about the room, while Zael, so like his father, sat in his father's place behind the huge carved desk, watching his younger sibling pace the floor.

'What a restless sea you are, Herod. Be still before you wear out the mosaic tiles and they blame us for that too.'

Herod turned hot eyes to his brother. 'You find it funny that they go after Antony with their lies. They say that a deputation met him at every stop in Bithynia, squealing tales of how you and I are seizing power.'

Zael shrugged, as if to say, what of it?

'They will turn Antony against us.'

'Not Antony.'

'You think not?' Herod drummed his fingers against the edge of the desk, as though he would have liked to drum them against Zael's head. 'Antony has little liking for kingship.'

'Then he has chosen odd allies in Octavian and Cleopatra.'

'There is still enough of the old Republican in him to be swayed by those Jews who are our enemies.'

'You say Jews as though we did not count amongst them.'

'Amongst our enemies we do not. Only see, Zael, how their eyes are locked on the past. So enthralled they are by what a Jew once was that they have no thought of what he might become. And our danger lies in the way they pique Antony's sentiment for the nobility of tradition. We are painted as usurpers, stripping Hyrcanus of all but the trappings of royalty.'

Zael stretched out his legs, pushing the chair back along the floor. 'You worry needlessly, brother. At Daphne a hundred of their most prominent leaders made their case against us. Now we are elevated to tetrarchs by Antony's command. Rome rewards us for weakening Hyrcanus. A puppet is a better friend to the empire than a man who moves with strength and autonomy. If Rome had wanted a king they would not have poisoned his brother.'

Herod frowned. 'You have a loose way of speaking.' The mention of poison had unsettled him. His father's death was still the haunting spectre of his nightmares, and it was rumoured that Cypros often crept to Herod's room to sit with him while he tossed and sweated out his fears during the deep hours of the night.

Zael pushed his legs out further. 'We have nothing to fear from Rome. Recall, Antony executed the latest embassy from Tyre as revolutionaries. The gold you stuffed in his ears seems to have deafened him to their pleas.' He looked at his brother coolly and enjoyed the flush that rose beneath his skin. The bribe had been a secret.

Herod pushed himself away from the desk, and began pacing again. 'Still, I did not like that Antony executed them. It does no good to our cause to have Jewish blood on our hands. It fills me with strange premonitions and apprehensions.'

'It is not the spilling of Jewish blood that causes your agitation.' It was Pheroras who spoke. Both the elder brothers turned to stare, having forgotten the younger's presence or simply having failed to notice it. But there he was, curled on a couch in a corner of the room, his nose buried in the writings of Ezra or Hillel or some such.

'What do you mean?' Herod demanded. His blood was up and it made him defensive. 'What causes my agitation?'

Pheroras, in the act of putting down the scroll he had been reading, glanced up, puzzled, as though he had already forgotten that he had joined the conversation. But seeing that an answer was expected, he blinked and replied, 'It is not the spilling of blood that troubles you so much as your desire to form a union with it.'

Herod's face darkened. He needed no reminder that Hyrcanus seemed in no hurry to complete the *kettubah*. Suddenly his eyes narrowed. 'You have heard something. A rumour.'

Pheroras shook his head. 'No.'

'I don't believe you.'

'I know nothing.' Pheroras glanced fearfully at Zael and repeated, 'Nothing.'

But Herod was coming towards him. 'You lie, little brother.' He grabbed Pheroras by the shoulders and dragged him from the couch. 'What are you hiding?'

Zael got to his feet. 'Herod, enough.'

'He knows something.'

'He only knows you are hurting him.' In three steps Zael was at Herod's side. He laid a hand on his brother's arm, gently enough, but it was clear that he was prepared to use force if force were called for. There was an instant when all futures were possible, then Herod flung the hand away. He stormed from the room, slamming the door behind him with such violence that all the delicate items set about the place —an inkpot fashioned from a single piece of bone, a peculiar double-headed oil lamp of great antiquity— shook in their places and a careful arrangement of reed pens upset itself across the desk.

Zael took a step in the direction Herod had gone then checked himself. He turned to

Pheroras, who was now by the desk, picking up the scattered pens.

'You should watch your tongue. He fears plots.'

'He fears the truth.'

'Think on it, he finds himself in an impossible situation. He craves the love of the people and it is constantly snatched from him.'

Pheroras paused, his hand hovering over a fallen pen. 'Perhaps he is the Jewish Tantalus then?'

'Indeed,' Pheroras agreed. 'And trapped in a very Jewish version of hell.'

A Jewish Tantalus indeed. Now I think on it, Pheroras told me that it was not for stealing nectar that Tantalus was punished, but because he sacrificed his son. I had forgotten that. You should not.

9

In which fates and fortunes are overturned

THE SERPENT HAS A COMPLICATED relationship with Israel. He is both friend and foe. Long, long ago we bowed down before the snake god, Nehushtan and made him offerings. And our prophet, Moses, is known to have carried a burnished serpent on a pole, which he used to cure the Israelites of snake bites. Yet, in my mother's eyes the serpent possessed no redeeming features, always an enemy, never to be trusted. She blamed him for our expulsion from the paradisiacal garden and the pain of childbirth visited upon her as the especial punishment of women.

Nor did she need to look far for proof of his treachery. Once, when weeding in the palace vegetable garden, a mole viper slithered out from under a patch of leafy black radishes. An insignificant creature, the colour of pitch. They were not usual in Jerusalem. Most likely this one had stolen passage from a caravan passing through the wilderness near Ein Gedi.

For a long while we stared at each other. I, so small, that I was excused labour and left to my own devices, the viper glinting in the sunlight, like a tiny dribble of ink. What happened next? Here mist rises over the landscape of memory. Did I reach out a chubby hand to stroke it? Or did I sit motionless, mesmerised by its jewelled, unblinking eyes? No matter, for in the next moment the snake was dead.

No word of warning, no cautionary cry. Suddenly the snake's head was cleaved clean from its body. In front of me it lay, tongue lolled, eyes dimming, until, shocked, I lifted my head, and there was my mother, a figure silhouetted black against the sun. She had taken on the magnificent proportions of giants, one of the Nephilim, those titans who once inhabited all Canaan. And she stared defiantly at me now, though I had uttered no word.

'Never,' she said venomously, 'never turn your back on a serpent. If you see one, kill it at once.'

Good advice. Since that day I have witnessed what the fangs of that tiny creature can do to a man when it strikes, not as the clean-made animals of the world, but obliquely from the corner of its jaw. Left unchecked, the poison spreads, the skin blackens, the flesh splits.

—Never, never turn your back on a serpent.— My mother was wise with the simple wisdom of simple folk. It is the kind of wisdom that slips through the complex lattice of intrigue and invention that is the hallmark of more sophisticated minds. How else can it be explained that in the great house of Hasmonaea, they have left a viper in their midst?

42 BCE

Cypros, her back against the reclining slope of a couch, used a long fingernail to break the wax seal on a letter and sat reading it, watched by the uneasy gaze of her daughter. Salome, seated opposite and uncomfortably on an upright chair of Grecian design, the arms of which were fitted a little too snugly around her generous curves, allowed a small sigh of disapproval escape her compressed lips. Cypros put the letter down and reached for another.

'What is the matter?'

She asked the question without looking up, and her nail tapped against the brittle red wax of the seal.

'It is only— It is just— '

Cypros' almond eyes flicked towards her daughter's pinkening cheeks. 'It is just?'

'Those letters are affairs of state.' Salome's hands twisted the delicate fabric of her over-dress into damp folds. 'Should not Zael open them now, now— ' The ghost of her father withered on her lips, and Cypros gave a dismissive laugh.

'Your brother has his hands full enough. He will welcome a little help.' She cracked the seal and unfurled the letter, and for three heartbeats there was silence then Cypros gave a cry and sat bolt upright. 'It cannot be!'

'Mother, what is wrong?' Salome's damp hands flew to her breast. 'What has happened?'

Cypros lowered the letter and looked her daughter squarely in the face, and even in the terror of the moment Salome could not help but bask in a focus of attention normally reserved for her brothers. 'Mother, tell me what has happened.'

'That serpent, the king's nephew— Antigonus has made an alliance with the Parthian satrap, Barzapharnes. He has bought their loyalty by promising them a thousand talents and fifty women if they will aid him in deposing Hyrcanus. And we are to be first amongst those offered.'

—*Ah, you are scratching your head. The Parthians, who are they? Indeed an odd breed. When Rome smashed the power of Alexander the Great's successors they birthed a strange unwanted bastard from the cracked skull of Hellenism. This child belonged neither totally to the east nor the west, and neglected by its father, turned on him with unbridled savagery.*

Rome sent one of its most lauded generals, Marcus Licinius Crassus, to face them at Carrhae. There he was defeated and his army destroyed. But do not waste tears on this defender of the civilized world. In killing him, the Parthians were merely snuffing out the life of the man who had snuffed the life out of the one known as, Spartacus. Crassus. The name is a curse on the lips of slaves. Still, the Parthians acquitted themselves poorly in victory, murdering long after surrender was a certainty and parading the mutilated head of Crassus' son about the camp on the tip of a spike.

Cypros knows that the choice between Rome and Parthia is not an easy one. Parthia is a dangerous enemy. But in the house of Herod they believe Parthia is a more dangerous friend.—

41 BCE

Look about! The sands are shifting, the tides are changing. A new wind blows across the dusty streets of Jerusalem. Antigonus has attacked the city at the head of an army generously bestowed by the Parthians. And the king's nephew leading a Parthian force can mean only one thing: Hyrcanus' rule has come to an end.

Herod —his face bloodied by a brawny Parthian foot-soldier, who had almost dragged him from his horse during a skirmish near the sheep market— walked along the passageways towards the chambers of the king. The corridors were empty, and sounds reached him only at a distance and then only strangely, in the way sounds normally came in dreams, —the high-pitched wails of a woman, suddenly cut short. The muffled barking of a young man, shouting out orders. Running feet. A door slammed several rooms away— Quick, echoing sounds but essentially meaningless, like a sudden flare of sparks amongst a fire's dying embers. Herod ignored them all.

He climbed the steps that led to the royal chambers two at a time, though his legs were bruised and aching. The pain, as with the goings-on in the palace, was a distant thing, and was also ignored. At the great cedar panelled doors he hesitated only long enough to give the most perfunctory knock, then entered uninvited.

Zael and Hyrcanus were sitting on the window seat speaking in low voices. At the sound of Herod's indecorous entrance they sprang apart and Zael jumped to his feet. He hurried towards his brother, a look of astonishment and admonishment showing in equal measures on his face. With a flick of his hand he dismissed the large Benjamite guard, known as David HaDov, David the bear, who was barring Herod's way. And the peremptoriness of the gesture, belonging rightly only to the hand of a king, was not lost on the younger brother.

'Herod.' Hyrcanus' thin voice broke in, as though only just recalling his place in the tableau. 'Come join us.' He gestured to the embroidered cushions where Zael had been sitting and Herod, remembering himself, executed a clumsy bow before enquiring after the royal personage's health. Hyrcanus gave a bony shrug. 'My sufferings are the sufferings of age,' he said, leaning over to lift the wine pitcher. 'And the best of my sages can find no cure for the affliction.' He filled a goblet by his own hand and held it out to Herod.

'Come. Sit.' And seeing him hesitate, added, 'Ceremony is the domain of diplomats and others who imagine that authority is man's to bestow rather than the Almighty's. Amongst friends it is a cold comfort.' He patted the cushions again, and Herod sank down on them with more weariness than grace. He accepted the goblet, but set it down hastily when he saw that it trembled in his hand. A look passed between Zael and Hyrcanus, ands Hyrcanus asked gently, 'How went the battle?'

Herod shrugged, moody now that he had been released from courtliness. 'It was no battle. The Parthians are well-disciplined, but unused to street fighting. Corner them in the alleyways, and they run. I could clear the suburbs in a day if it weren't for— ' He reached out and grasped the stem of his goblet, letting the unfinished thought hang in the air. *If it weren't for the Jews who fight on the Parthian side, who betray and slaughter their fellows for the chance to raise up a Hasmonaean usurper and bring down the Idumaean pawn.* Herod's hand tightened on the stem, squeezing it, as though he felt himself squeezing the throat of Parthia. 'Why do they hate us so?'

Zael cleared his throat. 'You are a great soldier, brother. But a poor politician.'

At this, Herod's eyes flicked up. 'I know he has been here. The Parthian General.'

Zael met his gaze. 'Then you know a great deal.'

'I know nothing at all save that he means us ill.'

'You misread him.' Hyrcanus spoke mildly, but his mildness masked rebuke. 'We will come to him presently. But you are wounded, Herod. Let me send for my physician. He was a disciple of Themison of Laodicea and there is none with greater skill.'

Herod, who had half risen to his feet, slumped back. He was a man who believed in the authority of kingship and dared not gainsay it. Moreover, his temper was most often a lightning strike, and once spent he was left weakened and self-loathing. So he sat silently and let the physician attend his wounds while Zael talked.

'The Parthian Satrap is no fool. He has been watching events play out. Our spies tell us that though Antigonus gives the appearance of command, he cannot keep control of his own men. And if we know this, the Satrap knows it also.'

'And he is a pious man for all he is a heathen,' Hyrcanus interjected. He met Herod's gaze then looked away, disturbed by the bloodied state of the wound. 'He respects the holiness of the Temple and fears the enthusiasms of the men Antigonus commands.'

'Furthermore—' Zael leaned past the crouching physician to pick at a dish of figs. 'The Parthians believe that kingship is rightfully invested by the gods. Whether it be Shamash or that eagle-faced one they call lord of heaven, the Satrap has respect for those divinely appointed; it will sit uneasily with him to flout the will of the Almighty.'

The physician pressed a poultice of dried herbs into the tear in Herod's thigh and Herod issued a low groan. 'What are his demands?'

'There are none.' Hyrcanus put a hand on Herod's shoulder and felt him wince. 'We are only advised to meet with him in person.'

'To what purpose?' In agitation, Herod half rose and the poultice fell to the floor. Tutting the physician pressed him to be seated once more, and seeing from the silence of Zael and Hyrcanus that answers were dependent on his compliance he fell reluctantly back on the cushions. The colour had drained from his face and he let his eyelids droop, so that he seemed a man disinterested or half dreaming.

Hyrcanus waited until fresh herbs had been applied before explaining, 'The Satrap is greatly disturbed by the chaos and confusion that follows everywhere in Antigonus' wake. He feels he has been grievously deceived regarding the state of affairs he might expect in

Judea. And talk of an uprising here in Jerusalem greatly troubles his conscience. Pacorus, his representative, —whom I found both virtuous and mannerly— assures us that his master is desirous to meet with men of reason.'

The physician found his wrist suddenly encircled by the strong fingers of a patient who a moment before had seemed barely conscious. Herod thrust the physician's hand aside and was, at once, on his feet.

'This is madness.'

'It is diplomacy.'

'Men who come with swords do not surrender to words.'

'Though it pains me brother, I must disagree.' Zael, who looked so much like his father sounded very like him now. 'It is men who answer with swords who cannot hear words of reason.'

Herod took an angry step forwards then swayed and was forced to grasp a burnished lampstand for support. 'This is folly. Antigonus controls the Temple. He controls the city. And every fool and halfwit with ambition follows his lead. To step beyond the palace walls is certain death.'

'Our king desires it, and I will not let him go alone.'

'You will defend him with words.'

'Death and life are in the power of the tongue, Herod,' Hyrcanus said gently. 'So the proverbs tell us. Besides Antigonus has promised us safe passage. I know my nephew. He is ambitious, but still an honourable man.' At the almost forgotten sound of Hyrcanus' voice the momentum of the brothers' argument was lost. Herod turned passionately towards his regent intending to use the power of emotion where his argument had failed. But there was movement in Hyrcanus' face. Eyes darting away, lips compressing, it was the expression of a man who does not want to see himself reflected in others. And with an empathy, rare in his character, Herod understood that here was Hyrcanus' fatal flaw. He was a king who wanted to die peacefully in his bed.

INTERLUDE, 4 BCE

SOFTLY NOW. WE ARE BACK in the chamber of a dying man, and the death of a king is not an easy one. Better to fall in battle or to embrace the traitor's blade. A king who wants to die in his bed corrupts his own destiny. Herod knew this when he looked into Hyrcanus' eyes and saw that watery plea for life. And to Herod in his youth, for whom life still stretched infinitely, the plea was a contemptible one.

And yet that rattling cough. The Galilean physician leaps back, wiping the spray of spittle from his face with a sleeve. In other circumstances he would have uttered an oath or covered the patient's mouth with a cloth, but the ruin in the bed is still a king. And the physician knows even a ruined king wields power over life and death.

Herod is trying to speak. Dry lips moving on the creased papyrus of his face. Fingers fret-

ting at the blankets. The Galillean supresses a grimace and bends low, but still he cannot hear. The mumbled prayers coming from the priest in the corner are louder, and so he straightens up shaking his head. Then Salome rises, from where she has been kneeling at the foot of the bed. She silences the priest with a disdainful glance and dismisses the doctor with a wave of her hand. Bending low, she presses her ear against her brother's lips, face drawn in concentration. Herod's voice is almost gone, but Salome has long been used to the shape of secrets, and their contours make sense even when their vibrations are lost.

'He is asking for news of the prisoner.'

—Ah, you remember that the prisoner has been mentioned before and your curiosity is piqued. You are right, of course. This Herod, writhing in agony at the threshold of death, can throw a man or a woman into lightless dungeons before sun up and have forgotten them by breakfast. Not even now, as the light fades, is he finished. Be certain of it; there will be more. None of us is safe as long as Herod continues to draw breath.

But why this prisoner, you ask. What is his special gift that causes him to be singled out from the faceless masses? You want his story, a name at least. But, no. Not yet. I think I will keep him to myself a little longer.

10

In which another side of Herod is revealed

HURRY! HURRY! *There is no time. A messenger has come from the port of Ecdippa. There he is before Herod now, a scrawny Idumaean lad, the gangling son of a goatherder, and not much use in the capital, except that he has a wide, astonished look about him that some mistake for innocence, and so has succeeded, where others have failed, in gaining Herod's trust. He stands there, his Adam's apple bobbing in and out, like the head of a sand lizard, while he gasps out his news.*

Zael and Hyrcanus are taken. The Parthians set a trap and would have sprung it sooner had they not hoped to arrest Herod before he got wind of it.

Salome cries out and Cypros unconsciously makes a gesture against evil, a very unJewish gesture from her childhood days in Nabatea. But Herod is very still. He is learning a new kind of anger, and his consciousness of it is almost greater than the words he speaks, 'My brother received no warning?'

'No, sir … I mean, yes, sir. A loyal Syrian Jew came to him and offered him a ship in which to make his escape. As you know, sir, Ecdippa is on the coast. But Zael would have none of it. He would not leave Hyrcanus or endanger you by forewarning the Satrap of his flight. He might have saved himself, but he went instead to the Parthian and denounced the plot. He said if it were a matter of money he would pay double what Antigonus had offered. But the Satrap only sneered at the proposal and had both him and Hyrcanus put in chains.'

Herod says nothing, tapping his knuckles against the arm of the chair, and his thoughts are not the thoughts that can be read on a man's face. Then the knuckles grow still and his look becomes decisive.

'We must do all we can to rescue them.'

'You must do no such thing.'

There is shock. This is a woman's voice publicly gainsaying Herod. Not even Cypros would dare so much. Heads turn, and slowly, Alexandra comes forward. She is stately in her subdued robes and her expression is unafraid. 'You must escape.'

'Surely a daughter of the house of Hasmonaea does not persuade my son to the actions of a coward?' Cypros' voice is without her usual cunning and her hand clutches tightly at her breast. But whether this is emotion or an attempt to hide a rather ostentatious necklace of turquoise and emerald is a matter upon which there can be no certainty.

Yet Alexandra appears not to hear the slight. Her words are addressed directly to Herod. 'To risk open attack is madness. You have too many enemies in Jerusalem. Your plans will be

61

relayed across a hundred lips and whispered in Antigonus' ear within the hour.'

Herod hesitates. He dislikes this woman, who does nothing to hide her haughtiness, and doubtless plots against him. But then again he is surrounded by demons, and this one's shape is at least familiar …

But Alexandra is not finished. 'If not for your sake then for the sake of my daughter. Or would you have the Satrap make her the prize of his harem?' Now here is craft. Here is incantation. Alexandra takes the amorphous form of Herod's jealousy and casts it in the shape of an unbearable future. For a frozen droplet of time they stare at each other —one certain she has dared to say too much, the other suspecting that she has not dared to say enough. Herod jumps to his feet.

'We leave within the hour.'

With these words fear erupted throughout the palace. Suddenly the creeping stillness was replaced by a frenzy of hysterical, almost absurd activity. The court was, for many, a point of unchanging permanence, like the heavenly bodies set in the sky's vault, taken utterly for granted. And for the court to crumble was as terrifying and impossible an event as the sun going out.

Expelled from their earthly paradise there were those who behaved with the naivety of children, packing jewels when they should have packed food, and packing food when they should have packed water. They had forgotten the part of themselves that came from the desert, and they viewed the thought of returning to that burning emptiness with blind, unreasoning panic.

And with panic came rumour. These were a people of the Word; their history, their mythology had grown out of their unique need to form themselves as the people of a continuing story. But for now, without context or perspective, this gift for storytelling unleashed itself, like an unstoppable force of nature. Amidst prayers and frightened female cries stories grew and became legion. The number of women Antigonus had promised his Parthian patrons jumped from fifty to five hundred. The king was captured. The king was dead. Antigonus had word of their escape. Antigonus had surrounded the palace.

Like a metaphorical Jericho, they built the walls of their stories up then found themselves trapped within. To stay was suicide, but they told themselves beyond the city walls their fate lay in the chains or death.

Panic begot rumour and rumour begot chaos. Soon the stately audience rooms, the sumptuous chambers, the sweltering kitchens, the laundry rooms and storehouses, all lay abandoned, their doors gaping, while men and women, regardless of rank, scurried down the corridors dragging sacks or chests, tripping over wailing, runny-nosed children, and crying out impossible, contradictory orders to one another.

Mind the gold. I won't leave it to those filthy devils.

Mama … mama …

Tonight you sup on sand, and you dress in silks and jewels. O the Almighty has given me a fool for a—

... every vessel with water—

Where is Micah? I can't see—

Don't leave her! She can't walk unaided ...

My stick! Who took my stick?

Thieves! Thieves!

Let them fend for themselves. Take the chests. Hurry!

Micah! Michah! Micah!

And in amongst this jostling press of bodies, which threw out elbows and fists, like the spines of a terrified creature, a slave girl, thin and tall, with yet more growing to do in her, was struggling to make headway. Held tightly against her chest was a worn sack containing all her worldly possessions, a wooden comb with broken teeth, a small stash of coins, their combined value no greater than a half-sheckel, a chipped drinking vessel and an alabaster pot with the dregs of scented attar of spikenard stolen from Salome.

Trying to reach the door to the great hall, where those bent on escape were to gather, she found herself buffeted again and again against the churning whirlpool of humanity, pushed back constantly against her will, further and further from her intended path until she found herself wedged into an alcove powerless to move forward or back. Tears of frustration welled in her eyes. Tears that, naturally, did not fall because she had learned from a young age that a slave's tears are invisible. But her situation seemed hopeless until a voice close to her ear urged,

Come! Quickly!

She turned in wonderment only to see a child of about ten run into its mother's arms. Then it struck Loshema in one of those moments of monumental clarity, which occur only at the eye of a tempest, that every single person around her, with the exception of herself, was running towards another living being. For all their gold and silks and jewels, their most precious possessions were each other, and the recognition of this was enough to make her knees buckle so that she slid down the plastered wall and sat with her sack between her bony knees.

And though she had known that her mother and sister were gone, and her father long gone, and she had mourned them and thought herself beyond such pain, a terrible, writhing despair opened up in her chest, as though all the while a viper had been sleeping there and had only just awakened. Suddenly the cries and yelps, the running feet, the press of bodies all disappeared beneath the collapsing walls of her misery, and the shape of the world diminished and grew very far away indeed.

'What have we here then?'

The words came to Loshema from a great distance and seemed to have little to do with her.

'A strange way to behave when everyone else is running for their lives. You must be the bravest lad in the palace.'

Slowly, painfully she lifted her head, and her hair, that fine northern hair so unlike the curling manes of her mother and sister, flopped forwards over her shoulder though not free of the woollen tie at her neck.

'Sincerest apologies.' The young man before her had the dreaming smile of a scholar, but there was no mockery in his tone. Her lack of response made him frown. 'Are you ill?'

A weak shake of the head.

'Then tell me your name.'

But instead a male voice called, 'Pheroras?'

'Here, brother.'

'You are needed by your wife— ' Herod broke off when he saw what had taken his brother's attention. 'Who is this?'

'A slave who cannot speak.'

'A woman with no tongue, a blessing indeed.' And Herod, who could only be relied on to do the unexpected reached down, and taking Loshema by the shoulders, raised her to her feet. He studied her face, his eyes narrowing, then pushed her back a little, seeming at the same time to have come to a decision. 'See her safe within the caravan.'

'With Salome?'

Herod raised an eyebrow. 'With someone who will treat her kindly.'

Pheroras nodded and the brothers shared a smile of knowing.

'Come.'

Because any other course of action was unthinkable, Loshema, who for all her quirks was slave born and bred, made a move to obey, but Pheroras leaned down and took her hand. The shock of a human touch, which was neither blow nor dismissal, made her gasp and stumble a little. But of this Pheroras appeared to notice little or nothing. Nor did he notice that this skinny, unusual-looking slave lifted her eyes from the floor and watched his face as he guided her to where the kitchen women were loading a cart, setting her down on it and patting her head absently before taking his leave. Even after he had disappeared into the crowd Loshema sat, legs dangling, watching the shape of his gone-ness, aware of a faint, pleasant tingling in her hand and arm, which was the memory of his touch, and the strange sensation of knowing that a part of her was still warm with the desire to go on living.

What have we here? A yawn disguised behind closed fingers, a disbelieving quirk at the corner of the mouth. Surely the previous passage was a piece of romance. Herod? The monster, the murderer, the decaying ruin lying in his own secretions on a bed of silks, is this the man who would notice the misery of a single slave while fleeing for his life? Yet that was the strange thing about Herod; he had the common touch. O yes. This man, who will shortly condemn his nearest and dearest to grisly fates, is the same man who will sell his precious possessions to feed the starving or halt a triumphant procession to press coins into the hand of a beggar. But you know none of this, of course. It is not, after all, the poor who pen history, nor the common man who records the fate of kings.

Ah, a frisson. The thought of the monster having another side excites you. Suddenly you see flesh where, before, only a shadowy outline existed. This Herod is becoming painfully real, and it's shocking to discover that he is a human being after all. A monster is easy to dismiss, but a man is a creature very much like yourself, and the soft underbelly of his acts, his generosity, his kindness, his need for love, whets your appetite. You need to know more because, if no force, earthly or divine, could prevent this man from becoming a monster what do you imagine will save you?

But moralising bores you I can tell. Come, let us move on. Where is Herod now? There, on a narrow rocky path above the dreadful shores of Lake Alsphaltitus, the Sea of Salt.

Lift your head; you are as weary as the rest of us, covered in a thick layer of fine white sand that penetrates the scarves about your face and neck, scouring the soft tissues of your nostrils and making your eyes run with constant, comfortless tears. Did you think, because you are a shade, you would not share in the miseries of travel? You are glad to have left the sand dunes but this desolate emptiness, where the blazing, ochre-coloured cliffs tower, like an immense temple dedicated to death, seems poor reward for the days of trekking. You have not slept; your neck aches from constantly craning behind, certain that Antigonus and his Parthian mob are in hot pursuit.

There is no army to protect you. The bulk of Herod's men have been left to defend the palace and to cover our escape. And all around that smell, a sulphurous, decaying smell, the stench of a dead world, and the refuge only to the hopeless and those abandoned by their God.

But what is this? Suddenly the thick, motionless air is ripped apart by shouts. The mules are pulled up, their hooves skittering on the rocky floor. The wagon in front halts without warning, forcing ours to veer from the path. Confusion and panic everywhere. —Brays of terrified animals. Fierce, ululating sobs from the women.— We came by such a circuitous route, avoiding Etam and Tekoa, not even daring to stop at the wretched little hamlets along the way where starving goats tugged listlessly at scrubs of yellow grass. Yet is it possible that Antigonus has headed us off?

Quickly, jump down; let's see what all the commotion is about. But it's hard to go fast enough. The sand rubs and scrapes inside your robe. And the fear. The great, dense fear. Not here. I cannot die here, at the bottom of the world, suffering the fate of Sedom and Amora, those inhospitable cities blasted by the Lord. Let me not end here, not in this creatureless wilderness, this valley in the shadow of death, where salt grows into pillars taller than the size of a man and the sky is a constant parched glaze of light.

It is not Antigonus, but Herod who holds up our progress. He is a madman. Turning this way then that. Tearing at his hair, his tunic. The scarf that covered his face lies discarded at his feet and his hand is on his sword. From his mouth comes a sound that is more agonised cry than human word.

Mariamme is off her mount. She takes a step towards him but his violence freezes her resolve. She turns towards Alexandra.

'What is he saying?'

Alexandra shakes her head. Yet she knows. We all know. There is only one word that can reach so deeply into Herod that it feels like a hand clutched about his heart.

'Mother!'

And now we see what has not been seen before. A wagon turned on its side. Nearby Salome sitting on a rock, a rag clutched to her bleeding forehead. She looks up suddenly, as though drawn by our gaze, but it is to Herod that she hurls her accusation. 'Because of you—' She gestures blindly at the fallen cart. And there, for all to see, is the small brown hand of a woman plaintively thrust out, and more plaintively still because its plea is frozen, lifeless.

'Because of … you—' she says again, but can get out no more words. There is no need. Her meaning is unmistakable. We all heard the argument between Herod and the captain of the guard.

—It is too narrow for the wagons. We must go by the lower track.—

—And be exposed to Antigonus' scouts? No, we will go by the upper route.—

—That is madness.—

—Then I am a madman.—

And here we have it, the alpha and omega of Herod's nature, his ability to leap beyond boundaries and taboos, to dance closer and closer to the flames of insanity, to look through that thin curtain that separates dreams of ambition from dreams of madness, and to read their augurs.

He is drawn by his own impulsiveness, is fascinated and defined by it, feeling it to be the great, strange mystery at his core. And though he would not admit it, even under torture, he is worshipful and a little in awe of this power he perceives within himself, as though he alone has spotted the divine spark and has endowed it with his own name. His anchor, his source, it is the thing that makes him stronger than other men, setting him apart. He needs it to be whole.

But now it has led him falsely, severing in the most brutal manner that most binding connection he has in this world. And to discover he has followed a fickle god unmoors Herod from his certainty. His inner light dims. He plummets, he plunges, casting about for the finger of blame only to find it pointed squarely at his own breast.

The culprit having been found, the sentence is inevitable as it is immutable. And for all the charges laid at Herod's door, he is no hypocrite. He draws his sword and would have done himself mischief except that Pheroras and the captain, leap to restrain him.

'Would you abandon these men, women and children to their fate?' Pheroras pleads. 'You brought them here, brother. Any impulse to self-harm now is both base-born and ignoble. Will you secure release for yourself from worldly woes and leave the rest of us prey to our enemies?'

Herod stops struggling, but he does not lower his sword. Pheroras and the captain look at one another uncertainly. Then a voice shouts, 'Look! Look! Her hand.'

Cypros' fingers are twitching. Herod drops his sword and races forwards. Two men rush over and hoist up the wagon, while Herod reaches for his mother and pulls her free.

'Water!' His order is unnecessary. Already a dozen jugs are proffered along with exhortations to the Almighty that He might spare a good and virtuous woman. Her ladies gather round, but he will have none of it. He wets a rag, allows it to drip onto her forehead, over her dusty lips and slowly, like a seed dormant in the sand, Cypros revives. Her eyelids flutter, she moans and her hands grasp at Herod's arm. He cradles her head, as though he is now the parent and she the child.

'Mother?'

Cypros' consciousness is quick, and mother and son share a moment of perfect communion before they are interrupted by a muted cheer, which is as much warning as it is an expression of jubilation. Herod nods and gets to his feet. 'Make ready. We will reach the safety of Masada by nightfall.' He lifts his mother and lays her gently on the righted wagon, oblivious of his betrothed's intense gaze.

Mariamme stands very still, watching him, the scarves about her face rippling in an unexpected breath of wind. Something has discomposed that naturally cool remote face. Perhaps she, too, has spotted a new side to Herod, something intriguing in the violence of his remorse, in the touching attempt to revive his mother. Does the softening of her brow suggest the beginnings of a new perspective, a bridge that might be built across their respective worlds? And, as Herod nears it seems she is moved to speak. Her lips part. But suddenly one of the scouts, a wiry, little Simeonite from Arad, bounds up out of nowhere, breathless and anxious to deliver his news.

'Antigonus' men spotted on the shore road, sir. Less than a single stade behind us.'

Herod pauses then turns to look back along the way they have come, and his thoughts require no priestly divination to make them clear. Antigonus is on the shore road. To have taken the wider path would have meant certain death. Thus, if his way was madness it was surely a righteous madness. With this thought the deep truth of his mystery stirs within him again. At once something reignites behind Herod's eyes and already he is striding past Mariamme unaware of her attempt to reach him.

Only later, much later will he confess to Pheroras, (who will eventually tell all to me) that, as he swings himself up onto his mount, he is assailed by a cold pang that makes him shiver, like a man coming down with fever. How differently the day might have ended, his bloated corpse abandoned in this barren wilderness, a feast for the pale-bodied desert spiders and clouds of black sand flies. He saw then that his true foe was doubt. Listening to its scaly falsehoods had nearly destroyed him. From then on he must root it out with the zeal of those great Israelite warrior kings, who slew the faithless Hittites and the Amorites, the Canaanites and the Perizzites, the Hivites and the Jebusites, even as the Lord God commanded. He no longer doubts that doubt is his foe … and from this moment on, to doubt him is to side with the enemy.

Part II

The Dream Of A King

11

In which Herod incurs the ire of a goddess

40 BCE

AT THE SOUND OF APPROACHING footsteps, the guards on either side of the imposing ebonite doors stiffened their backs then, bowing from the waist, opened wide the entrance to the lesser of the royal audience chambers. A moment later a woman appeared between them, standing framed in the threshold, her dark eyes as turbulent and unfathomable as the endless river of royal dynasties, of kings and queens, of lavish palaces and imposing tombs rising and falling over and over again, like the waters of the Nile, which culminated in this slender being known as Cleopatra VII Thea Philopater, Queen of kings, Younger Goddess and Mother of the Two Kingdoms.

To an untrained eye she might have been surveying the gorgeous trappings of the room — the smooth basalt floor, the narrow tapering columns, their capitols carved with individual delicacy in the shape of spreading lotus flowers and inlaid with gold, or even the brilliant hieroglyphic paintings, whose flattened perspective depicted the glorious triumphs, both real and fictional, of a line of ancestors that wound all the way back to the dawn of time— But Cleopatra was looking at none of this. Nor was she looking at the glittering courtiers, who had dropped to the floor as soon as her entrance had been noted. Cleopatra was used to splendour, and considerably more splendour than the lesser of the royal audience rooms could hope to offer.

She walked across the floor, which was at least sixty feet in length, with her head held high and her gaze in the middle distance, as though she was alone with her thoughts, which, with her courtiers crouched in obeisance and even her ladies walking with eyes downcast, was no more than the truth of it.

At the end of the room Cleopatra ascended five white marble steps to the throne where her dissolute and vicious father had once reigned. But if she was thinking of Ptolemy Auletes with his weak chin and lascivious eyes, with whom she had jointly ruled Egypt as his consort until his death, or indeed of her elder sister, Berenice, who had briefly tried to take her father's place after a rebellion and been beheaded for her troubles, no sign showed on the round, rather unremarkable, face.

She sat down and leaned back, allowing the throne's wide low design to display the tautness of her body to best effect. Her robe was of simple white cotton, so finely woven that the outline of her supple legs and the small curves of her breasts were visible in the way the tantalizing shadows of fish are visible squirming at the bottom of a sunlit pool. And to balance the striking simplicity of her gown and the informality of her pose, she wore the trappings of a queen in the heavy coiled bracelets on her wrists and arms, which were fashioned from the purest gold taken from her mines in Nubia. Upon her head was a diadem, also of gold, displaying but a single uraeus in keeping with the status of visitors entertained in the lesser of the royal audience chambers.

Glancing upwards she was in time to see the first rays of sunlight pierce the narrow rectangular window above the throne so that it appeared that the sun had moved with her desire to be illuminated by a single golden shaft of light. The thought pleased her immensely and she permitted herself a rare smile for the simple pleasure of it, a smile that was not for seduction or politics (indeed they were one and the same to her) but just for herself. Then, setting her hands on the heads of the twin sphinxes which formed the arms of her throne, she made a small tapping gesture with one foot. At once the lady in her service of most senior rank moved to the front of the platform and clapped her hands. The courtiers rose bowing towards the seated queen, and a bald, heavily-painted chamberlain approached and humbly enquired after the day's orders.

'Permit him to enter.'

Within moments of her command the doors opened again and a tall man was led before the platform. She watched his approach curiously, noting that he looked thin and worn-out in the way travellers often do when their path has been a hard one, and that he took in everything about the room yet neither cringed nor affected an arrogant disinterest to disguise his awe.

He was simply clothed, his head bare, and in amongst the perfumed wigs and glittering jewels of the courtiers the contrast was strangely pleasing, like a smooth, river-washed branch washed up on a shore of glittering stones. The chamberlain signalled that he should halt at the base of the marble steps and he obeyed. And though everything about him suggested that he was a citizen of Rome, he bowed before her in the eastern fashion and paid her the compliments due a queen of the oldest civilization in the world.

'We welcome you, Herod, tetrarch of —and here Cleopatra hesitated slightly, not because she had forgotten (she forgot nothing that was of use to her) but rather to indicate that a man, who was known to be fleeing from an invader could hardly take his title, little that it was, for granted— ... tetrarch of Galilee,' she finished lightly.

On cue the chamberlain beat his staff against the floor. 'State your business before the divine Cleopatra, Queen of the great Aegyptus, Lover of the Two Kingdoms, The Female Falcon and Adoratrice of Isis.'

For the smallest instant Herod drew down his black brows, as though the orotund phrases sat uneasily with him. —It was no light matter for a Jew to be in the presence of a god and one whose divinity was displayed in voluptuous female form.— But he recovered himself quickly, and bowing said, 'I have no business with Queen Cleopatra.' At once a rustling gust of whispers blew up behind him, which he ignored. 'I am on my way to plead the case for my king's grandson, Jonathan, before the Senate, and came only to pay my respects to another loyal ally of Rome.'

Cleopatra stiffened, and the room quivered, smelling blood. —Would the queen call for her guards, would she have him whipped or would she strike him down where he stood?— For a long time the round face stared down at the man who would have described himself in simple terms as a Judean. At last she spoke in a soft, rather husky voice, which to those who knew her, was both disarming and dangerous in equal measures. 'I have a question.'

He nodded in readiness.

'Are you arrogant for a Jew or arrogant because you are a Jew?'

His smile was rueful and fleeting. 'It is true that, as a nation, we have been accused of arrogance, though we prefer to think of it more as a straight way of speaking. But if I have offended I wholeheartedly withdraw my remark and wish only that I might have bitten out my tongue before giving insult before so gracious and noble a queen.'

'I believe you have said as much to a beggar woman.'

'Had I given offence, yes.'

Cleopatra raised her finely-shaped eyebrows and the green malachite on her lids caught the sunlight, giving her face an unworldly glow. Without another word she rose to her feet in a single catlike motion that was the signature of her ever-present sensuality, then turned to go. The room bowed low, and Herod, —who understood better than any of his countrymen the importance of 'when in Rome'— bowed also. The audience was over.

The base of the oaken staff belonging to the chamberlain appeared before Herod's lowered gaze and thudded three times against the floor. Herod lifted his eyes.

'Come.' No explanation or pretty flatteries. Only a single word loaded with the expectation of absolute obedience. Herod straightened his back and followed, outwardly confident, yet not entirely certain within himself that these might not be the last steps he took upon this earth.

The room, into which he was ushered, was smaller than the lesser of the royal audience chambers, but nevertheless outranked even the most stately apartment in the Hasmonaean palace. Through thick fumes of cardamom and root of orris, fanned into the atmosphere by a dozen naked slaves, Cleopatra could be seen reclining on the convex curve of a cedar-wood couch. In similar manner with her throne, the couch was set on a platform between two gigantic pillars, above which stretched a canopy embroidered with astrological signs and symbols. And being virtually the only item of furniture in the room it added to the intended impression that she was settled on a divine barge floating through a firmament of stars.

She did not look up as Herod approached, being —or affecting to be— too far away to notice. Faintly angered, Herod followed behind the chamberlain determination settling in him to give no impression of intimidation. Yet, less than half way across, the sound of his own ringing steps on the inlaid marble awakened in him an unacknowledged response to the Egyptian obsession with stone. There was a timelessness about Cleopatra that came from the towering edifices with which she surrounded herself, the soaring pillars that bore her name, the temples dedicated to her greatness, even the obelisks he had passed on his way to the palace, upon which were inscribed her past glories both mortal and divine. If the Jews had climbed the high places looking for the word of God then in the great Aegyptus the inhabitants had their immortality written in stone.

At the platform Herod bowed low, but did not await for the accustomed invitation to rise before straightening up again. He met the glittering eyes of the queen calmly, waiting for her to speak.

'So you have no business with me?'

'Indeed no. My only desire is that you will grant me safe passage when I choose to leave.'

'At Pelusium the captains refused to take you on board.'

'I was able to persuade them.'

'And the Arabian king. You recalled your debt and were refused again.'

Herod gave a tight nod.

'Yet you have no business with me?'

'I hoped only to present you with a few poor trinkets before leaving for Rome.'

Cleopatra nodded to indicate that she had seen the jewels —some of the finest pieces from the dowries of Mariamme and Salome— and she was not impressed. With a small gesture of her head, she indicated that Herod might sit on a low stool at the foot of the couch, and nodded to one of her ladies to pass him a cup of wine.

The goblet was fashioned from very finely wrought silver, and Herod attempted to pass off his hesitation as admiration for the design. But Cleopatra was no fool.

'You fear poisoning?' She silenced his protests with a raised hand. 'You're father, of course. We grieved to hear of it.' She turned her head. 'Agathodiamon.' A large, well-muscled Thracian slave stepped forward, and without having to be told, drank deeply from Herod's cup. He waited patiently for several moments then returned to his place apparently unharmed. Cleopatra smiled. 'I call him Agathodiamon for my amusement. Naturally you do not get the joke. Agathodiamon was a renowned alchemist in ancient times. They say the list of poisons he compiled is quite the most extensive ever written. His records are preserved in the library should you care to see them. We were lucky that the scrolls were not kept in the storehouses, burned by Caesar during his siege.' She gave a tinkling laugh.

'It is also true that poisoning has long been a royal pursuit, all the way back to the time of Menes I, he it was who cultivated the most vicious vegetation into a garden for his own purposes. But you need not fear the gift of a cup from my hand. Had I desired to kill you I would not have been obliged to take so subtle a course.'

Herod gave a little moue of defeat. 'I believe you could kill me with your beauty alone.' The compliment was extravagant, but Cleopatra was used to extravagance and paid no more heed to it than to the exquisite nature of Herod's gift of jewels. She stretched back on the embroidered cushions and tapped the rim of her cup with a nail lacquered red with a mixture of beeswax and henna. 'You come to me in sorrowful times. It is being said that your brother ended his life recently in a Parthian cell.'

Lowering his head, less in assent, and more in order to compose himself —he was well aware that he was being watched closely— Herod answered, 'That is what is being said.'

'But you do not believe it.'

Herod hesitated. There was a prickling under his scalp, an intense, animalistic awareness that he had underestimated the queen of the great Aegyptus. That she should have intelligence on his activities was to be expected. But the extent of her knowledge troubled him. She spoke with the assurance of a deity. Her enquiries were specific, her insight too accurate, the questions she put to him already answered before he had time to part his lips. How is it possible to remain guarded when all is already known? Then it came to him that he would approach her now as he had approached her in the lesser of the royal chambers, directly and simply and with the truth.

'I have met men like the king's nephew before,' he began slowly, holding steady the gaze of the malachite eyes. 'They are neither fools nor cowards. But they live for victory or, rather, it is better said that they live from it. With each triumph they grow taller. But defeat diminishes them. It causes weakness in their bones.

'When Antigonus heard that we had escaped, and that he had no prize to offer the Parthian Satrap in the shape of our womenfolk, he grew frightened. He saw the people turning against him and wanted vengeance. It was he who demanded that the king and my brother be brought before him.

'The king is an old man, a quality by no means assured in personages of royal status.'

Cleopatra's eyes narrowed, but she did not interrupt.

'He has reached his great age because he is pious and moderate, much loved and respected by the people. Antigonus knew this and therefore feared to be known as the author of his doom. He had hoped to discredit Hyrcanus by showing him to be weak in the face of a younger, more vital force. And now that his plan was failing he thought to destroy his piety and make him look ridiculous before the world.

'My spies tell me that, at once, Antigonus began to rant at his uncle and make threats upon his person. Hyrcanus, being no match for such an assault entreated the Lord —He whom we believe to be the one true God— to deliver him. This drove Antigonus into a wilder passion. He swore that the Lord was not listening to the babblings of an old fool. And when Hyrcanus remarked mildly that, old though he undeniably was, he still had ears to hear how the Lord might answer, Antigonus grabbed his head and tore the offending organs with his teeth until they were nothing but a bloody mess.'

He paused. Cleopatra was looking at him steadily, almost challengingly. It was hardly likely that a woman, who had poisoned her brother and ordered the execution of her younger sister, would be much moved by the story of a feeble king she had never laid eyes upon. Still her coldness chilled him, and he bent his head to take a reviving sip from his cup. Her voice interrupted his confusion.

'I am afraid, tetrarch of Galilee, that the arcana of Jewish custom is unfamiliar to me. How does mutilating a man's ears destroy his piety?'

Herod permitted himself a bitter smile. 'It is our tradition, going back generations that our kings are not only political leaders, but also given the office most sacred to us, that of High Priest.'

Cleopatra nodded, understanding well the sacerdotal demands of royalty.

'And such is the elevation of this role that we cannot suffer the bearer to have even the smallest physical imperfection. In mutilating his uncle Antigonus has effectively dethroned him.'

'And this was the moment when your brother took his life?'

The question was cruelly, deliberately formulated. He felt its poisoned arrow pierce his heart. And, unable to help himself, he glanced up, a naked look of anger showing on his face. It startled him to find no malice in her expression, but childlike curiosity. And suddenly he knew what they meant when they called Cleopatra a goddess. Mysterious in her directness, pitiless in her innocence and so removed from the common human lot that she might have been a falcon, obsidian-eyed, wheeling high above him in the endless blue skies over Alexandria.

His anger dissolved. Can you be angry with a force of nature? 'My intelligence is scant,' he admitted. 'But had you known my brother, lady, you would have understood that his resilience would not have given way so easily.'

Cleopatra stretched, letting her naked foot rest inches from Herod's face. He could smell the dark tones of her scent, myrrh and cardamom, exquisitely blended. His eyes never left her face. 'Zael was a man very much like my father. Their battles were fought with the points of their arguments.'

'And yet the rumour on everyone's lips is suicide?'

Herod shrugged. 'And again I would say, Antigonus is a man who thrives on victory. He must paint himself in heroic colours or lose himself to self-doubt. His attack on Hyrcanus had made him base in his own eyes. A second act would make him base before the world.' Herod paused and drew breath before saying in a tight, hard voice. 'My spies tell me that my brother was wounded during his capture. Antigonus sent his private physicians to tend him, which they did by applying poison to the open flesh.'

'And you hope for vengeance?'

'I hope for justice.'

'And you turn now to Rome for help?'

'I do what has to be done.'

'There is a price for seeking Rome's help you know that?'

Herod nodded grimly. 'Tell me, lady, what in this world is without its price?'

Cleopatra sat up and leaned her body towards Herod. 'You are aware, of course, that we have our own Jews in Alexandria.'

Herod nodded his assent. 'The community is the largest outside Judea.'

'They have been here since the founding of the city. Did you know that?'

Again a nod.

'And still they insist on sticking to their own way of doing things. They make use of the entirety of the Delta district for their own purposes. I find them an obstinate people.'

'That is no more than the truth.'

'Yet you hope to change them.'

'I have not the benefit of a royal education, but it seems to me that change is not something to be feared. We have often faced it.' Here he smiled and took a gamble. 'For without a willingness to change, we should still be breaking our backs dragging stones to build the great tombs of your ancestors.' Then he added swiftly, 'You say we are an obstinate people, and you are right of course. We are a nation whose only true point of agreement is that there is nothing upon which we can agree. And it is truly claimed that to start a war you need only put two Jews in the same room. But that is because, if we hate change, we love principle more. We braved the torments of hunger and thirst to chase the dream of freedom across a desert, and we tore down the idols of our ancestors to follow a vision of the absolute unity of the divine Word. Yes, Rome will come and the Jews will fight against it. But in fighting they will change without knowing that they change. And who is to say what might come of it?'

Cleopatra cocked her head towards one shoulder and regarded Herod side-on. 'You are not like other Jews I have encountered.'

'Not to my discredit I hope.'

She smiled and leaned a little closer. 'Do you grieve for your brother? Ah, I can see by your face that the pain is still raw. I, too, have lost brothers.' A shadow passed over her face. 'But it is different for those of us who rule in Aegyptus; our mother's milk is laced with cruelty. We grow up in the royal harems learning that distrust is a virtue and pity a fool's indulgence. If you can shed tears for your brother you have had a gentler upbringing than I.'

For once Herod was at a loss for words. Many things he had expected to feel towards the Younger Goddess of the Upper Nile, but pity was not amongst them. Then she added, 'You know of my sister, Arsinoe? I gave the order for her execution myself.' Her voice hardened. 'Don't be fooled by tales of a sweet demeanour. She may have gulled the common crowds in Rome with her tears, but she would have done the same to me given half the chance.

'I have shocked you, Herod of Galilee. Sororcide is a crime in your eyes. Yes? Perhaps you are correct. It is certainly so in the world of men. But here I now sit on the throne of Aegyptus with the great delta as my footstool and the sun as my crown, a goddess. And, remember, all things are forgiven those whose veins run with ichor.'

As though suddenly recalling the distance between them, she drew back a little, and the shadows slithered over the fine folds of her robe, exposing the contours of her body to new light. 'You grieve for your brother,' she went on. 'But I know you better than you know yourself. Your grief is not without knowledge. And an elder brother, no matter how loved, is always a rival.'

Herod did not reply. In the hot, cardamom-scented air something had opened up between them. Something rare and precious, a chasm of infinite possibility, and he was drawn towards this voluptuous gift she was offering, leaning forward despite himself, and seeing with fascination her carmine-stained lips tremble then part. And though he hesitated on the threshold, he felt himself reaching, as surely as that first glamoured man who had reached out for forbidden fruit.

Then, suddenly, he was struck by an awareness of the drama playing out between them, of their roles and positions in the world —he the suppliant prostrating himself before the divine queen of the great Aegyptus— The thought did not sit easily with him.

He drew back then, saying stiffly, 'You have been too gracious to a poor, unworthy traveller, my queen. I must not allow myself to further intrude upon your time.' Getting to his feet, he bowed. 'If you will do me the favour of permitting me safe passage, I will trouble you with my woes no longer.'

The silence ached between them. And when he dared to look up Cleopatra's eyes were slits. 'Go,' she hissed. It was a dismissal, but too late; already she knew herself to be the one dismissed, and by this strange, tall man, dressed as a Roman, who spoke like a Jew, but no Jew she had ever known.

A Deo et Romae rex

WINTER HAD ARRIVED IN ROME. And in striking contrast to the scorched atmosphere of Alexandria the skies were dark and stormy. Great forks of lightning had been seen over the Palantine, and a property owned by Octavian had been hit, killing an unfortunate steward, who was then denied burial by the local priests having been deemed the focal point of Jupiter's wrath, though no-one could be quite certain of the exact nature of the steward's crimes. But even this gesture of submission to divine caprice did little to abate the severity of the elements, and amongst the priests and seers, their robes dripping with the blood of sacrificial birds, rumours were rife of evil portents and changes in the direction of Fate.

During this time Caius the hunchback made his way down the stinking alley known colloquially as the *river of piss*, which lay behind the Porta Capena and near to Rome's Jewish quarter. It was a poor day for begging. The rain was coming down in sheets, and those who had the luxury of calling somewhere home were either already huddled snugly in front of blazing fires or heading back there, heads down, with no time to spare the pleading, out-stretched claw of a hunchback.

Caius stopped and raised his face upwards as far as he could, letting the fat drops plop into his matted hair and beard. A poor day, he muttered again without bothering to finish the thought. Even the rags he used to exaggerate the pathos of his hump were sodden, and their rain-filled weight continuously threatened to overbalance him. The best that could be hoped for on a day like this was that the rain would wash out the *river of piss*.

Feeling the strain in his deformed neck muscles he dropped his gaze to the ground and turning, smacked head on into a stranger who had appeared from nowhere while the hunch-back had been contemplating the sky.

At once Caius backed away dribbling apologies through his crooked teeth. The fault was by no means certainly his, but life had taught him that it was wisest to assume blame and seek forgiveness no matter what the circumstances, being already a hunchback and thus perpetually condemned. He waited, eyes downcast, expecting a blow or, at best, a stream of curses to rain down upon his head. But neither came. And, when Caius struggled to look up he found a gaunt man in a threadbare cloak with several days growth of beard darkening his chin. He looked at Caius steadily then asked, 'How is it that they treat Jews in this city?'

Caius was taken aback. There was nothing that marked him out particularly amongst the followers of Moses. True he was near the Jewish quarter, but that in itself meant nothing.

Then it occurred to him that the man might be asking for himself. He scowled and gave a grotesque, lopsided shrug. 'How are we treated? O, with great care. The emperor's very fond of Jews. He lets us send our taxes back to Jerusalem, and allows us to study the laws of our fathers. If you have money he loves you all the more. You can buy a villa and a citizenship and mingle with the best of society. And if you've no money you can live comfortably enough behind the Porta Capena drinking the shit-filled water they use to irrigate their fields and going out on days when their gods empty pisspots from the clouds, trying to beg a quinucunx to keep your ribs from sticking through your flesh.' He waved his empty cup in the stranger's face. 'Which is only the same as saying that the rich are blessed and the poor are damned, and so are all men treated the world over.' He broke off bitterly and looked down the alleyway. The rain was heavier and not a soul was about. When he looked back the stranger was still at his side, a smile playing about his lips.

'To my ears you seem more philosopher than beggar.'

Caius sighed. 'Show me a beggar who is not a philosopher. We are schooled by hunger and left to count the stars.' He moved restlessly. It was occurring to him that his luck might be better at the basilica where there were covered walkways. But the stranger was not finished. 'Is it possible that such a student of wisdom knows the way to the house of Mark Antony?'

At this astonishing request Caius raised his eyebrows, but the stranger did a more astonishing thing. He reached into his cloak and produced a gold coin which he held out to Caius. 'This is the last coin in my possession. Will it purchase your services as a guide?'

Needing no second invitation Caius took the coin, testing it thoughtfully between his malformed teeth, before saying in a wondering voice, 'Now do I bow to you and salute you with deepest respect, and offer what little service an unworthy, malformed creature, such as myself, can give. It would be an honour to be your guide in this great city, and an impertinence to inquire what business you might have with the great Mark Antony, hero of Phillipi and brother-in-law to our emperor.'

He paused, blinking earnestly up. But the stranger's smile had disappeared, and fearful that he had offended, Caius took several shuffling steps backwards, squirreling the coin into the deep folds of his robe. But the stranger merely shook his head. 'You ask my business with Mark Antony. Let us say only that when Mark Antony was in need, my father was his friend and that is the reason that your emperor is so fond of Jews.'

Mark Antony received Herod with warmth, a cup of wine held loosely in one hand, as though he had been drinking when Herod's arrival had been announced, and had forgotten to put the cup down. A big gruff bear of a man, he drained the cup then tossed it at a nearby slave before, first hugging the tetrarch of Galilee until he was breathless, then holding him at arm's length and grinning down at him, as though he had lost sight of a dear friend in battle and could not believe his good fortune in finding him still alive.

'By all the gods —even that one you Jews think so special— I thought they had left me a corpse on the doorstep.'

Herod smiled ruefully and gestured at his threadbare cloak. 'They might have better wrapped a corpse.'

'That they might. Do I see a man beset by bandits or furies?'

'Perhaps sirens would be a better choice. For in trying to reach Pamphylia a storm blew up, the like of which the sailors swore they had never seen, and we were lucky to escape with our lives.' The tiniest alteration in Mark Antony's face made Herod add hastily. 'While I hastened on myself, I have sent word back to my family that they must, with all urgency, forward replacements for those gifts I hoped to present to the emperor and yourself.'

Mark Antony's face relaxed. 'And you found no welcome in Rhodes?'

'Welcome there was plenty. But only in the sense that paupers will make a brother of one who shares their fate. The war with Cassius has left the place in ruins.'

At that moment a waft of something blew up from the kitchens and Herod grew a little pale and swayed on his feet. He was caught about the waist by Mark Antony, who was already bellowing orders at his scurrying slaves.

'Quick, bring food. Prepare a feast. Do we greet guests in my house then leave them to faint from hunger?' Turning to Herod. 'You must bathe and change then you will have the best we Romans can offer.' He caught himself, asking, with a solicitousness that sat preposterously on his bluff, soldier's face, 'But what is it you Jews eat? Are there not purifications, rituals or some such— '

Herod held up a hand. 'I will be honoured to partake in whatever you offer.'

A thudding hand clapped him on the back. 'That's the spirit. But I was under the impression that you Jews make a fetish out of every morsel?'

'You will find that we make a fetish out of our ways mostly when we feel our ways being threatened.'

'By the dog of Aegyptus. I'd wager they'd have your head for saying that in Jerusalem.'

'For saying much less. But it's true just the same.'

The dining room, to which Herod was led, was ridiculously large. Mark Antony had decorated the room with the spoils of his conquests, both in love and war and Herod found he could discern neither plan nor theme. There was an outsized Grecian sideboard taking up half a wall, a variety of urns, matching in neither size nor pattern, a beautiful little scarab fashioned from lapis lazuli, doubtless the gift of Cleopatra, and a rough-hewn statue of a Celtic thunder god, which for all its crudeness evoked an uneasy response in Herod and he consciously avoided its unsettling glare, turning instead to his host. 'You are a prodigious collector.'

This evoked a hearty chuckle. 'Another way of saying I have no taste. No. No.' He waved Herod's protests away, and it was suddenly easy to see why this man was a friend to those in power. Complex minds are drawn to simplicity, fascinated by the workings of a machine they perceive to be insufficient in parts.

Mark Antony patted a couch, surprisingly worn and showing tufts of wool poking through a faded striped fabric. 'Take this one. I am no appreciator of art, but a soldier learns to recognise comfort when he sees it. I choose to lie here myself. Take it, and I'll warrant your bones will ache the less for it.'

Herod nodded gratefully, suddenly too weary to attempt diplomacy. Since disembarking at Brindisium, he had left his men and ridden day and night to reach Rome on a nag, which might have been the very manifestation of Cleopatra's curse upon him, first dithering to the point of lameness then fiery and perverse, making every step of the journey an addition of misery greater than the sum of its parts.

Now, as he lowered himself onto the yielding embrace of the couch, still feeling the rattle of the cobbles deep within his legs and spine, he wanted nothing more than to lay his head down and to close his eyes. The instinct to alertness he had carried with him all the way from Jerusalem, fuelled by the awareness that he was little more than a hunted animal, was leaving him and he had to fight to remember that in some ways he was in more danger now than with the Parthians snapping at his heels or Cleopatra's maledictions ringing in his ears.

He stifled a yawn, glancing over at Mark Antony through watering eyes for fear of having caused offence. But Mark Antony's attention was taken with the dishes brought to the table by a comely young kitchen boy —a Macedonian by the look of him— who glanced up at Herod under long-fringed lashes as he laid a bowl of figs before him.

'Thirteen,' Mark Antony said watching the pert figure disappearing back to the kitchens. 'A beautiful age in boys.'

'By thirteen we are men.'

Mark Antony laughed, as though the customs of the Jews were beyond him and suddenly yelled. 'Bring the dancers. Our honoured guest is a man of the world. He shall have the entertainment of the east. From Alexandria.' To Herod he said in sotto voce, as though they were sharing a delicious secret. 'Couldn't show them to just anyone. Prudes they are in this city. But you're not offended.' Then yelling again. 'He's not offended.'

The door opened and a group of young men and women slid into the room. They had the sinuous movements of professional dancers and arrayed themselves quickly to fill the space between the couches, posing with arms and legs in stiff, architectural poses, as though the hieroglyphs of a cartouche, carved on the side of a king's grave, had come to sudden life. Two of their number were musicians, and between them, played the high straining notes of the lyre underscored by a darker more urgent rhythm beat out on a drum.

The dancers started to move, slow, languorous movements at first that drew attention to the snaking hips, the small naked breasts swaying with the rhythm of the drum. The beat grew faster and, with it, the dancers' movements. Now they jumped and spun, the men solid, like the pillars of a temple, between which the young women wound themselves in twisting vines of human flesh.

The room grew very hot. Shadows danced on the walls. From his couch Herod watched

Mark Antony watching the dancers, seeing how the older man's face glowed with a sheen of sweat, his wine cup held carelessly towards loosened lips. His need, which seemed more naked than the nakedness of the dancers brought out a flush of distaste in Herod that overrode his instinctual reaction to the proximity of so much gleaming flesh. He was not a man to whom sex is faceless, and the painted uniformity of their expressions made the dancers, to him, no more than animate lumps of meat. As well that the legs of lamb or the carcass of the chicken got up from the table to perform.

When the dance was over he clapped politely outdone by Mark Antony's rapturous applause. Then the tallest of the female dancers came forward and bowed with dignity before the general, asking if he wished the performance to continue. Her face was immobile, but she was panting a little, and Mark Antony shook his head, beaming, magnanimous. 'No, no. We will not risk the virtue of our young Jew further.' He roared at his own joke and produced a bag of coins, which he held out to her. She took it gracefully, but not before he had reached out and tweaked her nipple with his free hand.

Embarrassed, by such intimate exposure, not of flesh, but of weakness, Herod pretended not to see. And when he looked up again the dancers had gone and Mark Antony was changing the subject. 'Your first time in the Eternal City, I think. What do you make of it?'

Herod tore a piece of olive bread between his fingers. He was bathed and cleanly dressed for the first time in weeks, and it restored his flagging self-esteem, the sense of unworthiness that goes with uncleanliness, to which, as a Jew, he was especially sensitive. 'In truth I have travelled only through the back alleys and the slums. My guide favoured a discrete route. But if I have seen Rome at its worst then it rivals much of what I have heard in other places described as, best.'

'Flatterer. Did the wonders of Alexandria wash past you? Or is it impossible for a Jew to admit an Aegyptian has the better of him?'

'There were marvels in every direction, but my mind was otherwise occupied.'

Mark Antony looked down at his goblet. 'She is an enchanting woman.'

At once all sense of sleep left Herod. With care he replied, 'You must forgive me. I had forgotten to congratulate you on your marriage to the emperor's sister.'

Mark Antony's face darkened. 'Crows take you,' he snarled, all traces of his good humour gone. 'Do you think that you will sit across from me, Jew, and play the politician?'

'I did not— ' Herod began, but was cut off.

'Do I need a lesson in morality? You have the appearance of a Roman on the outside, but scratch the surface and the sanctimony comes pouring out. Have you never been with a woman who looks at you as though she's drinking in your soul? Well, have you?' He gestured with his cup and wine sloshed over the edges. 'To need her day and night. To live in terror that she will turn her affections on another man. I am Jupiter lost to the wiles of his Venus. She is a witch. I am beguiled.' A note of self-pity crept into his voice. 'And you talk to me of my wife.'

Herod slipped from his couch and knelt beside this great bear-like man, who suddenly looked like a whipped child. 'Forgive me.'

Mark Antony's head had sunk on his chest. He was staring dolorously into his cup. 'She will ruin me. I should cut her head from her shoulders.'

Herod put his hand out and gently eased the cup from his host's hand, shaking his head at a solicitous slave who approached to refill it. Mark Antony had grasped Herod's wrist; he was holding it tightly, and Herod felt the need to say, 'If I have misspoken— '

But Mark Antony suddenly turned his head, pressing his face close to the younger man. Herod could smell the must of grapes on his breath.

'You're my friend, aren't you?'

'I hope you will consider me such.'

Mark Antony reached out with his free hand and stroked Herod's freshly-shaven cheek. 'You should have kept the beard. You looked more like a king.'

'I— ' Herod was at a rare loss of words. At last he ventured, 'My loyalty is, of course, with the grandson of Hyrcanus, brother to my betrothed. He is the rightful heir to the Has-monaean line, and I am here only to— '

But Mark Antony's mood had changed again. 'You're my friend,' he said again in brus-quer tones. 'You must get rid of her for me.'

It was not altogether clear whether he was talking about the queen of Aegyptus or his wife. Herod cleared his throat, trying, at the same time, to release his wrist. But Mark An-tony only gripped tighter, a wild unfocussed expression blurring his fine features. 'You know it must be done. You will know how. They say the Jews are full of guile and cunning. O— ' He dropped his head onto his chest again. 'I am a man bewitched. She is so beautiful. You saw her!' Another swing in Herod's direction, and now something accusatory crept into his tone. 'Were you not moved by her beauty?'

Herod saw the trap and knew himself to be cornered. A man as passionately in love as Mark Antony cannot bear to think that the object of his affections is any less desirable to other men, yet, equally, cannot bear to hear that it is so. Affirmation or denial; either answer, Herod knew, would condemn him. Feigning a need to consider his thoughts, he allowed his gaze to wander about the room. The wicked stare of the Celtic god came out of the shadows, and Cleopatra's scarab shifted in the flickering lamp light. His thoughts were interrupted by a grunt from Mark Antony, and when he turned back, he found his host lost in slumber, his brow furrowed in a frown.

The next day Herod was awoken by a slave who informed him that Mark Antony was waiting for him, and would Herod please make haste as they were to depart at once. He sat up, blinking the sleep from his eyes.

'Where are we going?'

The slave, a spindly, somewhat fussy man whose scrawny body seemed insufficient to support his large dome-shaped head regarded Herod with distaste. 'Sincerest apologies. The master does not make me privy to the details of his plans.'

Herod suspected this was untrue, hearing the note of condescension in the man's voice, a common trait in high-ranking slaves who feel themselves better versed in the manners of their captors than those provincial barbarians with whom their masters choose to associate.

'I will bring you warm water to bathe in if —he paused delicately— you are ready.' Before leaving he glanced pointedly at the window where it was clear that the sun, in contrast to Mark Antony's guest, had been up for hours.

By the time Herod reached the atrium, Mark Antony was already dressed in his cloak and giving the dome-headed slave some final instructions. He gave a quick, one-eyed glance at Herod, who was hurrying down the stairs, still tugging at the generous folds of his borrowed tunic.

'So, the sun in the east rises at last.'

Herod smiled uneasily, never certain whether banter carried a subtext of rebuke. It was clear that this was not the Mark Antony of the night before. This man was alert and calmly in control, and Herod knew himself to have been a fool to assume that his host would suffer the consequences of his indulgence the next day; was Mark Antony's constitution not legendary?

'Do we go to Caesar?'

'Better. I sent messengers on your behalf last night. He has convened the Senate.'

Mark Antony had chosen the route along the *via Lata* towards the Senate building, which in those days was housed in temporary quarters behind the theatre of Pompey. It was no longer raining. Instead there was a clear, harsh beauty to the day, the sky sheathed in iron-clad clouds, except where winter sunlight broke through in blades of reflected light. Herod, whose blood was thinned to accommodate sunnier climes, found his borrowed cloak too light to keep out the sharp bite of the air. He fussed with the collar and with the length of his hair, wishing he had got the slave to cut it the night before when he had shaved him.

More troubling was Mark Antony's silence. He had withdrawn from the *bon homie* of the dinner party, answering Herod's questions with sharp military brevity designed only to deter further interrogation. And the sight of the theatre complex, looming over the campus Martius, like the harsh reality that follows too good a dream, did nothing to allay Herod's growing anxieties.

He had been caught up in his own game, playing everything on a single roll of the dice, certain that he could persuade Rome to accept the right of Hyrcanus' grandson —a boy of thirteen, and no more a man in the eyes of the Senate than a child hanging from the teat of his wet-nurse— to rule, over the right of the nephew, Antigonus. Yet, if Mark Antony's grim expression was anything to go by, he had failed even to persuade the one man he might call friend. The thought of Mark Antony's dissolution the night before chilled him. Not that it was unusual to see a man in his cups. But Mark Antony had spilled more than wine before Herod, and a man does not easily forgive another for bearing witness to the secrets of his heart.

They entered the complex through a huge gateway, colonnaded on four sides, then descended marble steps which led into formal gardens, flanked by temples to the minor deities and were reputed —so Herod had heard— to contain the artworks and treasures Pompey had brought back from his campaigns. Despite his worries that innate desire for the picturesque raised itself inside Herod, and he threw the shadowed depths a longing glance.

'Venus Victrix.'

This pronouncement flatly made by Mark Antony startled the younger man.

'Up there?' He followed Mark Antony's squinting glance to where a marble goddess stood at the apex of the theatre roof, her gaze aloof, one arm stretched out to suspend a laurel wreath.

'Pompey had to pretend the theatre was to honour religion. It was that or the old women in the Senate would have forced him to tear it down.'

'Tear it down?' The creative element in Herod's nature shrank at the prospect. Mark Antony shrugged. 'Lest our simple Roman virtues be sullied with Greek vanities. Surely this purity of spirit appeals to a Jew.'

'Amongst the Pharisees there is a tendency to renounce everything in the name of simplicity, but we Jews can recognise beauty in stone. You forget that Solomon built a temple, which while it stood, was one of the wonders of the world.'

Mark Antony gave Herod a sidelong glance. 'Are there many theatres in Jerusalem then?'

'No.' Herod's smile was strange and secret. 'Not yet.'

They entered the curia at the far side of the complex. Herod felt the draw of anticipation quicken his footsteps, but Mark Antony's pace slowed. He paused in front of the great statue of Pompey that graced the entrance, staring up through the pale shafts of winter sunlight that fell through the columned portico.

'It was there.'

He was pointing at the foot of the statue, and, for an instant, Herod did not understand then he said —not knowing what else to say— 'He did not heed the soothsayer.'

Mark Antony shrugged. 'Every time a great man leaves the house soothsayers crawl out of the corners predicting this outcome or that. We remember the ones who happen upon the truth, and forget that they contradicted themselves the day before.' He went on staring at the base of the statue, and Herod joined him, searching, without consciousness of searching, for the bloodstains which must surely be soaked into the marble for perpetuity.

At his side Mark Antony sighed. 'You should remember, most soothsayers are historians at heart, and all historians have a yearning to be dramatists. 'Already they are saying Calpurnia begged him not to go.'

Herod looked up. 'You know otherwise?'

'They argued certainly. Calpurnia ever had a scolding tongue. But who is to say what was said and what was not? Do you imagine Sallust or Nicolaus of Damascus sat in his apartment writing down his words?'

Herod raised a knowing eyebrow, but Mark Antony shook his head. 'Slaves will fashion their stories to match the value of coin crossing their palms. Their tales contradict each other worse than soothsayers.'

The sun went behind a cloud and Pompey's face was lost in shadow. Herod shivered. 'You were there?'

Mark Antony did not answer for a moment, and Herod, who had a strange sympathy for pain beyond his ken, understood that, for now, he was no more than a ghost, standing invisible and helpless, on a cold bright day towards the middle of the month of Martius. He drew in his breath and waited.

'Gave him no chance to defend himself.' Mark Antony went on, his voice hard and flat. 'Surrounded him, like a slavering pack, butchering him, with less dignity than you would kill a pig. Stabbing and slicing so wildly they cut each other in the process.' He swung round, as though suddenly hearing the question Herod had put. 'You ask where I was. I was there —pointing beyond the entrance— Outside on the steps, detained by that snake, Trebonius. 'And when I reached him he was no longer dictator of Rome, no. He wasn't even a man. Just a bloodied lump of meat. I bent over him. His eyes were closed, but his lips were moving. And now every gossip, who dignifies his name with the title historicus, is inventing tales of great words he spoke.'

'There were none?'

Mark Antony shook his head and looked back at the statue. 'You have been in battle, Herod. Does a man wounded in every part of his body make speeches? He calls for his mother if he still has speech in him. Caesar died. He just died. Without saying anything at all.'

They stood in silence. And Herod looked down on the scrubbed white marble, where no trace of infamy showed and wondered, not for the first time, how it was that great men so often belonged to Janus rather than Jupiter, constantly wearing the double face of saviour and monster.

Mark Antony, who had been hunched forward, looking older than his years, shrugged suddenly and some of his old heartiness came back. 'But he is a god now. That at least we could do for him.' He clapped Herod on the shoulder. 'You Jews should consider it. Does your one true God never get lonely all alone in his heavenly sphere?'

'That is why he created mankind.'

Mark Antony laughed. 'Then his tastes are strange. We must make poor companions for a deity.'

It occurred to Herod to point out that Cleopatra was now a goddess, but Herod had intuitions that often saved him, and he followed one now, saying nothing, and allowing his smile to appear to be in response to Mark Antony's humour.

They entered the Senate chamber, and from the first things did not go well. Octavian appeared impatient, as though he had been expecting them at an appointed hour and they were late. He did not look at Herod, but addressed himself directly to Mark Antony, who, in turn, made his greetings. But there was a coldness about it, and it was clear that these men held more respect than friendship for one another.

Herod stood stiffly under the scrutiny of the Senate, painfully aware that every eye, but Octavian's was upon him. He felt himself assessed and judged and found wanting, seeing, while pretending not to see, the heads turned towards one another, the comments murmured behind covered mouths, a low titter quickly disguised as a cough, and his awareness grew of how his hair reached past his collar, the extravagant manner of his bow, even the belt at his waist fastened just a little differently. A thousand indefinable traits marked him out as 'other', the Jewish wolf donning sheep's clothing so that he might slip in amongst the herd. Too dangerous, too cunning. Not to be trusted.

'Messala will speak first,' this announcement made by Octavian.

'A friend.' Mark Antony's whisper was in his ear.

Messala, a narrow wisp of a man with a receding hairline, spoke in a surprisingly rich melodious voice, his arguments constructed with the clean precision of a geometer, and finally, summing up what he described as the 'Judean crisis', in clear calm tones. 'It all boils down to one thing, gentlemen. Antigonus represents Parthia. He has sided with the enemy. With our support, the grandson of Hyrcanus has every reason to be a loyal ally to Rome.'

A bland-faced man in his senior years, his hair a snowy fringe, got up from where he sat near Octavian's side.

'Speak, good Balbus,' Octavian enjoined. Balbus bowed then patted himself down and looked about, as though he had misplaced some papers.

'Balbus?'

'Indeed, Caesar. Indeed.' Balbus stopped looking about, and turned his bland, rather rosy-cheeked, face directly to Herod. 'The question of Judea is not an easy one, you will agree?'

'No.'

'To the north there is Syria and to the south the great Aegyptus. Both nations consider you an aberration at best and an abomination at worst.'

Herod opened his mouth, but Balbus was not finished.

'And don't think that converting a few goat herders and penniless peasants in Peraea or Idumaea will protect you against the Arabs waging war from the east. But that is not the worst of it.'

Herod said nothing.

'Far from it. Your ruling family has become weak and corrupt.' He saw Herod's expression harden and smiled. 'O, we Romans know well enough that a family can survive the latter. Some individuals may even grow stronger because of it. But never the former. Your own people, the Hasmonaeans, pulled down the might of Greece when it attacked them. Do you know why?'

'Because they were righteous.'

Balbus gave a bark of laughter, which was echoed in the tiered ranks behind him. 'No, friend, do not play the pious Jew with me. You know well it was because their enemies, those Greeks called Seleucid, had become weak, a fatal flaw amidst the mighty. They fell to fighting amongst themselves. And how can you defend against an external enemy if the hand you trusted with a sword turns it against your breast? Do you follow what I am saying?'

Herod's face tightened. He should seize the moment. If he was to speak it must be now. But he was torn between throwing himself on his knees and offering himself up to Rome in all humility or shaking his fist to demonstrate the ardour of his strength. He searched his mind for some clever flattery or last-minute promise that might swing the balance in his favour then dismissed them all as hopelessly too late. And already Balbus had stepped back and Octavian was speaking; he had missed his chance.

'We request that you leave the chamber now and allow us to proceed in private.'

Herod understood that this was no request. He held a moment longer the iron-coloured eyes, belonging to a man, not yet four and twenty, who had killed clever Cassius with nothing more than the force of a lie. Then, at Mark Antony's light touch, he bowed and left the chamber with as much dignity as he could muster.

For the rest of the morning Herod paced the length and breadth of the covered walkways as a lion will pace its cage with the half wariness of the gladiatorial arena and the certain death that lies beyond. His instincts told him that there must be something he could do to change the odds, while his intelligence argued that the game was lost.

He stopped before the painting of a youth, which hung in a little alcove in one of Pompey's treasure troves. The boy was handsome, no older than Jonathan was now, and he stared back at Herod out of the portrait with clear, candid eyes. For his part, Herod felt no revulsion at the fine rendering of a human form. In common with the more sophisticated members of his society he obeyed the law concerning graven images, but in practice felt immune to their influence. It was the abstract, unreachable god that appealed to Herod's soul, and any attempt to draw God's face would have filled him with contemptuous mirth.

And looking at this portrait now he was struck by the way art reaches into men, and the worlds they inhabit, reflecting their obsessions in ways only an outsider has the privilege to see. In Aegyptus the stiff, unyielding figures spoke of a fixation with the past, while in Greece —Zeus casting his thunderbolts, Athena leaping with her hounds, Dionysus surrounded by adoring nymphs— exalted achievement only in the domain of the gods.

But here, in Rome, things were different. Herod's eyes narrowed with his thoughts. Here the art was on an earthly plane. The men and women portrayed gazed boldly back at the observer, as if their own flesh and blood was immortality enough, and Herod sensed the power of a people who were neither transfixed in bygone days nor dazzled by the clouds, but comfortable in their own skins, willing even to laugh at themselves if the satirists were to be believed. Herod's education, which was not truly equal to one of the nobility, had difficulty coming up with names, such as Lucilius or Persius, but he knew that a Roman could poke fun at himself in a way that neither a Greek nor an Aegyptian nor even a Jew could do at that time, and he felt his mind opening in new directions when he considered how the men and women of this city were satisfied with their own essential humanness.

Footsteps behind him made him turn sharply. Mark Antony was behind him, his face a mask.

'Come.'

Heart failing, Herod obeyed. They returned to the chamber, and this time his entrance provoked a deadening silence. Herod followed Mark Antony to the centre of the room, where he stood, feeling a smallness that not even Cleopatra, with her ostentatious wealth and her millennial lineage, could conjure. Octavian studied him, chin resting on the knuckles of one hand, whilst every atom in Herod's body fought an infinitesimal battle against his struggle to maintain rigid self-control.

'The boy is too young.'

The words came to Herod as the words spoken to a dreamer. He heard himself say, 'But with my guidance. I would seek to influence— '

Octavian interrupted. 'Rome is not blind. Do you imagine you are first to tell us of how it stands in Judea? But Jonathan is no Cleopatra; he could never withstand the forces of his uncle. The country would fragment into warring factions, and we would be forced to assume control.'

So that was it. All the dark dogs of doubt, he had kept so assiduously at bay since fleeing Masada, began to howl and slaver inside his head. He fought to stay calm.

'Jonathon's claim is legitimate.'

Octavian gave him a look that said, to hang with that, and Herod closed his eyes. He was choking with anger and sorrow. The oldest Roman families could not trace their ancestries back more than a couple of hundred years. Had he expected them to respect more ancient bloodlines? The Roman way was to burn then rebuild in their own image. Consider Carthage. Weep for Corinth. Suddenly the future stretched before him, vast and empty, and within it he was a tiny wandering figure without place or part. Octavian's voice came from far away,

'And so it is the decision of the Senate to confer the kingship upon you.'

Herod's eyes snapped open, but consciousness did not keep up.

'I— What do you— '

'The motion was put forth by Messala and seconded by Atratinus. Congratulations Herod ben Antipater, King of Jews. But make haste. We go shortly to make sacrifice and to deposit the decree in the Capitol. Tonight there will be a banquet in your honour.'

Herod still shaking his head looked to Mark Antony who laughed aloud at his bewilderment, and his laughter broke the tension in the room. It made Herod smile, his lips stretching back so far his face ached.

'I am at a loss. Give me your advice?'

Mark Antony clapped a powerful hand on Herod's shoulder then bent low to whisper in his ear. 'Grow back the beard. It makes you look the part.'

13

An interval in which death is snatched out of Death

INTERLUDE, 4 BCE

Y*ES, WE ARE HERE AGAIN. At the end. What did you imagine? That it is easy to become a king. Rome decrees and the world obeys? But Parthia is neither a backwater province, ready to be trampled, nor an ancient civilization fallen into debauchery and dissolution. Parthia is a force to be reckoned with, and its king, Pacorus, can summon a hundred thousand men to the battlefield with a snap of his fingers. You may be certain that Herod will have his hands full when he returns. But we will come back to that. Leave him for now to discover that to be gifted a throne is to be given, not as Herod thinks a noun, but a verb. It exists only in a state of action: of coveting, of taking, of retaining, of maintaining and sustaining, and of quelling and expelling the greedy hands who would push him from it, and there will be many of those.*

Well then, let him have his moment of unexpected triumph. The bright spokes of sunlight are pushing back the clouds as he heads towards the Capitoline, his shoulders bearing the affectionate weight of the two most powerful men in the world. He will never again feel such pure, unspoiled happiness, and his joy is increased by his ignorance of the future. Time then to draw your eyes away, and turn the decades, like pages, until we are back once more with the dying king—

—What is wrong? Ah, you thought me gone. But this is my story and I will tell it my way.—

There, now you see what I see, Salome sitting in the antechamber, staring at her reflection in a hand-mirror. Her expression is an unhappy one, exaggerating the droop of her face. Time has proved a traitorous friend, exacting a high price in sagging jowls and dulling eye for every second allotted from his miserly purse. Her hair —once her pride and joy now the colour of cobwebs and almost as thin— is disguised by an elaborate wig, and she stares despairingly into the burnished bronze searching for comforts in the distortions of its polished surface. The mirror can be kind in a way that the years are not. Her complexion softens, her hair darkens a little. Surely she is not made from the same friable stuff that lies corrupting in the bed next door. Utterly absorbed she sits until—

A banging on the door. She starts then composes herself. A quick glance back towards the main chamber then,

'Enter.'

91

Mordechai ben Jacob comes into the room, the captain of the guard, a powerfully built man in his fifties with the harassed look of a man promoted beyond his limits. He bows before Salome then does not seem to know what to do, looking down at his big hands, as though they might speak for him. And Salome, who has bulk, though not height, stares at him coldly, not because she is afraid of him, but because she is afraid of what he has to say.

'Well, don't stand there, as though your tongue has been cut out —for it can be if you continue to fail in your duties. What news do you bring?'

The captain of the guard starts to sweat. 'Peace be with you, lady, and upon this noble house,' he begins nervously.

'Peace be damned. Your news.'

'There has been an … incident. At the Temple.'

Salome feels the palms of her hands grow slick. —So it begins.— But she has lived long enough at her brother's side not to loose the reigns of power too soon. She stretches herself up taller and pulls in her stomach. 'What has happened?'

The captain of the guard mops his brow. 'The people weep for the state of the king— '

'Yes, yes,' Salome interrupts impatiently. 'We need not worry about the ones who weep.'

'Begging my lady's pardon, but I know different. In their grief, the ones who love your brother most have convinced themselves that he is no more than hours away from his final breath.'

Salome's mouth sets in a grim line. She wants to scream at the captain of the guard to stop staring at the floor and look her in the eye, but this she cannot do, so she says quietly, 'And this has made his enemies bold.'

A nod from the captain. 'The Pharisees, Judas bar Sepphoris and Matthias bar Margalus, they are learned men. And many go to listen to their teachings, especially the young. And they are much loved and respected and— '

'The point, captain.'

Ben Jacob's eyes slide across the floor. He mops his brow. 'They have been riling the young men up with tales of how the king's illness is a punishment from the Almighty.' And here the captain glances upwards, as though afraid that he might have caused offence in heaven. But the ceiling, with its pretty border of acanthus leaves, does not split apart, and he grows more confident. 'They say it's the eagle.'

—The great golden eagle Herod erected over the gates of the Temple, in homage to his benefactors in Rome.—

Salome closes her eyes. He built them a Temple, she is thinking. A temple beyond the dream of Solomon, a monument of surpassing magnificence that will stand for eternity as testimony to the glory of the Almighty. And they think him struck down for the offence of a golden eagle. But she says only, 'Go on.'

The captain is looking at his hands again. 'They were preaching that it was a splendid thing in the eyes of the Almighty to tear down the eagle, just as in ancient times Josiah tore down the poles of Asherah and destroyed her sacred groves and scattered the ashes with the bones of her priests. They were saying it was better to die young in a noble cause than be struck down, as those who have blackened their souls are blighted by disease and infirmity.'

How many years did he reign, thinks Salome. How many years did they crave his justice and his favour?

'And the young men were fired up by this talk, and they went to the Temple at midday, knowing there would be an audience for their misdeeds, and began hacking down the eagle with axes they had hidden in their robes.'

'How did this happen on your watch, Captain?'

Fear of death sends ben Jacob's inhibitions flying out the window. He looks Salome in the eye, his lined, sweating face attempting appeal. 'I did all that could be done, lady. As soon as I received word of what was taking place, I went with a force of men, and we fell upon them without mercy. Most ran in terror. They were only there to watch the spectacle, you see. '

'I see only that you caused a rout and panic in the holiest place known to man.'

The captain flinches then recovering himself. 'We captured forty who stood in defiance, lady. They are outside awaiting the king's orders.'

Salome pales and reaches out to grip the edge of a table. She is thinking, Two could be ignored, ten even we might have hidden. But forty. Dear God. Her gaze has dropped, with the immensity of it all, to the floor. She sees the captain's feet shuffling.

'What are my orders, lady?'

She takes a breath, knowing that in this moment she is more powerful than she has ever been. With her next words she can snatch a little more time from the angel of Death or she can sever Herod's reign as easily as one of her maidservants might cut a wayward thread. A quick glance over her shoulder towards the bedchamber. And there's the paradox. How much does she hate this brother she has also loved? Injustice fights a battle with gratitude inside her head, and the violence of it drives the nails of one hand into the palm of the other. But she has hesitated too long and the captain raises his eyes.

'Lady?'

She sees herself reflected there, a wrinkled matron of maturing years, vacillating in the rays of a dying sun. And now she thinks on it, isn't there something predatory in the captain's servile toadying? A dog crawling on its belly, ready to rip the flesh from his dead master's bones. And suddenly she has no stomach for the games people play. Only let things be simple. That is punishment enough. She watches him bow his head once more before declaring her verdict.

'Select the ringleaders. We will take them to the king.'

The prisoners were brought to the amphitheatre at Jericho. Their trial had taken place a week before, and now, for the ones standing ragged and chained upon the sandy floor, there could be no more hope. They faced the crowd, seeing for the last time the grieving relatives, who had gathered on the tiered, limestone seats and now sat weeping and wringing their hands or frantically offering up unanswered prayers. In the front rows, sat the nobles and magistrates, who had come only because they were aware that their absence would have been more notable than their presence.

At some unseen signal, there was the sound of drums and two Levites, dressed in blue, pulled apart the cedar doors opening on to the royal pavilion. Moments later the king was brought in.

— *Have you heard of a man, already dead, brought back to life? But, of course, you have. There is the one called, Lazarus, whom you consider so unique. Yet what of Elijah and Elisha? Have you forgotten that they, too, dragged fleeing souls back into their bones? Shaking your head? Such things are impossible. Yet it is a fact. I have witnessed resurrection with my own eyes.*

He is here, the king, Herod who was dead. By all that is dear to me I swear I saw his body without breath, beneath him, his resting place turned, in an instant, from bed to catafalque. And bending over him the Greek physician shaking his head. 'Lady, it is too late.' Yet how little he understood the mind of a Herod. Salome threw herself upon her brother's unmoving chest.

'Is this how it must be?' she hissed in his ear. 'You gone and the jackals tearing the king-dom apart. Leave me now, brother and all you have built up will become the ashes and salt of a new Amora.'

At this the dead man's eyes flicked open. The voice, which had not been heard for days, demanded wine, and when it was brought he drank greedily, as though his illness had been a fasting in the desert and now he had returned to the appetites of men.—

The couch was lowered. The drumbeat ceased and the king was plainly seen by all, a skeletal yellow figure, propped up on a couch, whose hands trembled beneath a thin blanket of lambswool. Salome took her place at her brother's side, half shielding him with her solid body. She was tight-lipped and pale, but still she faced the crowd with a sort of haughty forbearance, the indomitable face of House Herod. Behind the royal brother and sister were the usual mix of eunuchs, slaves, priests, freedmen and ministers et cetera that gathered in the background, knowing that their days were numbered, but still clinging to that which was familiar.

In a corner was a drably dressed woman, who went largely unnoticed. Though, if any-one had been looking closely enough they might have sensed something in addition to the desolation that made her eyes luminous, something fixed and resolute, almost as though she anticipated the executions, not as an act of righteousness, but more as a gladiator will face the ordeal of the arena.

—But the king is speaking—

'Is it me you imagine you have offended?'

That voice, still daring the listener to defiance. Hearing it, the prisoners shuffled, only one or two daring a fleeting glance upwards. This speech was not new to their ears. It had fallen upon them, like a storm, less than seven days ago, the king's rage a molten, uncontrolled flow that scorched hope from the air.

—Who had given them a Temple greater than the vision of Solomon? Who had filled it with the most sumptuary dedicatory offerings? Not the Hasmonaeans. No. In more than a century's reign to what expense had they ever put themselves? But perhaps they were indeed wiser. Only a fool would have wasted half a life time cherishing the thought that his incomparable achievement would grant him respect beyond the grave when it was plain that the common man in the street wished to insult him to his very face in broad daylight.—

Here, bar Margalus, the more diplomatic of the two Pharisees, (for the teachers have been taken too) attempted to intervene. It was not Herod that they attacked, merely the violations of Mosaic Law. 'If we are condemned it is not through any fault on our part, but only through our love of piety.'

— Piety? Did they dare to talk of piety? With the people looking on, they had laid hands on an offering he, their king, had set up, and this was more than any outrage against his royal office, this was an act of sacrilege!—

He had been shaking with rage, but now, at the word, *sacrilege*, Herod's face took on an expression of satisfaction. They had moved against him, and he had caught them in a trap of their own making. The listening magistrates might hesitate to convict men who offered insult to a king, even at risk to their lives, but to suffer an offence against the Almighty —He with whom they had a unique covenant made in flesh— that was to risk losing eternity.

Bar Margalus grasped at once the sleight of words that turned him from righteous hero into base villain, and glanced urgently at bar Sepphoris, who shook his head despairingly. At their backs the young men were still defiant, not yet understanding that their mentors were impaled on the claws of a wounded lion.

They stood, displaying the cocky certainty of youth, half hoping for the melodrama that an unjust death would bring them —*Kiddush hashem*, to sanctify His Name, and they would do it with the sacrifice of their own blood—. And yet, truth be told, they were more convinced that the crowning strength of their faith was not going unnoticed by the god of their fathers, who after all had plucked Moses, Jacob, Daniel and countless others from the hands of their oppressors.

The magistrates returned. The verdicts were read, and Herod watched closely the faces of the condemned as the death sentence was invariably passed. The announcement struck each man differently, and this seemed to interest him greatly. Bar Sepphoris stood silent and angry, while bar Margalus wept, not for himself, but to see so much youth destroyed for the sake of a Pharisee's arrogance and a king's pride. The young men reacted variously. Some looked about them in wide-eyed surprise, as though they expected the wrath of God to descend and strike Herod down, others closed their eyes rocking slightly with the force of their prayers. And most pitiful was a young boy —who later turned out to be barely sixteen— who blinked, as though coming out of a trance then started calling out to his mother and father to take him home. And, all the while, Herod watched grimly, alone and unloved, and filled with the pain of knowing he was unloved, even this victory soured by the knowledge that however many he put to death he would not be long in joining them.

And now there they stand on the white sand freshly scattered on the floor of the amphitheatre. The rabbis are to be first, the method chosen by Herod himself, SEREFAH, *death by burning.*

 Will you watch? Or are you above such voyeuristic extravagancies? How civilized you are. Turn the pages quickly. You will know the instant the story changes direction. Or stay and peep through the outstretched bars of your fingers; give in to the irresistible urge to see a man tipped into eternity. No-one will ever know you were here. And you will not be the first, I promise.

In her rough-spun robes Loshema was ignored by those around her. No-one took the trouble to speak to her, even shunning her slightly so that her view remained unobscured, and this was to her liking. Down below, on the freshly scattered sand they were thrusting ben Margalus into a deep hole, which left only his head and shoulders visible. There was no pyre. *Serefah* was not a death of the Roman arena, no pitch or *tunica molesta* were necessary.

Bar Margolus made no attempt to struggle, even when they filled the hole with shovelfuls of dung, and his restraint was achieved without protest. Behind him bar Sepphoris, who was to share his fate, looked on with his disciples, though, as all their faces were blackened and swollen with beating, it was hard to distinguish the teacher from his students.

Loshema, a sickening knot at the base of her stomach, allowed her gaze to lift upwards. The sky was overcast because spring was not early coming that year and the night had been chill, yet even so there was a crackling, hot atmosphere in the air promoted by the smell of burning charcoal. And, knowing there was no escape, Loshema let her gaze fall to where a sweating, bald man, whom she recognised as a blacksmith of the king's household, was struggling to maintain a fire, above which a cauldron simmered.

She knew him to be a large, simple man, who believed that the universe is a hierarchy where the Almighty ruled supreme and appointed the rest of mankind in ranked order. And finding himself very near the bottom of the pile, he followed blithely the orders of others, certain that his betters knew more about the world than he ever would. Yet, down in the arena he fidgeted and ran his rough hands through the thinning straggle at the nape of his neck in a manner that betrayed his discomfort with the current task.

Herod was growing impatient. Loshema saw him worrying the edge of the lamb's wool blanket.

'Devil take that man. How long does it take to melt a simple wick of lead? Does he want to join the fate of men who meddle with the Law?'

Salome moved to quiet him, but she shot a warning look down into the arena, and the captain of the guard nodded and hurried over to the blacksmith. But it was unnecessary. The blacksmith was already filling a ladle which steamed and hissed as the molten lead touched the cold metal. When it was full he stepped back, glancing up at the pavilion, as though awaiting permission. No signal was issued, but the drums started up again and the black-smith began to walk in the direction of the prisoners, the hissing ladle held gingerly before him.

At his approach the two guards fell to their knees behind the prisoner. Loshema could not see their expressions, but she saw the hopeful, eager glance one of the younger disciples threw them. And if she had not stoppered up her heart against pity she would surely have pitied him then, knowing as she did that he mistook their intention for sudden piety.

A length of cloth was produced and wound round ben Margalus' neck. He made no protest. His eyes were closed and his lips were moving slightly. Each guard held a loose end then the cloth was pulled tight in opposite directions. Ben Margalus' eyes snapped open and his mouth gaped. In the stands behind him, Loshema could see a woman —wife or sister perhaps— begin a wild, ululating weeping. At her side, an old man urged her to hide her grief. One cannot weep too loudly in the face of the king's justice.

A third guard approached carrying the blacksmith's ladle at arm's length. He halted be-fore ben Margalus, and the drums stopped. An aching silence rolled across the crowd. Necks were stretched, tears hung, suspended on eyelashes. Loshema felt her bowels tighten. Then suddenly, shockingly, it was done. In the space between one moment and the next the guard tipped the ladle and a lustrous stream of lead poured into ben Margalus' gaping mouth.

If there had been a scream it might have seemed a more natural death, a death con-ceived by man. Instead steam poured from ben Margalus' throat. His face turned livid and his eyes rolled up into his skull. At once the guards let go the ends of the cloth and the Phar-isee's head fell back with that strange emptiness of movement that marks death. Even so, the steam continued to rise in a steady column from his mouth giving the strange impression that he had become fluent in the subtle language of clouds.

In front Salome was stroking her brother's hand, while Herod shifted restlessly beneath his blanket, having discovered that dispensing death offered no vicarious relief, yet unwilling to give up the experiment, rather like a man who has lost his sense of taste, but cannot resist taking another bite of flesh. And suddenly finding it hard to breathe, Loshema gathered her robes in her hands and slipped, unnoticed outside.

In the gloom of the connecting corridor all the urgency left her, and she leaned heavily on the wall, eyes closed against the horror and the coming possibility of more horror. She was unaware of approaching footsteps until a voice said softly, 'This is an evil day.'

Startled, Loshema looked round and found Micaiah, a eunuch of Herod's household, standing a short distance off. She made no answer, instinctually glancing about, searching for the trap. Micaiah, his hands folded inside the long sleeves of his robes, ignored her reaction, or at least pretended to ignore her reaction, continuing on in the same soft tones, 'They say ben Margalus was the mildest of the teachers.' He paused to allow her to respond. But, when she made none, he went on, 'His acts of rebellion were meant only as torches to light the way to peace, and instead they are saying that he has set flame under a new face of Judaism where death will speak louder than life.' He shrugged, as though to indicate how little weight he gave loose talk then his eyes narrowed.

'I overheard the Roman ambassador saying that such a death as ben Margalus suffered would be considered too lenient in Rome. Dead in a heartbeat, no time to satisfy the blood-lust of the crowd.' He put his head on one side, as though considering. 'They don't understand, of course, the terrible irony at the heart of *Serefah*. The great inversion that snatches death from death.' His eyes flicked towards Loshema's frozen face. 'They say it destroys the soul but not the body. Do you believe that?'

What answer could she give? Instead the muscles of her face spoke for her, revisiting the habits of childhood and offering up only the expressionless mask of the slave. Micaiah studied her for some time then gave a dry laugh, as though he had been caught out in an act of foolishness. 'Ah, of course.' He bowed. 'No-one knows what Loshema believes.'

As he walked away her lip began to tremble, but he did not turn to see it.

14

In which Herod shows the followers of Antigonus no mercy and sends
his brother a gift.

39 BCE

*I*N THE DAYS OF WHICH *I speak, Jerusalem was a city lived for the most part out on the streets. Under striped canopies all manner of transactions took place, from the buying of simple, unleavened bread to the procurement of the costliest spices and silks brought in from the unimaginable corners of the empire, where the gods have many arms and legs and the eyes of the people are kept always half-shut against the sun.*

In Jerusalem's squares there were preachers who told poor men that the Lord had not forgotten them and preachers who told rich men that the Lord had blessed them. There were travellers and peddlers, politicians and beggars, whores and holy men, all doing business at the tops of their voices. And in the dusty corners, in doorways and beneath staircases there were children, children who gathered to play a game that was a great favourite at the time.

The game was a simple one. To play a quantity of pebbles was marked on one side with charcoal and placed blackened side up. One child was set the challenge of turning over the pebbles faster than their opponent could right them. If he could do this to more than half the pebbles then he was the victor. So it was for Herod as he tried to wrest Jerusalem back from Antigonus and establish the kingship conferred upon him by Rome. With each triumph, a dozen revolts and insurrections would turn over in his wake.

And there was little help from the Roman generals appointed as his allies. Hannibal, that prince of Africa, once called Rome a city for sale, and his words were not short of the mark. On more than one occasion Antigonus' agents were able to bribe the Romans into betraying their cause, and even when they rallied to Herod's side, their looting and destruction of the conquered cities led Herod to write despairingly to Mark Antony complaining that his victory would be a poor one if he was left a dominion of blackened ruins and king only to corpses.

But this is no way to bring that time to life. Not for me the historian's dispassionate eye. Let the story emerge as memories emerge, out of the surrounding darkness, peopled with larger-than-life figures, the colours too impossibly vivid to be real, the sounds magnified until they agree with our perceptions of what took place; for this is what we call history and there is only one way to tell it.

'King!' Alexandra spits out the word, as though it were poisoned. She glances at her daughter, who, as always, sits passive and unreadable, then back to the messenger, an experienced officer, time-served on the battlefield at Mark Antony's side, who nevertheless quails in the face of this onslaught by a matron of Judea.

Alexandra walks over to the window, which is nothing more than a crude opening in the stone walls of the fortress known as Masada. Far below she can see Lake Asphaltitus with its glittering surface and its poisonous depths, a metaphor for her future son-in-law almost too coarse to be borne. With monumental effort Alexandra controls herself. 'I am to understand that my father and my son, who have legitimate right to the throne in the eyes of the Almighty and the people, have been set aside by the will of the Senate?'

'That is so, lady.'

Alexandra cannot speak. Her face is patched in livid blotches, as though the news of Herod's promotion is a disease which has struck her down. Before she can say more the door opens and Jonathan enters.

'Mother.' Seeing her distress he rushes to her side this good son, who at sixteen, is now showing signs of manhood through the soft edges of his youth. The doe's eyes, the sensuous lips, he has been kissed by the same god who fashioned his sister. But where she is made up of light and shadow, he is as radiant and unspoiled as the face of the sun.

'Mother, what is it?'

'The Senate has declared Herod king of Judea.' The boy stares at her with wide, uncomprehending eyes, but in his presence Alexandra grows calm. She reaches up and strokes his hair, as he places a protective arm about her shoulders. Mariamme, watching them, does not stir from her chair, but seems to grow a little more still. Alexandra pays her no attention and turns back to the legate. 'How long until Herod returns?'

'Many weeks, perhaps months. He is dealing with an insurrection in Galilee. And Antigonus still holds Jerusalem. But he promises —a quick glance at Mariamme— that he will return to you at the first opportunity.'

Alexandra's foot taps three times then she permits herself a smile, a dry mysterious smile such as the sphinx of Aegyptus is said to wear. 'Please extend our congratulations to the king, and assure him I will write personally to Caesar to express my gratitude for his unparalleled interest in our welfare.' At this Jonathan lifts his head from her shoulder and gives her a shocked, wide-eyed glance. But he is too well schooled to speak. The legate takes this statement as dismissal and begins to make his parting bow.

'Wait!'

He looks up.

'Herod's betrothal to my daughter is not in question?'

The legate is confused. He shakes his head. 'It is my belief that Caesar welcomes the marriage. To join two great houses can only be a joy to him.'

'Two great houses?' Alexandra repeats the numeral as though the legate has misspoken,

though, in fact, his Greek is perfect. Understanding his faux pas, the legate colours and bows and flees from the room.

In the silence that follows, Mariamme is the first to speak, her question directed to her mother.

'Why?'

Alexandra, her fury returning, turns its focus on her daughter. Is she, Alexandra Maccabeus, the last of the Hasmonaeans blessed with wisdom? While she cowers inside the walls of Masada, hiding from the murderous intent of her own nephew and his Parthian horde, while her father is forced to seek refuge with the Jews of Babylon, did her own daughter expect that she would dare to insult Rome? But what could she expect from a daughter who had never shown a moment's gratitude in her whole life?

With a dramatic gesture she thrusts her son aside and snatches up writing implements from a little ivory desk. 'Shall I write to Caesar telling him that from this day forth he may consider the house of Hasomea his enemy? We will raise our walls against him as Fulvia did during the Perusine war. How well that worked out for her. They say she is buried in an unmarked grave. Shall I sign the letter Alexandra, scribe to her royal highness, Mariamme, queen of holy Judea?'

'Stop!' Mariamme is on her feet, her golden skin flushing with emotion. And this is an event rare enough to halt Alexandra in her tracks. 'It is no wish of mine to marry Herod.' Mariamme's eyes glisten with tears, and towards this beautiful girl whose unblemished nobility is no more than a yoke about her neck, it is hard not to feel pity. Hard, though seemingly not impossible. Alexandra throws her hands in the air. 'Is this the sort of daughter she has been cursed to bring into the world? Will she stand there and pretend that to refuse Herod is not to sign all their death warrants? If she has no feeling for her mother, who daily suffers the ravages of age and so doubtless needs no consideration, then what of her brother? As Herod's consort only she can protect him.'

'Protecting me for what, mother?' Jonathan has found his voice. ' Herod is king now.'

Alexandra sighs and lowers her hands. Her voice is softer now. 'We must be cleverer than this. Rome can make him king, but it can never make a High Priest out of him. Neither Octavian nor the Senate understands the Jewish mind. They think if he is a good administrator, if he rules justly then he will be loved; there will be peace. Think of them now, counting the taxes Herod has promised to collect. But they have made a mistake; they do not recognise that Jews will always choose sanctity over the secular. They will never accept this low-born half Jew as sovereign over them.' She reaches out and brushes her fingertips against her son's cheek. 'You will be king. Perhaps not in name, at first. But every Jew in the land will know it.'

'And Herod too; he will know it,' Mariamme says. But she says it so softly that no-one hears her, apart from the slave who is sorting through one of the large cedar chests containing Alexandra's wardrobe. And even she is not certain whether Mariamme has truly spoken or whether the words were merely part of her own secret thoughts and understandings.

Serene once more Alexandra sweeps from the room, taking Jonathan with her. Mariamme watches them leave, neither invited nor informed of their plans. With the closing of the door, all the fight goes out of her. She sinks back down into her seat and sits there staring into emptiness. And there is something moving about her sadness, all alone beneath the rough fortress walls of Masada. If she had wept it would have been one thing or if she had raged and cursed it would have been another. But she only sits there, like an abandoned child.

The slave sorting through Alexandra's fine dresses knows only too keenly how deep the well of misery plummets. But it is not her place to make comparisons between herself and this Jewish princess, two women so different in circumstance yet so much a part of their time. She turns back to the chest. Yet does she not also know that desolation is kindred to death in making no exception for rank, so hesitantly she leaves off sorting through Alexandra's fine dresses and takes a few uncertain steps towards her mistress.

The movement attracts Mariamme, who looks up, and for an instant their eyes lock. But there is no sisterhood to be found here; the chasm is too wide. All the intended words of sympathy die on Loshema's lips, and the hand she meant to place on the beautiful shoulder, just visible beneath a clasp of cabochon and gold, falls limply to her side. And suddenly it is clear that the fortress around Mariamme's heart is far thicker than the walls of Masada. She is locked up alone there and finds no echo in the commonplace wretchedness of a slave. Loshema drops her gaze and returns slowly to the sorting of the dresses. Mariamme continues to stare ahead, as though the motes of dust twinkling in the air have more to offer.

37 BCE

To every family one dreamer is allotted, and to the Herodians —for such they now thought themselves— that role was given to the youngest son, Pheroras. In so many ways unlike his siblings, taller than Joseph or Zael, his features thin and vulnerable, frown lines between the brow, his hair already receding at the temples. But this was not the sum of his difference. There was some quality he lacked that the others shared, a vitality and robustness with which they made the world tremble about them.

Pheroras, to the contrary, always lagged behind. He was too thin, he stooped, he forgot things, even breaking off in the middle of a sentence to consider other possibilities. He had the fragility of one who lives too much inside their head and walks through the world as a dreamer walks, and he had reached the age of nine and twenty strangely untouched by the lure of power and ambition that held his siblings in their thrall. In short, they lived in one world, he in another.

He was dreaming now, or at least that is how it seemed to the two slaves who laid the fire in the hearth, a crone and a girl of sixteen years. That he had not acknowledged them as they entered was only to be expected, but that he had stood, his back to them, without moving, his gaze seemingly lost in contemplation of mount Gerezim, became stranger the longer it went on. Only once or twice did he break this pose, glancing over his shoulder at a large oak desk, belonging to Netanel the Ephaimite, their host, upon which was a box, dusty and scarred from travel and a leather tube of the type used to carry scrolls.

The crone, stiff and arthritic through age, and the harshness of having lived as a slave to such an age, noticed nothing. This villa lost in the hills of Samaria was chillier than she was used to, and she wanted only to finish the job, as quickly as her maladroit fingers would allow so that she might return to the warmth of the kitchens. But Loshema noticed how, when Pheroras gazed at the box, he stood so perfectly still through the long minutes that she might have believed that he had shed his mortal presence as a serpent sheds its skin. And thus fascinated she deliberately tarried over her task, watching him slyly with sidelong glances. But the game was interrupted with the opening of the door.

'Pheroras.' Those soft sibilants, but Pheroras turned at once.

'Mother.'

Cypros slipped into the room. She was not quite the same woman who had walked with queenly grace throughout the corridors of the Hasmonaean palace. Her face was haggard, dark circles shadowing her eyes, and her dress, though far short of sackcloth, was an unbecoming rough weave, the dress of a mourner. She glanced deliberately at the scroll cylinder. 'Your brother sends a letter.'

Pheroras stared at it without moving.

'Open it. I would hear what he has to say.'

But Pheroras did not move. And Loshema, watching from the corner of her eye, understood his confusion. What letter addressed to him would the Cypros of old have deigned to leave unopened? Well went the epigram scratched into a pillar in the cellars of the palace in Jerusalem, *a mouse squeaks and Cypros turns her head.*

When Pheroras continued to stare, uncomprehending, she crossed the room with something of her old spirit and thrust the cylinder into his hands. 'My eyes are raw with weeping. Must I blind myself with reading as a woman without sons to rely on?'

A look of anguish crossed Pheroras' face and, without a word he broke the seal and lifting out not one, but two scrolls, began to read the contents aloud.

> Herod, *Basileus of Judea, and the territories of Idumeae and Peraea*, to his brother, Pheroras, in the third year of his reign.
>
> Brother, I write in this brief moment snatched from the conflict which keeps me from you. Firstly I must send my deepest sympathies on the loss of our brother Joseph. I have written to mother, whose share of our grief must burn like the hellish sun of Aegyptus, where all others feel only the cold pinpricks of stars

—Pheroras glanced up from the letter, but Cypros gave a weary shrug, as if to say, no letter had ever reached her.

'Does he say when he is returning to us?'

Pheroras coughed and went on,—

The Lord works in mysterious ways and it is not ours to question why. But I torture myself, brother, that I am to be found in some way at fault for Joseph's folly. He was too young to have been left in sole command in Judea. Many times I warned him to make no attempts against Antigonus, for, though I have found great nobility in the person of Mark Antony, the same cannot be said of his generals. Macheras, who was to be our ally has proved headstrong and more foe than friend. When attempting to breach the walls of Jerusalem (those very walls that father raised. O the grief it brings me to think of tearing them down) he was repulsed by Antigonus, and in his rage slew every Jew in his path murdering many of our own partisans, a deed I fear we will be held accountable for in the eyes of the people if not the Almighty in his infinite mercy.

You may have heard that I went straight to Mark Antony to make my complaint, and delayed with him to aid in his siege of Samosata. That Joseph should attempt to take Jericho while I was thus occupied was an act of madness. But Joseph always was the wildest of we brothers and now he has paid for his impetuous nature with his life. I know the fault will be laid at my door, but I swear before the Almighty, what else could I have done?

—Here Pheroras frowned then hesitated. He held out the scroll for his mother to view. At the fireplace the younger slave stood up, apparently stretching her back, turning her head, as if by chance in the direction of the letter. Unable to read, and at too great a distance even if she had been in possession of such a skill, nonetheless her sharp eyes spotted the shift from *sikra,* the red hue of a scribe's cinnabar-based ink to the smudged lop-sided scrawl done in the lampblack of *deyo.*

'I think,' Pheroras began then paused until Cypros' impatient snort woke him from his dream. 'I think this letter was written over many months, and not easily. His state of mind seems to change… '—

Forgive my delay in finishing this letter. Matters press heavily upon me, and there is no time to wait for a scribe. They are saying that you made approaches to Antigonus, offering to redeem Joseph's body. And, though I pray it may not be true, it is being said that he denied you and cut our brother's head from his body, displaying it before his troops as a sign of what he means to do to the rest of us. Know that I would have come at once, if only to tell mother that her son will not go unavenged.

—Cypros was staring at the floor. She did not look up, but her jaw tightened and an angry tide of breath swelled and ebbed in her chest —

But Antigonus' unspeakable act has caused unrest in places we thought already friendly to our cause. In Galilee, banditry is rife again, and many turned against us, seizing our men and drowning them in the lake of Gennesaret. I will describe the way in which

—'The text breaks off,' Pheroras said slowly. He paused a moment, as though deciphering difficult handwriting, then looked up with appalled eyes. 'I think there is blood staining the page...' At once Cypros was at his side. She snatched the letter from him and began to read the contents for herself.—

Forgive me yet again, brother. I have been hard pressed to find a moment to write these last weeks, and the men are so battle-weary that I have not the heart to demand one as my scribe. Not that scribes are plentiful here. My soldiers are good men, strong sturdy boys who are used to working the land or foreign mercenaries looking for adventure, but I would be hard pressed to find one amongst them one who could wield a pen as mightily as a sword.

I have written again to mother and also to Salome, but I have had not the merest line in return and fear my letters do not make it through. It justifies the length I am taking over this one, as it will surely vanish into nothingness the moment it leaves my hands.

But I digress and you must be eager for news, far away as you are in Samaria. As promised, we have cleared the heights of Jericho. But victory was not easy and I myself was wounded in the side. Tell mother she must not worry for what we lack in practitioners of the literary arts we make up for in men who are skilled in all methods of healing.

I have been attended by a Greek, called Aristrides, a huge brute who is all froth and fury on the battlefield, yet said to be learned in medical matters. He sewed my wound with stitches of flax and treated it with a poultice of willow and honey and I am doing well. But he fusses over me like a new mother and insists that I have a diet of celery and garlic, and would not be satisfied until it was promised that his will would be obeyed. Though where he imagines such things can be found on these ravaged heights takes the faith of an Essene to think it possible.

—It appeared that this was the end of the scroll, but not the letter. Cypros lifted the second scroll from the desk, unrolled it and began to read,—

Strange are the ways of the Lord. It is the only point upon which one can get agreement between Pharisee and Sadducee alike, but this once I find myself in perfect harmony with their claims. Such opposition and revolt have dogged the early days of my reign that even I have felt at times that the Lord had turned his back on me.

Swear that you will not divulge what I am about to tell you to mother, but my wound became infected. My life was in danger and they had to call a surgeon. Aristrides was beside himself and had to be physically restrained, while the surgeon cut out the infection. Another brute, called, Anaximander, whose skill at cutting flesh makes me think he is very likely the son of butchers. Afterwards Aristides bled me and fed me on a tincture of poppies and I soon recovered.

But my spirit was low. You will know that it is hard to fight for oneself in this condition, but to make others fight on your behalf is nearly impossible. I was near despair when two strange happenings took place. First off, I chose to have my senior officers to dinner, and we occupied an abandoned property. The talk was lively and we made merry as men will do when they fear to be alone with their thoughts.

Yet the wine jugs were not emptied when I was overcome with the strangest feeling that I must send them back to their tents, which I did and myself retired. Not an hour later but there was a rumble that sent us all running to find its cause, and moments later the whole house collapsed in ruins. Had we stayed but an hour longer then not one of us would have survived.

Of course the owner was tracked down, but he swore the house was sound and that it was only fear of the soldiers that had made him abandon it. And many who knew him swore likewise. Aristrides being Greek and something of a philosopher to boot, insists on quoting Leucippus and Arcesilaus and all manner of sceptics at me. Truly it seems that these Greeks have made Reason into a kind of god and can see the Divine spark nowhere in the machinations of the world. But whispers arose amongst the men that I had been specially favoured by the Lord as his anointed king and their spirits duly rose.

What I am about to tell you next is too horrible for the ears of the gentler sex.

—Pheroras cleared his throat, but Cypros silenced him with the arch of her brows. Nor did she dismiss the two women attending the fire who were, after all, slaves and did not possess the finer feelings of their betters.—

The next day our fortunes changed. Antigonus' troops harassed us with javelins and stones. I was hit in the side, but through the favour the Almighty is now showing me, it was but a graze. Seeing that we were not to be stopped the enemy tried to melt away into the nearby towns and villages, who favoured them and hid them in their midst. But we descended upon them, like Saul's army, capturing five towns and slaughtering all we found there.

It was then that news was brought to me that Antigonus' appointed General, Pappus —he who slew Joseph— was returning to confront me. I knew no reason then. I turned my men and we headed him off near a village named Isana.

Pappus' forces were formidable. And it does Joseph no dishonour to admit that Pappus is a courageous man and his attack was fierce and uncompromising. Yet now the tide had turned and men flocked to my side. We fell on them as King Saul in ancient days routing the Philistine horde. And if Antigonus' men thought I had been without mercy before truly they found what it is to bring down the wrath of the house of Herod.

Into the village houses they fled, for many of them were young and panicked by the taste of defeat. But I did not spare them. I had my men tear the roofs from these dwellings exposing the wretches huddled there, unable even to use their weapons. Then I had my own men climb up, while others gathered rocks, which are plentiful here, until I gave the order, whereupon they began to stone the miserable creatures below. Their screams were hideous.

And, believe me, brother, there is no more ghastly a sound than a man with neither teeth nor jawbone drowning in his own blood. The memory haunts my dreams. But then I stood unmoved in their midst, and did not suffer a single one to live nor would give the order to cease until the body of Pappus was brought before me.

I think the time has come that I might send this rambling epistle to you. But, before I do, I must tell you of the event which sows in my heart certainty that the Almighty is with us. After we were done in Isana, my scouts brought me news that the enemy had gathered in great numbers in the distance about the village, but in witnessing the ferocity with which I dealt with the captives they turned and fled, their spirits broken.

My men were of a mind to march to Jerusalem that very night such fires of enthusiasm had been lit under them, but the hour was late and the weather had grown inclement, thus I ordered them to take their supper, and would have followed but for a local magistrate —a man who had welcomed us from the first— who approached me timidly and offered me his house as a refuge where I might bathe and rest.

Pheroras, I know you to be a man of peace, who has never known war, and as such I commend and admire you, but O my brother, you will never know the celestial joy of a bath after months of perpetual uncleanliness. Whosoever claimed that we grow accustomed to the stink of human flesh is neither a soldier nor a Jew.

I took with me only one elderly body slave, a mute called Bartolemew, such was my arrogance in victory. And, when I immersed myself in the warm waters, I understood that sage, Hillel, who claims that to bathe is a pious deed. I had been there but a few minutes when, to my astonishment and horror, one of the enemy appeared from behind a curtain, where he had been concealed. He was a lad of no more than nineteen judging by his gangling frame, but armed to the teeth. Bartolemew displayed his bravery by cowering in a corner and pulling his tunic over his eyes.

The lad and I eyeballed each other, me in all my kingly glory and my sword unreachable at the other end of the room. Then the most miraculous thing happened, which must surely silence Aristrides and all his skeptics for if the Lord was not behind it, I can find no other explanation that fits. The lad turned tail and fled from the room. And while I stared, mute as Bartolemew, another two lads, similarly armed, slipped by me.

I waited for a commotion, for the clash of swords. But there was none. If it had not been for Bartolemew rocking in the corner, I should have sworn the whole thing a dream. What could I do? I talked softly to Bartolemew to tell him danger was passed then I leant back in the water and went on with my bath. You will think this story the stuff of legends, but I swear it is true.

The Almighty spared me again that night and so tomorrow I head for Jerusalem. Give my love to mother and Salome and my dearest Mariamme, whom I think of tenderly. I have sent a present to you all, which I think will not be displeasing to you.

—Cypros lowered the scroll. Her eyes moved from the box, still sitting on the desk, to Pheroras, who bit his lip and looked away. Cypros went on looking at her son, as though she did not recognize this creature as the child of her body. Then she threw the scroll down and called over her shoulder, 'Bring a knife.'

Seizing her chance, Loshema leapt forward, lifting a small paring blade resting near a bowl of fruit and proffered it to her mistress. Cypros took it without acknowledgement, and with four swift motions cut through the binding that held the lid. Casting it aside she peered inside, and Loshema, close by, could see that it was packed with straw.

Something dark lurked beneath the straw and Cypros reached in and seized it. In a rush something came out, and even in those brutal times, the sight of a head no longer attached to its means of locomotion evoked a kind of uncomprehending paralysis that denied, even as it accepted the horror of what it was seeing. For an instant they were frozen, Cypros holding the head aloft, like David clutching the head of Goliath then, at once, the ghastly decapitation had a name. Pappus. Pheroras turned white and fled from the room. Neither of the slaves moved, knowing that in danger their safest action was no action at all. And, Cypros, who knew that her son would be a king of Israel as no-one had imagined such a king, lowered the head of Pappus and turned to the window, smiling out at the dawn of a new age.

15

In which home is discovered to be the same yet altered

37 BCE

'SHE IS YOUR WIFE!' Cypros' hand slapped down on the delicate surface of an inlaid side-table, making a decanter half full of caecuban wine, the gift of their Samarian host, shiver and the goblets around it tremble violently. 'You cannot simply send her away.' She glanced at Doris, who was limply sat on a couch, her pleading stare directed at her husband's back, and, for an instant, Cypros shared some of her son's distaste for the passive terror with which this girl moved through the world.

Herod, his hand leaning against the stone casement of the window, his back to the room, noticed nothing of the appeal in Doris' eyes nor the little touches she had set such store by, dreaming that he might notice and find them alluring, the heavy ropes of rubies and pearls around her thin neck, the richly embroidered dress, which hung from the sharp angles of her shoulders —she had a reputation for fasting—shapeless as an empty sack.

'You cannot do this.' Cypros' voice had softened. 'How can you do this? She is the mother of your son.'

Her keen eyes caught something altered in Herod's posture. He began to turn towards her and she was thinking, —*Now is the moment when I have won him back to me.*— when the door opened softly and Mariamme stepped inside.

'O.' She was surprised to see them. And, in truth, she had reason to be, as the room was originally assigned to the Hasmonaeans, and only recently requisitioned by Cypros with the arrival of her daughter-in-law. The sight of her made Cypros' task more urgent and she turned back to her son. But it was too late. His face was aflame and he greeted Mariamme, like a man greeting the sun after an eclipse. And she, a little melted by the force of his joy offered him a shy imitation of his smile.

'I came to find my book.' And that Mariamme should offer an explanation unbidden was strangeness in itself. She swept into the room, her rose pink robe enfolding her rounded limbs, delicate as a petal or the wing of a butterfly imitating a petal. She wore no jewellery other than two ovals of sardonyx, which hung from the fragile lobes of her ears, and bore the emblems of her great great grandfather, John Hyrcanus, etched upon them in cameoed relief, yet the effect was to make her seem as richly jewelled as a queen.

As though he had forgotten the other two women in the room, Herod asked, 'What do you read?'

'Whatever I am fortunate enough to come across.' She was frowning down at a gilded chest of tamarisk wood, which had clearly been opened by a hand other than her own. She threw a quick, puzzled glance at Cypros then, recovering herself, continued, 'I am fond of the Greeks. But I lack discernment. Mother says she will send for a tutor to school me when we return to Jerusalem.'

'A grown woman does not require a tutor,' Cypros cut in icily with a deliberate glance at Doris. But Herod was deaf to her.

'You have a favourite author?'

'Sophocles,' she answered, lifting a scroll from where it had been placed near the bottom of the chest. 'These days I find myself drawn to tragedy, and I must confess most particularly to *Antigone*.' She raised her eyes to gauge whether he shared her joke.

—You do not see the humour? Antigone is the feminine of Antigonus. She can pun in Greek, this clever Jewish princess.—

Herod's laughter was as clear as a bell. And for a moment there was something Greek about the communion they shared, that instant grasped by Plato in which the consuming fire of passion gives way to a higher ideal and finds itself full circle in that purest of human bonds known as friendship. Herod would have said more, but Mariamme, more sensitive to the shipwrecked woman upon the sofa asked of Doris, 'Do you also enjoy Sophocles?'

'I do not read works by pagan authors,' Doris replied. Indeed she could not read at all and had felt Mariamme's question to be a calculated barb. At once the atmosphere in the room soured. Mariamme's face closed and she let the lid of the tamarisk chest fall shut. 'I have intruded too long.'

Herod would have argued, but Cypros was quick with expressions of regretful assent. And while Herod stood, transfixed by the sight of the door through which Mariamme disappeared, Cypros gave Doris a quick gesture of dismissal. Doris' eyes reddened, their expression hurt and protesting, but she was, as always, the dutiful wife and daughter, and such a stake she had put in her reputation for submission that obedience was her only armour in the face of attack. She got to her feet and slunk from the room, glancing piteously in the direction of her husband, whom she knew had already forgotten her existence.

Cypros and Herod were left alone in the room, Herod, his eyes still on the door, Cypros, her narrowed gaze directed at her son. When at last he turned, her expression was soft. The almond eyes blinked, like a cat who knows that it must beguile rather than show its claws.

'Of course, she is beautiful,' Cypros said and there was no need for Herod to inquire to whom she referred. 'You have been clever in this.' She turned, as though the matters they discussed were of little consequence, and signalled a slave to pour the wine.

—Yes, yes. I know I said they were alone. Would you have counted the presence of a mouse?—

'You are right to have her think that the betrothal still stands. Jerusalem will soon be yours and then we may act.'

Her eyes slid towards her son, gauging whether he had taken the bait, but Herod's face was unreadable. Cypros found herself forced to press a little harder. 'Once you are king in Jerusalem you will see that Doris is the right choice. She is a woman beyond reproach, and her piety will be a beacon to both Sadducees and Pharisees alike.' Lifting a hand she stroked his cheek. 'Have I not been as Naomi who brought Ruth to Boaz? Doris too will father kings.' She stood before him, looking up into the masculine echo of her own features, tenderly invoking the special bond that sometimes made them seem two reflections of the one person. He laid his strong hands on her shoulders.

'I will marry Mariamme.'

For a second she was dumbfounded then she threw herself from him, dismissing the slave, who held out a filled goblet, with such violence that the goblet crashed to the floor and a stain of amber liquid spread across the mosaic tiles. At once Herod went after her, issuing a curt order to the petrified slave to clean up the mess.

'Mother.'

She rounded on him. 'Have you lost your wits? Do you imagine they will accept you while there are Hasmonaean claims to the throne? They will be forever plotting your death. And the Grand Sanhedrin will be allies to their cause as they have been to Antigonus.'

Seeing only his stubborn expression she threw up her hands. 'You think she loves you? Did you not witness how she greeted us, with the emblems of John Hyrcanus dangling from her ears? She looks at you and sees an Idumaean thief who has stolen the Hasmonaean crown. Think!' She leaned into his thunderous expression, unafraid, like the reed bending itself to the shape of the storm.

'What would the issue be of such a match? The Sadducees are the nobility, the pillars of Hasmonaean power. They would see your son as a pawn in their hands worth a thousand times his volatile and unpredictable father. They would call him one of their own and turn him against you. And you would be a king who could not trust where the loyalties of his own child lay.'

'Such a heritage can never be proved,' Herod said softly.

'What need have they of proof? Have you forgotten the vast estates they own? And not only here. All through the empire, wherever Jews have made a home, you may be certain a Sadducee has an interest.'

Herod shrugged. But Cypros was not to be silenced. The infinitely complex nuances of Judean politics formed the air she breathed, and well she understood, as Alexandra also understood, that Judea was a seething furnace of dispute and divided opinion. Looking into the future she saw, with horror, that there was only one thing that would bind together the endless schisms, that divided one house against another, and that was a common enemy, a scapegoat for their own internal strife, and they would use her son, her Herod, as a melting pot into which they would pour all their hatred and enmity. She breathed out sharply through her nostrils and tried again,

'I see you have no fear of the rich and powerful. What then of the Pharisees? Well is it said that a Sadducee owns the property and goods of the common man, but the Pharisees own his heart and mind. They will fight amongst themselves for your sons, I can promise you that. First the house of Hillel will claim them then the House of Shammai. And they will never be done promising them greater and greater things. Do you not see, the Sadducean nobles will offer them a seat amongst kings. But the Pharisees will promise them the Kingdom of Heaven itself. What then would be the house of Herod to them?' She placed a hand on Herod's chest, her narrow fingers forming a cage over his heart. 'You would never be safe. And I should never sleep soundly again.'

'–And there they stand, a mother pressed up against her favourite son. And the intimacy of this moment is almost too vivid to bear. But don't look away just yet. What Herod does next will create the mould, not only of his future reign, but the cast in which history will shape him. And Cypros stands there, watching her child hovering at a crossroads and silently pleading with him to take the right path. And more than that she is pleading with him as a mother, her love so raw and fragile she is like a skinned creature left beneath the searing desert sun. Don't leave me. Don't take her hand and drop mine. My son. My son.

His dark eyes move across her face, as though each new line is a revelation then, with infinite tenderness, he bends down and kisses her on the forehead.

'I will marry her. I must.'

'You will die.'

'I will outlive you all.'

Antipater, ten years old, the first son of Herod, and his only living child at that time, sat on the edge of the bed he shared with his mother and watched as she argued with God. Was she not a dutiful wife? Had she not produced a son? Might she not, given the chance, produce many more?

She had been praying for several hours and he was not allowed to go to sleep until she was finished. And before she had begun, she had clutched his shoulders in her long bony hands, so tightly it hurt, yet he was too afraid to cry out. 'I will pray,' she had said. 'I will pray and you will see. You will see he cannot do this.' Then she had turned away, her arms outspread, her head tilted heavenwards. 'LSHMO T⊠·⊠IN·NA⊠ ʿAB·D⊠·KĀ'… Hear the supplication of your servant…

On and on, her voice rising and falling, long after they might have gone down to dinner, and he dared not interrupt her except with the growls of his stomach. In Jerusalem a watchful slave would have brought up a tray. But here in Samaria there was only a handful of the old retainers, and they were kept too busy by Cypros and Salome to remember Herod's forgotten son.

'Ă·ZAβ·TĂ·Nî.' He has forsaken us. Antipater, his large dark eyes watching anxiously through the thickening gloom, wondered exactly who had abandoned them. Were they lost to God as Joash the Abiezrite and his son Gideon had been amongst the Midianites? At the thought a strange sensation overtook him. And though he was sitting on the bed, his hands firmly gripping the edges, suddenly the substance of the world fell away, and he was overcome with a nameless terror, as though he had been sent spinning head over heels down, down through the absolute nothingness before creation.

A knock on the door broke his fall, and made his mother choke on her prayers. He watched as she lowered her arms, a naked flame of hope lighting her face.

'Enter.'

But it was only an unusual looking slave, a girl of about seventeen with hair the colour of a faun, sleek, light hair, streaked through with gold.

'What do you want?' Doris demanded. 'I did not send for you.'

The girl kept her gaze trained to the floor. 'I am here to help you pack, lady. You are to take whatever you choose from this room.'

For an instant Doris gaped at her, as though she did not understand then she exploded in a ferocious onslaught peppered by so much Idumaean dialect that Antipater had difficulty following her. Suddenly she was shaking him by the shoulders, her face made ugly by two angry rivers of tears excoriating her pallid cheeks.

'Do you understand? He is sending us away, casting us off, like Hagar and Ishmael, back to my father so he might marry his Hasmonaean whore!' Then, seeing his wide-eyed confusion, she clapped her hand to her mouth. 'Am I a mother to talk to my child this way?' She straightened and began to pace back and forth. 'Yet to send us away. To cover us with shame. Are these the actions of a father?' She paused then spun round to face Antipater, as if he had expressed some deeply held conviction. 'This is her doing. She has bewitched him that Jezebel, that Lillith. May the Almighty curse her family until the last member of the house of Hasmonaea is wiped from the face of the earth.' She fell to her knees and hugged him tightly against her breast. 'The Almighty will curse her and then he will come back to us. You will see. You will see, he will come back.'

And Antipater, who was only just realising that the father he barely knew, yet feared and worshipped from afar, was rejecting him felt the dizzying terror overcome him again. He lifted his gaze in panic and saw, over his mother's shoulder, the green cat's gaze of the slave girl watching him.

Yes, look about you. We are triumphant at the gates of Jerusalem. At last, Jerusalem on high, the city that hovers beneath God's holy breath, forever in the perpetual golden light of dreams and memories. Yet the leaves have turned and blow about our feet, and a thin cold mizzle closes in from the West, soaking our clothes, and bedraggling the victory banners, embroidered so diligently by the women of the house, so that they cease fluttering and droop, like beggars' rags about their poles. In this state we seem more funerary procession than triumph as we trudge along towards the palace and home.

Slaves, of course, keep to the rear, and we see last what Herod and his retinue first pass through. But it does not shield us from the shock. In the marketplace, where are the bright stalls, the heaving crowds elbowing each other to buy goods brought in from Jericho and Galilee, and from greater distances, Tyre, Alexandria, Askum and far off Barbarikon. Instead there is grass poking out between the paving stones. Placed across them are a few dirty blankets spread on the ground, their sad wares not worth a second glance. And surely that cannot be the street of bakers? The roofs and doors are torn off and the walls blackened by fire.

And, look! Someone is pointing. Is that the house of Joseph Shimeon? Joseph Shimeon! Surely you know the name. Is he not from one of the most powerful Sadducean families in Jerusalem, the owner of a thriving industry that manufactures ointments and perfumes from Jericho's famous balsam? His is one of the richest families in Israel, known in all the cities of the Decapolis. But now his doors are gaping and we must pick our way through a trail of potsherds and fragments of expensive coloured glass; the pristine painted shutters and fretwork that decorated his workshops are like kindling at our feet.

As we turn into the avenue of Kings a few Jerusalemites come out to cheer, but others, their faces twisted with looks of hatred, rend their clothes and pour dirt upon their heads. We cannot see Herod and his family. But it is not hard to guess the hard angry expression that tightens his face or the cold calculating stare of Cypros.

Later they will say that Salome looked frightened and that Pheroras only stared dreamily off into the distance noticing nothing, and, despite everything, there is something saintly about that one. But mostly they say, an Idumaean half Jew, who brought destruction on the city, now proclaims himself king while kindly Hyrcanus is still in Babylon. Lord, how have we offended thee?

It is still light outside when we reach the palace, but it seems dark within its painted walls. And small. How can it be so small this place that engulfed my childhood? The stairs to the kitchens, how often I cursed the misery of climbing them, but they number less than a dozen. Everything is strange yet familiar at the same time, which makes it stranger still. But the smell. Someone is baking bread, and suddenly, with a rushing of my heart, I am here. I am home.

'Morderchai?'

He appears from behind a pillar, his old face sweating from the heat of the oven. Youngest son to a shepherd family in Idumaea, he has served Herod's household man and boy. Ancient as he is, it is said of him that he is as nimble as a goat and as loyal as a lamb, and thus was given the great privilege of overseeing the kitchens in readiness for their master's return.

'Loshema? Can it be? Little Loshema?' *He is rubbing his hands on his apron, shaking his* head. And suddenly I am shy, clutching my bundle against me (which is scarcely bigger than the day I left more than two years ago, save for the carved lid of a scent bottle, retrieved after Salome smashed the vessel in a fit of temper, and a play by Sophocles, stolen from Mariamme, for what purpose I cannot answer, even to myself. But sometimes, when there is an idle moment to be found, I creep into a corner and trace the letters with a finger, and it draws out some great nameless thing inside me, some need or urge or longing that has been growing since our departure from Jerusalem.)

But now Morderchai has grasped me by the arm and is dragging me from place to place about the kitchens, showing how clean he has kept them and the little improvements he has made. And I follow him, nodding and smiling, but with a prickling behind my eyes, for surely this is what it means to be home, to be recognised and welcomed and shown the best of everything.

Eventually Morderchai grows sombre. 'Ah, child, you do not know what it was to be in the city in the last days of the siege. Antigonus was too proud. —Dropping his voice— There were too many who loved him. Herod tried to win their love. He let it be known that Antigonus had allowed fire to spread to the porticoes about the Temple. Yet still the people clung to him and did not censure his actions. Then Herod allowed that animals be given safe passage to the Temple so that the daily sacrifices to the Almighty might not be interrupted. But still Antigonus refused to surrender.' He leans a little closer.

'You see the Sanhedrin were behind him. And everywhere on the streets, Pharisees also proclaiming that Jerusalem must close its doors to the Idumaean usurper. And enough Sadduccean gold crossed outstretched palms to buy the loyalty of those who swithered, undecided.

'It was a poor time to be known to be of the house of Herod. They attacked us daily.' Suddenly the old man straightens, as though talking of a favoured son. 'But Herod is no fool. He left a phalanx of Ituraean mercenaries. Great archers they are, trained from the day they leave their mothers' wombs it is said. And the enemy soon learned a harsh lesson if they came too near the palace walls. Yet still— ' He breaks off, biting his lip. The great machinations of the world are too difficult for him to understand. He lives in a palace, but he is still an Idumaean shepherd's son inside his head. His is not to reason why.

'When Antigonus refused to surrender, what choice then did Herod have? He took the place by storm. Then the streets ran with blood. Yes indeed.' He lowers his chin onto his chest and squeezes his eyes tight shut for a moment. ' There were too many Romans, too many mercenaries, you see. And what is Jerusalem to them? A treasure chest? A rich man's purse to be picked?

'I went out afterwards. Crept from where I had been hiding and walked through the streets. Antigonus' men were all dead, a great heap of them at the gate. Then I made my way towards the Temple mount and there were families, men I knew, shopkeepers and scribes, doctors and musicians, and their wives, and children, infants still against the breast, and they were dead too. All dead. And the infants, not one did they spare. And everywhere there was *blood and the smell and the taste of death— '*

He breaks off to wipe dampness from his eyes with the back of his arm then, rallying himself, hurries on, 'Antigonus gave himself up that day to Sosius, the Roman General, and they have taken him off to Mark Antony in chains. But it was not enough.'

Seeing a pall of horror about my face, he pats my shoulder with his gnarled old hand. 'You are young. You think this is the worst that can happen. But what of Nebuchadnezzar when he led his Babylonian horde against us? Did he not destroy our Temple and steal away our people? And when Pompey came to restore Hyrcanus to the throne, do you think he did it with fine speeches? Twelve thousand he slaughtered once the walls of the city were breached, and they say the pool of Siloam ran red.

'No, they weep and rub dirt into their faces, but they have seen it before, and they do not tell that it was Herod who held the pagans from looting the Temple. Faced them down he did, his own men, with threats and force of arms. And he went to Sosius and demanded they put an end to the slaughter. But Romans —shrugging— what care have they of life when there is coin to be made. Sosius argued that a soldier has a right to spoils so what did Herod do then?' He pauses, a look of triumph lighting his old face. 'He offers to pay them out of his own purse. What king of Israel ever did that? Even Hezekiah could not manage to save Jerusalem without emptying the coffers of the Temple.'

His point is made. He steps back, face aglow. 'Yes, they are afraid of him for now. But they will come to love him. They will see— ' But, quite what they will see is not explained. Voices. Footsteps. And Morderchai hurries off to welcome new prodigals returning to the fold.

'They will fear him. But love him? No.'

The voice comes from behind me. Turning, I find an old man leaning on a staff who seems familiar and unfamiliar in equal measures. He has come from the kitchen gardens, but how long he has been there or how much he has heard I cannot say. He is dressed modestly in the style of the Pharisees, but the clothes he wears are not a poor man's garments. His fringed mantle is knotted and expensively dyed in the blue of Tyre and his tunic is of fine linen. A Pharisee in the house of Herod?

And it comes to me that this is old Pollio, with his bent back and his snowy beard falling practically to his knees. This is the doctor of the Law who spoke on Herod's behalf when they would have imprisoned him for his handling of the Galilean bandits. And, even while Antigonus reigned supreme, this same Pollio and his disciple, Samaias, spoke in favour of the Idumaean upstart rattling at the city gates. I cannot imagine how he has managed to appear, unnoticed. But he notices nothing of the recognition momentarily lighting my face. His gaze is directed towards Morderchai's retreating back, and when he speaks it is as though it was to him his words were addressed.

'They will fear Herod now he is king. And many will have reason to.'

16

In which Joseph, the husband of Salome, finds favour with the Hasmonaeans

37 BCE

ARIAMME, THE HASMONAEAN, WAS NOW a girl of eighteen years who was no longer a girl, but a woman. She was wife to a strange brooding man, who called himself king, but was no king in the eyes of anyone who counted. She was afraid of him and she despised him, and she loved him if only because of the way he looked at her, as though he, too, was a little afraid, and that gave her a sense of power over him.

Not that it mattered whether she loved him or not. That particular emotion played no part in the union of a man and woman in those times, particularly amongst the wealthier classes. There was too much at stake to allow such a vague and unpredictable bond, as love, to underpin the great unions of the day. And, besides, Mariamme knew that her marriage was a kind of sham from the outset, a matrimonial amulet to protect her brother's claim to the throne until they were ready to make their move.

Quite what her reward was to be, once her brother was king, was unspecified, but like most daughters of that time she had been groomed to be dutiful and obedient and to recall only subconsciously that, when it came to human sacrifice, it was written that the Almighty had intervened to save the son of Abraham, but readily accepted the daughter of Jephta. Her happiness, she had been assured, was a small price to pay for a kingdom.

That had been back in Samaria, shortly before Herod arrived. The tide of victory sweeping him along, he had demanded his prize, overriding all Alexandra's protests that he could hardly expect to marry a princess of the Hasmonaean line in a backwater province far from the holy streets of the capital. He had listened to her before, and now she stood before him, tall and regal in a simple gown of virginal white, pleading for her daughter.

'Would you see her married without the eyes of the people upon her, as though there is something hidden, something *shameful* about the affair?'

But Herod had stood his ground. And Alexandra turned away, understanding that where previously she held sway over Herod the tetrarch she had none over Herod the king.

Now it was many weeks later, and Mariamme was with her brother in the royal apartments in Jerusalem. Since becoming a wife she had retained that coolness which set her apart, yet on this particular morning there was a suffocating stillness to the air. Twice she had left off her spinning and wandered over to the window. She had paced up and down and sighed several times. Finally she turned to her brother, who was sprawled on a couch, his attention absorbed in the act of dissecting a pomegranate. 'Did my husband's uncle not say he would pay you a visit today?'

He shrugged. 'If he wills it?'

'What else should he do?'

'How should I know?' At that Jonathan pricked his thumb with the fruit knife. A bead of blood welled up and, at once, the ruddy-faced Jebusite woman, who had been wet nurse to them both, got to her feet and hefted her meaty girth towards him, murmuring soothingly, as though he was still her own babe to coddle. Mariamme glared for a moment then turned away. In the corner a slave girl with poker straight hair, lightened by the sun, waited, but Mariamme looked through her, as though she didn't exist. And this was only to be expected yet it hurt the feelings of this strange-looking girl, who remembered a time in Samaria when Mariamme had sought her out and secretly asked for her council.

The motive and the reasons behind this encounter were as simple as they were complex. Mariamme had been told she was to be wife to Herod. And understanding the role she must fulfil had wanted to know the method and the detail of how she was to play her part. But in this Alexandra proved unhelpful. As a mother she had absorbed the prevailing wisdom that knowledge in a girl is a curse capable only of spawning disaster and downfall. And thus all Mariamme's uncertain questions fell on deaf ears.

In desperation Mariamme cornered a maid one day, and bribing her with a coin asked, 'What is it like to be with a man?'

Loshema, who had, against the odds, managed to retain her status as maid both in role and substance looked at her mistress in confusion. Sex was an unknown for her, a formless horror that had been the ruin of her mother and sister. As she grew towards womanhood it became a thing that stalked her down corridors and leapt from shadowed nooks to grope her breasts and lick her ears. By the age of seventeen all she understood of sex was the chase and the struggle, the fingers probing the soft folds between her legs, the panic in her belly as she fought to get away, and she looked up at her mistress with the gazelle's wide-eyed terror on hearing the soft foot falls of a lion. But Mariamme persisted,

'What is it to lie with a man? You know. Tell me!'

Loshema started to shake her head. But there was something pitiful in this princess who had been told to become a woman yet not told how one went about it, and something more pitiful still in the way she must debase herself by seeking advice amongst the lowest of her household. So Loshema squared her shoulders and answered with more kindness than truth, 'To lie with a man is good, lady. Very good.'

Mariamme said nothing, no word of thanks or even acknowledgement, only nodded and left the room. Loshema stood watching her go, the coin growing hot in her hand until the voice of Mariamme's old Jebusite nurse sounded behind her. 'It is a *mitzvah* you have done.'

Loshema spun round, and staring at the wrinkled, rosy-cheeked woman, could think of no way in which lying to a virgin was deemed a commandment by the Almighty. But the

Jebusite was gazing towards the door, her eyes misted.

'He will not be gentle.'

'But he loves her!' The tiny spark of kindness extended to her by Herod and his brother had been kindled into a fierce brand of loyalty within Loshema, and she would not stand silent in the face of vilification. 'Look!' She gestured rather wildly at the room towards the gifts Herod had prepared for his bride, the gilded furniture, the gold-worked hangings, even the delicacy of the combs and scent bottles all laid out in anticipation of their owner.

The Jebusite shrugged then asked suddenly, 'How old am I?'

Loshema blinked. Was it a question, a trick?

The Jebusite gave a knowing nod. 'You are afraid to say. One hundred years, two hundred perhaps? You would have me walking out of the burning Sinai at Moses' side. I am, in fact, fifty two years of age, which may seem to a chit, like you, as old as the hills. But I will tell you this. It is not so old that I do not remember what it is to have a man, and that all men are not the same, and there are ways of telling what a man will be when he takes a maid. Do you believe me?'

'You say he will not be kind?' Loshema whispered.

The Jebusite paused to hike her skirts more comfortably about her hips before answering in a gentler voice, 'O, I do not mean that he is like the men of Rome, too superstitious to deflower a virgin so that they take their mewling wives in the arse on their wedding nights. Nor am I one of those who look at Herod and see only his great grandfather climbing the high places to worship the Divine Archer. There is much that is good and noble about him. But I tell you this —and if it is a lie then let the earth swallow me whole as it did Korah when she spoke falsehood— Herod is a man who does not understand women.'

She held up a hand to prevent protest. 'O, he loves women. Some might even say he worships them. Was there ever a son more dutiful than Herod? But he does not understand them. Not here.' She thumped her chest with a fist. 'Not with his heart. He is a man who knows men. That is why men follow him, why men have made him a king. But women are another thing. They exist outside his world. As angels exist, as ghosts, as things he cannot understand.'

'Can he not love without understanding?'

The Jebusite shook her head sorrowfully. 'You are young, but I have seen, that which a man cannot understand and is different to him, he must tear down.'

With that she was gone, and now they were in Jerusalem, and the wedding night was a thing past many weeks. Loshema had heard whispers that Herod had, indeed, not been kind, for what had prepared him for a shrinking virgin inside a body of glass, and, in frustration it was said, he mounted Mariamme, black and hairy as the starved wolves roaming the rocky slopes of Idumaea, who sneak down at night to tear apart the white limbs of lambs. Mariamme had screamed and Alexandra was seen in the formal garden in her white robe, stiff and still, as a column of salt, her face turned expressionlessly upwards towards the lamps flickering in the windows of the royal apartments.

Loshema had never found out what Mariamme thought of her advice; no more was ever said of it, and, when they met thereafter, Mariamme looked through Loshema as though she wasn't there.

A knock on the door and David HaDov appeared announcing that Pheroras wished to be allowed into their presence.

'Let him enter.' And this from Mariamme. Her brother glanced in her direction, but she was seated by the window, her face a cool and lovely oval.

So in he came, Herod's brother. The most unHerodian of the Herodians. He was thinner than ever, his shoulders the rounded shoulders of a scholar, and there was none of the grace of a Herod about him either. He caught his foot on his robe, barely managing to save himself from sprawling at their feet by windmilling his arms until connecting with a sideboard and nearly upsetting a vase containing lilies. Jonathan laughed openly, and even Mariamme covered her mouth behind the tips of her long fingers.

Blushing to the roots of his hair Pheroras attempted a courtly bow and stuttered out the usual flatteries until Jonathan stood up and went towards him, hands outstretched. 'Please, we are brothers now. Such formalities are unnecessary.' He glanced over at Mariamme, but she was absorbed in her spinning and gave only the coolest of nods. Jonathan made a little moue of puzzlement then turned back to his uncle. 'Have you brought us news?' He smiled up at the older man with great charm. 'It is so terribly dull here. No-one ever tells us anything.'

Pheroras coughed. 'I fear I am not here to make pleasantries. My brother flatters me with the title, scholar, and has asked me to discover the extent of your learning.' Then, mistaking Jonathan's look of disgust for one of disappointment he continued hastily. 'He intends to provide you with a tutor, some learned fellow from Greece perhaps. But in the meantime I must be a poor substitute.' He glanced towards the door that led deeper into the apartment. 'Perhaps there is a place we may set aside for the task.'

Jonathan shrugged. 'Why not here?' Then charming enough to recognize when he was not being charming, added, 'Unless, of course, you consider it unsuitable.'

Pheroras looked astonished then embarrassed. 'My fear is to disturb your sister.'

'Naturally, as a married woman, it is unfitting for me to have a tutor,' Mariamme said. Her words had a flat, rehearsed tone. Then something altered about her face and her voice fell almost to a whisper. 'But it would be my pleasure to listen.'

Pheroras said nothing, simply held Mariamme's gaze in that way men have when they discover beauty to be more than skin deep. Jonathan interrupted them with a boyish laugh.

'My sister fancies herself a philosopher and would be pleased if you would help her grow a beard.'

Pheroras blinked and seemed to remember himself. He turned to his pupil. 'Is philosophy unfit for the fairer sex then?'

121

'It is written that a woman's place is in the home, and her work is spinning.'

Pheroras' smile was engaging. 'And where is it written that she must not use her brain?'

Jonathan shot his sister a puzzled look. 'You are not suggesting that a woman can be a philosopher surely?'

'Am I not? Do you deny the Arcadian, Axiothea, studied at Plato's Academy?'

'But she dressed as a man.'

'What of Aspasia then? It is said she could hold her own with Socrates.'

'Yes. But she was a woman of … ill repute, a *hetaira*.' Jonathan's cheeks burned. He was filled with the prudery of a people who traced their origins to nomadic desert tribes.

Secretly observing them from her corner, it was hard for Loshema not to see the strange transformation that was taking place. Jonathan had begun to stutter and throw nervous glances towards his sister, whereas, Pheroras was suddenly the eye in a storm of ideas. Calm and measured in his speech, he had metamorphosed entirely, like those shadowy strangers, who turn out to be messengers of the Lord. He seemed to be deliberately teasing Jonathan to test his reactions, and without meaning to, Loshema lifted her head a little and listened more intently. Pheroras laughed, a surprisingly loud and natural laugh that filled the room. 'Are we to dismiss Theano, Arete of Cyrene, Hipparchia?'

'All pagans,' Jonathan muttered and looked away.

He doesn't like his own arguments, Loshema dared to reason then caught herself daring to reason. But Pheroras seemed to have been expecting it. 'Philosopher is not a word we have been overly fond of bestowing upon our people. But consider this. Where does the word come from? From the Greek *philein* 'to love' and *sophos* 'wise'. It would be a poor thing if we Jews claimed that we did not love wisdom. And we have only to look to our Torah to see Wisdom portrayed as a woman.'

'Yet that is allegory.' Mariamme said. Her head was bent as she tied fibres to her spindle.

'And what is allegory except an interpretation of the ideal. Let us look to flesh and blood then. Was Deborah not a philosopher of sorts?'

'A prophetess.'

'An old way of putting things. What is philosophy if not the search for that which is beautiful and divine? And a prophetess is but a vessel to accept the divine.'

Mariamme's head was still bent. She made a little motion with her shoulders, not quite won over. Pheroras nodded, as though her doubt pleased him. 'And if that does not convince you, let me tell— '

But at this David HaDov entered and announced that Joseph the husband of Salome wished to pay his respects.

In he came, bowing elaborately to all, and Loshema eyed him curiously from beneath lowered lashes having seen him but rarely. A fat man past middle life, it was, nonetheless, not impossible to see the resemblance with Herod's father. Yet he seemed the lesser of the two brothers, soft where Herod's father had been hard, restless where the elder brother had been steady. She caught him giving her a quick, appraising look, and even throwing a glance in the direction of the old Jebusite nurse before settling inevitably upon the golden presence of Mariamme.

'An honour to find myself in your esteemed company.' He seemed eager to please, but it was a cringing eagerness, the rejected lion who slinks behind the pack. And Loshema remembered that the younger Herodians shunned their uncle, not least his young wife.

'I mean you'd think a man of his age would be past that kind of thing.' Between mouthfuls of honey figs, Salome had taken one of the court ladies into her confidence. 'But he gawps at everything in a tunic past the knees.'

'The ambassador from Chalcis had best learn to gird his loins,' came the giggling reply. Then sobering, 'But really, Salome, can't you tell the king?'

'Pheroras forbids it. He says Herod would kill him for his roving eye, and there has been too much bloodshed in the family already.' Then, as if realizing that she had shared too much. 'Of course, it is a blessing to me that he leaves me alone, and he only looks. He doesn't actually do anything.'

'Uncle, how surprising to meet you here,' Pheroras said quietly.

Uncle Joseph started up in the middle of an ostentatious bow. As was often the case, the presence of his scholarly nephew had gone unnoticed.

'Pheroras, ah yes. A surprise to us both I daresay— ' He broke off in a forced cough and thumped his chest several times. 'So dusty here. You forget. It was breezier in Alexandria.'

'Of course, you have just returned,' Jonathan interrupted, suddenly excited. "We have never been anywhere worth mentioning. You must tell us all about it.' He took the older man's arm and Loshema noted how Joseph plumped up beneath such affectionate acceptance.

'Is it true that there were Jews at the founding of the city, with Alexander himself?'

Joseph smiled, showing white, even teeth, remarkable in a man his age. 'Alexander's tutor, Aristotle, made friends with the captain of the Jewish mercenaries in Alexander's army. So impressed he was with the man's manners and his education, that it is said that when Aristotle was pressed to join the antagonists of the Jews, he answered, I am occupied with human knowledge only and not with divine, and in that they strike me as an intelligent people, much given to learning and philosophical erudition.'

Loshema watched as Mariamme stopped spinning, her cool gaze fixed on Joseph. Pheroras was looking at the floor. Then Jonathan laughed aloud and clapped the older man's shoulder. 'If what you say is true I will one day find myself in command of the wisest army in the world. I— ' He broke off, colouring damson red at a warning look from his sister. And Joseph chuckled, delighted to have elicited such enthusiasm. But Pheroras shot his uncle a narrow, worried look then clumsily changed the subject.

'I am afraid you will find our company dull, uncle. Jonathan and I are at our lessons.'

'We are learning that women may philosophize.' There was a pleading look in Jonathan's eyes, as though he hoped Joseph might have the authority to overrule the lesson on the grounds of improbability. But Joseph nodded, and rubbed his paunch thoughtfully. 'It is the truth. Amongst the Alexandrian community they have their own women philosophers.'

At this Mariamme's glance went sharply to her brother, as if to ask, *did you know of this?* But Jonathan seemed baffled.

'Jewish women who philosophize,' he repeated.

Joseph nodded. 'They renounce family life, and their days are spent in contemplation and study.'

Mariamme expelled a puff of air between her lips in an expression of disbelief.

'You do not think it possible that a woman should devote her life to learning?'

In one of those moments that should belong to a dream, a scene dissolving from one reality into another, Loshema understood two things, one that Pheroras attention was not focused on Mariamme, instead he was gazing directly into her face, and, two, the dismissive expulsion had come from between her own lips.

There was a frozen silence, in which Loshema forgot to drop her gaze to the floor as was the obligation of an addressed slave. She stared helplessly into his eyes, finding them dark and intense and perhaps a little amused. He seemed to be waiting for a response, but behind him was the cool disc of Mariamme's face, its blank otherness speaking of the divide which Loshema should not dare to cross. At last she managed to drop her eyes to the floor. She felt, rather than saw him, shrug and turn away. The conversation moved on, but Loshema heard not another word.

There is an old phrase, **If a slave wants to keep his tongue he must forget he has one**. *The meaning is clear. A slave does not speak out. If a slave has thoughts —and there are those who would dispute it, only read the politics of Aristotle or peruse a line of Varro's, de rustica— he must keep them locked inside his heart. Better the couch or the sideboard share an opinion than the human voice of the slave dare to confront his master with the sound of his humanity. Who knew this rule better than I, who broke it? And, naturally, the punishment for my transgression was not long in coming.*

See how it is arranged. There is Mariamme getting to her feet. The day is unseasonably warm, she announces. Perhaps they should take the opportunity for a stroll in the garden, a proposition to which Pheroras nods and Joseph readily agrees. 'Hippocrates,' he says, 'wrote much on the benefits of exercise and, indeed, does our Torah not exhort us to remember that a wise man is full of strength, and a man of knowledge enhances his might.'

They leave together with Jonathan, and despite my shame I dare to follow Pheroras with my eyes hoping to inspire his curiosity again, his pity even. I will willingly take the dregs. He leads Mariamme past without a second glance; I am forgotten.

Once gone the Jebusite nurse boxes my ears then banishes me to the kitchen, where I am to stay, with the direst warnings 'not to be seen' still ringing in my ears, even after the pain of the blows has worn off.

Very well, we will go down to the kitchens. But permit the months to pass. Let what seems a lifetime to me, be an instant to you, for time moves slowly when the compass of one's days is entirely set by others. Lift, fetch, carry, serve! Such is the routine of a slave, a monotonous round that numbs the brain and weighs down the body. Aristotle tells us that subjugation is the natural state of the enslaved, yet he is silent on how we are to endure it. And, truthfully, I found it harder since I saw myself reflected in Pheroras' kindly, questioning eyes. Even outside in the fresh air, now sweetened with spring, I am in darkness. I think it has always been so, and, for an instant, he offered a glimmer of light. I need that light. I close my eyes and think, if only I could hear his voice.

'Yet that would hardly be wise,' he says.

And now it is only my slave training that prevents me from crying aloud. Because, of course, these words are not addressed to me. I open my eyes wide and look about, but no soul reveals itself. And I think myself dreaming when old Pollio says, 'To spare a man's life goes beyond wisdom.'

The voices are coming from my feet. Looking down I realize that, the spot where I am standing, has been cleared for planting, and in moving the top soil they have revealed a narrow grate once intended to ventilate a cellar. That Pollio and Pheroras believe that they are talking in private piques my interest. I lay my basket down and kneel upon the ground, pretending to be absorbed in some task, the appearance of diligence being a trick in which every slave is well versed. It is Pheroras' voice I hear.

'Do not be too quick to judge him. Too many do that. I swear that if my brother were a book he would best be read between the lines.'

Pheroras, dear Pheroras to whom the whole world is a book. It does not surprise me that Pollio has taken him into his confidence. Pheroras was always kindred with scholarly souls. To paraphrase that cruel jibe aimed at Julius Caesar, Pheroras could be described as every student's teacher and every teacher's student.

'But Mark Antony is set on having Antigonus march in his Triumph.'

Pheroras again. 'Herod cannot permit it. While Antigonus lives we will never know safety.'

'Yet to kill a king.'

'A false one.'

'A Hasmonaean ...'

'All the more reason—'

'But, do you not see, Herod is the victor yet he seeks to tip the scales of justice still further

in his favour. Such an act is a perversion of the natural order of things.'

'A moral error perhaps, but—.'

'Can you deny that creation is a matter of order? To violate the moral order is to adversely affect the natural. Was the ground not polluted after Cain's murderous act, did the Great Aegyptus not feel the wrath of the Almighty in hail and fire? What Herod chooses to do will affect us all.'

'Here in Jersalem?'

'In all Jewry. He will become the portrait by which all other Jews are painted.'

There is silence for a moment then Pheroras speaks in an exasperated, pleading tone. 'Must I be my brother's keeper?'

'You are. You must.'

'Herod is king now.'

'Does the Almighty not punish kings? Did Solomon or Saul or Uzziah or Jeroboam escape His Justice? He has been my protector, and before the Almighty my love of him is boundless, but you cannot deny that though Herod has won, yet his thirst for vengeance is not quenched. Pheroras— ' Pollio's voice rises, and though I have set eyes on him but barely, I can picture him, his lined face intense, his hand gripping Pheroras' shoulder. 'If Herod can do this, what else might he be capable of?'

There is silence again, longer this time. Pheroras is turning over the form and shape of the question in his mind, trying to reach the heart of what this Pharisee is asking. —What else might Herod be capable of?— A breeze rustles across the garden and the budding branches of an olive tree tremble. Suddenly the air fills with damp half-remembered scents, mint, camomile, cumin. And from behind, comes the sound of Mariamme calling Jonathan to join her. Distracted, I am on the point of turning away when, unexpectedly, Pheroras laughs. 'I understand you now. Rest assured, there is nothing to fear. I know my brother. He would never hurt her.'

17

A kingdom is laid at the feet of Mariamme

36 BCE

*P*ICTURE IT NOW. *The youngest of the kitchen boys comes running in through the door crying, 'They're dead … They're dead! … Out there. Soldiers…' The words are tumbling out of his mouth in an incoherent gabble. His face is red and tearstained. He is making no sense.*

Shlomi reaches down and cuffs the boy on the side of the head. 'Who? Who is dead?'

But the boy only stutters and gulps and points behind him. Shlomi's eyes grow fearful. 'They are killing here, in the palace?' Several women gasp and lift their aprons to their faces. But the boy shakes his head and points more frantically.

'Out there?' Shlomi asks. 'Beyond the walls?'

The boy nods. A stream of clear snot is running from one nostril. He takes a deep breath and croaks, 'The Grand Sanhedrin … all dead'

The gasps are not confined to the women this time. There is uproar in the kitchens. Wailing cries go up to the Almighty, who is known to have cruelly punished the children of Israel for lesser indiscretions in the past. The noise grows many heads, like the snapping skulls of a Leviathan, until Shlomi pours out a stream of invective rich enough to curdle the pitchers of ewe's milk set aside to wash down the daily ration of bread.

In the appalled hush that follows, Shlomi continues, red-faced, his great body shaking with emotion. 'Do you think soldiers who have murdered the holiest men in the city will spare a breath before they turn their swords on ungrateful slaves? You heard the boy; Herod is purging his enemies. The Sanhedrin are all dead!'

Then a voice, almost too quiet to be heard says, 'No, not quite.'

One of the maids cries out, 'It's Pollio.'

Everyone turns to follow her finger, for who in the company does not know Herod's friend, ancient Pollio. Little wonder he has been spared, yet somehow his arrrival in the midst of horror and confusion has the appearance of a miracle.

He seems on the point of saying something when he sways and is only saved from falling by the strong arm of an unusual-looking kitchen slave with green eyes and sun-streaked hair. Immediately one of the gardeners, a burly peasant lad burnt almost black from his days in the relentless sun, pushes forward to take her place. But Pollio, an exception in so many ways, does not share this fellow's misogyny. He shakes his head and tightens his grip on Loshema's arm. 'I must speak with Herod now.' He turns to Shlomi with disarming deference. 'If you will spare this maid to be my staff, I will make my own way up.'

But when they get there, Herod is with his wife. The two stand facing each other, separated by the swelling curve of her belly. — Come now, we will watch this scene unfold. In the corner is safest. Slaves are always found in the corners. No-one pays attention; we gather there, like dust.—

The sun is out in force this day and the drapes have been drawn to mute its strength. But a breeze lifts the fabric, opening up chinks so that the room ripples with shadows and scurrying patches of light. When Pollio enters, Herod and Mariamme turn to face him, a model of propriety. But look a little closer. See how the light reveals the bloom of blood that flushes Mariamme's throat or Herod's hand curled in on itself in a foetal gesture of anger. Words have been exchanged. Pollio bows low. Indeed so low that, for several moments it is uncertain whether he can rise again. But rise he does and makes his greetings,

'I bow to you and honour you. May peace reign over this house and may it be blessed with fruitfulness.'

'It is done?' Herod's question is too abrupt. He is still more soldier than politician. Pollio blinks then nods. 'Antigonus will find no supporters amongst the Sanhedrin now.'

'Dead?'

Mariamme's chin rises, as though her throat is tightening, but she remains the obedient silent wife. Pollio avoids her gaze. 'Most are dead. Some have fled, leaving their possessions behind, and glad enough to save their skins. Of the twenty six who remain, you can be assured of their loyalty.'

See how my shoulders stiffen, my gaze fixes rigidly upon the floor. I am unworldly, naïve as my cloistered mistress, but I understand the immensity of what Herod has done. He has cut off the head of the Jews as effectively as he cut it from Pappus' shoulders. The great judges of Israel, who sit in counterbalance to the power of the king are now no more than the cult statues brought out by the priests of Aegyptus, their hinged heads giving the illusion of nodding agreement.

Mariamme does not have the slave's privilege of looking at the floor, but she cannot meet her husband's gaze. Instead she pours wine with her own hand and offers it to Pollio. But she is trembling and the wine falls in little bloody droplets over her skin.

'Lady,' Pollio says gently. 'Your husband had no choice.'

Mariamme does not answer. She is afraid to speak, and Herod seeing that she is afraid is hurt by her reaction. He stares at her in pleading confusion for a moment, which she does not see, then turns and strides over to the window, throwing back the curtains so that his expression is obliterated in a white blaze of light.

From behind a curtained door, Uncle Joseph appears. He has come from one of the inner chambers, but it is clear from his face, which is sombre as a tomb, that he has overheard every word. He glances from his nephew to his nephew's wife with concern, and even spares me a narrowed-eyed glance that does not rise higher than the tiny peaked buds that pass as my woman's bosom. But it is clear he wants to demonstrate his usefulness and his first words are for Pollio.

'Dear Pollio, we are always in your debt.' *—By which he means, of course, that he is always in ours.—*

Pollio bows, looks about to speak, but Joseph is already addressing Mariamme. 'This good Pharisee speaks the truth. Those men who lie dead were your enemies.' *—By which he means they were Herod's.—* 'Your husband is king now and he must show a king's strength.'

Mariamme has locked eyes with him. It is as if they have forgotten Herod is present. 'Yet so many ... more than half— ' *—By this she is implying what everyone knows; Herod has wiped out the only power able to countermand the king.— Joseph sighs.*

'Is he alone in this? It seems to me that history tells us that this is an old story. Did not David hunt down and hang the sons of Rizpah rather than allow the pretenders to his throne to live?'

'What claim had the men of the Sanhedrin to be kings?'

'None, but we must be practical, my dear. Victory against Antigonus has not come cheaply. He is not dead yet and Antony will be swayed more by gold than eloquence. All that Herod does, he does to protect you ... and your child.' *The argument hits its mark. Mariamme hesitates, biting her lip, an arm held protectively over the swell of her stomach.*

'You have a persuasive tongue, uncle.' *They glance up, startled. Herod has left the window. He comes close to his wife, placing himself deliberately between Mariamme and Joseph. Taking her by the shoulders he forces her to meet his gaze. He is too rough and she flinches under his grasp, but he does not notice. When he speaks his voice is surprisingly soft and urgent.* 'Look at me.' *Then again more roughly.* 'Look at me!' *Mariamme blinks, then lifts her gaze.*

'Who do you see before you?'

'I see *—She falters. What does he want?—* I see Herod ... my king.'

He shakes his head. 'Rome has made me a king, but I am no king. My great grandfather bowed down in the sacred groves and burnt offerings to false gods. My childhood was spent with my mother's people in Nabataea. And when my father brought me to Jerusalem in my twentieth year it was to learn to be a Jew.' *Mariamme tries to say something, but he silences her with a finger to her lips.* 'I am no rightful ruler, not by blood, nor in the eyes of the people. But, for you, I would be a king. And know that I will tear down and destroy any impediment, large or small, that gets in my way. What was done today was done that I might lay a kingdom before you. Would you have me apologise for doing everything in my power to make you mine?'

Poor Herod. He is offering up severed heads as tokens of his love. He pauses, eager for her response. And Mariamme stares up at him with eyes as wide as Persephone as she trembled before the king of the underworld. Silence shrieks, like a fury, and Herod's expression begins to grow brittle. Hold your breath. What Mariamme says next will determine whether he kills her on the spot. Her eyes dart hopelessly. Where can she appeal? Who can she trust? Then the doe's

gaze widens and she clutches her stomach.
   'Help me.'

The cock crows and the sum total of beings on the earth goes up by one. Herod's mewling son, Alexander, has entered the world, a wrinkled pink nub of flesh that is the culmination of ancient blood and new. While, in Antioch Antigonus bows his head and holds out the little stretch of bone and gristle that is his neck for Antony's falling sword. And the sum total of beings in the world goes down by one. But no-one thinks of him. All eyes are on the infant. Here is a nation's hope all wrapped up in swaddling linens. A future king of Jews. There is rejoicing. Herod lifts his son with such reverence that the sight makes even the harshest of his dissenters grow tender-eyed. And, in all the excitement and revelries, no-one seems to remember that Herod already has a son.

As soon as Herod left the room, carrying his new son aloft to meet his paternal grandmother, Mariamme fell back on the pillows, her face sheened with sweat. And even here in the stink of the birth chamber, with her hair curling in damp tendrils and her belly distended, there was still a fragility and a loveliness about her that many women fail to achieve even on their wedding days, least of all forgotten Doris.

With Herod gone all the air seemed to be sucked out of the room, and her eyelids began to flutter. But Alexandra shook her wrist violently, and Mariamme groaned and struggled to come back to the world.

'We must act quickly.'

'Act?' Mariamme's eyelids were drooping again. A sharp pinch to her wrist made her start. Alexandra leaned in close.

'Convince your husband that he must bring back your grandfather.'

'Now? When the men of the Sanhedrin lie dead?'

'Is there a better time? No —another pinch— Can you think to sleep when we must act?'

Mariamme did not answer, but tears welled in her eyes. Alexandra gave an exasperated moan. 'Is your womb torn? Is your child dead? No. As always in everything you do, angels attend. Yet I ask the smallest thing, with only your good in mind, and am denied.'

Mariamme shook her head weakly. 'Mother, no. Please, mother. I will speak to him, when he returns with my son.'

Seven weeks later Alexandra went to see Herod. She was white to the lips and trembling, knowing that he had outwitted her again, and yet unable to back down in the face of this half-Jew's impudence. She found him in the chamber where her father, Hyrcanus, had given audiences. It was a long low room, stark and featureless in the Hellenistic style, lit from above by smoking torches suspended in candelabras of burnished bronze. Herod was seated at the far end, surrounded by his chamberlains and eunuchs. And the sight of him on her father's throne, and the purple *chlamys* he wore so casually over his tunic, made the muscles in her face pull tight so that she looked at him through a sort of mask of her own flesh.

He was dictating a letter to one of his secretaries, though he set it aside as she came in and looked at her enquiringly.

'Alexandra, how may I be of service?'

She fought to control herself. 'I wish to thank you for bringing my father home.'

Herod gave a small nod. 'I hope the journey was not too arduous for him.'

'On the contrary. My father is more robust than you may suspect.'

'And he suffers no ill effects from his nephew's savage mistreatment?'

She swallowed. 'Indeed. He is a little deaf, but, thanks be to the Almighty, he grows stronger every day now he is back in Jerusalem. And it is his wish that I convey his heartfelt gratitude that his unshakable faith in you as a son has been rewarded.' They stared at each other, and Alexandra waited for Herod to speak. When he did not, she went on, 'You will think this the foolishness of a woman to bring these matters to you yet ... I thought his return ... I had been led to believe ... ' A listening part of her nature recoiled in horror at the pleading supplicant figure she was making of herself. Shame shrivelled the words on her lips, but Herod was looking at her steadily and she fought to inject authority into her tone when she continued. 'Yet I hear rumours, which seem to suggest that Ananelus of Babylon came with him.'

Herod's lips lengthened. 'He is of one of the noble families.'

'The *minor* nobles,' Alexandra said. 'There is talk ... there is talk that you intend to ... '

Herod smiled encouragingly. 'That you intend to appoint him High Priest.'

Herod's smile broadened to a wolf's grin. One of the eunuchs tittered. And Alexandra knew she had lost.

In her daughter's apartments Alexandra gave vent to her rage.

'Opposite me he sat, like a smirking toad, saying that Ananelus would take over as High Priest. That my own father was unfit for the role. As though he was nothing but a mutilated old man, and not a thousand times more worthy in the sight of the Almighty than that creeping worm they dragged from the gutters of Babylon. Ananelus? Who had heard his name before your husband set him up with breastplate and *ephod*?' She brought her fist down on a side-table with such a crash that the slaves jumped and the infant, Alexander, opened his toothless mouth and howled with terror.

Mariamme handed him to the outstretched arms of a wet-nurse and attempted to placate Alexandra's rage as she might have attempted to hold back the tide. 'Did he not mention Jonathan?'

Alexandra made a gesture of futility. 'He uses his age against him. Jonathan is too young. Where is it written that a youth cannot take the sacred vows? Where?' Her violence seemed to demand an answer, but what answer could be given? She rounded on her daughter and suddenly she was laughing wildly. 'This is a monster you have married. A behemoth, a cockatrice.' She broke free of Mariamme's embrace and began to tear at her hair. 'Was there ever a mother so despised? My own daughter cannot control her husband. He will kill me— '

'No mother.'

'And you and your brother.' Alexandra's words fell to a moaning sob as she pointed at the infant whimpering in his wet-nurse's arms. 'Even he is not safe.'

'You cannot mean it. Mother.' Mariamme spoke soothingly, but there was fear in her eyes as she looked at her son.

Alexandra slumped down on a couch and covered her face. 'We have risen too high. Better we had stayed slaves of the great Aegyptus than remain here.'

And yet it was from Aegyptus —that place still synonymous in the collective psyche of the Jews as the embodiment of abomination and depravity— that the first glimmer of hope was kindled.

36 BCE

Letters

Her Majesty, Queen of Upper and Lower Egypt, Cleopatra, the vindicated, to her daughter Alexandra the Hasmonaean, dowager princess of Judea and the associated tetrarchies etcetera etcetera…

It pains us to hear that the usurper has treated you with dishonour. Yet we cannot say that we did not warn you; the impression he made upon us was an unfavourable one. As you suspected, this mediocrity from Babylon is entirely his puppet, and we share your fears for what he might be about. Our envoy, Dellius, who is a good friend to Antony, will shortly be with you. He will assess the situation and advise what best may be done. Rest assured that we make moves against the usurper, and it is only the love we hold for the *Magister Equitum* that prevents us from a more open course of action. Until such times that see righteousness redressed, may your One God watch over you and protect you.

Quintus Dellius to his friend, Mark Antony

My dearest, what a place you have sent me. Such strange perfumes, such wild sentiments and notions. Being forced to leave the hyacinthine realm of your arms was a curse too extravagant to be heaped upon such mortal shoulders. I am Orpheus to your Eurydice, cast out beyond the reach of my heart's delight. How the gods must hate me.

And to send me hither to such an alien realm. Indeed I would have ranged more willingly beyond the furthest reaches of the Indus, where it is said that the dogs are the size of lions, and monopods abound, like grotesque fungi, resting at midday beneath the shade of their singular extremity.

How alien everything seemed at first when I found myself upon such

Sisyphean shores, unable to imagine how one contemplates life as a Jew. Is it not said that their practices are entrenched in wickedness and self-interest? Many and earnest were the warnings I received to 'watch my purse'. Not in the literal sense —though cutpurses abound in the markets— but rather in the nature of the Jew, which readily connives to increase his own wealth to the detriment of others.

They are a closed breed, shunning almost everything that is natural in a manner as astonishing as it is perverse. They deny the gods and eschew from lying with any but their own kind, and yet amongst their own I have heard that they practice a relentless Olympiad of licentiousness with the sole desire of increasing their number in this world. And so entrenched are they in this desire that they even consider infanticide the deadliest of sins.

And so it is with a gleaming and naked astonishment that I find myself describing the twin pearl that is at the heart of this corrupted and stinking oyster. In these times when we are become so worldly and jaded, the wonder is that there is a sight still left which can bestir our stagnant souls. Yet, my dearest, you must put aside all the gaudy trinkets of Aegytpus, and send with all haste for the son and daughter of Alexandra the Hasmonaean.

O, I am Ariadne weeping with frustration on the shores of Naxos as I try to make my meaning plain. Truly the lovely epigrammatic musings of Euphorion or Catullus could not do them justice let alone a poor scribbler such as myself. Only let me say that, with their golden skin and ebonite hair they seem not mortal beings, but rather the offspring of some strange union between luminous Aurora and her saturnine lover, Lord Hades. The boy in particular has the dewy complexion of artless youth, while the girl purses her sensuous lips and gives the secret sidelong glances of one who is virgin no more.

Send for them, you, who have made pleasure an art. You will be the rising Phoebus of our age, holding Cassandra and Cyparissus in each golden hand, and then will your Isis Incarnate not see you as once, twice, thrice the lover she has come to expect?

I entreat you, Antony. Whatever delights you may have sampled thus far, I swear before the immortal gods, you cannot die happy until you have bitten deep into this gorgeous morsel of youthful flesh.

18

A clash of Titans

THE HOUR WAS LATE AND the lamps were lit in Cypros' apartments. And, in keeping with the strange contrasts of the time, where men could erect vast pyramidal structures to entomb their dead or bridges that spanned rivers and valleys, like the arched instep of a colossus, the lamps were a poor affair. They gave out an oily, flickering illumination that trapped the occupants of the room each in his own feeble halo of light. In the centre of one such halo Cypros reclined on her couch in the posture that made her seem most like a watchful cat.

In her hands was a letter and she read from it, holding it at a distance, for though her mind was as sharp as ever, her eyes were beginning to fade. Pheroras had offered to take the task from her, but she had turned on him with such fury that he had retreated to one of the crescent-shaped stools and sat there, helplessly in silence. Between them paced Herod, his mouth a thin line, his eyes fathomless in the shadows.

'Go on!'

Cypros read: '*... The boy in particular has the dewy complexion of artless youth, while the girl purses her sensuous lips and gives the secret sidelong glances of one who is virgin no longer—*'

'Enough!' Herod reached down and snatched the scroll from his mother's hands. He threw an angry glance at Pheroras, who blinked and made a hopeless gesture, pressing his fingertips together and bowing his head over them. Cypros leaned back on her cushions.

'It is no more than we expected.'

'You have read the other letters?'

'Naturally.'

'She refers to Cleopatra as "my mother".'

'It is the old form,' Pheroras interjected. 'Between royals of unequal standing.'

Herod ignored him, saying to his mother. 'You noted it?'

'I did.'

'And she has sent their portraits. They sit for graven images now.'

Cypros shrugged as if to indicate that she had suspected nothing less.

'Does she spare no thought for Alexander?'

'Did you imagine a grandson would mean more than her pure Hasmonaean son?'

Salome appeared in the doorway, dithering on the threshold, like an uninvited guest. Cypros threw her an irritated glance. 'Tell your brother how his wife's family honours us.'

Salome entered slowly, glancing nervously at Herod. She, more than her mother, understood that kingship had created a new Herod and that the bonds of kinship were no longer to be taken for granted. 'She ... your wife ... will not receive me. I have gone to pay my respects, but am turned away with excuses and ....'

'Lies,' Cypros finished. 'Excuses and lies. Your Hasmonaean relatives do not consider your sister fit company.'

'Yet they were gracious to both myself and Uncle Joseph.' Pheroras put in.

'They thought you a servant ordered there to tutor their princeling,' Salome snapped. 'And, as for my husband, he will toady to anyone but his wife.' Tears sprang to her eyes and rolled down her plump cheeks. Herod, the brother, would have wiped them away with laughter, but Herod the king looked at her with an ill-concealed disgust. 'Do we have time for women's quarrels when my kingdom is at stake?'

Rabbit-eyed, Salome looked to her mother, who gave the faintest shake of her head. Salome's lip trembled then she stamped her foot, like a little girl, and yelled. 'I only told him because you asked it of me!' Then, turning tail, she fled from the room.

Herod took an angry step towards the door, then seeming to remember himself, turned hotly towards his mother.

'Am I to put up with this?'

'Hush.' Cypros' voice was calming. 'We have bigger things to trouble us.'

Herod nodded. His body was tense, jaw, shoulders, fists all clenched against attack. One of the lamps guttered and a slave hurried forward to replenish the oil and trim the wick. Herod watched him with the glazed stare of one who does not see, only coming back to life when the lamp was once again throwing out its winking wolf's-eye of yellow light.

'Antony demands that I send Jonathan to him.'

'You must refuse.'

'How can I? Mark Antony made me a king. Now he expects his reward.'

'He is your friend. He will understand.'

Herod stopped pacing and looked at his mother. 'I never thought to hear you act the woman.'

'And I never thought to hear you play the fool.'

'Please,' Pheroras said. 'This helps no-one.'

Cypros ignored him. But Herod drew in a deep breath and spoke more steadily. 'Even if Mark Antony holds some especial love of me, he is caught in Cleopatra's clutches. Have you no eyes to see? With her conniving she has gained Chalcis, Orthosia, Berytus, Damascus, Antioch and every city and hamlet between.

'All the great riches that once benefited the Syrian and Nabatean kings now flow through Aegyptus' royal coffers. She is eating up the world and no-one can stop her. Malichus has been threatened if he does not give up Hegra and Nitzana she will seize Petra and deprive him from his trade in aromatics.

'And further, I have heard that she drips poison in Antony's ear, claiming that her illustrious ancestor, Cleopatra the first was gifted Judea by the Seleucids and to depose me is no dishonour as my kingdom was never Rome's to give.'

'She is wrong,' Pheroras said. 'Cleopatra the third made a pact with Alexander Jannaeus at Beth-Shean. She was at war with her son, Ptolemy Lathyrus, and needed Jewish help to raise an army against him. In return she was persuaded that there was no wisdom in incurring the enmity of the Jews by annexing Coele-Syria and …' His voice trailed off as he realised that his mother and brother were staring at him.

A smile of surprising tenderness lit Herod's face. 'Pheroras, if you applied yourself to politics instead of scholarship I swear you would be my most formidable rival.' Then he sighed and grew sombre. 'But this is to no matter. —O, I do not doubt you, brother.— But Cleopatra knows how to blot out old histories and write them anew. I have been in the great Aegyptus where the heads of statues do not match the bodies beneath them, and the painted panegyrics still glisten wetly over the old version of events.

'We must not forget that Alexandra sent the portraits at Cleopatra's request. This demand for Jonathan is a provocation; it is her doing.'

Cypros regarded her son steadily. 'Yet Mark Antony does not ask for your wife.'

Herod's eyes flashed violently. 'No matter, he will.'

Slowly, her languidness deliberate, Cypros swiveled round, placing her small feet on the floor and sitting upright, as a queen sits, stiff-backed upon her throne. 'You misread the situation. Mark Antony has done the equivalent of giving his goddess a bloody nose. He is a man whose carnal desires are legendary, yet he refuses to send for your wife. Herod, do you not see, he loves you.'

'Then I must send Jonathan?'

'No. Refuse even that.' Now, unusually, Pheroras took the reins of the argument. 'Mother is right. Mark Antony loves you still. But he cannot free himself from the witch's talons. He must appease his queen, and so he sends a lukewarm request, and leaves you to read between the lines. I tell you, brother, he expects you to refuse. Tell him that it would cause upheaval in the country. Mark Antony is still a Roman at heart; he will not risk insurrection along his eastern border.'

Herod pressed the tip of his thumb into his lower lip. 'And what of Cleopatra's demands for land?'

'We will deal with that.'

'And Alexandra's treachery?'

'Ah, you must deal with that yourself.

And deal with it he does. He throws a banquet, and the guest of honour is ancient Hyrcanus, whose hair and beard are now so white that the people whisper that he is a saint, and the more daring ones add that he is more truly the High Priest than any Idumaean-appointed puppet, and surely the Almighty would willingly overlook the deformity of his ears in the face of his piety. But if Hyrcanus is deaf to these whispers, Cypros is not. But, for now, she listens and says nothing and bides her time.

All talk is of the banquet at present. No member of the Hasmonaean household can refuse to be there, and, in truth, they are curious. Rumours abound that Herod will fill the palace full of abominations, golden statues that piss out wine, unclean foods, stuffed mice and suckling pig, and there will be the gleaming limbs of dancers everywhere, their oiled and naked bodies turning this holy city into a Babylon of licentiousness. And he would be the man to do it, would Herod. He's travelled to Rome and the Great Aegyptus, where everyone knows that Cleopatra seduced him on a throne inlaid with the ivory of holy men's skulls.

And so it is with trepidation and the sense of being caught in a half-waking dream that Alexandra leads the other Hasmonaeans down the tapestry-hung corridor to the great banqueting hall, to find themselves guests where once they were hosts.

But when they get there, they are pleasantly surprised. What greets them is a feast for kings, and very Jewish kings at that. The tables are groaning beneath huge platters of carved venison and platters piled high with the stuffed bodies of pigeons, partridges and quail. Pyramids of pomegranates, grapes, sweet oranges, dates and raisons, persimmons and figs tower over dishes of honeyed sweetmeats delicately arranged in the carved vessels of melons. And there is even a cake meticulously crafted in the image of the palace.

Arranged around the room is an almost obscene number of slaves, twice, three times the usual number. Half of them are holding wineskins, bursting at the seams with the full-bodied, purple-hued wines of Galilee, and despite their lowered heads, they are ready to spring forward to fulfill the smallest desires of the seated guests.

As the Hasmonaeans enter, Herod gets to his feet and the courtiers follow his lead. Alexandra notes the Roman ambassador exchange a look with the envoy from Chalcis. This show of humility impresses them. And when Herod offers his chair to Hyrcanus, murmurs of approval are audible.

Herod places Mariamme to his left, between himself and his mother. She moves forward, every bit the Jewish queen, in a robe that reflects the sky blue of priestly robes and intricately embroidered with doves and lilies, a robe designed for peace, a peacemaker's robe. Around her neck is not the heavy gold collar that Herod sent as a betrothal gift —that went to Cleopatra in their hour of need and she was not sorry to see it go— but three thin strands of rubies, winking on silver chains so fine they are barely visible to the naked eye.

'It makes her look as though her neck were slit,' mutters Salome and is hushed by her fat husband.

Alexandra is placed next to her father, and Jonathan between Pheroras and the incumbent High Priest, Ananelus. He smiles unctuously at the Hasmonaeans as they take their seats. Mariamme affords him a cool nod; Jonathan is too charming to be anything but polite, while old Hyrcanus misses Ananelus' overtures altogether, and his daughter pretends to do likewise.

Still, honour has been served. Herod claps his hands. Minstrels begin to play. The meal begins.

If success can be calculated, then Herod is surely privy to the equation. He is a charming host, attentive, witty, yet modest in his appetites. There are none of Mark Antony's excesses to be seen and reported. Although, it does not go without note that nothing passes Herod's lips that his taster does not sample first and then again.

Slowly the Roman ambassador's formality softens, like the cinnamon wax candles that are arranged in clusters about the table. Cypros had them brought from a caravan that had passed through Arikamedu on its way along the spice route, and they are a subtle and exotic reminder that Herod is no country bumpkin needing a lesson in sophistication. Even the ambassador from Aegyptus, a thin, balding man, known for the sour droop of his features breaks into something approximating a smile at a witticism from his host. Raising his cup he announces,

'Your good health, majesty.' Herod joins him graciously, though it is clear when the ambassador misses his mouth and dribbles good Galilean wine down his front that he has had a little too much to drink. A purple stain forms on his robe, which he dabs at disconsolately then, as if remembering himself, raises his cup again. 'And to the health of your father-in-law, the goodly Hyrcanus.'

Again Herod's acknowledgement is gracious. But the ambassador is not finished. 'I must confess that we have no great love of Jews in my home country. I tell you, as a stranger first come to this land, you have an unconscionably high opinion of yourselves. Everyone knows that your most renowned city could fit into one of our palaces in Thebes yet the beggar in the street considers himself above kings.' He gives the ambassador from Rome a knowing look that barely falls short of a wink. The Roman does not acknowledge the remark, but neither does he deny it. The Aegyptian goes on. 'Perhaps it is your great wealth that shores such confidence. After all, the breadth of your county is not two hundred and fifty stadia, yet your affluence is legendary. Cut a Jew they say and he will bleed gold.'

Mariamme's fingers go to the silver chains about her neck, as though searching for the collar that went to Cleopatra. Cypros' eyes dart towards her son. Herod's expression is still gracious, but he has become very still, as though it is not Herod who sits there, but some profane likeness made of wax. The ambassador becomes aware of Herod's stillness and coughs. He fingers the stain on the front of his robe, which is now the size and shape of a pomegranate.

'What I mean to say,' he says thickly then tries again. 'What I mean to say is that these were impressions gained BEFORE I was a recipient of your generosity. I won't hide that I've been impressed. The piety of the people is beyond question, and your brother, Pheroras, has made it his business to educate me in the history and customs of the Temple. How shall I put it … my experience here has been an education in the unorthodox.

'And when I raised a toast to your esteemed father-in-law's health, I meant it more truly as a compliment to yourself. In the great Aegyptus, May-It-Rule-Forever, a man in your position would quite frankly —he pauses delicately, choosing his words— rid himself of reminders of the old regime. Yet here you are giving pride of place to the king you have

replaced.' When Herod does not respond, he turns to Alexandra, a glint in his eye. 'You must feel comforted in the light of such largesse.'

And now Herod's moment has come. Anyone, who is not a fool, can see that this scene has been staged. The ambassador from Aegyptus is not drunk, his lines are rehearsed — though he has perhaps added an improvised barb further than Herod intended.—

Alexandra coughs. She is ruffled by the question, but does not yet see the trap. 'Indeed, we are well looked after,' she admits. She looks down as she says it, but an eerie, following silence forces her to lift her gaze. Herod is looking directly at her. Everyone else is looking at Herod. Despite herself, Alexandra feels her colour rising.

'I treat you well,' Herod says. It is not a question. Alexandra nods dumbly.

'Your freedoms have not been curtailed. I treat you with honour.'

Another nod.

'Then what explanation can there be for your desire to leave us?'

Heat drains from Alexandra's face. In a room humid with the press of bodies, where complexions shine with a gleam of sweat, Alexandra is suddenly cold. Her skin pimples; she fights the urge to shudder. Herod is waiting.

'I do not— I am not clear— '

'The question is perhaps too difficult. Let me ask another. The Hasmonaeans are pillars of our faith, are they not?'

Tight-lipped, Alexandra inclines her head. Herod's brows rise a little, as though surprised at her miserly response. 'After all,' he continues, 'when the monster, Antiochus, raised a statue to the god, Zeus, on the Temple Mount, was it not your esteemed ancestor, Judah the Maccabee, who had it torn down?' A thought seems to strike him. He makes a gesture towards the foreign ambassadors. 'That may seem an act of sacrilege in your eyes, but I assure you it was necessary if we were to obey one of the tenets of our faith. My mother-in-law will explain.' His eyes gleam in the candlelight. Alexandra, finding her mouth dry, reaches for her cup, but her hand is trembling too much and she dare not lift it. At last she rasps out the second commandment, 'Thou shalt not make unto thee any graven image.'

Herod sits back in his chair. With a sweeping gesture he indicates the frescoed walls, dimly visible through the flickering light, the acanthus leaves and ferns, the curling waves and many-pointed stars. 'You do not find human likeness here.'

'Indeed we are forbidden from producing such images as may be mistaken for a form of idolatry,' Ananelus butts in, unaware that even as High Priest it is not his prerogative to speak before invited.

'Yes,' the Roman ambassador says carefully. 'Your pieties are well known throughout the empire.'

Cypros' eyes slide towards him. She notes the use of the verb GNOSIS, knowledge, rather than TIMESATE, respect. Herod notes it too. His smile tightens. His gaze returns to Alexandra. 'Naturally as the daughter of our saintly Hyrcanus you are above reproach in these matters.'

Hyrcanus hears his name and gives a toothless nod in the direction of his daughter. He has followed little of the proceedings and is occupied in attempting to eat some soup, which is now dribbling down his chin. Alexandra looks at him helplessly then back to Herod. He has her trapped. With a word, he can order them all to their deaths. Her gaze roves wildly amongst the foreign ambassadors. The Aegyptian has already proved treacherous. The Roman regards her coolly, an observer not a player. A kindly look from the envoy from Chalcis, but would tiny Chalcis intervene and risk war?

Slowly she gets to her feet, steadying herself with the tips of her fingers against the table's edge. 'You know what I have done,' she says hoarsely. 'But before the Almighty and all those who sit here, let it be known that I acted only as a mother —a sly glance at Cypros— who must do all to protect her child.

'You say, Herod, that you have treated me well. Have I done less? What greater honour could I have bestowed beyond the joining of our two houses through my daughter? Was it too much to expect that you would honour my child.' A gesture of her hand indicates Jonathan. 'The High Priesthood is his right. The people expect it.'

At this there is a murmur in the room. Even Herod's gelded Sanhedrin cannot hide their longing. Alexandra grows a little stronger. But Herod's face is stone. He has killed Antigonus; he has executed the holiest men in the city. A few bird-like twitterings will not sway him. In her panic she looks to Jonathan, and he smiles, encouraged by her words, not understanding the danger he is in. Her daughter will not meet her gaze, but remains, eyes lowered, as though she had been forced unwillingly to attend a particularly distasteful play.

Herod shifts. He is about to speak, and then it happens. Mariamme does something seen only by Cypros and a single attending slave. She reaches under the table and puts her hand on Herod's thigh. In Aegyptus or Rome such an action between a man and his wife would garner little comment. But here in holy Jerusalem, it is charged with tensions that spark and sizzle, like arcs of lightning, leaping crazily all the way back through the generations until Eve stands naked and shameless, offering Adam all the fruits of forbidden pleasure she has gathered between her palms.

Herod pauses. He looks at his wife, who lifts her eyes to gaze up at him and speaks a single word.

'Please.'

There it is, the moment the tide turns, the wind shifts and a heart changes direction. This is Queen Esther pleading with Ahasuerus or wise Abigail abasing herself, face in the dirt, pacifying David's masculine pride. Herod does not answer instead turning his head back to his mother-in-law, but beneath the table his hand reaches out and encloses his wife's small wrist.

'Your words move me,' he says, but he says it in a flat, uninflected voice that gives Alexandra no clue as to what will happen next. 'I see that I have erred in overlooking your son. Yet I did so only with the thought of protecting one of such tender years from the rigors

of high office.' He gives his wife's hand a secret squeeze. 'Nonetheless I freely admit my fault and hereby declare that from this day on Jonathan the Hasmonaean will be High Priest over Jerusalem and Jews.'

There is a collective gasp of shock, none louder than from the current High Priest. The members of the king's council know that Herod has no authority to appoint and dismiss the High Priest, as though he was in service to the realm, rather than a servant of the Almighty. But no-one raises an objection when two of the palace guards lead Ananelus, who is now deathly white beneath his sweating face, out of the room. He will be back in Babylon before he knows it, but it will be some time before he counts it amongst his blessings.

Alexandra is still standing. She tries to summon words of gratitude, but sounds collide in her throat. Has she won or been outmaneuvered yet again? Herod's expression is a study of contrition. The ambassadors are impressed. At his side Mariamme is looking at her hands, which are now resting on the table, as though there is a new force exuding from the fingertips or as if she were holding the key to her husband's unreachable soul.

Suddenly applause starts up, though no-one knows from where. Then everyone is joining in. Cheers are heard, feet stamp, backs are slapped, and everyone has the feeling that they have personally contributed to this happy outcome. And the only one not wreathed in smiles, either true or false, is Salome. Her mouth is a downturned droop, and she watches Mariamme as if to say, You think you have won, but no-one can ride a lion's back for long.

19

The Fall

T HE FOLKLORE OF THE JEWS *tells of a demon who went by the name, Shabriri. He hid in deep pools, waiting. And when his hapless victims reached down to scoop the cool liquid into their mouths, Shabriri would strike and put out their eyes for that was the meaning of his name, Shabriri, blindness. Fear of this demon led some rabbis to warn against drinking from pools on Wednesdays and the eves of the Sabbath. And some were so afraid that they counseled against drinking from pools no matter what the night of the week. Beware still pools, mothers warned their children. Shabriri lurks beneath.*

And, in a similar vein, Herod thought of his kingdom in the days after Jonathan had been anointed High Priest. On the surface things were calm. His wife smiled at him. Their son was growing fit and healthy, if the thwarted howl that regularly came from his princely lungs was anything to go by. Even his mother-in-law was at pains to tell anyone who would listen that the High Priesthood was all that she desired for her child, and that she had no designs on the crown, indeed would refuse it if offered.

All was calm, yet Herod could not shake the feeling that if he reached out and let his fingers trail in the water, Shabriri would curse him and he would be left wandering his kingdom, blind and spurned, like that Greek hoarder of tragedies, Oedipus .

29 BCE

With her hand raised to knock on the door of Alexandra's apartments, Loshema froze. From within came the distinct tinkling cascade of breaking glass. Her instinct was to turn away, but her hand moved reflexively and she had rapped against the wood before she could stop herself. To her surprise the door was opened and she was ushered inside by the old Jebusite nurse. But before she could speak the Jebusite put a finger to her lips. Another splintering explosion and the inner door flew open and Alexandra stormed into the room, her daughter close behind.

'He dares— He dares— ' Choleric, panting in her fury, Alexandra could not get the words out. Mariamme tried to place a placating hand on her arm and was shaken off.

'Mother, think how he sees it.'

'He sees it as he sees everything, like the low creeping things of the earth and all of them living in Idumaea.'

'If you will only give it a little time.'

'Time?' Alexandra rounded on her daughter. 'I am the daughter of a saint, direct

142

descendent of John Hyrcanus. Am I ordered by the likes of your husband to keep to my quarters?'

'He said only that you must be accompanied.'

'It is beneath my dignity.' Alexandra's hair was disheveled and she clawed at one of her sleeves, which had fallen from her shoulder. Suddenly she was weeping. 'He hates me. He wants me dead.'

'No, mother. He is just afraid. You have made him afraid.'

Alexandra turned away and her shoulders heaved. 'But to be treated like a prisoner in my own home, like a … a slave! He watches my every move. Spies everywhere.' Her eyes lit on Loshema. 'You. What are you doing here? Listening to every word. Ready to scuttle back, a creeping Delilah eager to report what you've heard.'

Wild-eyed she crossed the room, forcing Loshema to back away until her shoulder blades connected bluntly with a wall and she could go no further. 'Lady, I am here for the soiled linens.'

'Lies.' She was so close that Loshema could smell the sour tang of wine on her breath. 'I know you. You were there when I spoke with my son-in-law and later when I was walking in the garden.'

This was untrue. At the time Alexandra took her evening stroll, Loshema had been in attendance to Mariamme. And Alexandra's mistake was a result of that arrogance of liberty, which allowed her to see all creatures stamped with the mark of slavery as one and the same.

Loshema looked pleadingly in Mariamme's direction, hoping to hear her contradict her mother. Surely there was some bond between them? Had Mariamme not sought her out before she lay with her husband? Loshema had been a human being to her then, a hand to grasp in the dark. But Mariamme stood blank and aloof, not even pointing out that Loshema, with her aquamarine eyes and lightened hair, would have made a poor choice of a spy amongst her doe-eyed, raven-haired sisters.

With nothing to deflect her rage Alexandra began jabbing a finger at Loshema's chest, her hysteria mounting. 'I saw you!' Then, mistaking inaction for a breed of insolence, began beating her about the head and face, all the time screaming, 'Vile filth … dirt beneath my feet. … Cowardly, disgusting, lowborn … —she gathered herself up to spit out the most damning word in her vocabulary— SLAVE!'

And while this was happening she was numb. Loshema was numb. She felt like the descriptions of sailors aboard storm torn ships, helpless and buffeted as she was tossed inside the vessel of herfself, aware of the crashing blows from outside, yet aware of them only as 'out there', and her pain coming not from punches or slaps, but from the piercing blades of words that passed through the thin sides of the vessel and degraded her essence, that part of her that existed in response to the acknowledgement of others.

Words are power and, at that time, no-one had refined the power of the word more so than the Jews. Without conscious acknowledgment Alexandra understood how words destroy, and while a living mind might armour itself against an onslaught, sooner or later something must pass through, the quick blade, the poisoned arrow, and then there is no longer a need to use physical force because the kind of death you have inflicted is inevitable, a slow creeping strangulation of the soul.

And this very much fit Loshema's state as, finally released, she stood, head lowered not in pain, but shame, shame for her knowledge that she was a coward who did not strike back for fear of death, shame for her aloneness in the world, where everyone else belonged and shame for her innate and filthy nature as a slave and the daughter of a slave.

Alexandra turned back to her daughter, as though Loshema was already forgotten, but she was panting, her face slack as if with sexual release. To crush a spirit completely is an erotic act and she glistened with almost palpable pleasure.

Now it was known that the obliteration of the sense of 'I' leaves behind a hollow vacuum where death or religion often pour in to fill the void. But for all her knowledge, acknowledged or otherwise, she had forgotten that in rare cases a stranger process takes place. A person, who has suffered more than a person can suffer and remain whole, transforms and emerges from the flames of their own conflagration unrecognizable, and in the words of the Law, it is as if they were *swept away in the dream of death only to awaken the next day, like new grass, stretching towards the sun.*

It was thus for Loshema, who began her stunned, newborn stumble out of the room, yet stopping for a half moment to glance backwards, as though trying to make sense of what had taken place. In later years she would come to think of it as the instant when she no longer thought of herself as a slave, as if such self-knowledge can be immediate rather than, what it more truly was, the beginning of a long process of self-revelation. But, in turning, she saw also the quick, furtive movement of the Jebusite nurse's meaty hand as she thrust letters under a casket, as though in response to some warning look from her mistress. Loshema stared, swaying a little, her eyes emptied and vacuous, and when she turned back to the door there was no attempt to stop her.

Daylight was not kind to Pheroras. The columns of light that streamed into the cramped little room, he was pleased to call his *tablinum* in the Roman style, only highlighted how deep were etched the lines about his eyes and mouth, as though he had taken on his brother's worries as his own and magnified them in the process.

Set squarely in front of him were letters, which he read, not looking up until he was finished, and then only long enough to reorder them so that he might read them through a second time. At last he set them down and sat back, studying the girl who was standing before him, hands clasped, waiting for his response.

Loshema had come to him silently, but not tentatively. She had not approached him as a slave approaches, but had simply walked up to his desk and laid the letters down. Now she waited patiently, yet with something desperate and hectic flickering in her pale eyes. He wanted to question her, and at the same time he did not want to hear what she had to say. He rolled up the scrolls and got slowly to his feet.

'Come with me.'

They found Herod in his chambers surrounded by his favourites, preparing to go out on a hunt. A handsome youth, with the remarkable dark auburn hair that was sometimes found amongst the tribe of Judah, was engaged in helping him to dress, and Herod was watching him with a tender, amused expression, as the youth bent a little too close to fasten a leather cuff about his wrist. He raised his free arm, splaying the fingers of his hand as though considering caressing the youth's bent head, but, at Pheroras' warning cough, he pushed the young man away and got to his feet.

'Brother?'

Pheroras said nothing, the quick lightning dart of his eyes communicating more than words. Herod clapped his hands and gave a roar more suitable to the battlefield than the bedroom, and the favourites scurried from the room, none quicker than the auburn-haired youth. Pheroras handed Herod the scrolls, but as he took them he held his brother's gaze, saying in a low incredulous voice, 'She has dared?'

'Only read what is there.'

Herod searched his brother's eyes a moment longer then unrolled the first scroll with a violent motion of his hands and began to read.

'It is still to Cleopatra she turns.' It was neither a question nor a comment that invited response, and Pheroras remained silent. 'My mother-in-law,' Herod said disbelievingly after a while. 'She is a she-serpent in thin disguise.'

Pheroras shrugged. 'We expected as much.'

'But so soon. She has no shame.' Herod lowered the letters and his sharp gaze fell on Loshema, who trembled a little, but did not lower her head.

'You knew what was in these letters?'

A quick shake to indicate no.

'Yet you brought them to my brother. Why?'

Loshema reached for her voice and found it hiding deep inside her chest. She gave a choking cough then managed to say, 'Because he showed me kindness.' And then because she could feel Pheroras staring at her in amazement, she added, 'And because I am loyal to the house of Herod.'

Herod stood, looking at her, tapping the edge of one fist against his lips. And Loshema knew he was taking her measure and weighing her worth. What had she expected? That he would clasp her by the shoulders again and order that she be treated with kindness? *He is less the man now,* she realized, *and more the king.* But she held herself straight and did not cringe as a slave cringes. She felt him studying her split lip, the bruises on her face. 'You are loyal to the house of Herod,' he repeated and there was a dangerous edge to his voice.

Not trusting herself to speak again, she nodded.

'A spy might bring me these letters to gain my trust. Or they might be fabricated as an act of vengeance. In Rome a slave is tortured before he can give evidence because, by nature, his word is doubtful.'

'Brother. We are not Romans.' Pheroras intervened, his voice a soothing balm. 'I watched her face closely. She is an innocent. I would stake my life on it.'

'Then your life can be of little worth to you if you would wager it so lightly,' Herod snapped. He turned back to Loshema. 'My brother reads a good deal and finds out nothing. You, on the other hand, read nothing and find out all.'

Loshema did not answer. She was a mote of dust spinning in a glaring beam of light, yet in some dim part of herself she sensed that Herod was a man who imposes his own narrative on a situation, and to attempt to set the facts before him was to risk being in defiance of his singular interpretation. The air grew heavier and the floor began to sway beneath her feet. What demon had possessed her to steal back to Alexandra's chambers to take the letters? A thousand scenarios where she acted differently thundered through her head and echoed in the beat of fear pulsing through her veins. She felt, rather than saw, Pheroras shift at her side. 'You will arrest them?'

Herod's glance flicked towards his brother, and Loshema felt air rush back into her lungs. He gave a short, mirthless laugh. 'You are right, brother.'

Pheroras started to speak, but Herod went on, 'We are not Romans. And we will not deal with it in a Roman way. There will be no spectacle. Let them play out their drama. We will be ready.'

The dawn light is chilled. Wraiths of mist rise from the street as the cart bumps and rattles along the city streets. Its load, two coffins, plain, unadorned paupers' coffins, are secured, but still they shift and strain against the ropes which constantly threaten to break and set free their load. In front a hunched hooded figure sits, egging on an ancient ass, who plods grudgingly along, his resentment fueled by ancestral memories of perpetual toil. At the city gate he stops.

This is not the great Nablus Gate, with its double arch, the entranceway for kings and foreign dignitaries, nor even the lesser Horse Gate, where beasts might be watered to fortify them for a journey across parched landscapes, but rather a mean and unadorned little archway, barely wide enough to allow a cart to pass through. Yet, for all its insignificance, it has its purpose, for this is the death gate, the entrance to the great cemetery of the Kidron valley, where not all who enter will be destined to return. This is the final exit from golden Jerusalem for the poor, the nameless, the foreigner.

The gate is poor, but it is not unguarded. A man blocks the way, a soldier, a retired veteran more likely, but he's been in the king's guard at some point; he has the look. And his helmet and spear have a glinting professional polish that catches in the torchlight.

'State your business.'

The hooded driver cocks his head to the back of the cart. 'Bodies.'

'Burial at this time?'

'Paupers. No tomb. They'll go unmarked into the field.'

The guard comes a little closer. 'And no funeral procession. Even a poor man has mourners.'

The driver shrugs. 'A potter and his wife. No family.' He leans forward as the guard puts his hand on the cart. 'I heard whispers from the women who washed the bodies; there were boils.'

The guard pulls back his hand, and the driver lifts the reins. But he has presumed too much. The guard's hand darts out and encloses his wrist.

'Open the coffins.'

The driver gasps, but he keeps his composure. He lets his hood fall back, revealing a man much younger than his voice has suggested. He is a handsome boy, and the guard recognizes the epicene features from his time in the palace. Locking his gaze with the guard, the youth reaches into his cloak and pulls out a purse. He holds it out. 'I must take these bodies clear of the city.' He leans a little closer. 'When I am done I will return.' The promise of his words lingers in the air, like scent.

The guard's gaze moves briefly to the purse then to the youth's damsom-coloured eyes. He smiles and stretches out a hand. The youth smiles back, placing the purse in the guard's upturned palm. Then, in one swift motion, the guard has the purse and the lad inside the iron vice of his grip. The lad gasps. But it is too late. He is lifted down and, in response to a low whistle by his captor, more guards appear on the scene. They look the lad up and down, who is now pale and shaking, and lament that their orders require immediate return to the palace. One climbs up on the cart and takes the reins. The sun is still not up as they clatter off, and the guard, with his hand firmly grasping the trembling lad by the collar, blows his clouded breath into the morning chill and dreams of warming himself inside the spread buttocks of youth.

It is still early by the time they reach the palace, but Herod is waiting. A crowd of yawning courtiers stands with a group of white-faced men in priestly vestments, watching as the coffins are placed on the floor before their king. Pheroras is there, his face drawn, his eyes troubled. And, on either side Herod is flanked by Cypros and Salome. In their eagerness, their eyes have the look of overripe fruits. You could imagine their pupils splitting and all the resentment pouring out. Salome can barely keep still and keeps casting Herod yearning looks.

At the far end of the chamber the door opens and a sleep-tousled Mariamme enters. Unlike Cypros and Salome she has had no warning. A blanket is thrown over her shoulders, her feet are bare. She looks at her husband in bewilderment. But when her gaze falls on the coffins the colour washes from her face. She tries to say something, but instead, stumbles and is caught by the Jebusite nurse. Then, with an effort, that is visible to all who are watching, she masters herself and asks Herod,

'Who is in there? Who is dead?'

And, in one of those strange reversals which make Herod the unpredictable character he is, he might have been moved to take pity on his disheveled, sleep-befuddled queen with nothing to adorn her, but the crown of her tumbled black curls, but his mother snaps,

'Enough of this play acting. Do you deceive my son then think to treat him like a fool?'

And with Mariamme's mouth effectively stopped by this unexpected venom, Cypros demands, 'Let the lids be prised open.'

And now the true drama begins. First Jonathan then Alexandra are hauled out, gasping and sobbing, and deposited at Herod's feet, like fish caught in a net. Out from the coffins the guards pull ropes of jewels and bags of gold and set them on the floor. Alexandra is dragged to her feet, and stands supported between two of Herod's guards. Dressed in a cloak, she manages a certain dignity despite the fact that her hair has loosed itself from its tight net and greying locks stand up about her head, like a gorgon's serpentine coils. Lightning flashes of fear illuminate her eyes, but she keeps her voice steady, lifting her chin to announce, 'You have taken my servant, Aesop. I demand his release.'

'You demand, do you?'

Mariamme, who has summoned the courage to cross the room, but not enough of it to approach her husband, stands a little apart from both parties. Nonetheless she sends her mother a warning glance.

She turns next to her husband, but Herod's face is filled with fury. She does not recognize him yet is transfixed by the primal power of his rage. He is a storm king of old, back, back to the beginnings of time when the gods were new to men and kings thundered across the flat plains of Canaan brandishing their weapons of black iron ore, worshipping nothing but the tumultuous heavens filled with their burning pitchforks of divine white light. He is still looking at Alexandra, waiting for her to respond.

'Aesop is an innocent in this,' Alexandra persists. It is known that she favours her servant. After Jonathan, Aesop has her heart, and she is fond of him in the way later generations may be fond of a faithful family pet. Herod regards her in a manner that makes ice run down the spines of several of those whose role is no more than spectator.

'Then you should have muzzled this innocent before you let him abroad,' he says. 'Less likely then that he would have given away your plans to your friend, Sabbion.

At this my head snaps up. —O, I am there, summoned with other house slaves to perform menial duties or perhaps to add to the weight of humiliation heaped upon the Hasmonaean heads.— But did Aesop really blab? Sabbion is known to have wanted to wheedle his way back into Herod's good graces. Yet it does not ring true, and for an instant I believe that Pheroras is looking directly at me, a glint of complicity in his eyes. Yet this subterfuge is surely not for me. Ah, I see it now. Better to be betrayed by the word of a free man than a slave's dubious tongue.

Believing that her friend has betrayed her, Alexandra falters. She casts about for excuses. If only Herod had honoured her.

—Was the High Priesthood bestowed upon her son not honour enough?—

If he had not treated her as prisoner. If he had trusted her.

—And what a worthy vessel she has proved herself to receive trust.—

Argument and counterargument. Alexandra has been caught red-handed and hasn't the wit to admit it.

Treason.

It isn't clear who says it first. But soon it's being whispered about the room. APATÊ TOU DÊMOU KAI KANóN *The educated ones murmur the words in their Greek form. Deceiving the people and the king. Mariamme hears it first and looks wildly at Herod. There is no escape from this. What can come from this, but death? But he hasn't heard yet. He is poised, waiting for that final nudge to cut the bonds of his rage.*

She is moving, Mariamme in her nightgown and her bare feet, is crossing the floor. As she passes her mother she sends her mother a quick warning glance, let me handle this. Alexandra's babbling dries up. Noticing her approach Cypros clutches her son's arm. Salome, too, notices and opens her mouth. Too late. Mariamme falls to her knees. There she is, down on her knees, begging her husband.

Her words are soft and do not carry. Herod listens, expressionless. And the whole room finds itself straining forward, repelled and attracted by this act of submission. For this is no Chana weeping in contrition for her childless state before Elkhana, nor Samson's Philistine wife begging for proof of his love. This is a proud and beautiful woman, a queen, down on her knees groveling before the brutish power of a primitive and unforgiving man.

Herod listens to the soft, imploring words. Once or twice he glances at the wan faces of Alexandra and her son. He says something to Mariamme and nods his head, and Mariamme's shoulders slump with relief. At once Cypros, her face drawn down in a scowl, pulls at his robe, as if to drag his attention towards her. But Herod, Herod who always does the unexpected, shakes her free then he reaches down and takes his wife by her black curls and forces her face into his loins.

He lets her go almost at once. But the action is there, burning on the pupils of every onlooker in the room. And for me, for Loshema, forgotten, overlooked Loshema, the sight of Mariamme's arms flailing uselessly, her surprised gasp cut short, is more than a deliberate act of humiliation; it is a knife in the heart. Because, as he did it, as he desecrated this living temple to the proud and ancient honour of the Macabees, he looked at me. He looked directly at me so that our eyes met, and I understood that this was my reward.

20

In which we begin again and the end comes nearer

INTERLUDE, 4 BCE,

The heat in Jericho was a living thing, already pulsing in the morning air. Even the surface of the fish pool, where members of the royal family had gathered to cool themselves only a day ago, now caught the light and splintered it into scintillating fields of diamonds too livid for the eye to bear.

Salome had retreated indoors and lay languidly on a couch, allowing two slaves to fan her, and alternately yelling that all they did was move the hot air about or that they fanned so slowly she might as well have been a roast on a spit waiting to be turned.

A dog, which had been heard whimpering and pawing at the gates during the night, was found dead outside the palace walls, its tongue protruding and blackened. Everywhere touched by the sun's rays was parched and desiccated until the great palace itself, with all its classical lines and modern comforts, seemed to shrivel beneath the relentless pressure of light bearing down from the heavens. Yet Herod shivered.

A fever had come upon him during the short journey from the amphitheatre, where he had watched the rabbis, who had dared to tear down his golden eagle, die their horrible deaths. Now he lay on sweat-dampened sheets, unable to find a single position in which to rest, with no comfort save for the murmurings of the physicians and the soothsayers, the priests and the prophets, all who visited then backed into the shadows shaking their heads and muttering that this was the work of the Almighty who does not hesitate to punish evil-doers.

Of their number only one offered hope, a young rabbi from Magadan, in Galilee, who was rumoured to have worked wonders with lepers.

'Majesty,' the young man said earnestly, 'I believe that the warm springs of Callirrhoe, have curative properties.'

Herod opened an eye. It was rheumy and yellowed, the pupil vast with pain. 'You think you can cure me? An evil man, like me?'

Being young and from the north, the rabbi had developed no ear for danger. He merely nodded earnestly and talked of how Naaman, was cleansed of leprosy by Elisha. 'Seven times Elisha ordered him to bathe himself in the Jordan, and when he emerged he was whole again and clean.'

'So now you come to me as a prophet.'

'No, majesty, never that.' The Young man was very humble. 'But I have some reputation as a physician, and the springs are restorative. I would stake my life on it.'

A dry wheeze that Loshema, standing silently in her corner, recognised as laughter.

'You stake too little that is of value to me and too much that is of value to you. What will they say if you cure me? That you have suffered a devil to live, that you have given pestilence a human form to plague them the rest of their days? Do you understand what it would be to cure a Herod?'

The rabbi shrugged. 'What people will say I cannot predict, having no skills in sooth-saying. I only know that I will have cured a sick man and eased his pain. It is my privilege to be a follower of Hillel and I believe he would say the same.'

Herod's other eye opened. 'I know this Pharisee. He does not believe in the Law.'

The rabbi moved uncomfortably. 'It is not my place to correct kings.'

'Then do not correct a king. Only correct a dying man.' Herod shifted on his tangle of sheets and groaned. 'Dying men long to be corrected.'

The rabbi coughed and cleared his throat, glancing at Loshema, whom he had just noticed was staring at him intently. 'Hillel was famously challenged by a pagan to explain the whole law to him while he stood on one foot. Hillel agreed to the challenge and told him, that which is hateful to you, do not do to your neighbour: this is the whole Torah; the rest is commentary. He believes in the Law, majesty. But he believes that its practice amongst common men is more important than endless dissection by scholars.'

'How much easier to be a Pharisee than a king,' Herod said with bitterness. 'To hang with wars and famines and politics. All that is asked of me is to love my fellow man. Am I also to love the men who do hateful things? Yesterday I burned two rabbis who offended me. Would Hillel have forgiven them?' He paused. 'Would he have forgiven me?'

The rabbi was silent for some time, thinking. He glanced again at Loshema before continuing. 'Many call Hillel a saint, and with reason. Am I to speak for a saint? Let me send for him.'

'No!' From somewhere Herod found the strength to rise to a sitting position. 'There will be no saints in this house. You must answer for your pedagogue, and I advise you to do so quickly. Would Hillel have forgiven me?'

Again the rabbi was silent. At last he said. 'I am a poor repository of my master's wisdom. But Hillel teaches that the Almighty abounds with mercy. If you cannot forgive a man his sins, you cannot see his underlying nature. And if you cannot look at a man's true self, how can you sit in judgment over him?'

Herod fell back on his pillows. 'Is this your answer?'

'It is the only one that is mine to give.'

Herod's eyes narrowed and Loshema felt a pricking in her thumbs. The shaft of sunlight or the lightning strike; one never knew with Herod.

'You!' Loshema jumped, her mantle of invisibility sloughed off and lying in tatters about her feet.

'Well, do you stand there, saying nothing when your king addresses you or is everyone grown bold now the great beast is wounded?'

At that Loshema hurried to the bedside. But Herod was suddenly beset by excruciating cramps in his legs and moaned and writhed, arching his back piteously, as though it were possible to stretch himself free of the pain. The rabbi was at Loshema's side. 'I will fetch a tincture of red Squill. It will help with the limbs which have become dropsical.' He touched Herod's foot very gently and nodded to himself. 'And perhaps a drop of the poppy to settle his stomach.'

'Wait!' Herod spoke through gritted teeth. The rabbi hesitated and the dying king turned his head to the woman who was now kneeling to one side. 'Should I trust this man?'

Loshema blinked. 'Majesty?'

'Shall I take his cure?'

'I will fetch your sister.' Half rising, Loshema found her wrist encircled in a yellowed claw. The grip —which had severed the heads of men in battle— was weaker than a child's. She could have broken free easily, but she did not. Gently she said, 'You do not wish my opinion, majesty.'

'But I do.'

Even with her head turned she could sense the rabbi looking at her curiously.

'Majesty, I am only— '

'I know who you are.' A fit of wheezing took his next words. But he recovered himself. 'You, Anonyme —he addressed her in the Greek, but still, No-Name— You, alone, want nothing of me, ask nothing of me. And so you will tell me. Should I trust this man?'

Outside, in the corridor she walked rapidly, carrying a bowl of Herod's phlegm to be disposed of, her excuse to leave the room. But a voice called after her and she turned to find the young rabbi hurrying towards her. She stopped, but looked at the floor even when he had drawn level.

'Thank you.' He paused, but when she did not answer he went on, 'We will cross the Jordan tomorrow. It is best done sooner.'

She shrugged and would have moved off, but his next words snared her.

'He was wrong, though.'

Ah, he was sharper than he looked. Slowly, she lifted her gaze.

'There is something you want from him.' Their eyes met, and for a moment Loshema wanted to ask if Hillel truly believed it was possible to forgive all sins, that mercy was unbounded? Or was it all just words, pretty words falling like snowflakes on the swollen tongue of humanity, soothing, but ultimately without point.

She closed her eyes for a moment, and when she opened them again, she saw a very young man, whose beard had barely begun to sprout. He was looking at her with concern, as though the entire world was his problem to fix. And she wanted to weep, weep for all the poignant hope of youth and his belief that everything can be resolved through the simple action of love. But even as she felt the desire she knew she would not, because she was beyond such drama and mindful that she would do only what needed to be done.

She reached out a hand and patted his arm, a gesture unthinkable in a maiden, but he was looking at her only as a good son might look at his mother, and she was surprised at how much the awareness hurt her. She withdrew her hand and forced a smile. 'Yes. You are right. I do want something.' Then, knowing he was waiting for more, she turned and walked away.

The next day Herod was taken across the Jordan to the springs of Callirrhoe. But he was shivering so badly that two of his senior physicians insisted on putting him in a bath of oil to warm him. The cries of his servants brought them running back into the chamber, where they found the king, with his head fallen back, quite senseless, but not, as feared, dead.

Then for seven days they helped him to bathe in the springs, one or two of his favourites joining him. But it soon became clear that their light-hearted frolicking, when he could feel nothing but pain, only made his mood bleaker and they soon stopped. Like the young rabbi the priests, who watched from the banks, began to quote the prophet Elisha. But the words were not of miracles. '*Spiritual barrenness,*' they intoned, '*Like a giant shadow falls over our land. The streams that water the land are poisonous. The land is cursed.*'

On the eighth day Herod demanded to return home. The young rabbi pleaded with him to try a little longer. But Herod turned on him in a frenzy of rage, and had his guards drag him away with orders to '*Put him next to the prisoner so that their iniquitous natures might keep company with each other.*'

Loshema first became aware that Herod had returned to Jericho when Salome burst into the chamber where she was sitting. She stormed past Loshema without seeing her —but this was nothing new— throwing herself down on a couch sobbing uncontrollably and burying her head in a heap of silken cushions. Knowing when it is time to leave, Loshema got stealthily to her feet. But, at the creak of her chair, Salome sat up, blinking at her through her tear smeared face.

'O, I did not see you.'

Even after all these years Loshema had to bite back the desire to look about to see who was being addressed. Instead she smiled a blank, meaningless smile and enquired, 'How does the king?'

A fresh bout of weeping. 'He is dying. My brother is dying.'

A blind claw gripped Loshema's heart. 'It is near?'

Salome's ample shoulders heaved. 'Closer than before.'

'Then there is no hope?'

Something in Loshema's voice made Salome lift her head. The pouches beneath her eyes were swollen with weeping and the whites were bloodshot. She looked at Loshema, like a drunkard suddenly lucid in his cups. 'I never liked you, you know.'

Loshema said nothing. What was there to say? Salome suddenly lunged out and grasped the younger woman in a clumsy embrace. 'But you care about him. I hear it in your voice.' Her fingers tightened on Loshema's flesh. 'He is grieving. He is out of his mind with grief.' She let Loshema go and looked round wildly to see who was listening, but they were alone save for three slaves, who stood about the room, silent and unobtrusive, staring at the floor. Salome went on,

'My brother has always been a man who defeated the odds. How often would Judea have starved or been overrun by the pagan horde if not because Herod stood alone against convention, against wisdom, against tradition.' There was hostility in her voice, as though Loshema had raised an objection, where, in fact, she had said nothing at all. Her passivity, however, did not deter Salome, who was now warming to her theme.

'O yes, we Jews love our traditions. We cannot take one breath without being reminded of our ancient customs. We celebrate Passover in memory of our slavery in the great Aegyptus. Sukkoth, lest we forget we wandered the desert for forty years. And what is Hanukah, but celebration of that sanctimonious Hasmonaean victory in the Temple. It was my brother, who first made it clear to me. We do not remind ourselves of these events in order to stand still. If we have a tradition at all, it is that we celebrate *change!* We are a people always in flux, forever reinventing ourselves.'

Again Loshema felt the claws tightening in her heart. 'What has he asked of you?'

Salome flung away from her. 'You, boy,' she snapped at a male slave easily fifty years old. 'Do you stand there while your mistress dies of thirst?' Then distractedly she added, 'He grieves. He is full of grief.' A goblet of wine was held out to her. She snatched it and drank noisily before rounding on Loshema again. 'Can you imagine what it is like for him? They thought him dead in a tub of oil, and when he awoke he saw them covering their mouths. Not out of sorrow, but to hide the smiles they had given one another when they thought him deceased.'

'And now?'

'He thinks of nothing but vengeance.' She threw the goblet down and covered her face with her hands. 'O, you do not know what he has had me do.'

The room began to spin, but Loshema forced calmness into her voice. 'Tell me. I might help— '

'Help?' Salome began to beat at her breast. 'What help can you give? It is I, I who is to lure every prominent man the length and breadth of the country and have them assemble in the hippodrome.'

'And then?'

'Then he will have soldiers surround the place with secret orders that, when he breathes his last, they are to slaughter everyone inside, even those who are innocent of offence.'

Loshema, who had lived all her life in the shadow of the Herods, who had seen murder and intrigue and miracles all under the same roof, and expected only the unpredictable, now shook her head in confusion. 'But— for what purpose?'

Salome began to laugh, a low bitter laugh, as though she was too weary even for hysteria. Then she shook her head and gave a long painful sigh. She looked almost tenderly at Loshema. 'My foolish one, my brother knows what they say out there. They utter, Herod, and spit upon the ground to cleanse their mouths. Pharisees lead prayers for his death. Sadducees write to Rome, denouncing him for this, that and the next thing. Half the time they contradict each other, and nobody notices.

'He is not loved. And he knows himself not loved. All he has left to him is the great void of death, and I think even there he fears to hear their laughter. His pride—' She shook her head. 'That great stupid Herodian pride is the last part of him that is still alive. And he will incur the wrath of the Almighty by murdering guilty and innocent alike to fill the hours after his death with the greatest lamentations this land has ever seen.'

Loshema let her gaze drift to the floor, wondering why, when the heart has become a barren desert, pain still manages to take root and flourish. At last she looked up and found Salome staring at her curiously.

'Tell me something.'

Loshema nodded.

'Did you ever have love, true love, the sort they say is a kind of holiness?'

Loshema did not answer for a long time, wondering how Salome knew, then she nodded once briefly.

Something envious flitted across Salome's face. 'Then you have been luckier than I.' She made as if to turn away.

'Wait!' Things could not be left this way surely. 'Will you do it? Will you send for all those men?'

Salome stopped. 'Of course.'

'But why? You, yourself, said he is almost through Death's door.'

Something almost like amusement lifted the pouches in Salome's face. 'Because, foolish one, it does well to remember that my brother, blackened and worm-riddled as he is, has always been a man to defeat the odds.'

21

In which Loshema learns the dubious nature of reward

35 BCE

A LEXANDRA IS CAUGHT IN A *trap of her own making. Of my own making. Since spilling indecorously on the floor before her son-in-law and his courtiers to watch the Idumaean ape publicly humiliate her daughter, her world has become very small. She no longer has her ladies. They have been replaced by ones chosen by Cypros. Some of her choicest pieces of jewellery have been confiscated, and this has been explained to her as a practical measure now that she will no longer require to be in attendance at state functions.*

—The thief, she rages. The jealous, thieving, low-born, Nabataean camel-driver's daughter— Such are her epithets for Cypros. But no-one hears, save for her own four walls and the selectively deaf ears of her slaves. Alexandra is trapped. She cannot even leave her apartments now without permission. Her world has become very small, whereas mine, is about to grow curiously large.

O, don't think of me as without feeling. I have been accused of that often enough, and there were times, with my eyes hollowed out and my throat raw from weeping, that I have wished to possess a heart as cold and calculating as that of Athaliah, who could slay her own grandchildren to satisfy her cherished ambitions. Yet I feel every slight or wrong I visit upon the world magnifies itself ten-fold in my heart; it is my weakness (Pheroras used to say it was my strength.)

And watching the Hasmonaeans brought low, —Mariamme with her shocked, white face, Alexandra's fists drumming from inside her apartment as Jonathan stands shaken and helpless, refused entry by the guards— gives me no pleasure. Nor did a sense of satisfaction flood my veins when Herod looked at me across the audience chamber, his queen's face mashed against his loins.

All the anger, all the resentment I had felt at Alexandra's ill-treatment —and if truth be told the greatest hurt was Mariamme's indifference— all that vileness oozed from me that day and left behind a bitter, empty feeling, like the bite from a promising apple whose taste turns out dry as dust. Herod's expression was quite pitiless. He blamed me, as much as his mother-in-law for Mariamme's flailing dishonour. And while his courtiers, waking up from their shock, forced their necks to duck in approval and a pattering of applause rose and fell, I crept from the room, chin-to-chest, knowing I had lost more than I had won.

Now, it is hardly new to a slave to know sorrow or guilt, but unshakable inside my head was the certainty that there was more to come. I sensed it in my dreams full of the rippling wings of avenging angels, their hot breath waking me in Damoclesean agony, certain the blade was about to sever my neck.

In the presence of the Hasmonaeans I kept my head lowered, afraid to see myself reflected in their eyes, yet they treated me much as before, a beast of burden, an imperfect tool, blunt and ill-suited to its purpose, in all senses of the word a slave. They do not suspect me of being instrumental in their downfall any more than they would expect the teeth of a comb to bite.

'Girl!'

At the shrill imperative Loshema freezes. Her gaze will not lift from the floor.

—*Yes, yes. We have taken a step back. Better to be in the 'now', with the pain of the moment dilating your pupils and your heart pumping white heat through your veins than to sit, dry-eyed, watching the colours fade on 'long ago' and 'then'. To live is to constantly seek out pain. You don't believe me? Tell me, what ecstasy exists without a pinch of death in the mix? We spend our lives searching for these moments of excoriating vivacity. You know this. And if you do not, you're younger than you look*—

Loshema cannot lift her eyes to meet those of Alexandra. She is thinking, she knows. She knows what I have done. And how could she not? The sequence of events is painfully clear. The slave unjustly beaten. The harboured resentment leading inevitably to the betrayal of secret plans. There is only one possible explanation. And only one fault in Loshema's reasoning. Alexandra, does not think she has behaved unjustly.

'Fetch my physic chest.'

Almost unable to believe her ears Loshema hesitates, almost welcoming the pinch that stings life back into her and the scathing words that harry her out.

'I am given spies for waiting women and fools for slaves.'

When she returns Mariamme has joined her mother. Alexandra takes the chest without thanks and opens the lid.

'It will be here unless some filthy —she gives Loshema a hostile glance— Yes. Yes, here it is. —holding up a bottle half full of cloudy yellow liquid— This came from Olympos, Cleopatra's personal physician. He won't give me the recipe, but it contains cedar oil, which will clear his lungs.'

Mariamme's face is pinched and there are dark circles beneath her eyes. 'I wish he would let me bring him to you. His skin is hot and dry and he coughs day and night. And my husband sends nothing but quacks and charlatans. The last two were from Persia, and muttered nothing but abominable incantations and filled the room with such clouds of stinking incense that I could barely breathe let alone a sick child. When I feared my son could take no more I called for David haDov and had them thrown from the palace.'

Alexandra looks up. 'You defied him?'

'I had no choice.'

'You forget that it is not only your life that hangs in the balance.'

'No, mother. I do not forget. How should I forget when you are here every day to remind me?'

The slam of the physic chest lid makes Loshema and Mariamme jump. Alexandra's jaw works with righteous anger, but before she can give vent to it the door is knocked and a small slave boy enters.

'Forgive me, lady. The king's brother— The king's brother— (This slave is very young indeed.) He wishes to see—'

Mariamme steps forward. In common with her husband she has a way with the lesser mortals of the earth. But, to everyone's surprise, the boy shakes his head. 'No, lady. Not you. Her.'

He is pointing a bony, nail-bitten thumb at the tall girl with the mineral-coloured eyes.

Pheroras was alone when Loshema made her nervous entrance. And this was the more notable because his aloneness was in the true sense, the sense in which a man has no other company than himself, and not, as was to be expected at the time, that he should be surrounded by glassy-eyed attendants whose main purpose in life is to pretend that they are not there.

He did not look up when she approached, his head bent over a litter of unravelled scrolls that lay heaped about his desk. Yet there was no coldness about his indifference, no artifice of superiority in his manner, and when finally he noticed her presence, this least Herodian of the Herodians, greeted her with an absent smile.

'Ah, good. I am glad you are here.'

Loshema stared. He had summoned her. Where else should she be?

'I have something to ask. Do you still serve in the Hasmonaean apartments?'

Loshema nodded.

'That cannot be pleasant for you.'

Loshema nodded again uncertainly. Her position in life had made her wary of kindness and the appearance of kindness. Did it matter that she should find it pleasant?

Pheroras picked up a shaker and sifted some sand onto a freshly inked scroll. She noticed that his hands were very large, not like a scholar's hands at all, and that the tips were blunted and stained lampblack, as though he was forever spilling things or knocking them over. And she had no sooner finished thinking this than he knocked over a clumsily heaped pile of documents and sent them fluttering to the floor.

While it was true that a new version of Loshema was emerging, released by Alexandra's indefensible attack, it takes more than a purging of the self to eradicate years of slave training. At once Loshema fell to her knees to retrieve the scrolls, and, immediately, knocked her head against something hard. Stunned, she sat back on her heels and found herself looking into the dazed eyes of Pheroras, who had bent to help her. He was rubbing his temple.

'Apologies.'

She gaped at him a little afraid. Did he think you apologised to slaves? She recalled that there were those who whispered that he was a saint, and others who muttered that the difference between a saint and a madman was not the width of a hair on an infant's head. At least he did not attempt to help her to her feet. Quickly she gathered the scrolls and laid them on the desk. Pheroras had resumed his seat, but was fidgeting uncomfortably with his tunic, and she half suspected he had forgotten the reason he had sent for her.

'You did not know the content of the letters you brought to our notice?'

The sudden change of direction made her start then shake her head.

'Yet you brought them.'

'Yes.'

'Why?'

'I am loyal to the house of Herod.'

He was studying her face, a faint frown deepening the lines between his brows. And there was something troubling about his eyes, something that she could not escape, even by letting her gaze drop to the floor.

'To demonstrate your faithfulness through an act of disloyalty. Surely you left yourself open to misinterpretation of your motives.'

She did not answer, could not. She understood suddenly that he was looking at her, and she felt *seen*.

'It was a dangerous undertaking. Some might even say a desperate one. Did you hope to gain favour?'

She gave him an open helpless look. Favour is the currency of those who live their lives in bondage. What slave does not look for favour? Pheroras tapped an ink-stained finger against his chin. 'Ah, well perhaps that question is unfair.' He leaned his elbows on the desk, knocking over a dish of pens without seeming to notice. He frowned. 'And I am frightening you? I did not intend that.'

She was trembling, but she could not have explained that it was his kindness that frightened her. Part of her longing to be a friend to Mariamme had come from recognition of what it was to wall your heart off from the world. And since then the certainty that kindness was a gift only received by others had made its possibility recede in her consciousness until it became as inconceivable as thoughts of her own death.

Now the brother of the king sat there and was 'glad she had come' and apologised to her and was sorry if he made her afraid. It unlocked doors and opened her up in ways too painful to contain. And suddenly she was weeping, as openly and unreservedly as a child. She heard the scrape of his chair and felt his hands upon her shoulders. And then her face was against him and he was stroking her hair.

'There. There now. You have nothing to fear. We, of the house of Herod, know what it is to act out of desperation. When you had gone my brother, the king, turned to me and said, *Surely, she is some bastard child of our line.*' He raised her chin in his hand and smiled. 'If not for you, the king would have suffered a severe loss of face. Your deeds are not forgotten, and they will be rewarded.' He let her go and stepped back, eyes bright. 'What do you say?'

It was too much. It was as though she had been starving all her life and had now been presented with a feast. He might offer her anything, power, position, freedom. Yet she baulked at this last. Freedom is the dream of every slave. But what would freedom be to a very young woman with no trade to ply and no family or connections? How long might she last living off her wits before she was beggared or selling herself on street corners for the price of a loaf of bread?

When she had control of herself again, she looked into his face and found that he was waiting for her reaction.

'Rewarded?' It was a slave's response, and she heard its venal tone and wished she could have spat the word out on the ground before she gave it shape. But Pheroras only smiled.

'I am going to teach you to read.'

She blinked. Then she looked down at the scrolls unravelled across the desk, and, after a moment, she lifted her gaze back to Pheroras and shook her head slightly, as if a mistake had been made and he was obviously addressing the wrong person. He chuckled.

'You do not see it now, but this is a reward worthy of your deed.'

Her face fell. So this was a punishment for her treachery.

'Loshema, why so downcast?'

But this was wonderment and only added to her confusion. He knew her name and therefore knew also that she was nameless.

'Loshema?'

But how could she answer. Her eyes filled with tears again and she saw his smile vanish. He seemed lost in thought for some time then he sat back, sighing. His ink-stained fingers tapping the desk. 'On scroll or tablet words are my friends. But when I try to make myself understood to another being something —he made a helpless gesture with his hands— something becomes lost in the air.' He sighed again and his eyes took on their familiar faraway look. And when he continued he seemed almost to be addressing an unseen audience.

'The world is full of ignorance. Everyone agrees that learning is precious, then, like gold or jewels, they try to keep it for themselves. The wealthy horde knowledge from the poor. Politicians and priests hide their meaning so that they may seem to speak plainly, while keeping truth for themselves. Even fathers prefer to keep their daughters illiterate lest men tumble from their pedestals and walk shoulder-to-shoulder with their wives and sisters.'

He paused a moment trying to read something from her blank expression then went on. 'We Herods are often castigated by ignorant people for our actions. It is easier, after all, to follow the man who leads you down the beaten path than the man who breaks a path through the tangled wilderness.' He coughed.

'I believe I am trying to say that it is hard to be the one who stands alone, who does the terrible deed because they see further than other men and know it must be done.'

Nothing he was saying made sense. Loshema shrank inside herself. Was he referring to the taking of the letters or to something else? At that moment, if she had been given a choice between this mental torture and the lash of Shlomi's whip across the backs of her legs she would have knelt down and kissed the cord. He was looking into her face again with that wistful expression that filled her with the contradictory urge to hide her face from him in shame and to slap the foolish nobility out of it. But her thoughts seemed opaque to him for he carried on,

'You have seen for yourself that my brother, the king, does not shirk from his vision of how things must be. And today I will follow his example. I will choose the dubious route. The Law tells us that the world fell into chaos when woman gave man the secret of knowledge. Let us see what happens if we reverse the roles and I, as Adam, hand you the seeds of your own revelation.' He stopped speaking, but there was a pride in him, as if he had held out some cup of miracles and was urging her to sip.

Suddenly she was gripped by an immense anger. She had risked so much and been offered so little. To learn the art of reading. What possible use was that to a slave, and worse than that, a woman. A male slave might earn the role of secretary to a man of position. Once freed, he could eke out a living selling his services in the marketplace. There were many who would pay for the work of a scribe. But who would trust a woman with a pen?

Pheroras had talked of women scholars in Alexandria. Well, Loshema had certainly never seen any in Jerusalem. She was entirely of a mind to think it was fantastical, like a tale brought back by sailors of people who walked about with their heads under their arms, a tale suitable for an audience half drowned in their cups, but an insulting trick to pretend it was real and true.

Nothing had been said for several moments, and the new Loshema, the one who no longer thought quite as a slave should, met Pheroras' challenge and also took precedent into her own hands. 'If you have no further use of me, I must return to my duties.' It was blatantly insolent, and she saw the shock of it register in Pheroras' eyes. He blinked at her, as though he had not quite understood, and his Adam's apple bobbed in his throat. After a moment he nodded tightly. 'Yes, you may go.'

She felt a stab of remorse. Surely she should thank him. After all he had meant well. She opened her mouth and tried to force gratitude to take shape on her tongue, but Pheroras had bent his head —a little stiffly she thought— and did not notice her attempts. She nodded, as if in answer to something then turned to creep from the room. At the door she glanced back. Pheroras was still bent over his reading. On the desk the scrolls looked like lilies unfurling in the sun.

22

Death of a prince

35 BCE

THE YOUNG WOMAN STARING OUT of the mirror was a stranger to the owner of the reflection. The dress she wore was a hand-me-down and darned in several places. Nonetheless it was finer than any she had ever possessed. On her wrist was a bracelet of carved shell beads, and though one or two of the beads were missing, she looked down from, time to time, in open admiration before returning her gaze to the mirror.

Now and again the sea-coloured eyes blinked just for the pleasure of discovering themselves anew. Set in a face too long to be exactly oval, but now prettily framed by curling plaits of hair, a shade or two lighter than the pelt of a young fallow deer, the eyes were agog before the astonishing clarity of their own youth, the narrow waist, the curve of the tiny breasts reflected in the swell of the hips; if Loshema, the boy, had been pushed aside by Loshema, the girl, then Loshema, the woman, had swallowed them both.

The sound of a woman's voice from the chamber next door had Loshema scurrying to obey. But, at the door, she paused momentarily to compose herself and to recall that a lady's maid does not barge into a room, like a goatherd who has lost his flock. Taking a breath, she turned the handle and entered with self-conscious dignity. Pheroras was there with his wife. His wife glanced up, when her maid entered, and requested that Loshema find a particular silk shawl from one of the chests they had brought with them to Jericho.

'A gift for Salome,' she explained to her husband as Loshema searched. 'The poor thing spent too long in the sun yesterday and her arms are beginning to resemble the skin of a pomegranate.' This last was said quite without art. She was older than Pheroras by a good ten years, and older in her attitudes by ten beyond that. In the parlance of the day she was a plain, reliable woman of good family who accepted her scholarly, scatter-brained husband, as she did all things in life, with equanimity and not much interest.

She lifted a shaggy bundle of flax, and tied the teased fibres around a spindle while she talked. 'Of course we were all taken by surprise. So soon after the Feast of Tabernacles. Still, Alexandra must have been pleased. Stuck down here, not able to see her own son perform the sacrifices. Though I doubt she expected the entire royal household to descend without a moment's notice.'

Pheroras nodded. He had the telltale sleepy look that Loshema understood meant he was thinking of other things. But his wife showed no sign of noticing, and went on, 'I'm not a sentimental woman, as you know. But to see Jonathan in his vestments. I held him in my arms, that little wrinkled baby. And now a man.' She arranged the yarn against the whorl, looping it around the shaft then under the hook. With unconscious grace she dropped it, setting its hypnotic motion spinning between them. 'When he approached the altar I could see the crowd going mad with excitement. At least until that woman, Naomi bat Shimeon, stepped in front of me. You know who I mean, don't you. The Captain of the Temple's wife. I do not like to be unkind, but I swear she takes the commandment to go forth and multiply as a decree to increase her own girth. Not a soul in the woman's gallery could see a thing.' Pheroras' wife stopped talking and the spin of the amber whorl slowed. 'Pheroras, did you hear what I said?'

Pheroras blinked and moved his eyes from the corner of the room where Loshema was occupied. 'You said, "Not a soul in the woman's gallery could see a thing." '

His wife nodded and adjusted the tension of the yarn. 'Well, I exaggerate a little, of course. Not that it was necessary to see. You must have felt it yourself. The atmosphere. In all my days I have never experienced anything like it. The air was actually crackling. You know the way it does before a thunderstorm.'

Behind her back, Loshema took a moment to stretch her back. She did it in profile, allowing the youthful arch of her spine to curve, like a bow. The affect achieved, not entirely by accident, was reminiscent of the way, in which it was whispered, the Idumaean goddess, Asherah was taken by the Divine Archer in intercourse.

Pheroras' wife was adjusting the tension of the yarn. 'I mean, I have never seen anything like it. Sadducee beside Pharisee, gravediggers and dung-collectors, shoulder to shoulder with the highest ranks of society, cheering and weeping and hugging one another.

'The king himself —She caught herself.— Of course, I mean the previous king, Hyrcanus, he could not have united the populace, like that, even with all the love they bear him. It was such a shame to bring it to an end so soon. I can't imagine why your brother was in such a hurry for us all to go east. It's so hot here. And it isn't as if it were cold in Jerusalem. Another few days and we will all be the same pomegranate red as Salome.'

She smiled at Pheroras, who was smiling at her jest, or so she thought, for his eyes appeared never to leave her face, and, besides, how could she know that Loshema was standing in the background, brandishing the requested shawl, like a soldier holding aloft an eagle captured in battle, or that her husband was smiling because he shared the most wonderful secret with her maid.

I c- a- ca- can r- r- read. Ev- er- y day I g-et be- bet- better.

O yes, I can admit my refusal to learn came from arrogance and fear. But I was younger then. And now I am nineteen, my youthful follies fall from me, like withered leaves. There is a spring in my step and I am always singing. The wife of Pheroras looks at me shrewdly and makes sly comments about young men and love. And, of course, she is correct; I am in love. But not with some pimply youth eager to deflower an unprotected girl; my love is far older than that. I am in love with words.

Words, words, words. *Their meanings loaded arrow-tips able to pierce the thickest breast-plate. Some say that, when wicked Eve bit into the forbidden fruit, the first thing to happen was that her mind filled with the desire for new words. (And this explains the endless need of women to talk.)*

No-one, who grows up in a palace, fails to understand the power of words. Words are weapons. Words can be used to bring down men who think they rule the world. With words the impossible takes shape. The voiceless speak. New worlds are revealed and old ones brought into question.

Pheroras has even likened the flesh of the Almighty to a single glorious word, the Logos. And he has told me that this thinking comes from Jewish philosophers in Alexandria, who are less narrow-minded than their Jerusalem counterparts, and who talk of uncovering an underlying continuance of principles between our Law and the Greek philosophies. When our prophet, Moses, speaks, his words are not merely truths to be applied to the chosen few, but universal truths that apply to all mankind.

And these things I have learned because I have studied, not only our Law, but the works of Homer and Pythagoras and Aristotle and Diogenes of Babylon. I have read, too, our own dear Hillel and his opposite Shammai. And by reading them I have learned that great men may tackle the same problem yet reveal truths that conflict with one another.

And, in reading these works, I have discovered, not only the minds of the scholars who scrape their pens across papyrus, but all the ideas and wisdom of the men who were their influences. Once written down, an idea is like the trunk of a tree; it divides and sprouts into an infinite number of branches, so that each idea becomes like the great tree of knowledge at the heart of Paradise. And the more I read the more ideas come to my mind, spiralling up, up inside me until they burst from me in my skipping step and smiling mouth. And then the wife of Pheroras looks at me and whispers, she is in love.

I do not know how it happened, determined as I was to shun the useless art of literacy. Perhaps it was when I discovered that I was to be maid to Pheroras' wife, a promotion un-dreamt of in an orphaned kitchen slave. And, when a new dress was set before me, I wept, as I had not wept for my mother in many years. At once, I went to find Pheroras, wanting to thank him, and discovered him, of course, at his desk pondering a lengthy papyrus scroll. He looked up as I edged around the door, and his tired face lifted in a smile. 'Ah, Loshema, here for your first lesson.' And how could I disabuse him?

But it was not easy. My mind was agile. —Do you imagine I survived to nineteen a maid without wit?— But my hands were used only to the coarse tasks becoming to the lowborn. I had strength but no dexterity. I held the stylus Pheroras put between my fingers, as though I were wringing the neck of a chicken. The wax tablets splintered and cracked under my delicate touch and my letters cut so deep the implement in my hand might have been considered more dagger than pen. 'I cannot be taught,' I wailed more than once, but he would go on.

'First your name,' he said. 'What are you truly called?'

And truly I answered him, 'Loshema.'

'No-name?' He frowned. 'Out of all the creatures given to our forefather, Adam, you alone are nameless.'

I bowed my head in shame.

'Then you are unique.'

'Some say I am godless because of it.' —And by some, of course, I meant Shlomi.— Pheroras frowned. 'Give me your hand.'

I flinched. He was my mistress' husband, brother to the king and overlord of all that I did or was permitted to do, but I shrank, knowing only one use a man has for the touch of a woman's flesh. My reaction surprised him. He studied me a moment, one long finger stroking his upper lip then asked, 'Why do you think I ask you to give me your hand?'

It was a simple question to ask, but hardly a simple one to answer. In my world the divide between men and women stands like the chasm separating heaven from earth. So strange are we to each other that there are men who cannot find love anywhere but their own image, and men who see purity in their wives and daughters, but think of every other woman as a harlot in the making. Even Mariamme's fingers on her husband's thigh was an act so brazen it changed the mind of a king. And so, when Pheroras sits there, asking why he must take my hand the answer is, after all, a simple one, though it wrenches me to say it.

'Because my mother was a whore.'

In all my years in the palace I had never seen Pheroras angry, not even when an old, illiterate slave-woman used one of his precious scrolls to kindle a fire, yet he was angry now.

'Loshema,' he said in a voice I had never heard him use and trembled to hear it now, 'That is no word to describe your mother.' I wanted to say that I spoke of her only as she was spoken of, and over the years the word had lost its sting until it was no more charged than the words that describe the whorl of a spindle or a pitcher of wine. But his eyes were so cold and, for the first time, I saw the Herod in him.'

'I knew kindness from Batia when I was young.' —Wonder of wonders. He knew my mother's name.— 'She was a good woman, much misused.' He spoke slowly, ponderingly. 'It has always been a mystery to me, that the men of this world, who boast so proudly of murder and carnage, who heap honours upon themselves for every particle of the destruction they rain down upon the earth, smashing and plundering their bloody way through all that is beautiful and civilised, will not recognise their role in a woman's ruin, preferring to lay blame upon the broken gourd rather than the act of smashing it. Have we truly fallen so far from innocence that you cannot offer me your hand without fearing violence?'

I did not answer, so shocked I was at this Pheroras, who sat before me as judgmental as a prophet and sad-eyed as a martyr. Mistaking my immobility for sanction, a look of pain crossed his face. Suddenly he turned from me, and even I, who was illiterate, could read dismissal in the hunch of his shoulder.

'Please.' The words slid out on a plangent note of self-discovery. He turned his neck and encountered my outstretched hand. 'I am Batia's daughter, and I haven't seen my mother since I was a child.'

He was looking at my hand, which had begun to tremble a little, but there was still doubt clouding his expression, and he remained still.

'I would write my mother a letter.'

The words, now spoken, were suddenly obvious in their absurdity. Better to ask him to fashion my arms into angel wings so that I might fly. Then suddenly he made a move or perhaps it was I. No matter. For his hand was round mine, and together we drew the first letter of my name, a LAMED for Losema, its shape the curving body of the archer's divine bow pulled taut. Or perhaps it was a hook, because from that day on I was pulled from the narrow confines of a life, bounded by slavery, and into the worlds hidden inside the heads of men long since dead.

And in these worlds I might have stayed, and been happy there, with Pheroras' chaste hand to guide me, if tragedy had not struck soon after.

Come now, we must rejoin the action, here in Jericho less than a week since Jerusalem went wild at the sight of Jonathan in his priestly robes. The days have shortened, but the nights that close over our heads throb blood warm, and the balsam trees still shiver and fill the air with their spicy scent.

And, here strides Herod into the scene. He walks like a king these days, hands clasped behind his back, lord of all he surveys, and more, for nearby, at the mouth of the valley, he is constructing a palace of his own with all the embellishments of Roman modernity. He wants the world to think of him as a man who builds, and not, as he fears, another evil king remembered only with a shudder.

At the atrium he stops. The lamps are newly lit and outside he can see his guests streaming out between the limestone pillars eager to enjoy the night air. He makes a move to join them, but a maid steps out of the shadows.

'I bow to you and salute you, my king.'

Herod frowns. The words are servile, the expression is not. This is surely the expression of a girl who can write her own name, and who secretly reads Diogenes of Babylon during the bewitched hours of the night. But before he can show his disapproval she speaks again. 'The queen sends her deepest regrets and apologies, but your son, Alexander, is running a fever again, and she fears to leave his side.' —I do not add "in the company of quacks" as Mariamme did, but something in the set of my shoulders conveys it.—

Herod had been smiling; now he is scowling. 'The doctors cannot relieve it?'

'Majesty, they seem powerless, and she fears a return of the exanthem.'

Something about Herod diminishes. A rash, he knows, is a common side effect of poison. He saw it on his father's body, and it is rumoured that Cleopatra's enemies often die with *a constellation of purplish pinpricks erupting across their torsos. Would his enemies stoop so low? Without a word, Herod pushes past the maid and is already half way to the queen's chambers when she thinks to lift her skirts and run after him.*

The guard has no time to announce the arrival of the king before the door to the queen's chamber is thrown wide. Herod sees his tiny son lying on a bed in the centre of the room, and seeming tinier still because he is lying in the middle of a bed intended for the body of a king. He is white and sweating. When he hears the door, his eyes swivel towards his father, but their expression is glassy and he does not lift his head. Mariamme is at his side, dabbing cucumber-scented water at his temples. Beside her kneels Alexandra, holding the bowl. Both women get to their feet as soon as the king enters. He looks to Mariamme.

'Is he... Is it...'

And though an empire would be lost in the gap between these two, Mariamme understands him perfectly. 'No,' she says. 'Your Greek physician, Aristrides, assures me that nothing artificial is at play. He insists, that it is not unknown for some children to suffer a trial by the gods in infancy if they show great strength of character when born.' She forces a laugh. 'Of course, such talk is just pagan nonsense, but we should not fear poison.' All the time she is speaking her eyes are wide and static, locked with Herod's, knowing that they are both thinking how wrong the Greek physician is, but what if he is right?

Alexander's choking cough breaks the spell. He draws a breath, in, in until his chest swells taut, like a straining wineskin, but then he cannot get the breath out. It shifts and roils between his thin bones, stretching his ribcage and making the veins on his forehead stand out, while he pants pitiful empty gasps that bring no relief. Above him, Mariamme's hands flutter, like birds' wings, frightened that her touch might bring ruin.

Herod has turned to stone. There are roughly seventy million people inhabiting the earth at this time, and he would give up every one of them just to save this fragile little life. Only Alexandra has the wit to run to the door, crying for help.

It comes in the shape of Aristrides, the Greek, and two priests. The priests take the foot of the bed, eyes closed, arms outstretched murmuring to the Almighty in the hope that the sins of the father might not be visited upon the son. In other circumstances they would be flayed for their impertinence, but Herod has eyes and ears only for the dying infant on the bed.

Aristrides bends low to examine the boy then calls for an inhalation of black henbane to be brought. It takes too long. The seconds drag. Alexander's face turns puce then blue then, finally, drains. He turns the chalk white colour of dead things; his eyes roll.

All her reserve forgotten, Mariamme begins to ululate. A wild arcane sound coming from a place deeper than memory, and the rhythm is taken up by the maids in the room, until it echoes round the chamber, harsh and stinging, until it feels like the excoriating sensation of sand blown into the soft membranes of the eyes.

Aristrides holds up his hand for silence. He is a man of science, as his gods know, and he cannot have weakening feminine vapours in the room. If she were not the queen he would have shooed Mariamme and her maids outside long ago. A page rushes in with a steaming bowl. Aristrides indicates that Herod should tilt his son's head. The bowl is held under his nose.

Mariamme buries her face in her hands. As long as she does not look, her child cannot be dead. While she has strength she will not search for the shape of Lilith, devourer of infants, amongst the shadows. Time flows, like water under ice. Aristrides frowns. The drapes lift in the cooling night air. A fly buzzes into the room then back out the open window, or is it his son's soul escaping? Herod follows its path with his eyes then turns a murderous gaze on the doctor. If he dies, he thinks, if he dies—

But he does not die. There is a gurgling, hiccoughing sound as air rushes out of Alexander's lungs then a gasp as he draws it back in again. In. Out. In. Out. No-one dares to look away in case the spell is broken. Not until Mariamme lowers her fingers and lets out a cry of disbelief and joy. The tension in the room implodes, and everyone is at pains to take credit for this miracle. The priests are already praising the Almighty. Aristrides sends a silent prayer to Urania, muse of science. And Alexandra rushes forward, her chest puffed up with grandmotherly pride.

'The Lord is merciful to those who honour His Will.'

Through his relief Herod notes the barb. 'Your prayers are more fervent than mine?'

Alexandra does not see the trap. 'A mother feels her child's pain, a grandmother doubly so. Is it strange that the Almighty would heed a woman with the blood of High Priests in her veins? My family knows the meaning of sacrifice. How many of us were lost before we threw the Greek from our land?' At her back Aristrides stiffens, but no-one is paying attention to him.

'The Almighty looked into my heart and saw that I am true to my kin. To save my grandson I would have done anything.' She is almost spitting the words at Herod. ' I would have given up that which is dearest to me. Can you say the same?'

Herod does not answer. But something alters in him, some tiny nuance so at odds with the expected response that she is stopped in her tracks. Alexandra knows; she knows, even before the door is thrown open with the timing of a cheap melodrama and Pheroras stumbles in, wild-eyed and gasping. His clothes are soaked through, rivulets of water running from the folds. He does not speak, only stands there, staring at Herod, as though they have met in a dream and he cannot be certain of appearances.

Herod takes a step towards him, but Pheroras shrinks back a little. Herod stops then throws a puzzled glance over his shoulder at the frozen onlookers, as though one of them can explain things to him. What happens next is unclear, and later the facts are so heavily embroidered that it is hard to see the colour of the truth underneath. Suddenly everyone is running, following the dripping Pheroras downstairs and across the courtyard and through the peristyle and out into the warm evening air.

There are fishponds around the castle. They contain pike and trout, freshwater salmon, musht, biny, mackerel and herring. We Jews like our fish. In the north, in Galilee, they ferment the innards to produce the pungent sauce that spices the dishes served to Octavian in faraway Rome.

—Pheroras once told me of an old Semitic fish god, called Dagon, almost forgotten, his temples buried, his idols smashed. I think he felt a certain affinity with him because Dagon was brother to the king of the old gods, and often overlooked next to his more exalted sibling. From the waist down he had the body of a fish, and once, when Pheroras was a boy, a local fisherman had landed a pike almost the size of a man on the shores of lake Hula, and in the thrill of the moment yelled out, Look, look! I have caught Lord Dagon.

Now, here in Jericho, Lord Dagon lies sprawled on the ground, his black hair dripping onto his gleaming torso, his waist and legs concealed fishily in long pond weeds. We, who are made in the image of a God, know that we do not look like the old gods with their feathers and tusks, their cat's eyes and scales. This god has skin, like poured wax. We know also that the gods go by different names. Dagon is sometimes Enlil, Osiris, Zeus, Dionysus, Pan. And here too, he has a different name; he is called, Jonathan.—

Alexandra starts forward then falls to her knees. She pats her son's body, like a mother trying to wake a sleepy infant. And when he doesn't respond, she begins to tear at her hair and her clothes. Mariamme crouches down, trying to comfort her, but she shrinks away, arms wrapped around herself rocking back and forth, a high-pitched sound escaping from her lips, a sound like breaking things, a fracturing, splintering sound. We stare, transfixed. How can it be possible that this is Alexandra, that proud, vainglorious woman now weeping with the baffled soreness of a child? It seems even a dead god can bring about transformation.

From behind me comes a low groan. It is Herod; he is weeping, his body slumped against one of his men-at-arms. Suddenly everyone is talking and weeping and keening, as if grief were an emotion for company, like laughter. Alexandra is forgotten. All gazes are directed at the king. Except for mine.

—You see, young as I am in this scene, I have seen the magi and prophets, who gather on the steps of the Temple, performing their miracles for the crowds. Some cure the sick. Others pull doves and lilies out of the air. But, of one thing you may be certain, when you are directed to look towards something, it is because there is something else they do not wish you to see. So, when attention turns to Herod, I, alone, turn my eyes the other way. And there is Pheroras gazing at his brother with eyes filled with fear. —

23

The beginning of endings

34 BCE

THE PALACE IS ALIVE WITH *rumour. It thickens the atmosphere and muffles sounds. Enter a room unexpectedly and there is a shocked silence quickly followed by a loud, self-conscious exchange of hollow nonsense. And so it has been these last several months.*

Everyone has a theory, and neither name nor rank prevents them from giving voice to it. Of course, in the king's presence no-one dare do anything but pay lip service to the official version. Boyish horseplay in the water, a prank gone too far. The culprits are paraded and shed tears, almost on cue. They never fail to remind their audience that it could have been any one of them. Any one! But, behind their backs the whispers go on—

The signs were there if anyone cared to read them—

Herod was smiling. Whoever saw the king smiling in Jericho—

Not since Antony gave the territory to Cleopatra—

He wasn't smiling at the feast of Tabernacles when the crowd cheered Jonathan—

It's the way Idumaeans deal with their enemies—

Savages to a man—

But didn't the old king's brother and nephew try to do the same—

That was different. A fight between the blood of the royal house.—

And out in the open. No lowborn, pagan treachery—

They've been Jews for three generations—

Then it's still skin deep—

Only Pheroras was silent. Now that I could wield a pen with as much skill as most women have with a needle he kept a respectful distance during our lessons. But there were times when I caught him looking at me in a troubled way, then he would open his mouth, as though about to divulge a secret, only to close it again. And I longed to offer him my hand once more, but my skill had grown between us.

Alexandra was not silent. She had lain in her bed almost unmoving in the days that followed Jonathan's death. She attended the lavish funeral, insisted upon by Herod, where she stumbled vacantly, like a blind woman, leaning heavily on Mariamme and the wife of Pheroras. But no-one was looking at Alexandra.

All eyes were on the king, and Herod was magnificent in grief. The crowd, lining the dusty streets of Jerusalem, looked where he wanted them to look, at the rents in his clothing, at his feet, bare as the humblest of beggars, visible as he followed the bier with its decking of cloth

170

of gold. Some said he went barefoot because he was mad with sorrow. But others muttered it was a penance for murdering the holiest child in Israel. And thus love and hate grew in the capital intertwined, like the trunks of two trees competing for the light.

And Alexandra went back to her bed, and lay there until the rise of the next full moon when the light that laminated her apartment was the same light that her son had drowned in, and then she called for writing materials to be brought to her. She wrote with gusto, describing the body of her son as the body of a young god. A dead god, a drowned Osiris.

And her description paid off, for the living embodiment of the goddess, Isis, sent a command to Herod, in no kind terms, that he come and give account of himself regarding Jonathan's death. And it was pleasing to hear that Herod had grown pale, and consulted his advisors in the hopes of finding a way to ignore the summons. But none was found.

Alexandra watched from one of the tower windows as he rode out of Jerusalem, and gave up a prayer that she might finally have rid herself of the Idumaean upstart once and for all. Though the price had been too high, too high.

The sky had been moving in ominous patterns throughout the day. Alexandra stood at the window watching, and eventually called old Pollio to read it for her.

'A day for portents? Miracles?'

But this had angered him. He leaned on his staff and his old voice shook. 'Is the Lord some petty trickster playing with the shapes of clouds? Do you imagine he is like a snivelling pagan deity to whom you can dictate?' At the door he turned and looked at her. 'Be careful what you pray for, lady. The Lord does not obey commands. You will be the instigator of your family's destruction.'

When he had gone Mariamme asked. 'Was that wise? To provoke him so?'

Alexandra was still staring at the clouds. 'I wanted to know if he was still Cypros' creature.'

And yet it seemed that Alexandra's perception of oracles had been correct for later in the day Jerusalem was agog with the news Cleopatra had put the Jewish king to death.

Uncle Joseph it was who brought the news to the royal apartments. 'Alas.' Plump tears rolled down his plumper cheeks. 'I fear Antony has given way to his harsh mistress. They are saying that he would not listen to Herod's arguments, that he had him tortured then killed.'

Alexandra, who had been staring at the floor, while she received the news, looked up. 'Should I shed tears for the man who murdered my son?'

'Madam.' Uncle Joseph was shocked. 'Your grief deranges your mind. My nephew was with you at the time the accident occurred. He loved the boy.'

'Can accidents not be arranged? Is Herod so impoverished that he must stoop to do his own foul deeds?'

'Madam,' Uncle Joseph said again then found he had nothing to add. Absently he patted Loshema on the bottom as she passed.

Mariamme entered through an internal door and Joseph's eyes lit up at once then assumed an air of sorrow. 'My dear. I bring sad tidings.'

Mariamme looked at him coolly. 'You need not trouble yourself, uncle. I have heard.'

'Yet you do not seem— If I might venture to suggest— '

'I cannot play the hypocrite. Would you have me weep for a man who holds me in the lowest esteem?'

'My dear.' Uncle Joseph took several steps towards Mariamme, his arms outstretched. But his resolve withered beneath the sternness of her expression and he stopped short, drawing his hands back, like a child caught reaching for the honey pot. He rested them on his paunch. 'My dear, you misread your husband. He loves you to distraction. He is besotted, I assure you.' He tapped the side of his nose. 'I am entrusted with secret orders that leave me in no doubt of the depth of his feeling.'

'Orders?'

'Well,' Uncle Joseph suddenly felt himself trapped. 'As I say they are of a secret nature. But I promise they are motivated by the purest feelings of love.'

It was Mariamme's turn to move close. Uncle Joseph stood blinking and rubbing his paunch.

'What orders are these?'

'Really, my dear. You cannot expect me to divulge the king's secrets.'

'The king is dead.'

'May his soul know everlasting shame and contempt.' Alexandra joined her daughter and they gazed at Joseph with the same uncompromising expression. Beneath its combined glare, Joseph began to sweat. He glanced between the two women and his forehead glistened. 'The king's orders,' he said helplessly.

'And yet my husband is no longer here.' Mariamme's voice was gentler now. 'And, as his wife, I have a right to know his mind.'

Uncle Joseph dabbed at the back of his neck, and at the same time, let his gaze fall to the comforting height where the Almighty placed bosoms. 'It is true that in his place, you are the authority. And I confess the knowledge is a troublesome burden— '

Mariamme took his sweating paw in hers. 'We are good friends are we not?'

Joseph followed an invisible thread, which led from her hand up into her face, then nodded, as if half hypnotized.

'Then tell me. And only we three shall know of it.'

Nodding, both at them and to himself, Joseph told them what he knew. And when he was done both women were ashen and for a long time speechless. Alexandra was the first to recover.

'There is a Roman legion outside the city walls. We will go there and ask for protection.'

Uncle Joseph shook his head. 'Roman protection?'

'We cannot be certain of the mood of the people. You! —she pointed an imperious finger at Loshema— Gather our things.' Her attention returned to Joseph. 'The Romans have freed us of a Tyrant. They will desire stability as soon as possible. But my encounter with Pollio today has shown me that we cannot count on the full support of the Pharisees.

'If Cypros gets her way, they will lay claim to Alexander as a Herod and doubtless rid themselves of his Hasmonaean mother. Besides, we are playing Cypros at her own game. Did she not once advise Herod to seek out Sextus in his time of need?'

Uncle Joseph turned to Mariamme, who met his gaze, eyes wide with appeal. 'I know you are their kin, but you will not betray us. Salome affords you no respect. Come with us and offer us your protection.'

Joseph chewed at his lower lip then bobbed his head up and down, as though answering a question only he could hear. 'You are right, lady. We should fly at once. We— '

But he got no further, for at that moment there was a wild knocking at the door, and the youngest page Loshema had ever seen allowed in the royal apartments lunged through the door. 'Lady,' he addressed Mariamme in a high, piping voice. 'News from Lattaqia. The king wishes you to know that he is in good health and leaves with the blessing of Rome. He asks after your well-being and that of his son …'

O, irony of ironies. The critics would tear Homer apart for including the twists of fate that are commonplace in this story. Herod's life is a cornucopia of coincidence. And timing and chance seem the only plot devices. Only the Almighty would dare to pen a narrative with such cliché. Yet He has talent when it comes to characterisation; there we have the assuredness of a virtuoso.

Watch Salome waddling with plump indignation towards Mariamme. They meet on the marble staircase that leads to the formal gardens. Salome is climbing up, while Mariamme is coming down. Neither woman has expected the other and they momentarily freeze, considering then dismissing the possibility of flight. Then Salome bridles and, fearing to be at a disadvantage pants her way up the steps to be level with Mariamme. The Hasmonaean still has six inches on her, but to go higher would reveal childishness in her motive. Instead she leans in close, breathing a faintly repellent smell of half-digested cloves over the other woman (for she has been in at the sweetmeats).

'We know what you've been up to.'

Mariamme simply stares. It is not even insolent, simply blank and indifferent. It drives Salome into a passionate fury. 'Our spies are everywhere. Be certain, that when my brother returns he will know the colour of your loyalty.' She is gasping and her bosom heaves. She swings wildly for the advantage. 'Did you not imagine that we would have our spies?'

'No.' The word is so decisive that Salome does not respond, only stands there, her mouth hanging open slightly. Mariamme waits, as though allowing a polite interval to pass then adds, 'I never imagine what lowborn people get up to.' And, lifting her skirts, she glides downstairs.

Herod is angry. When in the full grip of a passion he trembles slightly, and in this condition only Cypros' embrace can calm him. But Cypros is not here. It is his wife who faces him, from her couch, and she is looking at him like something the dung-collectors overlooked. Herod collects his anger. He had been in triumphal mood when he reached the palace. But he has come from his mother's apartments.

'There are rumours.'

'There are always rumours.'

Herod stares. He is not used to this new Mariamme. Always there was a remoteness about her —it was part of her allure— but now she is so cold, he might as well be conferring with a block of ice. Not even when he humiliated her, and afterwards there had been tears and recriminations, had he encountered the chill she exhales in his direction. He gathers himself up again.

'Uncle Joseph has been visiting you in your apartments.'

A shrug.

'You did not consider that such a show of intimacy would distress my sister.'

'I should think it a relief to her. Is she not always complaining that she must sleep through the day as there is not room for them both in the same bed?'

Colour surges into Herod's face. He closes the distance between them in three strides and clutches his wife's arm in the circle of his fist. He pulls her roughly to her feet.

'Did you not consider that your intimacy would reflect upon me?'

He is hurting her, but she makes no attempt to free her arm. 'You put him in charge. Was I to dismiss him when he brought me the day's affairs?'

For a moment they look at each other hotly then Herod relaxes his grip. 'And you swear there was no intimacy between you?' *There is a pleading note in his voice. Mariamme, who hears and feels nothing, except coldness, shakes herself free.*

'O there was intimacy enough between us. But not of the kind your sister's ill-bred tongue devises. There was talk of love. Your love. And how it could be scarcely called love, but rather a form of hate.'

The colour has drained from Herod's face. In some way he is withdrawing from this assault. You would believe that he is backing away when, in fact, he is standing deadly still.

'He told you?' *he manages through dry lips.*

Mariamme's colour is high, her eyes flash; she has never looked so beautiful. 'He told me. Such love my husband has for me that, if he went to his rightful death at the command of Rome, I, too, was to be slaughtered. Not even as a sacrifice. Only the living may make sacrifice. But as a farm animal, a breeding heifer with no more use now the bull is gone.'

She had known he would hit her. Yet when the blow comes there is still the explosion that wipes out everything else, the exquisite shock. Her resolve to stand her ground disintegrates under its force and she is thrown against the couch. Herod drags her up by her hair.

'He knew you. He had knowledge of you!'

She spits the blood in her mouth into his face. The second slap throws her sprawling facedown on the couch,

'No. No! Please!' *The voice is not Mariamme's. A girl with eyes the colour of peacock feathers throws herself in front of the stricken queen.* 'He did not know her. He had no knowledge of her. I swear.' *And understanding words are not enough to stop a king in a passion, Loshema closes her eyes to await the blow. Three seconds, three lifetimes later, she dares to peek out from under her lashes. Herod is gazing down at her.*

'You?' *Recognition comes slowly.*

A nod. Should she speak? Loshema is caught, like Aesop's ass, between the decision to plead her worthiness or to remain silent. Behind her, she hears Mariamme struggling to right herself. Herod's eyes stray towards his wife and pain crosses his face. He returns to Loshema, his expression contemplative. 'Uncle Joseph and his ways are known to me. But you, you have not given me reason to doubt you yet.' *With that, and no more, he turns and heads for the door. At the threshold he pauses, looking over his shoulder.* 'I do not forget loyalty.' *His brow darkens, and he seems on the point of saying something more when he shakes his head and leaves.*

'He would have killed me.' *It is Mariamme who speaks, but she seems to say the words to the air. Loshema fetches her wine, which she accepts, but her eyes are blank and hopeless.*

Loshema is still there, later that day when there is a knock on the door. Two men-at-arms enter and lay a basket at Mariamme's feet. 'A present from the king,' *one announces.*

'Thank his majesty,' *Mariamme says tonelessly. But the two guards are already bowing their way from the room with indecorous haste. Mariamme looks to Loshema.* 'Open it.'

Loshema kneels down and prises open the lid. It comes off easily, and a sharp smell arises, straw and bitter herbs. She stares for an instant at the basket's contents then slams down the lid. But it is too late. She has seen, and behind her Mariamme has seen also. The head of Uncle Joseph nestling in the straw. His eyes are open, and with a pang, Loshema realises that, in the instant before she slammed down the lid, they seemed to be looking at her breasts.

24

In which seduction and death are never closer

34 BCE

'WHAT DOES IT MEAN?' HEROD pointed to the reports on his desk then looked up at his ministers. In the weeks since his return, the skies above Jerusalem have turned black and pitchforks of lightning have left one of the towers of the palace smoking and ruined. From Jericho there have been reports of hailstones, big as pearls raining down on the hot dry soil, and shepherds on the slopes of Gilead have told of tremors in the earth and the mysterious disappearance of healthy animals from their flocks.

Herod asked again, 'What does it mean?'

The ministers eyed one another uneasily then the wisest of them declared, 'Sire, these are not matters upon which we can speak with authority. You must call the priests.'

The priests were less circumspect than the ministers. They quoted Job and Proverbs and Leviticus; they remembered the grim words of Jonah and Samuel and the dark meteorological prophecies of Kings, all with the intention of proving a different point. And never had it held so true that the only things two Jews could agree upon was that there was nothing they could agree upon. They scratched their beards and shook their heads, arguing with each other over the perceived meaning so long that in the end Herod lost his temper and sent them scurrying from the room with imprecations that would have given the lowest foot soldier cause to blush.

He called for his brother then, and, together, they defied the elements and climbed the steps to the highest point of the remaining tower above the royal quarters. There, they stood watching the endless curtain of rain falling in sheets so that the hills seemed to move closer and the view of Lake Asphaltitus was obscured.

Herod was first to speak —he was always first to speak—. 'You know what they are saying?'

'Ignorant people will say anything.'

'And what of the ones who are very far from ignorant, who sit on my councils and preside over the Temple sacrifices, and still say the same thing?' His voice was rising, and Pheroras, always helpless in the face of violence, stood biting his lip and looking out over the view that was not there.

'She has no power here,' he said at last. 'Were we not delivered from the great Aegyptus?'

'Do you know what he did?' Herod asked suddenly. 'I stood before Mark Antony and he read the charges against me. Then he laughed. He said that in Rome the talk was only of why I had not done it sooner. They are many things Romans, but never accuse them of being hypocrites.'

'Brother, did you— '

'O Pheroras.' Herod shook his head. 'You too? Let the Almighty strike me down if I speak an untruth, but I was not responsible for Jonathan's death. That I have benefited from tragedy I cannot deny. But if that is to make me a sinner then so is every recipient of an inheritance. If the son becomes richer because the father is dead, is he now to stand accused? They said the same thing about Zael's death. They knew the Parthians had killed him a hundred stades from where I stood. But still they whispered it was my doing.' Herod paused, his eyes and lashes wet, but whether from the strength of his emotion, or simply the moisture that hung suspended in the damp air, was unclear.

Pheroras, who seemed to carry the portion of pity belonging to all the family, searched for words of comfort. At last he said. 'There is talk that Mark Antony is awakening from his enchanted sleep. After you had been released he visited Cleopatra upon her golden barge in the Nile and told her, in no uncertain terms, that she must keep out of the affairs of men. And Cleopatra wept before him, like a scolded little girl.'

'And when he had left, the witch-goddess flew into a rage and swore vengeance on my kingdom.'

'She cannot harm us here. We are His chosen people.'

Herod looked across his kingdom, where already the skies had darkened until the promise of early morning had been obscured by a fading light more like dusk. 'The age of miracles is behind us now. And, though we fear to say it aloud, is not the Great Aegyptus a land known to be steeped in sorcery and ancient magicks?'

'The Almighty would not free us from Pharaoh only to see us enslaved once more.'

Herod turned to his brother, and embraced him tenderly. 'Pheroras, you are the best of us.' But secretly he was thinking, could the Almighty be called upon to stir himself a second time, for an Idumaean, and a half Jew at that?

Cleopatra is coming. The missive arrived several weeks ago stating her intention to visit. Herod read the letter, stony-faced. O, but when he had finished, then the fur and feathers flew, for Herod would meet her within the walls of his own palace or not at all. 'It cannot be done,' the arichtects wailed. 'The building has scarcely begun.' But Herod, who expected no miracles from the Almighty, needed to prove to the world that he could perform a few of his own.

—Come, we will return to Jericho where they have gathered in the great hall of Herod's new palace, the king and his courtiers—

There he is, surrounded by the most eminent men in the country, and though it is not unusual, it is no accident that there is not a female face amongst them. Nor is the richness of their attire merely chance —the linen from Aegyptus, the Indian cottons, the damask lining of a cloak, the hemline in cloth-of-gold. If Herod is to meet the queen of the great Aegytpus then he will meet her as a king.

She is late and the court grows restless yet does not dare to show it. Forlorn glances are directed at the king, who sits, like marble, upon his throne, while, his subjects, his favourites and even his dream-eyed brother surreptitiously stretch out a limb or shift their weight from foot to foot.

A sound, the ram's horn's unearthly note. So familiar, so well anticipated that even Herod starts. She is here. Cleopatra is walking across the courtyard at the head of her entourage. The tension in the hall is exquisite, like the tension in an archer's arm as he waits to see the whites of his enemy's eyes. Time hovers over them on stretched wings then, finally, Herod gives the signal. The great panelled doors at the end of the hall are drawn open by bedecked slaves and Cleopatra appears between them, as though summoned on cue.

Any other woman, any other queen —even aloof Mariamme— would have faltered before a summons that appears orchestrated by the gods. But this is Cleopatra, who thinks nothing of drinking a pearl dissolved in vinegar, and she misses not a beat as she crosses the threshold. Herod gets to his feet. How else can he avoid being diminished by the retinue of the Aegyptian queen, which is already clearly outnumbering his courtiers?

Cleopatra stops a few paces from the dais, not in supplication as Herod well knows, but because it allows the light from the clerestory windows to catch the jewels threaded into her robe. They flare and the golden sun disk balanced on her tripartite wig —so luxuriant, it must surely have come from the shaven heads of a dozen slave girls— catches fire in the same moment. She is a burning effigy of herself, and her expression tells Herod that she isn't above a theatrical trick of her own, this new Isis of the Nile.

Herod steps down from his dais and bows low. When she gracefully entreats him to rise, he whispers that they should speak alone. Herod is wily enough to know when he has been outmanoeuvred.

In an intimate chamber off the great hall, Cleopatra accepts the couch Herod offers her. She makes no comment, but her eyes rove round the room, noting the mud brick construction, the plaster cleverly painted to resemble marble, but all the same, not marble. She is unimpressed.

He wants to tell her that the walls of this palace were barely the height of a man's shoulders when he received news that she was coming, that she is sitting in a miracle of ingenuity and engineering rivalling even the great Imhotep, long revered in Aegyptian memory as the architect of architects. Instead he joins her on a couch perpendicular to her own, so that they rest on the curved backs, their heads close, but their bodies turned away; he forces a smile. 'Some refreshment? Your journey has been an arduous one.'

She shakes her head. 'A little wine only.'

Herod waits while the wine is splashed into a golden goblet. He says nothing when the taster takes the first sip, and he continues keeping his counsel when Cleopatra shakes her head and insists that the taster drink more deeply. Clearly she wishes to provoke. At last she takes a disinterested mouthful, and sets the cup aside.

'The wine is not to your taste?'

A shrug. 'It is not what I am used to.'

'I will send for something different.'

'Thank you, no. My palate is more suited to our Aegyptian grapes.'

In fact Herod's wine is of the best quality. Many a Roman household toasts their victories with grapes grown on Judean slopes. But they are fencing, Cleopatra coming at him with her sword unsheathed, making little parries to weaken his defence, while he, Herod, sidesteps and feints. The victor will be the one who tires last.

Herod savours his wine then puts the cup down. 'How does Mark Antony?'

Only the very astute would notice Cleopatra stiffen. 'My husband is still abroad. He has business with the Armenian king.' A malicious smile spreads over her lips. 'My husband does not suffer slights to our person without consequence.'

'Nor should he.' Herod's eyes never leave the face of the Aegyptian queen. She is first to look away.

'I wish to inspect the plantations now that they are mine.'

'I will arrange it first thing tomorrow.' Herod lifts his cup and takes a long satisfying draught. 'Though I fear they will be a disappointment.'

And a disappointment it most certainly turns out to be. Cleopatra walks at Herod's side, her mouth drooping with displeasure as they pass through groves of ill-watered date palms and balsam shrubs tangled and uncared for. She examines the walnut-like fruit of a palm, known to grow only in this region, then throws it away in distaste.

Herod stops beside a balsam bush and picks one of its small red flowers. He offers it for her inspection, and, because she mistakes the gesture for a gift, she reaches out to take it and their hands accidentally touch. She withdraws immediately, the flower now in her possession. But there is connection. For an instant these two feel something ancient, as old as mankind and deeper than love, the bond that unites two old enemies. For they are a pair, you need only see them together. How the iconographers would love to cast them as Nephtys and Erebus, Lord of the Darkness and Queen of the Night.

Cleopatra is first to recover. She looks about the ill-kempt grove and her eyes narrow. 'You have a proposal.'

Herod inclines his head. 'We call the resin these trees produce the balm of Gilead. And nowhere in the world exists its match.' He finds Cleopatra looking at him, her eyebrows arched.

'Was it not Sheba's queen who gave them as a gift to your king Solomon?'

Herod, as always, is surprised to find an educated brain occupying the skull of a woman, even a queen, but he goes on smoothly, 'It is as you say. But we have cultivated them for generations. And now Jericho monopolizes the market for balsam throughout the east. The cosmetics you wear, the medicines your physicians supply, all contain balsam of Gilead.'

'Yet the plants wither and die.'

Herod fingers a drooping branchlet, releasing its deep perfumed notes into the air. 'The trees require great delicacy of care. It is not a task that can easily be managed at a distance.'

Cleopatra says nothing, which means she is dangerous, but Herod presses on. 'Allow me to lease the land from you. Your profit will be assured and the management of the plantations will be upon my shoulders.'

Cleopatra begins to walk; she is thinking. Herod follows her. She enters a little clearing, a grove within a grove and stands with her back to him. Herod is holding his breath. Will she take the bait? She stands in silence, and he is beginning to consider himself dismissed when she turns and faces him. Something has changed. She is more simply dressed today, her ornamentation, her face paints designed to suggest a dash of colour rather than the saturation that was on display yesterday.

She seems younger; there is a hint of the innocent young girl who never was (she murdered her brother at the tender age of twenty three). But here in the inner sanctum of trees Cleopatra is remade. She seems to sense it, and something wistful enters her expression. 'I wish— ' she begins then falters. She, who never falters. Herod takes a step closer. She looks down and fiddles absently with a band of gold on her index finger. 'I wish life were simpler.'

A breath of wind enters the grove and stirs the leaves. Herod is aware that his men and Cleopatra's —the courtiers, the bodyguards, the slaves— all are standing beyond this holy of holies. They cannot squeeze inside. He is alone with the queen of the Nile. She cannot have planned it. Opportunity? Chance? Fate? Cleopatra lifts her heavily fringed eyes. 'I wish we might be friends.'

Herod is caught off guard. She is so close. —Did he move or did she?— He can smell her perfume beneath the scent of the trees. It makes his head swim. Her face, upturned catches the light. But those eyes. He can look at nothing else. They are the colour of basalt, liquescent, twin black pearls dissolving in vinegar. He knows they have melted kings greater than he. He swallows, but his throat is dry. His head is drooping towards the shining disk of her face, and her breath moves against his cheek, like a divine wind.

'After all we both love him.'

He is plunged into cold water. He rears back, though it is the worst thing he can do. Inside his head he hears Mark Antony's words. "She is a witch. I am beguiled." He must break the spell before it is too late. She is staring at him, too shocked to react, and he tries to continue, as though these last moments they have not stepped outside time. 'You will lease me the plantations?'

The liquid eyes harden. 'No.'

But he cannot leave it like this. Without Jericho he will be a pauper king begging indulgences from Rome every time he must raise funds to repair a leak or fill in a pothole. A desperate man, he acts desperately. 'I will guarantee the revenues from Malichus.'

Cleopatra says nothing. She is assessing him, weighing up his chances of success with the Arabian king against her immediate desire to punish him. She is like her jackal-faced god, balancing his heart on a set of scales. Struggling to keep his composure Herod holds her gaze. He is thinking, all the talk is of her eyes, but it is her mouth where the true danger lies. If he had an artist's skill he would paint her almost entirely as a mouth with full unchaste lips and a rapacious maw constantly devouring men and kingdoms and still slavering for more. She is insatiable, ruthless and she never forgives. He has revealed too much of himself.

Herod's lips are cracking in the heat, but he forces himself not to let his nervous tongue moisten them. The scales are stacked against him. He sees how his pride will bring about the destruction of the kingdom. He should have kissed her feet, declared his love, and prayed she didn't run to Antony crying rapine. But perhaps it is not too late. He licks his lips, takes a tentative step towards her. Perhaps—

'Very well.' Herod blinks. Cleopatra is addressing him. 'I accept your terms.' She seems done, but then adds maliciously. 'Be aware, there are heavy penalties for failure. My husband will be ill pleased if you break your word to me.' She sweeps past him, and Herod follows her with his eyes.

'I should kill her.' Herod paced back and forth the length of his mother's apartment, as though he has been caged there and could find no escape. 'He asked it of me when we were in Rome. He begged me to kill her.'

Salome and Pheroras exchanged glances. Cypros slid from her couch and attempted to comfort him. 'Such action would be madness.'

'It would be for the best. It is the only thing that will save him. Antony will come to see that.'

'Is that what you imagine?' Cypros' tone has an exasperated ring to it. 'Is your crown so tight that it has addled your brain?' —Who else would dare talk to Herod in this way?— Herod's brow darkened, but he does not interrupt.

'For all the rumours, Mark Antony is as bewitched as he was the day he first set eyes upon his whore queen.' Cypros paused, rearranging her tone. She placed her hands on her son's heaving shoulders, and looked up into his bullish expression. 'Do this, and Antony will kill you first and thank you later.'

His jaw working, Herod averted his eyes, burning the tapestries at Cypros' back with his gaze. He was undecided.

'Herod. You are a soldier and a king. All your life you have followed Death and Death has followed you. But you do not know Death. You think killing Cleopatra is like killing a soldier in the field. Let me tell you, it is not so simple to kill a woman, especially a woman who has invaded your most intimate thoughts.'

He tried to shake her off then, but she gripped his shoulders more tightly. 'Do not deny it. I know what Cleopatra does to men. Herod, listen to your mother, men are born for extinction. Women, on the other hand, are the very antithesis of death. They alone bring life into the world. Even the Cleopatras of this age. If you kill her you will kill part of yourself. And that is too great a sacrifice.'

For a moment longer Herod was mutinous then his jaw slackened and his shoulders slumped. Cypros opened her arms and he laid his head on her breast. 'Mother. O, mother.'

25

In which the world becomes a more uncertain place

31 BCE

BUT VERY SOON HEROD HAS *more on his plate than even a king can stomach. Antony needs him. Octavian has got his hands on Antony's will and neither he, nor the Roman public, like what they see. Open war has been declared between these two, and all thoughts of killing Cleopatra must be laid to one side for the present because Anthony is in need of all the friends he can get.*

Herod goes to her. He goes to Alexandria to Cleopatra.

—I am here to help. I have an army, equipped and paid for, good men ready to join Antony's cause.—

Cleopatra looks down at him from her throne. Her throne rests on a dais that is reached by seven steps. Her throne is supported by four golden legs so high that she must rest her small jewelled feet on a footstool to prevent them from dangling. She looks down at Herod, as she might at an ant crawling across the floor.

—Where are my rents?—

—I have paid in full.—

Cleopatra nods to her chamberlain, and the man moves forward fussily, unfurls a scroll. —There are two hundred talents outstanding.—

—The Nabataean king ... Malichus he ...—

—You guaranteed Malichus' debt.—

—Antony needs me.—

The kohl is so thick around Cleopatra's eyes that it looks like the shadows of sleep, but there is nothing dulled or blunted about the sharp edge of her voice. —Antony needs men he can rely on. Men of their word. Go, collect Malichus' debt. Bring us proof of the quality of your friendship. Then we may talk of armies.—

The air in Jericho was hot and still, and it was hard to believe that elsewhere the great pillars of the world were about to topple. But Loshema was young and full of her own sense of purpose and the war between Rome and the Great Aegpytus was something she understood only in the abstract. For now her thoughts were shaped by her mistress' decision to go, with her senior maids, to visit Alexandra at the palace of the Hasmonaeans. It meant a day of relative freedom for the younger maids and Loshema knew exactly what she would do.

Without knocking she let herself into the *tablinum* and found, as she had suspected,

Pheroras asleep across his desk, his head pillowed upon a curling roll of papyrus. Clearly he had not gone to bed. Shaking her head, she began noisily sorting through the items on the desk until the sound brought Pheroras out of his dreams, and he sat up, the papyrus plastered to the side of his face. 'Did I fall asleep?'

'Yes. Without going to bed. Not for the first time either.' Loshema reached forward and gently peeled the papyrus from him. 'I will send for some wine, and bread and figs.'

'I have no appetite.'

'You will be hungry by the time it comes.' She turned away, avoiding Pheroras' doubtful face, and knowing that, if she got him to take a bite he was likely to forget to swallow. 'You should not work all night.'

'Loshema.' His voice was filled with reproach, yet still she felt a certain thrill to hear her name spoken aloud. 'How can I rest when my brother suffers every day in the field to collect Cleopatra's debt.'

And suffers in his pride to be sent like an errand boy when he would be at Antony's side, Loshema thought. But she said nothing. Instead she pointed. 'Are those the reports?'

'Yes, and they read ill. Malichus is wily. He uses every tactic to prolong the incursion, knowing that if Aegyptus falls his debt will be forgotten.' Pheroras sighed and ran his finger along the dry edge of a wine cup. Loshema took a step closer. 'There is something else.'

Pheroras started to protest then shook his head. He smiled. 'There is little I can keep from you.'

'What is it? What is wrong?'

'With my brother away, the voices of dissension are growing. They attack him through me, deliberately misconstruing my orders and sowing the seeds of doubt in the populace. Even with Salome's strength I do not know how much longer we can contain a revolt.'

'Then you must write to your brother. Implore him to return.'

Pheroras stared. 'Are you mad? My brother is in the thick of a battle with the Arabian king. Am I to heap more worries on his head?'

'That is not the point.' Loshema felt her temper rising. Yet to raise her voice was unthinkable. A slave, no matter how familiar, does not raise their voice to a master. But Loshema had forgotten how to be a slave, and within that inner sanctum she shared with the king's brother, her belief in herself as a being whose ideas and opinions *mattered* had taken deep root. 'If you will not write to the king then you must deal with the insubordination yourself.'

A hunted look had appeared in Pheroras' eyes. Out of Cypros' brood of kittens only Pheroras was born without claws. And there were times she loved him for it, and others, as now, when Pheroras' helplessness made her want to pull the hairs from her head. Trying to control her voice, she said, 'You must round up the ring leaders and make an example of them; imprison them if you fear to execute them in the king's absence.'

Pheroras backed away. 'I cannot.'

'You can. You must!' Loshema slammed her hand against the desk with such violence it shook. 'To do otherwise is to tell the world that the king's brother is a coward.'

The shock on Pheroras' face doused the blinding anger that had seized her. She blinked at him, like a drunkard, who wakes from his wine-soaked stupor and finds his wife broken and bloody on the floor. A voice in her head was screaming, this is the king's brother; this is Pheroras, who lifted you up from the lowest place to which a human being can sink, who taught you the magic of words, and now you have used those words to speak the unspeakable.

She half opened her mouth, wanting to gulp down all the ugliness of the last few moments. But the knowledge that it was too late made her dizzy.

'I— ' She went towards him, her hand extended, but the coldness of Pheroras' expression made her knees go weak. 'Please— ' All her wisdom, all her words had betrayed her. What use was reading Diogenes of Babylon or Artapanus of Alexandria if you did not know how to apply the knowledge? There was an acidic taste in her mouth, and she had a sudden, vivid image of herself as ancient Eve, juice running down her chin, while the pillars of paradise collapsed about her. There was a rumbling inside her head.

And then it was no longer inside her head, but beneath her feet and the floor shook. She saw the coldness in Pheroras' face change to surprise, and together they looked in wonderment at the desk as it swayed back and forth sending its load crashing to the floor. Then a tall vase of Oriental origin toppled and smashed into pieces on the floor.

Another tremor and Loshema and Pheroras were thrown together then torn apart. Loshema's back hit the doorframe with a jolt strong enough to make the muscles of her stomach contract, and she lay, curled, on the floor, a terror-stricken animal overwhelmed in the face of the unknown.

Struggling to his feet, Pheroras managed to grab the edge of a couch that was bucking violently against the desk. 'Get out!' he yelled. He made an attempt towards the exit, but the swaying floor sent him sprawling again. His voice, still the voice of a master, called to something in Loshema, and she responded, clinging to the door frame and dragging herself upright, though by now even the walls were swaying in rhythm with the floor.

'Go!'

But she hesitated. Her ears were filled with the deep groans of the earth and the sound of breaking glass. Beyond the door there were stairs, just a few feet away leading to the Western exit from the palace. If she could reach them she might make it to safety. But what of Pheroras, this clumsy, fearful man, who broke off mid-sentence and then forgot to start again, who thought you could dream through life and never choose sides, who had shown her that we cannot be alone in the world as long as we can reach the minds of others; how could she possibly leave him?

With an effort of will she fought the base animal inside herself that was screaming, *Run!* , prising her fingers from the solid sanctuary of the frame and throwing herself towards Pheroras, who had been knocked to the ground again.

She didn't make it.

When she awoke it was as if she had opened her eyes on some senseless dream. She was looking at open sky where once there had been a ceiling, and the creature, who bent over her saying her name, was featureless beneath a shroud of dust. 'Loshema! Loshema, can you hear me?'

She responded dreamily, which is to say that she did not respond at all. Then strong hands reached down and lifted her up.

'Pheroras?' She needed the certainty of his name.

'Hush, you are safe now.' With difficulty he carried her over the wreckage of the room and down debris-covered stairs out into the nightmare of the world.

In the years to come, Loshema would try to remember all the details of that fateful day in Jericho when the earthquake struck, but her mind chased in circles, dropping more than it gathered, and what she remembered was so mixed up with what she thought she remembered and what she later heard, that only a few fragments stood out with all the effulgent glamour of authenticity. The broken pillars, the blank mounds of dust, which, terrifyingly, opened round holes where eyes and mouths should be, and pleaded with them for water as they passed.

'Put me down. We must help.'

Reluctantly he did as she asked. She hid from him that it was all she could do not to let her bruised legs collapse beneath her, and taking a deep breath took a few tottering steps towards a shapeless heap lying upon the ground, who held out a hand and moaned.

'We must find a vessel that is not cracked and pray that the wells are not all destroyed.'

But Pheroras was looking at her strangely. 'I must find my wife.'

At once a crushing guilt made her breath catch in her chest. 'My poor mistress. I will come— '

'No. Stay here where you might be of help. I will be quicker if I go alone.'

But he was gone many hours. And Loshema worked through the filthy heat of day and into the night, learning the meaning of horror and loss until she was numb in the same way extreme cold transforms and swaddles a body in a blanket of disbelief so that it thinks itself warm again. And when Pheroras returned he found her sitting weeping beside a family, who had been dragged out dead from the collapsed foundations of their home.

He knelt down before her and wiped her tears. 'Do not weep. The palace of the Hasmonaeans is no more in Jericho, but your mistress is alive and well.'

But if she noticed that he imparted this news a little flatly she made no show of it, but only went on weeping. 'Loshema, what is wrong? Are you hurt?'

She shook her head.

'Then what is it?'

'My dress,' she said despairingly. 'It's torn.' And exhausted as she was, she found the strength to finger the fabric. 'I will never be able to mend it.' She looked up at him with such a sense of loss that Pheroras gave her a half-exasperated, half-tender look. 'I will buy you a new dress.'

And the offer, so simple and well-meant, struck her as a kind of miracle, and she began to weep again until Pheroras lost patience and lifted her to her feet. 'Come. We can do no more.' She tried to protest, but he was firm. 'Tomorrow we will begin to set things to rights. And tonight we will be as children who sleep peacefully and do not know that the world is a place that can be shaken to its core.'

26

In which the king of conquests makes a decision

31 - 30 BCE

*I*n the days that follow the great quake bringing destruction to Jericho and Masada, and drying up the spring that serves the holy community at Qumran, there are aftershocks that bring down more masonry, take more lives. But none so great as the shocks that are exploding across the civilized world. Cleopatra abandons her lover to his fate and flees Actium with Octavian's ships in hot pursuit. Some say when she made shore she was distraught to think Antony dead then more distraught to find him alive. Octavian will reach no truce while Antony still breathes.

In Jerusalem Herod feels the earth shifting beneath his feet. He has devised a generous plan to restore Jericho, but all his acts of generosity, his loyalty, his alliances will count for nothing if he has backed the losing side. Now Cypros comes to him and they talk long into the night.

—Go softly when you enter. Only a candle illuminates this room and your eyes must adjust to the sudden darkness. See, there is Herod drawing his knees up to his chin, like a child.—

'I cannot.'

'You must.'

'They think Hyrcanus a saint. And even those who do not, see only a toothless old man whom they love. I will be the most hated man in the kingdom.'

Cypros lays a hand on his head, seeing, with a pang, that there are threads of grey appearing within the black. 'A king cannot fear to be hated. When the Almighty rains down death and destruction, does He fear the Jews will turn their backs on him or does he do it because it is His Justice and all must abide by His Law?'

Now, a week later, here is Pheroras, in his chambers, weeping, and we can make no move to offer comfort because his wife is already at his side. Ever practical, she says, 'What else could he do? He betrayed him.'

Pheroras chokes on his indignation. 'A saint. He has killed a saint. Do you imagine Hyrcanus actually plotted to escape to Arabia, to throw himself on the mercy of Malichus? He can barely take two steps without stopping for breath. You did not see his trial. Half the time he could hardly hear the accusations and the other half he hardly understood them.'

His wife pats his arm. 'Alexandra was behind any plot of Hyrcanus to escape. Everyone knows that. Why your brother does not take her in hand is a mystery.'

Pheroras shakes himself free. 'Cleopatra is not yet dead. There is the answer to your mystery. But he has gone too far this time. He has shown himself to be afraid of a pathetic, feeble old man.'

'Hush. The king knows what he is doing.' Pheroras' wife is no fool. She knows slaves, as well as walls, have ears. But she is wrong. I am the only slave present, and I would rather cut out my heart than betray Pheroras. Or, at least, so I think.

Mark Antony and Cleopatra are drinking down the dregs of their lives, while Octavian's agents hunt down their son, the king of kings, the boy who promised new beginnings, who married Greek and Aegyptian and Roman in his blood, now a fugitive running from the one they hail as the king of conquests.

Herod is afraid of Rome. Alexandra is afraid of Herod. Everyone fears everything, except Herod's children to Mariamme, of whom the living ones now number four, two boys and two girls. Alexander and Aristobolus, Salampsio and Cypros. See how they run about the court waving their fingers in the air, their high-pitched squeals, like the chirrups of tame birds.

They do not sense the hawks and falcons, the owls and crows, wrapped in the dark cloaks of their wings, all around, watching. And because they think they are free, they are free, free from care or dread or that terrible envy that leaves its owner always on the outside looking in. How unlike Herod's first son they are. Think of poor Antipater, head down, following his bony, rejected mother out into the bleak terrains of exile.

Yes, Herod is afraid. And with good reason. Octavian has called him to Rhodes to give account.

They were jeering at him in Judea. This Herod knew and understood, and even at times imagined he could actually hear, as he neared the pavilion where Octavian had taken residence. He was aware of the eyes of the legionaries as he made his way through the camp. They went about their tasks busily enough—checking the straps on a cuirass, mending the split shaft of a pilum— but they were watching him. To his left a half-naked legionary was hammering in a tent peg. Herod glanced at the sweating back and saw it stiffen then the hand move down as he adjusted himself. No need, for a Greek anatomist to open a body to discover which organ quickens at the sight of a man's demise.

As he stepped onto the wooden platform upon which the pavilion sat, the sentries barred his way. Did they know who he was? He had come alone with neither his bodyguard nor the gold circlet upon his head.

'State your business, Herod the Jew.'

He is known. Most likely they were sour because the betting had been laid off. After all, who would be willing to risk coin in his favour? Herod felt a certain sympathy; he wouldn't place money on his chances either. They said there had been good odds for Archelaus of Cappadocia and Amyntas of Galatia. But they had possessed the wit to ally themselves with the winning side. But not Herod. Never Herod. At home they called him a half Jew behind his back. They were wrong. He shared in full that peculiar characteristic of his countrymen, that need to stand apart, to display an independence of thought so at odds with the world that it is often misinterpreted as aloofness or pig-headedness.

He glanced at the hard, lean faces blocking his way, and for the first time in his life he no longer felt young. It was a dangerous indulgence. The fresh wave washes away the old, such was the wisdom of the times. He pulled himself up straight. 'I am come at Caesar's bidding.' They stood aside.

The front compartment of the tent had an austere soldierly quality about it, a distinctive smell of animal hide and sweat, a wooden desk, benches, dispatches, maps. Herod was comforted by the sight. Behind the desk Octavian was studying a letter. He did not get up as Herod approached, no gesture of recognition or welcome —Antony would have embraced him in his bear-like arms, chided him for his girlish good looks then called for more wine.— Octavian put the letter down and raised his eyes expectantly. If he would ask for something, Herod thought desperately. Demand something of me. Order it. But Octavian went on staring; his eyes had the hard, blank look of unpainted marble.

Biting the inside of his lip Herod made his bow. Had Octavian noted that he no longer wore his diadem? He could read nothing in those marble eyes. He cleared his throat. 'I do not come to excuse myself. I ask for no mercy. I am here as Mark Antony's friend.' The coldness of the younger man's face made Herod speak coldly. 'I have done all in my power to aid and abet Antony's cause. Had I not been refused permission by Cleopatra I would have joined him at Actium.' Even as he formed the words he asked himself what madness was this? Cleopatra had inadvertently saved him by blocking his open alliance with Antony. Now, here he was, giving up that advantage, to a man they said wept no tears and smiled more rarely. Well Herod was a soldier, and once you had drawn first blood there was no going back.

'I openly confess that I sent him money and corn, and considered it a poor show of friendship in comparison with what I owed him. My father, who you knew as a loyal ally to Rome and to Antony, taught me that if a man owns himself to be another's friend, and knows him to be his benefactor, he is obliged to hazard everything, to use every faculty of his soul, every member of his body and all the wealth he has, for that friend.'

His mouth was dry. Antony would have had him down at least two cups before he allowed him to speak. By contrast, Octavian's desk was a desert of parchment and vellum containing not the slightest luxury or comfort, not even a pitcher of water. Herod tasted rot under his tongue, but forced himself to say, 'You will be asking yourself if I regret my actions.' He paused to allow Octavian to interrogate him, but the younger man said nothing and Herod found himself supplying his own answer. 'I regret only that I have failed him as a comrade at arms, and more especially, as a counsellor. For when I advised him that the only way to save himself was to slay the Aegyptian queen, he shut his ears to me and barred the way to all advice.'

Octavian sat back in his seat. 'You have come all this way to tell me that you are a friend to Antony?'

'I have come to tell you that I am a good and loyal friend to those who would have me.'

'I do not lack for friends. What else do you offer?'

Inside Herod's mouth was the taste of blood. There was a tension in his limbs, like a man who knows he will be forced to jump a ravine he reckons to be just too wide. 'I cannot offer you either a crown or a kingdom,' he began. 'Those were given to me by Rome and Rome has the right to take them from me. Naturally I have brought a few paltry gifts, and to you, personally, there awaits eight hundred talents— ' Antony would have fallen on his neck with gratitude, but the thought of a king's ransom did not move Octavian. His unblinking eyes kept Herod as the centre of their focus.

'I am uncertain of my opinions concerning Jews,' he said at last. 'My tutor, Apollodorus, does not speak highly of your kind. He thinks that you put yourselves above other men and your loyalty is suspect.'

Herod's eyes burned, but his voice was cool. 'I have heard the charge before. As a soldier I can only admire his shrewdness. Suspicion is a formidable weapon. It draws no blood yet is sharp enough to defeat the strongest of men.'

Just then the flaps of the tent were pushed aside and a man in the dress of a prefect entered. He was of middle years, tall and well-made with several visible scars on his face and forearms. Ignoring Herod, he saluted Octavian and offered a leather roll presumably containing dispatches. Octavian took the roll in one hand then paused, as if a thought were occurring to him. 'This officer, you see before you is Lucius Flavius Saturninus. Does he look familiar to you?'

Herod shook his head.

'Yet he knows you. He fought at the battle of the Nile, where your family came to the aid of Rome. I am surprised you don't recall him. Saturninus is a formidable soldier. I have seen him in Spain kill two men with one hammer blow. Do you understand what I am saying, I trust this man.'

Herod looked at the Satuninus again, who stood between them at attention somehow conveying by his mere presence the inert gravity of a rock. Herod wondered whether to feign some degree of recognition to win the man over, but Saturninus did not look like a man to respond to pleasant flatteries. Octavian was watching the interchange. He addressed his next words to his officer. 'You have seen this man fight?'

Saturninus nodded. 'Yes Caesar.'

'Tell me, in the heat of battle, would you place him before you or behind?'

Saturninus did not move, but his eyes flicked towards Herod. If Herod had met marble in Octavian, here was slate. The eyes flicked away. 'Behind. He is a man to have your back. As were his father and brother.'

At the mention of the dead a great sense of loss filled Herod's heart. He felt the fight go out of him and a terrible weariness descend. Let them take him away and lock him in some windowless dungeon or let them thrust a sword blade into his gut. Only get it over with and God grant him a little peace. He half opened his mouth to say as much, but Octavian was continuing to stare at his prefect, as though they carried on in silent conversation.

After an eternity his eyes narrowed, as they will do when a conclusion is reached, and he turned back to Herod. With a middle finger he tapped one of the dispatches.

'The governor of Syria also speaks well of you, concerning your help in the matter of the gladiators.'

Avoiding the desire to bow, Herod held himself rigid after the manner of Saturninus.

'And I am also informed that you sent your mother and sister to the safety of Masada.'

'Indeed Caesar.'

'Yet your wife and mother-in-law were sent to Alexandrium.'

'Caesar sees all.'

'There is strife in your household?'

'It is only a matter of the women.'

Octavian made a slight motion with his eyebrows that may have been a frown. He was impossible to read, which was no more than his detractors claimed. There was none of the splendour of Julius Caesar, none of the passion of Mark Antony. Beneath the glacial stare even Herod's fire seemed antiquated and out of place. Was this the future, a world ruled by men who observed all, but felt nothing? But Octavian was speaking,

'Do not underestimate the power of women to do damage. Mark Antony serves as an example to us all.' Suddenly changing he asked, 'What do you consider makes a great leader?'

'Caesar?'

'We set much store by military prowess. Above all things my stepfather called himself a conqueror. And Antony was never done boasting that a man's honour is forged in the heat of battle. Yet I do not consider myself a soldier of great skill.' Octavian made this pronouncement quite flatly, a simple statement of fact. 'I rely on those beneath me to know their jobs. My role is to judge character. A leader must be a good judge of character. Do you agree?'

'Yes Caesar.'

'Good. It is important that we understand each other. I did not mention that I had a second tutor, Arius Didymus. He was an Alexandrian by birth and a Stoic by choice. He lived near the Jewish quarter and claimed to see great parallels between Judaism and Stoicism. The rigorous training of the mind, the control of passions, *askesis* he called it. I think he would have liked you.' With that Octavian placed his hands palms-down on the desk, and Herod tensed, sensing that this was the point of no return. His breath was painful in his chest, but he could not let it out.

'Very well then. I have decided to trust Saturninus' opinion. Keep your throne, Herod, and be a good friend to Rome.'

Herod allowed himself the indulgence of a bow, snatching the fleeting moment when his face was hidden to compose himself. When he stood upright again, Octavian's attention seemed to be back with the dispatches, and taking himself to be dismissed, he turned to go, yet Octavian's voice halted him. 'In the matter of your household, you might take warning from Virgil, if your Latin compares to your Greek. *varium et mutabile semper femina.*'

Herod answered after a pause, 'Woman is always a fickle and changeable creature?'

Octavian gave a curt nod. 'You have the gist.'

The shoes of Herod's horse send tiny fountains of sparks across the cobbled courtyard of Alexandrium as he pulls the sweating beast to a halt. He is grimy and exhausted from the hard ride, but he hardly notices now that he is almost home. For that has been his revelation on the long journey from Rhodes, home is not to be found in the vast, echoing halls of palaces, nor in the pillared walkways or the gilded reception rooms. Home, instead, contains a heart beating with a human rhythm, its windows light up to accommodate your longing gaze and its doors are flung wide to gather you in.

Soemus, the man he left in charge, is already rushing out of a gatehouse, ready to take the reigns as Herod swings down.

'Tell— '

No need. She is here. Hot on Soemus' heels. Mariamme pulls herself up short, and points to his diadem, which catches the light in a nimbus of gold. And suddenly they are laughing, so hard that tears run down their faces and they have to grip one another's shoulders to stay upright. Soemus stares as though they have gone mad. Ignoring him, Mariamme reaches for Herod's crown and he catches her up and spins her around.

To the east he feels the sun's warmth rising over the Gilead mountains, those strange peaks of ancient name, Abarim, Pisgah, Nebo, and Peor, the birthplace of prophecies and the wars that follow prophecies. But this day is golden, quivering, numinous and the world is full of new beginnings.

—Such is the dream of Herod and it would be a pity to wake him.—

27

In which Salome's victory brings Herod terrible loss

29 BCE

T HERE IS HEROD, TWICE INSTATED king and the loneliest man in Judea. *You must hide your surprise when you see him, unwashed, slumped upon his throne, his gaze fixed upon a broken column of sunlight slanting across the inlaid floor. He is alone; he will have no-one with him. No-one to witness the black despair that drives claws into his shoulders and neck, making him think of carrion-faced Anubis, Aegytian god of death.*

His eyes are red and filled with grit; he cannot sleep. When he tries he is woken by a thunderclap of terror just as he slides over the lip of oblivion. By his feet a goblet lies on its side, the dregs spilling in red rivulets down the marble steps of the dais. The sight makes him finger his throat then run a dry tongue over drier lips. He would like to call for more wine, but he cannot bear the way people look at him now, even the slaves, who must perforce avert their eyes.

Sometimes he sees his mother in the shadows. He has started up several times. Or, if he is nearer sleep, frozen with the hammer blows of his heart resounding in his chest. Because that cannot be his mother hovering in the cobwebbed twilight; Cypros is no more. And it is not earthquakes, but death that has shaken Herod's foundations.

It happens thus, in Tishrei, the seventh month, with a sliver of new moon hanging above Jerusalem. Herod is hosting a feast to mark Yom Teruah, the feast of trumpets, and beyond the palace the streets are thronging with excited men and women, their numbers swollen by pilgrims carrying their harvest offerings to the Temple, and foreigners, from as far afield as Tarraco and Rome, drawn by the lure of spectacle.

For hours the city has been vibrating to the sound of ram's horn and the voices of the crowd, which have merged over time into one continuous leonine roar. Everyone is smiling, even Mariamme, who has been so sullen and unwelcoming since her husband's return. Only Cypros cannot bear it. She complains of a headache and how it is impossible to escape the endless blasting of the trumpets.

'Can something not be done?'

Herod looks at her in surprise. 'Am I to lift my staff aloft and part the swell of the people's praise?'

'You are king. You may do as you please.'

But, of late, Herod has been feeling the burden of a king's power to do as he pleases. Before his journey to Rhodes he sat with his mother and sister to decide the question of his wife.

Cypros was adamant. 'If Octavian does not spare you, Mariamme cannot be left to rule.'

He got up angrily then, paced across the room, like a caged thing. At last pleadingly, 'There is precedent. Salome Alexandra ruled after the death of her husband, Mariamme is of her blood.'

Cypros and Salome stared at the mulish hunch of his shoulders then Cypros cleared her throat. 'If you let her live other men will come for her. You saw how Alexandra tried to lure Antony. Do you imagine they will suffer your children to take the throne? Other men, Herod. Think on it. She is not the type of woman with strength enough to resist.'

And so it was done. Soemus had his orders. If Herod did not return, Mariamme was not to be spared. And he swore an oath of blood that he would not reveal this plan while she was in his care.

'It would frighten her,' Herod said. 'The Almighty willing, she need never know.'

Mariamme does not know, cannot know —Soemus denies all— yet she is so cold. She comes to him, so lovely, she might be a dream of his dream of her, until her face twists and she flings ugly accusations in his face. 'Can you look at me and pretend to love me?'

He tries to explain, to reveal to her what he has barely revealed to himself, that he cannot bear to live without her, worse still, how can he be dead and she go on living? It is not his children's fate that sets every particle of him on fire, but the thought of her cloistered in another man's arms; it makes him burn. He has seen how every man is aflame in her presence. May the Almighty forgive him, he wishes he was a Pharaoh of old who could take his wife with him into the tomb. He looks at her helplessly. Is not some part of this torture shared? Can she not feel the torment of a flame that is all consuming yet not consumed?

She stares at him. 'Love? What room is there in your heart for love? It is a shrivelled thing, incapable of so large a feeling.'

Later he sits, with his head in his hands. 'Can she know?'

Salome and Cypros exchange a look over his bent head. 'There is only one way,' Salome says.

'I will not believe it.'

So now he is king, but his wife still does not love him, and Cypros is standing before him complaining of the noise. 'Shall I part the clouds so that the stars may light your way?' he asks. 'Or shall I command the sun to rise as I am king and may do as I please.'

'More likely you will do it than please your mother,' Cypros snaps. They stare at each other, each wanting comfort but too proud, too alike to ask. As well to stand in front of a glass and ask your reflection to make the first move. Cypros feels the sting of tears behind her eyes; she gathers her skirts and walks stiffly from the room.

He is listening to a speech by the Roman ambassador when a maidservant runs in. She is stopped by one of the Galatian bodyguards he has inherited from Cleopatra. But Herod hears his mother's name and beckons her forward. She is pale and sweating. His first thoughts — always his first thoughts— are of poison. But the girl is only wild with fear.

195

'Come quickly. Before it is too late.'

But it is already too late. Cypros has lain down and closed her eyes, and if she opens them again it will not be in this life. Herod falls to his knees and clasps her hands. He is weeping without realizing it. 'She looks so small.' Salome puts a hand on his shoulder but he does not know she is there. 'We parted in bitterness.'

Now in the throne room, Herod sits alone. A cloud passes over the sun, the shaft of golden light flicks out, the shadows stir. Grabbing up the fallen goblet he dashes it at the emptiness between two columns. 'Be gone, shade!' He hears the ringing metal note as the goblet tumbles across the tiles. For a moment the echoes play with the sound then there is silence. His mother has vanished. But there are other ghosts waiting.

Herod curls up on his throne, like a child, and gnaws at the raw knuckles of one hand. He thinks of what has been given to him, the balsam groves are his once more, the coastline returned, and more, the towns of Jamnia, Azotus, Hippos and Gadara; he is king of a kingdom as big as any Hasmonaean king has ruled over and it means nothing, nothing. The irony strikes him in the chest, like the hammer of a bell and he begins to peal with laughter. And soon he finds he cannot stop.

His mother is standing in the shadows, watching him, and he wishes she would share the joke. It is such a strange feeling to be impossibly light and unbearably heavy at the same time. The shadows part and, not a ghost, but Salome emerges. She says his name, as though it is a question, 'Herod?' He does not answer. He is crying with laughter or perhaps he is laughing with tears.

She comes closer 'Herod?'

He turns his head away, knowing that she is asking if he is still there, does the man she knows still exist somewhere inside himself. He stops laughing, turns his face into the gilded wood of his throne, and hears her creep closer. 'Herod, please. I need you.' She tucks something soft around him, a blanket of soft Galilean wool. It has a comforting smell, hilltops and horizons and the dizziness that comes from lying on your back searching for God in the immense emptiness of the sky. He blinks at the concerned face hovering over him and seems to focus for the first time. He smiles. 'Send for Mariamme,' he says. 'Send for my wife.' And Salome starts back, as though he has bitten her.

In the days that follow Cypros' death, and after the funeral lavish enough to set the gossips tongues wagging from Ashkelon to Hazor, Salome was assailed by a curious contradiction of feelings. Like her brothers, she discovered a hole in herself now that her mother had gone. But she also found a feeling of lightness, as though the place her mother occupied had been heavy and she had carried the burden of it, unknowing, for years. A new weight settled on her shoulders, that of responsibility, and she went with it eagerly to her mother's desk, ready to sit on Cypros' chair that, all who were in the know, understood bore the phantom outline of a throne.

But when she got there, Mariamme was sitting behind the desk. She was reading the morning's despatches, and did not immediately notice her sister-in-law's entrance. Salome saw at once that she was very simply dressed, a plain dun-coloured robe, her dark curls caught up at the nape of her neck in a wooden clasp. For a moment she could think of nothing to say then she blurted, 'Do queens now dress as paupers?'

Mariamme looked up, surprised, and Salome, who felt her bosom grow more shapeless beneath its halter of stretched silk, knew that anyone in possession of a set of exquisite amber eyes had no need for the adornment of jewels.

'How can I help you?' Mariamme asked, ignoring Salome's outburst, which only made her sister-in-law hate her all the more.

'I wish to look through my mother's papers.'

'The kingdom's papers,' Mariamme corrected. She smiled, and her teeth shone, like pearls.

'My brother was glad to have her help,' Salome snapped.

'As were we all. No-one could doubt the great —the smallest pause, as though she searched for a word — dedication Cypros applied to her role. We all mourn her loss, but, as the king's wife, it is fitting that I take on these duties now.'

Salome felt something loosen in her backbone. As always, when challenged directly, the fight went out of her. 'I could be of help,' she offered, at the same time despising herself for stooping so low as to offer.

'How kind you are,' Mariamme said. 'But there is no need to trouble yourself. I can manage the king's affairs quite well myself.'

'Of course.' Salome gave a smile of pure hatred then turned and left the room.

It was not the next day or the day after, but some indefinable length of time that separated what was to follow entirely from what had been, so that they seemed disconnected and unrelated, rather than, what they truly were, the one the consequence of the other. On the day it happened Herod was in mellow mood, and despite the disappointments of the past, he called to his wife to keep him company in the warm, lazy hours of the afternoon.

She came to him warily, but Herod was determined to ignore the pain he felt when she looked at him without smiling or her habit of choosing the couch furthest from wherever he was seated. Besides, she had brought the children, and it was hard not to be infected by their bubbling innocence and the memories of innocence they evoked so that he looked at them chasing and rolling about, like puppies, and wondered how it was and when it had happened that innocence was lost once and for all from his life.

From her couch Mariamme watched him, noting that he lavished as much attention on the girls as the two sons he was so proud of. In an age where fathers often saw girls as God-given drudges, or, if they were rich enough, pawns in the games of marriage contracts, Herod was strangely even-handed. Such a contradiction of a man. It was as though he carried the natures of Cypros and Antipater quite separately inside his skull, and was entirely unconscious of the one when he behaved as the other. His tenderness was sincere, his wrath limitless. And so much he had done was unforgivable, wasn't it?

Yet he swore that Jonathan's death was an accident, that his hand had been forced when it came to her grandfather's execution. And hadn't he spared Alexandra who had provoked him, most of all? She was enough the princess to understand that the enormous sums he lavished on Roman interests and Roman wars, were bribes that kept Judea from suffering the fate of Carthage or Pergamon, now mere provinces of Rome. But it was in Jericho that she saw true proof of his largesse.

They made a state visit at the end of summer. Herod was not a king to sit behind the walls of his palace, and soon insisted on visiting the reconstruction of the city personally, and Mariamme declared a desire to accompany him in order to distribute bread to the poor, though secretly she longed to see a little more of the world than the pale walls that surrounded the royal enclosure.

A small group of the poor, carefully vetted by the royal bodyguards, was brought before her to receive the gift of bread directly from the queen's hands. Her upbringing had been within a cage, but a gilded one, and she was struck at once by how thin and old —even the young ones— looked, with the lines of sorrow deeply etched into the coarse, sunburnt skin of their faces. They were awed in her presence, and though Mariamme was used to that, she was strangely touched by the simplicity of their wonder.

She lifted a loaf of bread and held it out. The eldest of the group, a wizened old man in a striped woollen cloak that had seen better days, came forward shyly, bowing so continuously that it was a feat of timing to place the bread in his hands.

'Peace be upon you, lady and may the house of Herod know many blessings in memory of his kindness to the people.'

And then a woman cried out, unbidden. 'Tell the king we love him and the Almighty sees his good works.'

Mariamme stiffened. She was not used to hearing her husband as the object of spontaneous praise. Yet signs of his goodness were all around her in Jericho. She had been well aware that it was from Herodian quarries that the limestone came to rebuild the houses and municipal buildings. And Herodian money funded the architects and artisans, who were employed, not only in the reconstruction of Herod's palace, but in the restoration of the humblest homes. Even the little synagogue, with its Grecian columns and its red terracotta roof owed its resurrection to Herod's coffers.

All this she had known yet somehow she had not connected these deeds with the man who stormed through her life as changeable as the *qadim*, those scorching, unbearable winds from the east that left you breathless and exhausted. This was a different Herod, a man more gentle than she had thought possible, and after Jericho she looked at him anew.

Yet change was not easily achieved. The walls between them were many times thicker than the walls that were being erected in Jericho, and so Mariamme now sat, watching him playing with their children, and wondered if there was still time to find a man in there she could love.

Just then Alexander, who was re-enacting the battle of Actium charged his younger brother, who fell, knocking the four year old Salampsio off her feet. She collapsed, not particularly painfully to the floor. But the shock and the indignity of the attack made her open her mouth wide in a wail of bitter reproach.

'Alexander.' Herod's voice was reproving. He scooped his daughter up and set her upon his knee.

'It wasn't a hard fall,' Alexander said sulkily, knowing it to be his fault.

'Nonetheless it is unprincely to ignore the pain you have caused your sister.'

Alexander coloured. 'What does a half Jew know of being a prince?' He looked down as he said the words, muttering them into his chest, but Herod's hearing was keen. He put Salampsio down and got to his feet. 'Where did you hear that? Who is claiming these things?' In two strides he was at his son's side, forcing his chin up. 'Tell me.'

But seven year old Alexander was too frightened to reply.

'Answer your king!'

In fear Alexander's eyes slid towards his mother, and Herod had his answer. A terrible silence followed. Mariamme felt she should say something, but an outright denial rang false in her ears. There was talk enough in the Hasmonaean quarters of Herod's base origins. And if she had never said so outright, the words had certainly come from Alexandra. Mariamme clamped her lips tight shut; to say anything was to condemn either her mother or her son.

A knock on the door sounded like a clap of thunder.

'Enter!'

Epiktetos, Herod's cupbearer appeared in the doorway. He was carrying a goblet, which steamed gently with aromatic vapours, which he clearly intended to present to the king. But the sight of Mariamme and the children seemed to startle him, and he froze, blinking through his long-fringed lashes until Herod ordered him forward.

He came slowly, reluctantly almost. But it was known that he was a great favourite of Herod's, gifted to him by Antony in happier days. A youth of great beauty, Phrygian by birth, he delighted his new master with tales of Midas and Gordias, whom he spoke of, with such warmth and spontaneity they might have been close personal friends. Around the court he had the nickname, *omuoraon*, balm, for his soothing effect on Herod's nerves, and Mariamme seized the opportunity, signalling to her faithful Jebusite to shoo the children from the room.

Once the children were gone Mariamme breathed a little easier. She did not fear violence. Herod, had never so much as raised a hand against his children. But all knew Doris and Antipater's fate. And exile from Jerusalem, the golden city that vibrated in the blood of the Hasmonaeans, would in itself be a kind of living death. Let him become calm, she thought. Then we will talk. In keeping with the habits of the day she ignored the favourite and took herself into one of the inner chambers. And only later did she wonder why the Almighty sent no sign to delay her.

There were whispers, voices deliberately lowered. And this was strange because Herod was a man of great power, and men of such esteem in those days saw no shame in the admiration that was natural between men. An order, barked too quickly for her to catch. Then the sound of running feet. Mariamme walked towards the door then paused when she made out Epiktetos' hushed voice still on the other side. Time passed. The creak of a door and more footsteps.

'Wife!' The summons had a brutal finality about it. Not her title, or even her name, but *wife* as though she was an object to be fetched.

Mariamme entered the room behind the mask of her most remote expression. Yet it was hard to show no round-eyed surprise at seeing Salome and Pheroras there and, stranger still, to see one of the grooms holding the collar of a hunting dog.

'Husband?' She threw the term back at him. But Herod was looking at her, like a stranger. He held up the goblet Epiktetos had brought in.

'What is the meaning of this?'

A trick, a trap, a snare? She shook her head.

Herod's features tightened, as though her silence had confirmed his suspicions. Then suddenly, 'Epiktetos, tell the queen what you have told me.'

Now Mariamme was a royal child. Amongst her ancestors were good kings and bad kings, gentle queens and schemers and even a prince who could starve his own mother for the chance to feel the weight of a crown upon his head. She was, thus, far from naïve when it came to the machinations of court intrigues. Yet, even so, she had always believed that liars were apt to give themselves away in any one of a thousand little mannerisms, eyes that would not meet the accused, a fidgeting finger, a tapping foot. It was thus a shock when Epiktetos looked her in the eye, and stated quite baldly that she had instructed him to present the goblet of wine to the king, within which she had concealed a love potion.

'And you knew the provenance of this potion?'

Epiktetos shook his head. 'For that reason I could not allow your majesty to consider taking it in ignorance.'

Mariamme was watching him closely. Not the twitch of a muscle, not the slightest hesitation in his speech. She tried to catch her husband's eye, —surely there was some secret communication that existed between a man and his wife— but he turned his back and commanded. 'Give it to the animal.'

The dog, a molossus, muscles straining under its thick powerful body, lapped up the treat without demur. A silence laced with expectation and meaning followed. And like precious moments left to the dying, it could be counted in breaths. In. Out. In. Out. In—

Mariamme looked coolly, some said later disdainfully, at Herod. But Herod's eyes were on Epiktetos, whose features had become strangely frozen, and it was remembered afterwards that his top lip had glistened with sweat. In. Out. In— Maybe a dozen or so more breaths then the dog began to shake. Those closest took an instinctive step back, but the animal was rooted to the spot. Its muscles went rigid and it fell to the floor uttering a strange, almost human wail. Then it was fitting, a red froth appearing around its muzzle.

Epiktetos was so relieved he threw an unguarded look of complicity in Salome's direction. She appeared not to see him, but something in her posture made the sweat on his upper lip break out anew. At his feet the dog had begun its death throes, but Herod was satisfied.

'Enough!' His tone was strangely, madly triumphant. 'Take it away. I have seen enough.'

Two slaves rushed forward to drag the twitching animal away. Herod watched them go. And, once they were gone, he was left standing in the circle of his courtiers, unspeaking, lost in thought.

In the profoundness of his isolation no-one dared approach him, and there was almost a physical sense in which he retreated, as though they watched him turn and walk, alone, down a long dark corridor. Eventually, without having uttered a word, he left the room. Mariamme took a step after him, but Salome stood in her way. If her brother's victory had been pyrrhic she intended to enjoy the spoils in full.

'You cannot expect to remain in the royal quarters.'

Mariamme looked at her coldly, pityingly. 'You need not posture, Salome. You have won. I curse you only with the consequences of your own actions. You have sown thorns and you will surely reap pain.'

Ugly red patches appeared on Salome's cheeks. 'You have brought this upon yourself.' She spoke loudly enough to be heard by everyone in the room. 'You have only yourself to blame.'

Mariamme kept her face utterly still and impassive, as though Salome's threats were no more than the buzzing of a fly, even when the guards stepped forward and the cold touch of iron circled her wrists.

—*Come. We must hurry ahead. Take a breath then look about you. No longer in the palace, we are within the Temple precincts in the hall of Hewn Stone, where trials take place. How very simple travel is when you are in a dream. Only, remember, this is no dream. What will happen is real. For these are not characters beckoned by imagination; but creatures of flesh and blood.*

The light is dusty in here. The Temple is not the thing of beauty it was in Solomon's day, but look, there is Herod on his throne, stiff and stern, a wax effigy of himself. Around him sits the Grand Sanhedrin. At the back is ancient bar Ahab, the oldest member of the court, rocking gently and muttering to himself. He does not seem to know where he is and a trickle of drool runs unimpeded down his chin.

And there, two rows down, is his great grandson, Yoni, who barely looks old enough to let go of his mother's skirts. He keeps looking round to see what everyone else is doing, especial-

ly at ben Gamaliel, who sits at the front, hunched like a hawk. Ben Gamaliel is new blood, and eager to seek advantage. And do not make the mistake of thinking that these three are exceptional. Herod has picked his advisors with care from a vast pool of toothless, weak and ambitious men.

Now, look to your left. Here comes Mariamme with her mother and her maid.

—Yes, I am there. Mariamme's maids are deemed suspect. Pheroras has offered me in an act of compassion. 'Loshema may do it.'

'Loshema?'

'My wife's handmaiden. She can be trusted.' Salome's eyes fall upon me, narrowed and suspicious then she nods. 'So be it.'—

The royal women move with the stiff, slightly inhuman gait that shows they are exerting rigid self-control. Note how Alexandra clasps her hands to prevent them from shaking. Keep close as they approach Herod, and watch for the moment when, for the first time in days, the eyes of husband and wife meet.

There is a flash of pain. Colour rises and sets in Herod's face, while in Mariamme's neck, a fragile little vein beats frantically with blood. It looks like the wings of a butterfly still trapped in its cocoon. Never have they been so real, so alive. Undeniably their existence in this scene is less questionable than yours. You find that surprising? Yet every scribe knows that ink is the logos of magic; it summons the dead.

And now they are reading the charges. They are not unknown to her, adultery, treachery, treason. There is something almost trite in their predictability yet her hands clasp and unclasp on hearing them read aloud. She is addressed by Yehoshu ben Fabus, the High Priest. He is a small man, the days of his youth long gone, but his eyes, deep set each in an ammonite spiral of wrinkles, seem wise.

'What is your answer to these charges?'

'I am innocent.' Her voice echoes a little in the hall, and she cannot help remembering standing in her chamber with her finger tips pressed against the window panes, asking her mother or the green-eyed maid or perhaps addressing herself to the Almighty himself, 'Who will believe me? Who? Who? Who?'

The witnesses are brought in next. Ganymede, her favourite eunuch, stumbles between two guards. His embroidered robes, which he famously posed and postured in more delicately than the ladies of the court, are tattered rags about his waist. But it is the burn marks, where the hot irons have touched his skin, that make Mariamme gasp and take a step towards him. Two Temple Levites bring down their ceremonial spears and block her path.

The Eunuch's confession is rambling, confused. He cannot look at Mariamme, but he nods when he is asked to confirm that the queen confessed to using her wiles on Soemus. 'She said she had lain with him and that it was no great ordeal to her, as she had plied the same trick on her uncle Joseph'

His voice is toneless, a dead man speaking, but still his words evoke a gasp. In these times to voice doubt over a woman's purity is to tarnish her for surely a virtuous woman is beyond reproach. Ben Fabus clears his throat, 'What was the queen's purpose in seducing Soemus?'

'She expressed a desire … a wish to discover what the king intended as her fate. She was of a mind … of an inclination that Octavian would look unkindly on the king's alliance with Antony. Soemus knew. … He was the key she said … to know the king's mind.'

'And once she had discovered the secret Soemus was withholding?'

The eunuch drops his head.

'Louder please. The court must hear.'

'She swore to kill him.'

'By 'him' do you mean to imply the king?'

A nod.

The eunuch is led away beneath the mutterings of the audience. Mariamme's eyes are wet as she watches him go, but he does not turn round.

Next is Soemus. He must be dragged in then supported by the guards. Where his feet once were, now are two bloody pulps. His head droops and he is dragged up by his hair. But he is barely conscious, and does not seem to know where he is.

'Water. Bring him water!' ben Fabus cries. He turns, appalled, to Herod, who returns such an inhuman gaze that ben Fabus shudders and averts his eyes.

The water is brought and Soemus revives enough to understand his circumstances. He looks about him and finds Mariamme's face in the crowd. His lips flop against broken stumps of teeth and he makes a few whimpering noises that, in his head, may be words.

Ben Fabus draws in his breath and scans the watching faces. There are no allies there. He must continue on alone, his dream of a better world shattered. 'You confess you have had adulterous relations with the queen?'

Soemus makes a gibbering, chattering noise that is taken to mean, yes.

'And do you also admit that you were aware that the queen harboured resentment against the king and openly discussed her murderous intent?'

There is a pause then Soemus begins to laugh. It is a blood-chilling sound, a jackal's bark, mirthless and hollow, the sound everyone is afraid they have inside themselves. Ben Fabus shakes his head and Soemus is dragged away. Was that yes? No? It does not matter anymore. The queen is condemned.

Mariamme is led out into an antechamber while her fate is debated. It is a small bare room, intended only for the purpose of allowing attendants to wait, out of sight, in antici- pation of the king's command. The door is made of cedar planks, planed paper thin, and the sound of the debate can be clearly heard.

'He will divorce me, as he did Doris? He will send me away?' Mariamme asks these statements as questions. But neither her mother or the green-eyed maid answer. Mariamme and the maid press their ears against the door. 'What if I am not allowed to see the children? What if he disinherits them?'

'The witnesses did not mention me,' says Alexandra 'Do you think that was noted? That I was not mentioned?'

Outside the men's voices rumble on. 'The king has suggested exile. There are a number of strongholds where the queen might be kept.'

'And knowledge of the queen's incarceration will cause riots in the street.'

Mariamme glances at her mother. Is this high, slightly affected voice, the voice of a friend?

'Nonetheless exile is the king's wish.'

Ben Fabus clears his throat. 'There is the matter of the divorce to be settled first. This should be a matter of procedure only, as it is my interpretation of the Law that a husband may divorce his wife at will if she has displeased him.'

A rustling sound, a creak of bones and benches. 'There is another interpretation.' Another unknown voice, but from the far end of the chamber. They must strain to hear. 'That is the conculsion of Hillel. But our dear Shammai —may his soul repose with the Lord— would argue that a husband cannot divorce his wife without due cause.'

'Antenuptial incontinence is the charge. Where is it written that a man must keep an adulterous wife?'

'Yet I would query the evidence. Does the Law not require two or more witnesses in such matters?'

'We have heard the testimony of two.'

'Yet the eunuch was privy only to confidences. He cannot be held to be a witness.'

'Why does the king say nothing?' Mariamme whispers. She presses her eye to the door, where there is a knot-hole just wide enough to glimpse the chamber. Herod is silent and remote on his throne. He cannot admit that Mariamme is a flame he longs to douse, and so he gives the impression that he is subject to the Law and must await their verdict.

A small scuffle, a series of groans. Mariamme steps back from the peep hole then looks again. 'Bar Ahab is on his feet.'

Bar Ahab, that ancient incontinent, who seemed to walk with the angel of Death, has got to his feet. His voice is like an eddy of sand against rock. 'The matter of the divorce is without relevance. Mariamme is a queen of royal blood and cannot therefore be divorced.'

There is silence. Mariamme is still standing with her face to the door, though she is no longer looking through the peep hole. Without divorce Herod will be forced to go through his life with the ghost of his wife presiding from her empty chair during every banquet, audience or reception.

The affected voice pipes up again. 'The people will never tolerate the thought of the queen in exile. They will rise up. Everything you have built will be torn down. They will trample upon your name, your deeds.' Not a friend then. This is surely a voice lubricated by Salome's gold.

Ben Fabus' voice is a deep well of sadness as he announces, 'Then we need only consider *the charge of conspiring against the king's life.'*

Mariamme stops listening. She does not look through the peep hole again, not even when the shrill cries of a local woman, known to some as Hagar the witch and to others as Hagar the poisoner, is questioned about the advice she gave to the queen concerning the properties of deadly plants. Poison, there is no more unforgivable threat you can make against Herod. He still wakes with the sight of his father's empty eyes staring down at him. Had an assassin been sent, sword in hand, he might yet have found some subtle route to reconciliation. But not for poison, never poison. Only someone who understood his deepest fears would choose to use poison.

When they call her she already knows. She walks into the centre of the chamber in shocked silence, which will later be described as her dignity. As the sentence is passed she tries to look at Herod, but neither of them can meet the other's eyes, as though it is all some embarrassing scandal in which they are both complicit.

Only when she learns the form of her death does she reach out for her mother's hand. But Alexandra is not there; she has fallen behind, and Mariamme grasps at air. So now she takes her maid's hand, clutches it like a frightened child. Mariamme is twenty six years old and her life is already over.

—Wait! Here comes ugliness. Alexandra is trying to save her own skin. 'Wretch!' she screams, tearing at her daughter's hair and slapping her face. 'Do you dare turn upon the king, who has been our benefactor? How great is my grief that you ever issued from my womb.' She is growing theatrical in her turn of phrase. Mariamme does nothing to defend herself, only stands looking at her mother with a sad kind of knowing, as if it is more than her life she is losing that day.

And now there is no time to think. Everything is in fragments. Alexandra's self-pitying bleats die away as a Temple Levite drags her off. Two stone-faced guards approach the queen, hands on their sword hilts, as though she is a dangerous animal, who might spring forward and tear them to pieces. At the sight of them Herod grips the gilded arms of his throne, as if he will rise, as if he will put a stop to all this madness. But no, he stays. And Mariamme stands, like a moth with its wings folded, until the moment when her fingers disentangle from the fingers of her maid, and with a final squeeze, she finds herself alone and surrounded by enemies.

They talk later of her 'dignity', her 'royal demeanour'. But those are the writers of legends. The same authors will claim that Herod mourned his wife so greatly, he embalmed her body in wild honey. But, here and now, Mariamme is a woman of fragile flesh, who, in that instant, realises that all her favours, her beauty and her immaculate lineage, have led only here, to death.

She starts back and looks about, as though searching for a means of escape or a champion to defend her cause. And, only close up, does the maid see what others can't, that Mariamme has been playing a part her entire life, and has only just woken up.

The guards are on either side, but Mariamme cannot move. In Greek legend this is the moment when she would transform into a laurel tree or a swan. But the Almighty is not given to these transmigratory discretions. And Mariamme remains rooted to the spot by the force of her own sheer terror. There is not a sound in the chamber. The guards exchange a look of unease; this is still a queen. But Mariamme cries out suddenly, 'What of the children?' and makes as if to bolt in the direction of the king. This is all that is needed. The guards grasp her under the arms and look towards Herod. The king's face is sick and pale, but he does not countermand the order, and so they half escort, half drag Mariamme away.

When they reach the end of the chamber, two Levites spring forward to open the doors and the room is suddenly flooded with the warm familiar rays of the sun. For an instant Mariamme and the guards are caught in silhouette then they are gone. The queen is gone, and all that is left is the resounding clang of the door as it swings shut and cuts off the light.

Part III

The Queen of Heaven

28

Pheroras releases an avarshina

Y OU SHALL HAVE NO GODS *before me. So the Law tells us. Yet in ancient days it is known that the Almighty was not alone in his heavens. Some say He had a wife, and that she was worshipped as the Queen of Heaven in groves sacred to her name until she was chased away by men who saw the image of divinity only in their own reflection.*

Yet we, the descendents of a jealous god, did not entirely forget her. This loving mother goddess is still there, still visible between the letters of our Law.

Once she was worshipped in the form of a living tree, and still her form is visible in the shape of the menorah, the sacred candlestick that represents the tree of life, and there she is again in the story of creation, in her lonely place at the centre of paradise, her branches laden with the heavy burden of knowledge, both good and evil.

Great Goddess, Fecund One. She was mother to seventy sons and wet-nurse to kings. We honoured her in Israel, laying sweetened cakes upon her altars, for she is a wise one, this earthy goddess of the earth, and her love is boundless. How kind she seems, how infinite her charity. But it is not so simple. It is never so simple. Here, in this corner of the world where the dried bones of the earth stick through, a goddess wears more than one face. Those who look upon her gentle smile, her warm and giving breasts, would do well to remember this same goddess can bring death. She stands on the backs of lions with writhing serpents in her hands. She commands the sea. She is an engulfer, a swallower of men.

INTERLUDE, 4 BCE

Herod's condition is worsening. Since the failure of the hot springs he has fallen into despondency. He cannot bear the light, and the heaviest drapes, lined with the thick Galilean fleeces, have to be pulled across the windows at all times. Salome has ordered there to be no more than two candles lit in his chamber, and still he cringes if the smallest illumination falls on his face.

He has begun to see the dead. His father and brothers come to him at night, ghastly, blood-stained. They tell him that they are disappointed in him, that he failed to save them. Then he is piteous and calls for his mother, but she does not come. Of late he has been seen clutching at his throat, meaningless words garbling and frothing from his lips.

What do you see, Herod? Is it your wife? Lovely Mariamme, who is lovely no more. Not even beauty such as hers could stand the strangler's rope. Is that what you are thinking of, my king, your wife tied to a chair, her dark curls hacked off to allow the executioner free reign at

208

her neck.

Did they bring you descriptions of her face, the tendons stretched to breaking point, her tongue protruding between her lips, like an obscene jeer at fate? Tell me, does she come to you now, Herod, with bulging tortured veins on her forehead and blood running down her nose, and a wide appalled expression in her exploding eyes? Tell me this is how she comes and this is how you see her each time you go to sleep.

From the foot of the bed Salome watches. She is so rigid and still it is possible to forget she is there. Then she bites her lip or frowns and suddenly you remember.

'Brother?' Herod is clutching at his neck again. 'I have done what you asked.' He does not seem to hear her, but Salome presses on. 'They are all there, in the hippodrome. The most prominent men in the land. As you wished it.' Herod moans then murmurs Mariamme's name or possibly it is AemaA he says, mother. Salome's chins wobble; she is near tears. 'Herod. Brother, the soldiers are holding the men captive. Do you truly mean they should be executed once you are gone? Think, there are good men amongst them, men who have never spoken out against you.'

—My, my. This is dangerous even for Salome to say.—

'They have families, loved ones. I am so tired of death. If there is any pity left in your heart, order their release.'

Herod's eyelids flutter, but he does not respond. And with a great sigh that shakes the flesh at her shoulders, Salome leaves the room.

But we cannot let this lie. We must know. Here now at Herod's side, bend forward and search that ravaged face. 'Is there, Herod? Is there pity left in your heart?' His eyelids lift slowly, and, with visible effort, he focuses on my face. He holds my gaze and lets me look deep into those burning pupils. Is there pity there? No? Good.

28 BCE

It was in Samaria that Herod first fell ill. The news reached Loshema in Pheroras' appartments, as she sorted through his wife's belongings, still packed in chests unpacked since their arrival a week earlier. And her first thoughts, after hearing the breathless page boy gasping out his summons, was, *how has it taken so long?*

They went to Herod's chamber at once, Pheroras, his wife and the slaves who had been in attendance. On the way there Pheroras' wife said, 'It was madness to let him go hunting in this weather.'

Pheroras gave a shrug. 'How little you know my brother. I might more easily have held back the rain.'

Salome was already there, kneeling beside the bed and she got to her feet when they entered the room.

'This is your doing.'

Loshema saw Pheroras stiffen. He shook his head. 'I did only what you asked.'

'Did I ask for this?' Salome jabbed a finger at the figure in the bed, so frail and still, it hardly seemed possible that this was Herod. His lips were moving, and she fell to her knees again. The voice was rasping, but Loshema made out the words clearly.

'Am I poisoned?'

Salome dipped a cloth in a bowl of warm water then dabbed it gently at his temples. 'No, not poisoned. The physicians are certain of it.'

'Then I am cursed.'

'No, not that. Never that.'

But Herod groaned and pushed her hand away. He tried to prop himself up on his elbows, looking about him with a kind of dazed bewilderment. 'This is not Jerusalem.'

'No, brother.' Pheroras had found his voice. 'There is plague in Jerusalem. That is why we came here.'

Herod nodded, and for a moment seemed comforted then his eyes grew wild again. 'My friends … all dead. The city … they are saying Jerusalem is dying while the king is out hunting and feasting in Samaria.'

'Hush. You could not stay in Jerusalem.' Salome attempted to soothe, as though a moment ago she had not accused Pheroras of being behind the move. 'What good would it do to stay behind and die of plague? A kingdom must have a king.'

'The Almighty destroys my kingdom. He destroys me.'

'It is not so. Is it, Pheroras?'

'It is not,' Pheroras agreed. But, standing behind him, Loshema saw him secretly make Cypros' sign to ward off evil.

That evening Loshema went to find Pheroras. It was not easy to pick her way through the unfamiliar colonnades and courtyards. With the king ill, few lamps had been lit, and the great pools of darkness that lay between the pillars had an evil expectancy about them. Hesitantly, she made her way through the gloom, afraid yet determined, holding to her breast, like an infant, a napkin covering a round loaf and some thick yellow cheese.

She found Pheroras, as she had expected, in one of the tower rooms, in which their host kept his library, a room he boasted, which contained no fewer than twelve books. Pheroras was sitting on a bench gazing at a scroll, which depicted a large ornate building. 'The Temple in Solomon's day,' he said, as though they had been in the middle of a conversation. 'It is surely not a true representation. Even the temples in the great Aegyptus are not so grand.'

'I brought you food.' She laid the napkin on the table, careful to avoid the unrolled scroll. 'You were not at supper.'

A shadow passed across Pheroras' face. 'Was my absence noted?'

Loshema began slicing the cheese with the knife Pheroras used to break wax seals. 'They talk of nothing but the king.' A pang in her chest prevented her from adding, that Pheroras figured so little in the game of power that no-one had mentioned him.

'Do they talk of the queen?'

Loshema gave a tight little nod, raising one shoulder in an attempt to suggest the talk was inconsequential.

'For all their courtesy they must hate him.' Pheroras began rolling up the scroll. Then after a pause, 'You, too, must hate him.'

Loshema concentrated on the cutting of the cheese. Did she hate him? What had Mariamme meant to her or, more importantly, what had she meant to Mariamme, a woman who could seek her advice one day and forget she existed the next. Yet there was still that last squeeze of her hand. At night her fingers sometimes tingled with the memory. Her silence had gone on too long.

'You do not understand him as I do. He had no choice.'

Unable to bring herself to answer, Loshema banged the knife down on the table. It was a gesture that might have earned her a flogging, but Pheroras only lifted a piece of the bread, as though that might appease her, continuing gently, 'It was not enough for him to be king and master over her. He loved her so deeply that he needed his love to be returned.'

Loshema, who was stiffly arranging the bread and cheese, did not notice the particular intensity that Pheroras put on these words. Only later, in the fullness of time would she replay this scene and see what she had missed. Pheroras went on, 'You see a ruler, a king, but Mariamme often looked at him with disdain. She called him the half-Jew behind his back. And knowing, as he did, that she might have married a great and powerful prince, he always felt unworthy of her.'

Loshema turned sharply. 'Do you hold bread or do you eat it?'

Pheroras blinked and glanced down at the hunk still in his hand. Absently he took a bite then continued almost pleadingly, 'Doubt is a disease with my brother. There is something fertile in his mind that makes its seeds flourish. Over time he came to believe that if she could not love him, she must be compelled to kill him.'

Loshema stared. 'You are suggesting that he murdered her to prove himself undeserving of love?' Pheroras only spread his hands in that universal gesture of futility then hung his head.

When Herod returns to Jerusalem he finds he is entering a city of death. No-one comes out to greet him, and his scouts tell him that the bodies pile up so high that they cannot be buried within the customary period. Expressionless Herod nods and gives his litter-bearers —he is still too weak to ride— instructions to bear him to the Antonia fortress, the great grey fortress, which he had built upon the Temple mount, and in happier times dedicated to his now dead friend, Mark Antony.

They ride past wailing women and past men dragging corpse-laden carts towards the Kidron Valley gateway. His subjects do not greet him, but move silently and determinedly, their eyes staring blankly ahead. And everywhere that Herod goes he sees death and hears of death and thinks of death so that he might be any underworld king, Nergal, Aita, Osiris, returning, unloved, to his dismal throne.

That he has returned at all is miracle enough. For a week he hovered on the brink, indifferent to the pleadings of Salome and Pheroras. But gradually his senses returned and his breathing eased. The king is not dead. Long live the king.

But if Death is done with Herod, Herod is not done with death. The bones of his skull are visible through the sunken flesh on his face, but his eyes burn hotly in their sockets. He calls for his scribes and his first act is to sign Alexandra's death warrant. O yes. Alexandra has been up to her old tricks.

With her son gone, her daughter gone, you might think the life has been bled out of her, but, even as she lies clutching her wounds, she never takes her eyes off the throne. There is a quality of ruthlessness that appears at least once in each generation of the Hasmonaeans, and she is the embodiment of it. While Herod hovered between life and death, she almost had Jerusalem under her control. And even as they drag her through the streets to the place of death, she cannot believe that this monstrosity, this half-Jew has risen from the dead to destroy her.

But Herod is not finished.

Pheroras was not a man given easily to anger. He did not shout or rage as his siblings did. Yet, watching his hands curl around the scroll upon his desk, wringing the life from it as he thought he had living flesh beneath his fingers, Loshema understood that it was frustration, not sadness, that brimmed in his eyes and rolled down his cheeks.

'Master, what is wrong?' For all that they had grown closer over the years, she still did not address him by his name. Yet she liked to feel that she spoke it in a uniquely tender manner, quite without the drop of acid that laced her normal pronunciation, and made Salome stare at her with narrowed eyes.

Pheroras shook his head and wiped a hand down the side of his face. 'The king has issued warrants against Costobarus.'

Costobarus, the second husband of Salome. That she had grown tired of him was an ill-kept secret. She flaunted her distaste openly. Yet Costobarus clung to his connection with the king and would not grant a divorce.

'A warrant,' Loshema repeated. 'On what grounds?'

'That he has been harbouring the sons of Baba.'

Her hand flew to her mouth. If this was true then Salome would be a free woman in a matter of days. Had these men not rallied to Antigonus' side when Herod came to claim Jerusalem? They were Hasmonaeans, and with Alexandra gone, their claim to the throne was considerably strengthened. Rumours of their survival had abounded for years, but now it was clear.

Costobarus was known for his attempts to ride the wind in both directions. Despite Herod's generosity he had made an ally of Cleopatra, and it was clear that he intended to have powerful friends should Herod fall from grace. And was Herod ever more weakened, unloved, without a queen, even Death, it seemed, did not want him. Loshema bit her lower lip. 'How did the king find out?'

'Salome knew. She let it slip.'

'What word ever fell from Salome's mouth that she did not first craft?'

Pheroras looked up sharply. 'That is my sister of whom you speak.'

'Yes master. Of course, master. How right you are, master.'

'Loshema, do not play the humble servant. It does not suit you. Salome did right to tell him. It was only a pity she did not speak sooner. But now my brother is falling into such a pit of despair that I fear he will pull his entire kingdom down with him.'

'You must go to him, reason with him.'

Pheroras pushed the crumpled scroll at Loshema. 'Would you have me write my own warrant?'

Loshema looked at him helplessly. Pheroras, dear Pheroras, who was her only true friend in the world. Could he possibly think she wished him dead? And he was right, to question Herod was to condemn yourself. Why, why was she always sharp where other women were soft? She tried to say something that would take back her words, but Pheroras had turned away.

Yet only a few days later Pheroras changed his mind. Loshema was with him when he entered Herod's apartments. Herod was seated, or more accurately, slumped, on a chair while one of his Greek boys worked on his beard, combing and perfuming it. Pheroras addressed the boy, 'Get out.'

The youth's eyes widened and he glanced towards the king. A little fire flared in Herod's eyes then quickly died. He dismissed the youth then, taking the towel from his neck, turned to Pheroras. 'What troubles you, brother?'

'These.' He snatched the papers Loshema had been carrying and proffered them under Herod's nose. 'These are warrants for more than a dozen men's lives.'

'Traitors.'

'And where is the evidence? Every man knows that all he must do to rid himself of an enemy is whisper, conspiracy.'

'Do you question my judgement?'

Loshema, who had been keeping her eyes on the floor, glanced up in fright. This was too far surely? Pheroras paused, his Adam's apple bobbing in and out before he drew in breath and went on. 'I question, not your judgement, but your loneliness. You have turned your backs against us all. You sit alone upon your throne and shut your ears to those who love you.'

Herod's silence went on so long that Loshema dared to observe him from beneath lowered lashes. In the last few weeks he had recovered somewhat from his illness yet still there was something skeletal about his face. He looked like one of the hermits, who crawled out of the desert from time to time, after forty or so days of deprivation, fleshless, inhuman, scorched to the soul. And when he spoke, he spoke like those inspired madmen, his voice trembling in the way that the earth trembles before it releases its pain, 'Take a close look at me, brother. I am almost in my sixth decade. Older than when father died. And in that time I have outlived a tyrant. I have outlived a goddess. And surely I have outlived the need to love.'

The silence that followed was so profound it felt like a weight on the back of Loshema's head, and she began to fear that the noise of her beating heart would be taken for impudence. But eventually Pheroras lifted his head and speaking with quiet authority, said, 'I cannot believe that the Almighty spared you for no reason. You have purpose yet on this earth. I am certain of it.'

Herod gave a long and mirthless laugh. 'You were ever a fool, brother.' But he said it gently, almost kindly.

But Pheroras, who so rarely insisted on the last word, shook his head. 'That I am a fool may only be the truth. But the Romans are no fools. They made you a king because they saw in you someone unique. Someone set apart. You are an *avarshina*, Herod, the same bird the Greeks call the phoenix. Does Job not claim this quality when he says, *I shall die in my nest, but then I shall multiply my days as the sand.*' Pheroras leaned forward and laid his hand on Herod's shoulder. 'Time and again the world will think you destroyed, brother, but I know you better than yourself. You will rise up; you will build anew.'

29

Pheroras' Wife

THE DECADE 29 BCE … 20BCE

*I*T IS THERE FOR ALL *to see, Herod's great amphitheatre, the curving walls rising, like a mirage, from the plain. As soon as it comes into view Herod reigns in his horse and allows the royal litter a chance to come along side. He waits while the curtains are drawn back.*
'You see,' *he says.* 'It is as I described. Better.'

Building is the king's new passion. All over the country, at Masada, Sebaste, Herodium, fortresses, palaces and towns are being erected. He names his soaring structures Hyrcania, Mariamme, Kypros, as though he hopes to make eternal that which is gone forever. Little wonder the length and breadth of the empire, they are affectionately calling him —and some not so affectionately— the Jewish Pharaoh.

Mariamme sticks her head through the gap in the curtains and squints in the glare. 'It is wonderful, my dear. Truly, a marvel.'

—No, do not rub your eyes. I did indeed say, Mariamme, but look more closely. After building, the king's new passion is for wives. Not queens. He won't make that mistake twice. This is Mariamme II, his fourth, or is it fifth, wife? She has auburn hair and eyes like melting ambers. The poets proclaim that the king and Mariamme fell in love with each other at first sight, while the cynics grumble that her ambitious father used her as a pawn to win the High Priesthood. Herod does not even bother paying lip service to this sacred office now. Everyone knows the High Priest is Herod's man, and he can be replaced at the king's whim.

This new Mariamme falls back on her cushions. The day is hot and she would rather be sitting near one of the cooling fountains at the heart of the palace built for her by Herod. 'I cannot bear this heat,' *she says, fanning herself then she pouts, like a little girl, and Herod, who has enough years under his belt to be her grandfather, feels his heart beat a little faster.*

'It is only a little further.'

'I cannot stand it.' *She makes a face. It is the same face she made when she could not bear to have Mariamme's sons strutting about the palace, overshadowing her own son.* 'Send them to Rome,' *she pleaded.* 'Boys should be educated abroad. It is good for them.'

Now in the sunshine Herod looks down into that perfectly heart-shaped face. 'Only a little further.'

'I cannot.'

He considers anger. But, perhaps it is for the best. This amphitheatre, with its nude gymnasts and its wild, prowling beasts, is a harsh enough blow to those pious Jews who preach against pagan extravagance. Perhaps it is not the time to parade his consort too much in the Roman mould.

'Very well. As you know, I can refuse you nothing.'

She simpers and blows him a secret kiss. As the litter turns Herod watches, and something in the way it hastens away from him leaves him feeling lonely. He misses his sons so far away in Rome. And, for the first time in a long while, he thinks of his eldest son, still in exile with his mother, Doris. Antipater will be a man now. But what kind of man? He shakes the thought from him, and turns his horse to ride on. In the distance, a figure emerges from the amphitheatre and begins riding towards them at full tilt, the beast's hooves sending up clouds of ochre-coloured dust from the road. Herod exchanges a look with one of his German bodyguards. 'Who is that man?'

—Ah, but I won't tell you yet. I am not part of this scene, and I have taken too many liberties. Come, we will return to Herod's beautiful new palace, and witness how I learned the fate of the man riding towards Herod with such haste.—

Loshema did not know that she had been asleep until the sound of a commotion in the central courtyard made her jerk upright. She had been spinning wool with Pheroras' wife, and making a show of joining the other maids in singing to accompany the work. But her mind wandered far and free across countless dunes of sand to the halls of the great library of Alexandria, which Pheroras had described to her so many times in glowing terms. 'It contains more than seven hundred thousand scrolls,' he had said. 'And that is even after the store houses were accidentally burned by Julius Caesar.'

The thought that she would never have the chance to see the library with her own eyes made her ache inside, and she had to fix her eyes on the amber whorl to prevent tears from welling up. But the whorl was hypnotic, and she was drawn into a kind of waking slumber by the subtle fascination of its rotation. Then there were shouts and running footsteps, and suddenly everyone was on their feet.

The maids rushed to the window, though Pheroras' wife sat down again almost at once. 'Calm! Do we cackle, like a gaggle of geese? You —this at the tallest girl— describe what is happening.'

Loshema turned. 'It is the king's party. They have returned early from the theatre. Something has surely gone wrong.'

For answer Pheroras' wife began to cough. She had begun to cough these days and there were dark circles under her eyes.

'I will fetch you a tincture of rosemary and liquorice,' Loshema suggested. But the older woman shook her head. 'Not now. Go, find out what you can.'

Needing no second bidding, Loshema bounded from the room with unmaidenly swiftness and threw herself down the tower steps to reach the central courtyard.

There were more people than ever flooding into the quad, but her height was to her advantage and she had a clear view of the king in the centre of the furore. Pheroras was at his side, though he made no attempt to acknowledge her, not even secretly, and this was strangeness in itself. Loshema felt herself jostled on either side, but she held her ground and strained forward to hear, sieving through the excited babble for nuggets of information. '… an attempt on the king's life.'

'… at the theatre doors. But he had warning.'

'The Almighty be praised. The king is alive.' A ragged cheer went up, which ended on something of a question mark when the king did not respond. Loshema saw Pheroras put his hand on his brother's shoulder, but Herod shook him off. There was a dangerous look in the king's eye. It made Loshema think of lines from the Aeneid, which she had just finished reading, *Now to the realm of light it lifts a cloud, Of pitch-black, whirling smoke, and fiery dust…*

Then Herod was pushing himself through the crowd, like a man who cannot breathe, and Pheroras was at his side, trying to hold back the forest of hands and arms threatening to engulf them. 'Stand back. Stand back. Let the king through.'

'You.'

Loshema felt a jolt go through her spine. The king had stopped but a few feet away. He regarded her with neither pleasure nor amusement. Was he remembering her at Mariamme's side? 'Whosoever seeks trouble need only look to where you stand.'

Tears welling up in her eyes, Loshema lowered her head. But Pheroras spoke hurriedly, 'Hush brother, this maid only rejoices in your fortunate escape.'

Herod did not look at Pheroras. Instead he took a step closer to Loshema, waiting until the pressure of his silence made her steal a peep through her lashes. 'Perhaps she should rejoice more in having made such powerful allies,' he said sourly before moving on.

She should not have followed. The king had shunned all company, save for his brother, even barking at his bodyguards to keep their distance. But whether this was because he felt secure back within the palace's thick walls, or because they, too, were under suspicion, no-one could say. But as he made his way through the colonnades, Pheroras at his side, Loshema could not help but slip into step a few paces behind. She was afraid for Pheroras. It was one thing to fall under the king's suspicion, but it was known that Herod reserved a special hatred for those who came to the defence of the accused.

Fortunately they were heading to the royal quarters, which was only the direction she should be taking, and her hearing was keen.

'And you say ben Eli brought you warning?'

Herod nodded. 'He took a horse and reached us before we made our entrance. They were waiting in the corridor to the royal pavilion. Ten or more led by a fanatic called bar Lamech.'

'The blind prophet?'

Herod drew up short and Loshema was forced to dart behind a column.

'Yes, brother. They would rather follow the blind than follow Herod.'

'It is not so.' Pheroras' voice had that quality of gentleness considered a weakness by both his siblings. 'They love and admire you. It is only that you are moving too swiftly. A palace hanging from a cliff; a great harbour where none existed? And if that was not enough, when the Almighty did not provide you with a location for a fortress you gathered up the earth and built the mountain yourself.'

Herod gave a mollified grunt and began to walk again. Pheroras matched his pace. 'The people recognize your patronage. But here, in Jerusalem, it is too much. A hippodrome at the centre of the city. An amphitheatre in honour of a pagan emperor, an emperor who is worshipped as a god no less. You are tearing down what the people hold dear, what they believe is their righteousness. If they believe a blind man sees further than a king, it is because they fear that you are turning from the Almighty, and they will suffer the consequences.'

Herod turned angrily. 'Am I to be made a fool of in my own kingdom? They have come to the games in honour of Caesar. They have watched wild beasts tearing men apart in the arena.'

'They have protested.'

'Indeed, they have protested. They have shaken their heads and tutted their disapproval. But was it enough to make them think to murder their king?'

Pheroras shook his head helplessly.

'Then what? You do not answer? I will tell you then. It was wooden poles.'

'Do not jest— '

'Look into my eyes, brother. Do I jest? All around the arena there were poles made of wood. They had been adorned in silks and decorated with displays of armour in honour of Caesar's triumphs. The fools mistook them for idols and their 'righteousness', as you call it, gave them a taste for blood.'

There was a silence, and Loshema almost dared to creep from behind the pillar when Herod went on in a low, despairing voice, 'We are a people who cherish freedom, who hold in our hearts our escape from the Great Aegyptus. Yet we are a little nation. Aegyptus still exists. And if I build theatres and hippodromes to appease Rome, I also build fortresses. Do you not see, Pheroras, I do not destroy their freedom; I preserve it.'

There was no chance for Pheroras to answer for the Captain of the Guard appeared, his face wearing the solemn mask of bearers of bad news. Herod was immediately alert. 'Speak!'

The man stood at attention. 'It is the spy, sire.'

'Ben Eli? The one who gave me warning.'

'Once you were gone, word got out. The crowd turned on him.'

Pheroras asked, 'Is he injured?'

The Captain of the Guard bent his head. 'They tore him to pieces.'

Some span of time later, Loshema was combing her mistress' hair when there was a knock at the door. Everyone froze. For days now the Antonia had been filled with screams.

The Captain of the Guard had rounded up a number of suspects. And when the men would not give up the names of those who betrayed ben Eli, the king ordered that their wives be tortured.

Pheroras had dared to argue and been banished from the king's sight for his troubles. Loshema had not seen him for days, and time and again found herself listening to the screams, terrified that she might recognize the timbre of his voice in one of them. But all she learned was that human pain is anonymous, and one frightened animal sounds very like the next.

But it was not the Captain of the Guard at the door, but a small slave, who bleated out a summons for Loshema to attend on Pheroras. She nearly sobbed with relief then threw her mistress a guilty glance. 'I must finish here first.'

'No.' the older woman reached up and took the comb from her. 'You must go. My husband has called you.'

'At once, lady. As you will it.' She was speaking extravagantly to cover the pang in her chest when she met her mistress' eyes. Each time Pheroras sent for her, which he did increasingly, she was afraid that Pheroras' wife would choose to put an end to it. Yet she said nothing, only watched Loshema with sad eyes and went back to her spinning. Loshema often wondered if she knew that he was faithful, that in the strict sense of it he had not betrayed her. He did little enough to show it. His neglect was common gossip. And Loshema longed to offer that small morsel of reassurance. He does not touch me, she wanted to say. But the words sounded incredible, even to her own ears.

She pondered the conundrum as she hurried up the stone staircase, remembering how she had waited, with a mixture of fear and longing, year after year, but he went on treating her as a dear child who shared his passion for the written word. Yet, when she caught sight of herself in her mistress' mirror, the swelling of her bosom and the planes of her face, revealed a little more with each season that passed, she knew herself to be no child. She was a slave who did not think like a slave. She was a woman yet she was a scholar. She was a marvellous animal who had no place in the world of earthly things, and, now she thought of it, perhaps it was little wonder that Pheroras was indifferent to her charms.

She found him in the library. He looked up and smiled to see her in the doorway, understanding her fractional hesitation at the threshold, how she was allowing her senses to fill with that curious combination of intimacy and strangeness, dry rustling scents, leather, papyrus, ink. But when, after a moment, she still had not moved, he looked at her curiously.

'I thought ...,' she began. 'I feared ... When you angered the king ... '

A cloud cleared from his face. 'Do not fear my brother. He would never hurt his own flesh and blood. *(—Remember this!—)* He spread his arms. 'Come.' And she hurried inside.

The room was stuffy. Behind Pheroras the window was thrown open to allow a thin, nuzzling breeze to enter, which did practically nothing at all to lower the temperature. As she approached, she noted that several scrolls were already lying on the floor. Cushions, too, had been roughly consigned to a corner and more scrolls lay across the benches where they usually sat. Loshema laughed. 'Are we to work standing?'

Pheroras gave the chaos a distracted glance. 'There is a great deal to do.'

She laughed again. 'What has happened? Are we expecting an angel of the Lord to pay a visit?'

'His name is Nicolaus of Damascus. And he is no angel.'

Her smile disappeared. 'Then what is he?'

'A tutor to Cleopatra's children and a distinguished academician. And now my brother has offered him patronage in Judea.'

Still the name meant nothing to her, and Pheroras went on, while he put a selection of scrolls in order, managing in the process to send more fluttering to the floor. 'He is prolific in his works, a philosopher and the author of numerous respected commentaries.' Pheroras attempted to catch a scroll that the breeze had twitched from his grasp, but it escaped over the desk's edge and he gave up on it. 'He has penned a treatise on Plato's allegories and several commentaries on Aristotle. He is also known for his plays, comedies and tragedies. And there is a rumour that he is working on a vast universal history.'

Loshema bent down and began retrieving the fallen scrolls. 'And he has found time in all that to visit Judea. We should be honoured.'

Pheroras did not smile. 'He has expressed a wish to see our library and the king is anxious to make a good impression. There is talk of a memoir.' And seeing her confusion he added, 'There is quite a fashion for it now. Great men understand the need to get their version of events inscribed before their deaths. History, as they say is rarely written by friends.'

He turned away, and she sensed that, anxious as he was about the Greek's arrival, he was also hurt that his brother should turn to a stranger to compose his memoirs.'

Just then a slave appeared at the door, and in one of those moments weighted with premonition, Loshema was glad the scene was as it should be, and she was down on her knees, simply a slave gathering fallen scrolls. The slave bowed to Pheroras and requested that he join his wife.

Frowning, Pheroras shook his head. 'I am busy at work. Tell her I will be along shortly.'

'She said you would say that, sir. And I was to tell you to come at once.'

Pheroras stiffened, and Loshema felt her heart miss a beat. She scrambled to her feet. 'I must go to my lady.'

'No. Stay here! I will return shortly.'

Loshema flushed. She opened her mouth, as if to argue then closed it again, watching mutely as he left the room.

Once he was gone a wave of dizziness washed over her. This was the moment she had feared all these years to give shape to, the moment when her mistress finally opened her eyes and was displeased by what she saw. She tried to imagine what had happened, but it would not play sensibly in her head.

In the past, whenever she had tried to create the scene, she had always supposed being in the room at the moment of reckoning, using her clever tongue to talk herself out of danger. Or sometimes, if she was feeling dramatic, she thought of herself on her knees, martyred, allowing blame to be heaped entirely on her head, Pheroras watching from a corner with his sad brown eyes, regretting he had not done more to save her. But none of her musings had her as she was now, left behind and overlooked. She began to go over every nuance of speech and manner when she had last attended Pheroras' wife. Had some slip, some eager look, given her away?

She fell to her knees again and began gathering up the scrolls. Pheroras would want them in order, and perhaps this was the last time she would ever be allowed to touch them. Her fingers froze and she could not bring herself to continue. She got to her feet and began pacing. Of course, it could be nothing. After all, everyone knew that the flames of invention are fanned by a guilty conscience.

An hour passed. And then another one. She began to feel angry. Perhaps, after all, it was none of her doing. Might Pheroras, with his clumsy manners and clumsier tongue, not have given the game away? A careless word? A glance that lingered too long. It would be just like him to address his wife by Loshema's name. It was only a miracle that he had not done it sooner. And now everything was lost.

She wept a little then, and another hour passed in self-pity. But, after a while, even that became tedious. Opening the first scroll she had to hand she tried to read, but the words would not stay still. She got up and peeped out of the door. There was nothing to see but the stone staircase and a patch of light that led out to the courtyard.

She fell asleep in a corner of the room, her back against the heaped cushions, and when she woke it was dark. For a moment she forgot where she was until a cold awareness opened in her mind, and shivering, she got to her feet and lit a lamp. There was a jug of wine on the table, which miraculously Pheroras had not managed to spill, and she downed a cup feeling its strength seep through her stiffened limbs. Was she forgotten? All the intimacy, all the shared moments, what had they meant if she could be cast off at a moment's notice?

The answer lurked, like a dark shadow, below the surface of her consciousness, an insistent prickling behind her temples. Slave. A memory of her mother flashed into her mind, her mother smiling and nodding, certain that her eldest, Gomer, would not live a life of bondage because her father had deigned to give her a name. A name, Loshema now understood, born of irony and jest. And how was she, Loshema, any different? She was just another slave living off crumbs.

The blackness of the sky was cracking open on a grey line of dawn before Loshema heard footsteps approaching. She had vowed tearfully during the hours of blackness that she would treat Pheroras with aloofness. She would play the slave, respectful and distant, bowing, obeying without question, staring blankly at the ground when spoken to. But when she heard the footsteps she ran to the door and flung it wide.

It was not Pheroras, but one of the household slaves, who saw her dishevelled state and said disdainfully, 'You are to return to your master's quarters at once.'

'But my mistress?'

The slave looked at her strangely. 'Your mistress is dead.'

30

In which the king's wishes are thwarted by his brother

20 BCE

Yes dead. All around me life snuffing out, like candles. Had my mistress known she was dying? That dry, rustling cough that sounded like leaves blowing over a grave, and, now I think of it, hadn't she grown more still over the last months, rarely walking in the gardens as she once had, choosing rather to pray for long hours in private. One of the older maids, who treated me always with a thinly disguised hostility, was overheard whispering that her mistress had attended a Greek physician several times, but what he told her she confided to no-one.

And so she died. On the day I languished in the tower library, full of my own preoccupations and slighted dignity, my sweet, kind lady began to cough up strings of black sticky blood and could not stop. She called for her husband, but was unconscious by the time he got there. The physician was sent for, but there was nothing he could do. And so she died as she lived, a quiet woman who caused no ripples on the surface of humanity, and sank down beneath it almost unnoticed.

No, don't look at me like that. My arrogance has been the undoing of me more than once. And I fear that the cup of my follies is not yet full. I took my leave, carelessly that morning, with no thought but that she would be there when I returned, sitting in her chair, spinning her wool and singing softly to herself. Now she was gone, and it was a harsh reminder of how we walk constantly in the shadow of the angel of Death.

Herod's son, Antipater, once said that life is akin to looking up at the night sky and watching the stars go out one by one. No matter how attentively you kept vigil it would be impossible to tell which one would go out next. But, though he was right about many things, in this particular matter I must tell you, he was wrong. There are times when we do not wait, but reach up and pluck a star from the heavens and extinguish its light for ourselves.

But we are not here to philosophize. You will shed no tears over a woman who died millennia ago and I have shed too many. Let us move along. The days that follow my mistress' death are a mixture of formality and chaos. The funeral is dealt with without fuss or fanfare. Pheroras weeps a little, but his clothes are rent only for form's sake; he pours no ashes on his head, and the loudest wailing comes from her maids for a slave's fortunes follow that of her mistress.

Two of the maids are lucky —or perhaps unlucky enough— to join Salome's household. But one, a pretty dark-eyed Hibernian, is sold beyond the palace to a wealthy Pharisee, who

223

took a fancy to her. Rumour has it that the Pharisee's wife took less kindly to the new addition,
and she has found herself consigned to the kitchens, scrubbing pots.

And me? What has happened to me? For that we must leap forward and at the same
time backwards. Quickly now I will meet you again in the tower library. It is a different day
and Pheroras has been a widower a week. You see, I have not travelled very far since we last
met, but I am about to travel beyond my wildest dreams. Yes, yes, I am speaking in riddles,
and it is a poor writer who tells what should be shown. Better to see for yourself.—

Seven days had passed and the official period of mourning was over. And not once had
Pheroras sent for Loshema or, indeed, met her gaze, not even when she was alone sorting
through her mistress' things and glanced up to find him standing on the threshold. He had
been watching her bent head, but the moment she raised her eyes he turned away and closed
the door. For a while she took his behaviour to be no more than a mirror to her own guilt
and distress. But, as the days wore on, it became clear it was more than that, and that he was
deliberately going out of his way to avoid her.

She grew more lonely and frightened, and wished she had a friend to confide in. But it
came to her that she had distanced herself from the friendship of her peers. The other maids
were stout, loyal women, but they were illiterate, and their gossip and endless superstitions
left Loshema cold and unmoved. She was quiet in their presence, slightly aloof in her manner, which, she realised with a pang, was probably the reason her mistress had warmed to
her, at least in the beginning. But now she was alone again, and her life seemed destined to
remain an empty desert where all that grew there withered and died.

On the seventh day of mourning she sat with the maids, watching them chatter with a
mixture of excitement and fear, wondering what their new lives had in store for them.

'And you?' one asked Loshema. 'What is to be your fate?'

'I await word,' she said carefully. But one of the older maids eyed her shrewdly. 'The
king's brother has surely spoken to you.'

Loshema shifted uncomfortably and did not answer. She kept her eyes on the floor,
knowing that looks were being exchanged over her head. Then a sharp-faced maid added,
'Of course our betters have more important things to worry about than the fate of a slave. It
is a blessing that we have each other.'

It was a cruel barb, crueller still for the sting of truth within it. For wasn't it known that
Loshema had always sought out her betters, first Mariamme then Pheroras; it was rumoured
that she had even spoken directly to the king. A proud slave, who had looked beyond her
station, and now she was to be discarded and passed along, like the rest of her mistress'
household items. The other maids looked at her pityingly, and suddenly she could stand it
no longer. Getting to her feet she headed for the door. At her back one of the maids called,
'Wait! Where are you going?' But another one insisted, 'O, let her go. She'll learn soon
enough.'

There was an almost dream-like quality in the air as she crossed the courtyard then made her way up the warm limestone stairs through cool pools of shadow until she reached the door to the tower library. She lifted her fist to knock then changed her mind. With a hand that trembled so much that the door handle rattled in her palm, she eased it open and took a step inside. The room greeted her, like a contented sigh. All was as it should be, slanting columns of light, the sharp tang of ink and wax, the dry smell of papyrus beneath. And Pheroras. Pheroras was sitting, where he always sat behind his desk, his shoulders hunched, his nose buried in a scroll.

She had not rehearsed what she was going to say, and now she could think of nothing better than, 'I have come.'

She waited for his reaction. He barely looked up. 'Yes. Good. I have promised Nicolaus of Damascus details of our family history for his biography. I wish you to transcribe them for me. I do not mind admitting that your hand now exceeds mine for neatness.' He gave a false sort of laugh then patted a fresh papyrus on the desk. Loshema let her glance follow his hand, but when she looked back at his face, he had already lowered his gaze and was engrossed in the document he had been reading when she entered the room.

She hesitated a moment, feeling that she had missed something then sat down beside him at the desk and lifted her pen. How often had they sat like that, almost touching, the closeness of their bodies an exquisite torture? But now the shape of Pheroras' dead wife was between them, and they sat in uncomfortable postures avoiding one another's gaze.

Suddenly, with no warning Pheroras slammed down the stylus he had been using with such force it broke in two. In panic Loshema got to her feet. 'I will fetch another.'

'No.'

She sat back down and lowered her gaze to the floor. She heard Pheroras get up and begin pacing the room. 'If I take you as you are now they will call you a whore, like your mother.'

Loshema stared at him. The way he was speaking, so matter-of-fact, talking of 'taking her', as though they were discussing an obscure point of philosophy. And suddenly she did not recognise the man, who stood staring coldly across the room, as her own dear Pheroras. Panic seized her again and she scrambled to her feet.

'You must not— ' she began. But he started pacing again, speaking as if to himself. 'Yet, if I free you, you could not stay here. You have no family, no position.'

Loshema felt her legs go weak and she reached out to the table for support. Pheroras had stopped pacing, and now he looked at her over his shoulder. 'I am a rich man. I would see to it that you lived in comfort.' His expression grew hopeful. 'I would come to you.'

And now it was her turn to grow cold. 'You would come until your wife put a stop to it.'

Ugly red patches appeared on his cheeks, as though he had been slapped. 'I will not marry again.'

'The king will insist.' And fury made her add, 'You are not the man to gainsay him.'

He was in front of her in three strides. The gentleness of Pheroras often made people forget that he was a tall man, and for a split second she thought he would strike her or grab her shoulders and shake her. Instead, he took her arms then he sank to the floor on his knees, his head pressed into the soft flesh of her belly. 'I must have you. I must. I have played the dutiful son long enough. There must be a way. I cannot go on living unless there is a way.'

In Herod's palace the walls of his audience chamber are decorated in the masonry style, panels coloured to look like marble blocks and painted columns in yellow and white, which suggest to the untrained eye alcoves and passages that are not there. At the far end Herod sits on his gilded throne, which is set on a low dais so that, even sitting, he is at eye level with his courtiers. His mood is a good one.

With some amusement he observes the Roman ambassador taking note of the scars on his throne, the places where the gold ornamentation has been hacked off and the bare wood is visible. He has refused to allow the artisans to disguise the blemishes. They are a reminder to his courtiers of how he dealt with evil.

Suddenly aware that he is noticed, the Roman ambassador makes a stiff bow in that self-conscious way that Romans have when they attempt manners. 'It is true then,' he says. 'All over Rome they are telling of Judea's king, who cut up his ornaments to feed the people.'

Herod smiles. 'Only your lord Pluto enjoys being a king of corpses.'

'It was a bold move,' the ambassador concedes. 'I have heard it was a famine of unprecedented severity, the worst for a hundred years.'

Herod makes a small gesture of acknowledgement, and encouraged, the Roman ambassador asks, 'Do the people attribute its severity to your god's wrath?'

Behind the ambassador's back looks are exchanged. The question is provocative. When the harvest failed for a second year there were prophets in the streets proclaiming the Almighty's dissatisfaction with the house of Herod. Herod had them whipped and thereafter forbade gatherings and groups of more than three men. And so, when the ambassador speaks of God's wrath eyes widen and shoulders tense in anticipation not of God's fury, but of Herod's. The ambassador is lucky. Today Herod is in a good mood.

'To speak of the motives of the Almighty is not for mortal men,' Herod says, though something in the way he says it hints that he may be an exception to this rule. 'Perhaps it was the displeasure of the deity or perhaps it was simply one of those cyclical evils, which visit mankind from time to time. Who can say?' Herod turns to share his smile with his wife, who sits on a lesser throne at his side.

—What is wrong? Ah, of course. You are correct. This is not Mariamme first or even second. When Herod returned from the great Aegyptus, his wagons laden with grain, the people lined the roads cheering and calling him a 'patriarch of the people' and 'a new Joseph for our times' and their words evoke in Herod for the first time a touch of saintliness. He carries it with him into the palace and crowns this new feeling by putting aside his frivolous wife and

taking a bride from Samaria, a pious girl who prefers to veil herself in the company of men. It causes talk, but the growl of empty bellies speaks louder. And while we are on the subject of empty bellies, here comes the king's brother.

As always, he has a sombre, distracted look about him. His tunic is fresh, but already there are splashes of ink on it. His feet are shod in sandals that do not belong in a pair, and, if you have known him long, you will see that his face has a lean hungry look about it that was not there before the famine. More than once he has pushed his plate away, saying, 'I cannot eat while other men starve. Give my share to the poor.' The plates were removed and he never noticed that over time the cheeks of the kitchen boys were growing plumper even as his grew thinner.

And now, though he is a tall man, the courtiers ignore him until the king catches sight of his brother and orders them to give way. Pheroras makes a clumsy bow. 'I greet you and honour you.'

Herod nods, satisfied, then frowns. 'Brother, you have grown thinner?' There is no need for Pheroras to answer; his appearance speaks for itself. He looks like a little boy lost inside the folds of his father's tunic. The king shakes his head. 'Little brother,' he says, and his tone is surprisingly gentle. 'Your wife was a good woman. But it has been six months. You take your mourning too far.'

Pheroras glances up sharply, but it is never wise to argue with Herod's interpretation of things.

The king beams. 'Marriage is the natural order of things. It is a great comfort to godly men.' He bestows a fond glance on the stiff, veiled figure at his side. 'After all a wife of noble character is her husband's crown.' He is attempting piety and it sits oddly on his lined killer's face.

Pheroras looks flustered. He glances at a man, who is seated near the dais scribbling furiously on a tablet of wax. He is dressed in the Greek fashion, his beard shaped and pointed perhaps to hide a face that is unusually ruddy amongst the sallow complexions which surround him, and when he looks up, which he does from time to time, his eyes are pale and almost lashless, never still, but darting from spot to spot, taking everything in. This then is Nicolaus of Damascus, tutor of Cleopatra's children and already busy taking notes for his memoirs of a Jewish king. He spots Pheroras' confusion and hesitates, stylus poised in the air. Herod is speaking again.

'It is my duty to ensure the sanctity of the kingdom. I must be an example of piety to the people, and naturally those about me must be seen to follow— '

Pheroras makes an attempt to interrupt, but if it was hard to check Herod when he was a monster, it is impossible now that he is a saint. Herod gives a look at Nicolaus, as if to say, Here is something for you to record. Then he begins, 'My eldest daughter, Salampsio, is of an age to be betrothed. Fortunate child, she carries the blood of Hasmonaea and Herod equally in her veins, and there is talk of a brilliant match for her with one of the great houses here in

Judea or with some foreign prince of standing.' Again Pheroras tries to speak, but Herod is bestowing a complicit look on the Roman ambassador and does not notice. He turns back to Pheroras. 'We deem it time you had a wife. And such is my regard for you that I will forgo all the honours and offer you, my brother, the most precious gift a father can bestow. How do you answer?'

There is a terrible silence. Pheroras seems dumbstruck. Nicolaus of Damascus sits, his stencil poised in the air, while the Roman ambassador frowns and glances at the king. He is wondering if this whole display is staged. Are we to believe that Pheroras is overcome with the magnanimity of the gift? But the warmth is fading from Herod's smile. 'Brother?'

Pheroras clears his throat, but his voice comes out as a croak. 'You honour me far beyond my worth. But— '

The king's hands tighten on the scarred arms of his throne; his hands seem tipped with ivory at the knuckles. 'Go on.'

'I cannot accept.'

'Cannot?'

Pheroras flounders. 'It … is a great honour— '

'But you cannot accept?'

'I cannot accept.' Pheroras lowers his gaze then looks up at his brother, pleading with him to understand. 'Because I am already married.'

Nicolaus drops his stylus. It falls to the floor and the noise jerks everyone from their frozen positions. There is a shuffling of feet, shoulders rub as necks crane forward. Herod drops a single syllable into the air.

'Who?'

For answer, Pheroras turns and, as he does so, the courtiers part like a human sea, to where a tall young woman with sun-streaked hair and eyes, the blue green colour of Ethiopian opals, stands in the doorway.

31

In which Loshema receives a gift of two pearls

20-17 BCE

A ND SO YOU SEE DEAR READER, *I married him. A simple ceremony it was, conducted by a rabbi, with whom Pheroras was on friendly terms. There were no guests. I signed my signature on a document of emancipation then we made our commitment to one another before the Almighty. But you are shaking your head. You don't believe it. Pauper to princess is surely the stuff of romance. You have been cheated. You were led to expect genuine insight, historical truth, and instead you have been served up a syrupy tale too fantastic to digest.*

I do not blame you. So many things in life seem the stuff of invention. It is a wonder that the writer of histories can persuade anyone of anything. How can I convince you? You want proof. Well, I am there in the history books. Nicolaus includes me in Herod's memoirs, and later another Jewish historian, one Joseph ben Matthias, known as Josephus to his Roman audience, will mention me again. With unconscious irony neither of them went to the trouble of giving me a name. And so I remain down the centuries, as anonymous in death as I was in life. But still, I am there all the same.

Ah, now your curiosity is piqued. You want the grisly detail. Stay there at the door then and witness, how, once the rabbi has gone, Pheroras, my husband, sweeps me up in his arms and carries me to his bedchamber.

With the shutters closed the room is filled with a dusty twilight, that wan shade which comes just before the breaking of dawn or the gathering of the night, a crossing place it is, the beginning of new beginnings. And through this light comes a heady scent of willow and yellow jasmine from tall vases set around the room so that the senses are dizzied with thoughts of open fields and midnight gardens.

Down I am set so that the dress he bought me, (the most costly gold silk embroidered with flowers and vines in green and red, a dress fit for a queen) splays out across the blankets and catches the chinks of light, a miniature paradisiacal garden rustling against my open thighs. And now he pulls the veils from my hair letting it fall about my shoulders. And my unbound hair is a gift more potent than the baring of my breasts. At once his lips are on my forehead, his whisper nuzzling my ear. 'One day, I swear, I will place a crown upon this brow.' Then he throws my skirts over my head before, remembering himself, he goes to lock the bedroom door.

You are disappointed. I have left you out in the cold. Now surely you did not think to accompany a virgin maid on her wedding night. It would be a poor thing if literature has made a voyeur out of you. I will tell you this though, Pheroras was not one of these men who turn from lamb to wolf in the bedroom. He was the same gentle, clumsy being he was in daily life. On that night I had to have courage for us both, and had there been witnesses they would have been forgiven for thinking Pheroras the virgin and me the accomplished widow.

Of course Herod could have dashed our hopes in the blink of an eye. Did you not see me tremble when the courtiers parted to reveal me as the wife of Pheroras? Come, I will take you back there. Stand for an instant in my shoes. O, it is not so easy is it, when your bones have turned to liquid and your belly is on fire. Herod is so shocked he has risen to his feet. He looks at his brother and his expression says, What have you done?

Then he is coming down from his dais, towards me, his face as blank as unpainted block of stone. Behind him Pheroras looks stricken, but he does not move. No-one moves. Herod is the only animate being in the chamber, as though the Almighty has chosen to turn everyone else into pillars of salt.

He stops an inch from my face, so close that his features are blurred and I can smell his hot lionish breath, the foetid scent of the meat he pulled apart with his teeth during dinner. I should fall to my knees, lower my head, wash his feet with my tears. But I am a rabbit caught in the twin lamps of an eagle's stare, and I can do nothing but watch as his jaws part.

The sound that comes from the dark depths of his throat is so unexpected that it seems to belong neither to Herod the monster nor Herod the saint. It is a raw primal sound, oddly out of place, like a clap of thunder indoors. It is laughter. The courtiers exchange glances. One of the eunuchs ventures a titter, and when Herod does not strike him down but goes on laughing, others join in. And soon the whole court is in uproar, until only Pheroras and I stand frozen and aghast.

Herod shakes his greying head and holds up a beringed hand. The laughter stops. He is still looking down at me, as though I might be a desert mirage, which will disappear as soon as he turns away.

'Extraordinary,' he announces. 'The situation is exceptional. It appears that my brother has taught us all a lesson.' He pauses and the courtiers nod vigorously, though they have no idea what that lesson might be. Herod enlightens them. 'My brother has looked beyond what is accepted in the ordinary way and has created something marvellous in its place.' His eyes narrow. He fingers his beard. 'Perhaps it is time, after all, for the older brother to learn from the younger.' And that was that.

O this was a happy time. The world both receded and advanced. Everything was new and old pains no longer mattered. Pheroras presented me with a wardrobe of gowns so finely embroidered, so delicately made that I feared the merest sneeze or clearing of the throat would be enough to blow them away. And when I asked timidly if I might touch them, Pheroras took my hands and smiled, saying 'Loshema, you are a free woman now. These are your robes. You may choose to do with them as you will. Take a knife if you please and cut them to shreds.' Then he laughed to see my scandalized face. And it was good to see Pheroras laugh.

There was so much to learn about being free. Because, of course, no-one, but the birds and the hermits in the wilderness who neither see nor speak to any soul during their endless days, is ever truly free. As a woman there were sometimes strictures on my movements that had not existed when I was enslaved. I could not, for example, visit the market as I was used to, skipping from stall to stall admiring the wares. Nor could I run down corridors and across courtyards, but must walk at all times at a ladylike pace.

When Pheroras and I walked abroad the people stopped their business and stared.

—Why are they cheering?—

—Because they love you.—

—The do not know me.—

—But they know that I love you, and that is enough.—

And now I was part of the royal retinue there were endless customs and conventions to master. Where should I sit at the royal table (for Herod adopted the Roman custom of having men and women sitting together). Should I stand when another person of the royal family entered, even Salome? I should have liked to ask Salome's advice, but naturally she was displeased by my promotion and made it known that I was a person to be despised, though she was careful to never voice this opinion within her brothers' hearing.

I did not blame her. Half the court considered her an Idumaean upstart, and to fraternize with me would only make matters worse. Besides, I had learned from Mariamme's fate that Salome could be a dangerous enemy. And so I adopted no airs in her presence, but bent my head and kept my lips sealed, even when she entertained, spinning her stories, like flax, when I knew my clever tongue could spin gold. And gradually, if she did not warm to me, she at least showed some little signs of thawing —a small acknowledgement, the tolerance of my presence in a room— the first trickles of water beneath a frozen puddle.

All was vigour and action. Herod announced his most audacious project yet, inspired he insisted by his younger brother's daring. If Pheroras had taken a base foundation (I took no offence) and transformed her into something noble, could he not take the Temple (so disappointingly reconstructed after the fall of the Babylonian empire that it was said that each new High Priest wept afresh for the loss of Solomon's original) and build it afresh? Could he, Herod, who had constructed whole cities out of the dust and had tamed the sea with a magnificent artificial harbour, not reconstruct a temple that would be the most marvellous tribute the Jews had ever made to their unique and mysterious deity?

Of course there was shock amongst the holy men, Sadducees and Pharisees for once joined in their protests. Such daring smacked of blasphemy. They raised objections.

'The risk is too great. What if unclean hands were to be involved in the construction of so holy a building?'

'Then we will train an army of Temple Levites as stone masons and carpenters.'

'But the sacred rituals. They cannot be interrupted.'

'Nor shall they be. They may continue even as we build.'

'Such an undertaking will take years, decades. You will never live to see it completed.'

At this Herod bowed his head piously and it was left for his audience to recall that those favoured by the Almighty's grace, Abraham, Moses, Noah, Enoch, may live for centuries. The holy men look at each other. A house of God that would make pagan temples shrink to the size of mouse-holes? Who were they to stand in its way?

And so it was begun, and Pheroras and I used to climb one of the great towers in the Antonia fortress to watch the progress and sometimes to laugh at the sweating faces of the Levites, who were more used to gentle tasks of ritual than the hard labour of shaping stone and timber.

O, a happy time it was. And I took it all for granted, growing so comfortable in my new shape as a freed woman that I could barely recall a time when I had not worn silk or called for a maid to fashion my hair. So natural my new status became to me that I often allowed myself to become irritated over the inconsequential vexations that plague human life, snapping at a page for being slovenly in his manner and even scolding Pheroras for his slow way of drawing his speech to a conclusion.

And so the weeks turned to months and the months to years, and I have no great passions or catastrophes to make your eyes widen or your tongue protrude to wet your lips. For so is the trickle of ordinary life, which we let flow past us, almost unaware. And when we look back we see only the events that shaped existence. We forget the dead empty spaces between. We forget that happiness is not always to be found amongst the thrusting mountains and the raging torrents, but sometimes in the vast emptiness of the sky.

And when did it change? Was there an event, a single moment when the sun was obscured by cloud or was it not a slow, slow erosion, a falling pebble, the sliding of a few grains of sand, signs almost imperceptible before the land begins to slip.

'Boy, tell my wife I would meet with her.'

'Here, husband.' Loshema came from her chamber, still with too excited a step, and aware of the frown thrown her by one of the passing ladies of the court. She looked eagerly into Pheroras' face, recognising the fond crinkle of his eyes as a hopeful sign. 'You have something to show me?'

He tapped her nose. 'What should I have to show a presumptuous wife?'

'Is it presumptuous for a wife to know her husband?'

'No. Only hazardous to her husband's dignity.' But he was smiling too broadly to maintain the stern facade. He held a hand out to her. 'Come!'

They descended the stairs together and out into the enclosed garden nearest their apartments. Pheroras halted, and Loshema, blinking in the strong sunlight looked first about the ornamental bushes and trees then at her husband. Secretly she had been hoping for some new jewels, earrings to match the magnificent rope of pearls he had given her to celebrate their anniversary. Pheroras made a small gesture with his head and Loshema followed the direction of his motion. Trees, bushes and a couple of old women standing in a corner. Was he making fun of her?

'I do not— ' she began then something in his expression made her turn her head again. And suddenly she was running across the garden, skirts bunched indecorously high in her hands. 'AemaA, AemaA!' Mother! The younger of the women tugged the elder one's sleeve, making her raise the brown prune of her face just as Loshema skidded to a stop before them. 'Is it truly you?'

The elder woman made a deep bow, a slave's bow and began muttering apologies in a piteous beseeching tone until her daughter dragged her upright, saying roughly, 'Mother, can you not see who it is? It is Loshema. Our Loshema.'

'Loshema?' the old woman repeated, blinking. 'Loshema!' Then the next moments were lost in weeping and questions too numerous to be answered. Pheroras joined them and Batia, Loshema's mother, had to be stopped from going down on her knees to kiss his hand.

'But how?' Loshema asked when she could breathe again and was no longer weeping and exclaiming. Pheroras reached out and tugged one of her earlobes, his expression wry. 'Did I not promise you two pearls?'

Her avarice, so easily read, made colour rush to Loshema's cheeks, but she managed to lift her face, still glittering with tears, and hiccough. 'You have made me the happiest of women this day.'

Pheroras looked at her fondly. 'Then I am counted the happiest of men.'

Yet it seemed the day was not replete with surprises. An hour later, as Loshema's sister, Gomer, recounted how she and her mother had lived on an estate close enough to see the walls of the holy city shining in the distance, yet never allowed more than a step from the kitchen gardens, and that they had not spent their days as whores, but as the lowest, most despised work slaves —Truly, I do not think our mother could have survived another month if your husband had not found us— the door opened and Pheroras entered, his face flushed, as though he had hurried all the way. For an instant he looked at Batia and Gomer, as though wondering who they were and what they were doing in his chambers then he found his wife's face amongst them and blurted, 'The sons of Mariamme have returned from Rome.'

Loshema got to her feet. 'Alexander and Aristobolus are back?' This was news indeed. Although wife after wife had provided Herod with sons so that it was said that Octavian (who now styled himself Augustus) envied the Jewish king his wealth of heirs, it was an open secret that Herod favoured the sons of Mariamme over all others. And now they were back. Loshema felt a little shiver travel down her spine, a strange consciousness that something had shifted and that the air was different. Then she looked towards the weary, lined faces of her mother and sister and the here-and-now grew large in her vision and blotted out all else.

And, indeed, in the weeks that followed little seemed to change. There was much rejoicing that the princes had returned home. Here was the blood of the Hasmonaeans embodied in the vigorous youthful bodies of two young men, for men they now were. Even Aristobolus, the younger had passed his thirteenth year while in Rome, and could be considered to have reached his majority. And if it could not be denied that they also had the blood of Herod in them, it seemed to have caused them no ill effect.

Herod seemed happier than he had appeared for a number of years. He smiled more often and seemed to have developed a taste for the rigours of abstract thought. He was regularly seen walking with Nicolaus of Damascus, discussing the three genres of rhetoric or Aristophanes' development of dramatic irony. Indeed his latest wife almost seemed chosen as a demonstration of his grasp of irony, being named Kleopatra, and henceforth always referred to as Kleopatra of Jerusalem lest there be some confusion with the long dead lover of the viper's kiss.

And yet for all that life had begun to resemble the tranquil waters of a great peaceful lake, there were undercurrents. There were mutterings below the surface, which Loshema felt when she walked about the palace, murmurings that could not be quite heard yet felt like ripples along the surface of her skin. But such was her contentment that she chose to ignore her instincts until the day Salome came to visit.

It had not been the easiest of days. Batia was finding it hard to remember that she was no longer a slave, and had to be repeatedly reminded that she was not to leave when the maids were dismissed. Gomer, on the other hand, recalled too well that she was by rights the elder sister and her tongue was as sharp as ever. She stood now with her hands on her hips, her expression mutinous. 'So we are freed from our bondage so that we might drudge for you?'

Loshema bit back her own sharp reply, knowing that if her sister's speech was tart it was due to fermentation in years of bitterness. 'I asked only that you help me with a little mending. I wish to read the commentary my husband has left and I have promised him my notes no later than sundown tomorrow.' It was the wrong thing to say. Gomer's eyes began to fill with angry tears, which spilled over and collected in the deep crevices under her eyes. 'Of course we are never to forget that you are learned, above us in rank and station and education!'

'Gomer— ' Loshema began, exasperated, but the door swung open and Salome swept into the room, unannounced.

'I wish to see my brother.'

'Peace. I am here.' Pheroras' calm voice sounded behind Salome. He entered behind her, carrying a number of scroll cases under his arm. Salome turned to him at once. 'Something must be done about it.'

'About, sister?' Pheroras laid the leather cylinders carefully down on a table. He seemed distracted, but Salome was having none of it. 'About Alexander and Aristobolus.'

'What of them? They seem pleasant, well-mannered boys.'

'They are not boys, Pheroras. They are men.'

'Hardly.' Pheroras was busy arranging the scroll tubes, which kept getting away from him. 'Alexander is not quite fifteen.'

Salome rustled her skirts in annoyance. 'What of it? At fifteen Zael was fighting alongside father.'

A shrug. 'It is different for them.'

'Different because they are Hasmonaean princes?'

Loshema stood, frozen to the spot she had been standing in when Salome barged through the door. It was humiliating to be ignored in this way in her own apartments. But Loshema had long given up the hope that Pheroras would take Salome up on her rudeness. —She does not mean it, he would say afterwards when Loshema was burning and breathless with indignation. It was always difficult for Salome to be a woman. His eyes would narrow. Surely you can sympathize.— Loshema's usual practice was to leave the room. But Gomer was watching the argument, open-mouthed, her own grievances forgotten, and Loshema did not dare leave her. Salome was in full thrust, her ample bosom thrust forward, like the prow of a warship. 'These boys, as you would have it are a danger to us. I can see it if you cannot. The Hasmonaean dream is reawakening. And the people are becoming restless as I predicted.'

Pheroras glanced at his sister. 'Did you not welcome them when they arrived in court? I remember your speech on "prodigals". '

'Am I a fool? Do you think I would dash our brother's dreams to his face and pour salt on the ruins? But I have been listening.' She took a step closer to Pheroras. 'I hear their complaints.'

'What boys of their age do not complain? They think the heavens were made as their playthings. Do you not remember how Herod would rage the moment it rained, as though the clouds were compelled to part if he shouted loud enough?'

Salome rolled her eyes. 'This is not the foolishness of youth. They go about claiming that their mother was unjustly murdered and that they are forced to live amongst her murderers.'

The mildness left Pheroras' expression. He glanced at Loshema and Gomer, as though suddenly remembering their presence, and sending a pang through his wife's heart at seeing herself recalled absently in the way the presence of a slave is brought to mind. She saw him consider dismissing them then, frowning, turn back to his sister. 'This is dangerous talk.'

Salome threw up her hands. 'What choice have we? I counselled him against giving his new wife the best of Mariamme's finery. But he insisted. Apparently Kleopatra had her heart set upon the course and he could not refuse her.'

'Our brother who can see plots in a stone can see no wrong in a woman he loves.' Pheroras gave a sad smile. 'He will grow tired of her then everything will be solved. I have heard talk of Pallas, eldest daughter to a noble family that finds itself without sons.'

'There is no time. Alexander and Aristobolus think to use the Cappadocian king as an ally.'

'What use is the Cappadocian king to two stripling princes?'

'O use your head, Pheroras. He is a loyal friend of Augustus. They mean to go to Rome with him and lay charges of murder against their father.'

'You have proof of this?' Salome made an exasperated noise in the back of her throat. 'Do you think they write their plans down and have the scribes send me copies?'

'Then there is nothing we can do but wait until we have proof.'

'By that time we will be dead. No-one will be spared.' Salome suddenly swung round and pointed a plump finger at Loshema. 'No-one.'

And so it is decided. Pheroras and Salome will approach Herod, brother and sister united by a common cause. Pheroras is worried. 'Will Herod listen?' But Salome dismisses his fears. 'Do I not know our brother? Have I not shown myself the one who best understands him?' Of course she means she has persuaded Herod to rid her of two husbands and his own beautiful wife. Yes, Salome has learned to turn the demons inside Herod to her own use. All she need do is reveal to her elder brother who his enemies truly are. And so it is with confidence that she goes to Herod with whispers that his sons are plotting against him. And it is a pity, that with all her understanding she fails to recall that the only thing that is predictable about Herod is that he is unpredictable...

32

The calm before the storm

13 BCE

A STORM WAS APPROACHING. LOSHEMA could feel it in her bones and in the strangeness of her body, which now had everything that might satisfy it yet yearned constantly for some unseen thing she could not quite grasp, as though she walked through life with a hand constantly outstretched. She knew that Pheroras, too, sensed the approach of a storm and it was making him sick.

During the night Loshema awoke to find her husband was no longer at her side. The room was neither light nor dark, but some halfway place belonging to neither, and for a moment she believed herself still dreaming. If this is real, she thought, then I am unreal. Then a movement, caught in the corner of her eye, had her scrambling backwards in fear, for who did not know of the *iyrin,* who were made before men, and who walked the earth as watchers, not all of whom were of good intent.

But it was only Pheroras, her husband, who was pacing the room in a hunched, agitated way, his thin fingers worrying at the neck of his robe.

'What is it? What is wrong?' She had the sense of speaking from beneath water or of not speaking at all. But Pheroras started and threw her a glance over his shoulder. 'Three weeks,' he said.

Loshema felt a cold shiver down her spine. Three weeks since Pheroras and Salome had gone to Herod and pointed accusing fingers in the direction of his sons. And in that time all that had come from Herod's chambers was a deathly unbroken silence. She got out of bed and went over to her husband, reaching up tenderly to touch the wiry hair of his beard. He looked at her with the dull eyes of a somnambulist. 'Fetch Salome.'

Loshema let her hands drop. 'You are certain?'

'Yes. No. I do not know.' Pheroras shook his head violently then began pacing again. Over the last weeks brother and sister had seen each other practically every day, seeming compelled to seek one another out, yet finding no comfort in the other's company. They argued continuously, and almost always the argument was the same. A sullen silence then Pheroras would say, 'We should never have gone.'

'And then what?' Salome was sharp because she was afraid. 'My spies tell me that Alexander and Aristobolus are already boasting that they will turn all Herod's wives into peasants, and that his family can assuredly hope for even less mercy.'

'Perhaps, if we were to say we had changed our minds— '

'Shall we tie the strangler's knot too!'

'This was your idea.'

'You dare! You dare— '

Plates or other small breakables would crash. Doors would slam and the argument would begin anew the next day. At first Pheroras spoke angrily about the situation. 'Go to him,' Loshema counselled. 'Speak to your brother directly. Herod admires strength.' But Pheroras shook his head. 'The strength of a warrior not a scholar.'

'It matters not.' She touched his arm. 'Words may be sharper than swords.' But Pheroras shook his head and turned away.

Now Pheroras was awake in the half light of dawn, and pacing the room.

'We must leave. Yes. Yes.' Nodding to himself. 'We will leave at first light.'

'Leave? Where are we going?'

He started, as though he had forgotten she was in the room. 'Peraea.'

'I don't— You do not— '

'I am made tetrarch there. Or do you forget?'

Loshema shook her head dumbly. No, she hadn't forgotten. Herod had heaped honours on his brother's head. But they were titles without weight, and an army of administrators carried out the real work. She rubbed her eyes thinking, 'O, my husband, you could no more rule Peraea than an unborn child.'

He had begun pulling items from chests, piling them randomly on the floor. 'It will be fitting to take a trip. It need raise no suspicion.'

Loshema watched helplessly, her eyes glistening then she went over and took hold of his shoulders. 'Husband.' He paused in his frantic sorting, but did not look round. She smelled the sour, animal smell of him, the desperate need for flight. 'If we go now, we will condemn ourselves without ever saying a word in our defence.' He was silent. 'Your sister will go to the king as soon as we are gone. And she will not think twice before she points the finger. She is not afraid.'

This was cruel, and she wished the words back in her throat as soon as she had said them. But Pheroras' shoulders slumped, and she was able to guide him back to bed, where they lay, he in her arms, until she heard the gentle rise and fall of his breathing, and knew him to be asleep. But now sleep was lost to her, and when she was sure that he would not awaken she slipped from the bed and, wrapping herself in a shawl, silently left the room.

It was still early. The corridors, which felt so solid when filled with sunlight, had an eerie uninhabited feel, like the buildings that stuck halfway out of the sand in ruined Jezreel. Loshema was suddenly filled with the need to be outside.

The nearest exit took her into one of the smaller gardens. Fruit trees had been planted here, peach and fig and sweet-smelling lemon. The trees were mature, though the palace was only a few years old. People marvelled at them in the king's presence, but, in truth, they were not greatly impressed. Herod had already proved that he was more than a match for Nature, and this was one miracle amongst many. A pale little breeze rippled through the branches, and when she looked up the night sky was almost gone and only one or two stars were still visible.

Her gaze was clearer when she looked down, and so she saw the man, who had been with her in the garden all the while she had been standing there. He was a few feet away, and she could see the strong clean lines of his profile as he stared up into the fleshy depths of a fig tree, unaware that his solitude had been broken. There was such a proprietorial expression on his face that for a moment she mistook him for one of the gardeners. But, even in the half light, she knew that to be foolish because his robe, though simple, was too finely made. And there was something else—

As though her thought had been audible, the man suddenly turned to face her. And as he did so she felt a shock of recognition. Then the feeling shrivelled and was replaced by confusion. It was like coming across a long forgotten painting only to find that it was quite different from the cherished memory of it. She knew this man yet did not know him.

They did not speak, but his eyes held Loshema's, and they were unlike the eyes of anyone she had ever encountered. They were bold eyes, taking her in, in a way that made her tighten the shawl about her thin shift. But the eyes also contained an element of fear, an old fear that had never left him, the kind of fear that exists only in adults who have suffered as children. And recognition of that fear jumped, like a spark, across the distance between them before either had time to acknowledge it. He looked on the verge of saying something, but Loshema suddenly remembered that she was a married woman, wandering alone late at night, and lowering her head, she turned and fled.

The next day Herod called his family together to make an announcement. It was done informally in his apartments with everyone crowded together on couches with only a slave or two on hand to serve chilled wine and dishes of dates and figs. The atmosphere was genial, and the only surprise came when Salome made a move towards a vacant couch.

'Not there.' Herod's voice brooked no argument. And Salome was forced to join Phero-ras and Loshema, which she did with ill grace, waggling her generous hind quarters against Loshema until the latter was almost pushed to the floor. Opposite sat Mariamme's sons, while Kleopatra sat with her father, who was the incumbent High Priest.

Herod, as was his right, stretched out on a couch by himself. He seemed relaxed. Yet Loshema was struck by the air of isolation that hung over him. Here he was surrounded by his loved ones, and yet the more his family expanded the lonelier he seemed to grow. And not for the first time she had a sense of how the outline of the king was swallowing up all that had been the man.

Herod cleared his throat. 'I have come to a decision with regard to Alexander and Aristobolus.'

Salome shot Pheroras a triumphant glance, but even through the glitter of her smile there was a damp sheen of relief. The two young princes, sitting opposite, kept their faces expressionless. Herod shifted his gaze to his brother, which made Pheroras twitch uncomfortably then attempt a smile, which manifested only as a spasm that bared his teeth. Salome poked him in the side and he stared down at his feet.

'Pheroras.' The king's voice was honey. 'You would be one to extol the virtues of marriage?'

Pheroras made the smallest inclination of his head. To agree with Herod could sometimes be the more dangerous course.

'Even at the expense of my wishes.'

Loshema felt the colour drain from her face. It had been foolishness to imagine that Herod had forgiven the slight to his daughter. She glanced at her husband, but Pheroras seemed to have lost his tongue. There was a dreadful silence then Herod leaned back on the couch and reached for a fig, and there was something in his expression that reminded Loshema of a cat, who has temporarily loosened its claws about the soft furry body of its victim just for the sport of it. His smile glistened.

'Well, let us make no more of it for now. My intention was merely to underline the importance of marriage for are we not told that "it is not good for a man to be alone"?' He turned towards his sons. 'It is with this in mind that I have chosen wives for Alexander and Aristobolus.'

The boys remained expressionless, and the only sound was a faint hiss from Salome that reached no further than Loshema's ears. Salome drained her cup, and when she looked up her lips were bloody with the purple stain of the grape. She held the cup out for more, and when it was filled she lifted it in toast to the princes. 'What noble sentiments. My congratulations. May I enquire who we will be welcoming into the family?'

'I am to marry Glaphyra, the daughter of the Cappadocian king,' Alexander answered flatly.

—O, this is well played. The princes thought to make an ally of the Cappadocian in the suit against their father. But now his daughter will be a hostage under Herod's roof. Salome knows this too. Her silks rustle and heave against my thigh as she battles to gain control of herself.—

In a voice like breaking glass, Salome asked, 'And you, Aristobolus, who are you to marry?'

The boy blushed and glanced at his father. 'I— Aunt, please, I am to marry your daughter, Berenice.'

There was a deathly silence. Salome's jaw worked. Then she said haltingly, 'The honour is too great. And besides Berenice is not ready— '

'Ready enough,' Herod interrupted.

'She is only a child.'

'Older than our mother when she married father.'

Salome was on her feet now, the rustling of her skirts audible with her trembling. 'I am her mother and I say it will not happen.'

Herod looked at her calmly. 'Will you defy your king?'

'Am I the one who defies you?' Salome spluttered. 'How many years of loyalty have I shown you? In all Israel name the counsellor you could trust more. While they— ' She broke off to wheel round and point a finger in the direction of Pheroras and Loshema. 'They sit there in open defiance of your wishes yet you do nothing.'

But Herod would not be moved. And, Salome, thinking to storm from the room, took a step towards the door only to find it already opening to allow the entry of an elderly woman and a much younger man.

Salome looked towards the empty couch then back again. 'Doris?' The name, once voiced, lifted a curtain, and suddenly everything fell into place. This gaunt, grey-haired woman was indeed Herod's first wife, Doris the Idumaean. And the young man, Loshema realised with a sort of implosion in her chest, was the same man she had encountered under the fig tree in Herod's garden. So this was Antipater. The skinny frightened boy, who had sat on the edge of his bed watching his mother wail over the prospect of exile, had disappeared. Herod's eldest son was well made, though not as tall as his younger brothers. Still he had a presence, that dark Herodian presence, not yet visible in Mariamme's sons.

'Sit down, Salome,' Herod barked. 'Permit me the kindness of welcoming family in my own chambers.' Salome threw him a furious glance but she returned to the couch and sat heavily down. Loshema could feel her ragged breath against her side.

Herod stood up and spread his arms. 'Welcome.' And Doris walked cringingly towards him.

'I prayed to the Almighty that He might let me back into your presence one day.' She hesitated. Her hands worried each other, as though if not occupied with prayer she was unsure what to do with them. 'I also prayed that you find happiness with your wife.' She gave Kleopatra a bow, and few noticed how her voice trembled on the last word. Her greeting was carelessly acknowledged by the younger woman. Kleopatra was wearing one of Mariamme's robes, and Loshema wondered if Doris recognised it.

But Herod was speaking. 'You have been wronged, Doris. And you have suffered greatly.' He managed somehow to imply that these wrongs were not of his doing, but the result of some unnamed party. Doris did not look up, and Herod's gaze was forced towards Antipater. 'And you, my son, have been kept too long from court.' Across the room Alexander and Aristobolus stiffened and exchanged glances. They were beginning to understand the noose that Herod was drawing round them, for in these times the succession was not fixed in Judea, and Herod was at liberty to choose whom he pleased as his heir.

Antipater bowed. 'I honour and respect you father. All I ask is the chance to prove myself.'

A snort from Salome had everyone turning and looking in her direction. She quickly turned it into a clearing of her throat and raised her cup, which was full again. 'My, what a touching scene. A father rewarding the loyalty of his sons. A pity we are not allowed graven images. We could distribute the likeness of today under the title, *familia supra omnia*.'

—And so the marriages went ahead. And contrary to expectations the young couples seemed happy. Glaphyra worshipped handsome Alexander and Berenice was similarly enamoured of Aristobolus, though afraid enough of her mother to keep her happiness to herself. For a short time peace reigned. Salome, in a kind of disgrace, sulked in corners. And Pheroras, relieved that Herod's disapproving eye was focussed on his sister, slept a deep dreamless sleep that is usually experienced only by the very young or those innocent of where events are leading them.—

On a day, not long after the weddings took place, Loshema went seeking her husband in the library. And no longer requiring to knock and wait patiently when called, she threw the door open only to find that Pheroras was not there. Instead, Nicolaus of Damascus was standing at the table, his hand stroking his pointed beard, while he contemplated a scroll laid out in front of him. Antipater was there also.

'Forgive me.' She started to withdraw.

'Please, stay.' It was Antipater who spoke, when by rights, it should have been the older man. She avoided his eye. 'I cannot. I have no escort.'

'But you are my uncle's wife. We are family.' Antipater came round the table and extended his arms in welcome. 'Come. Your husband is never done boasting of your talents as a scholar. And I am in need of rescue, as this Greek finds me a poor ignoramus, and will soon judge all Jews the less for it.'

Nicolaus' pale eyes looked at Antipater drily. 'I fear I shall think Jews are liars, as I have done nothing but praise the astuteness of your mind.'

'Ah well,' Antipater said with a shrug. 'Better a clever liar than a speaker of impoverished truths.'

There was something shocking in his manner, which struck a chord inside Loshema. It made her think of wild, trapped things. Claws fastening about bone, or the beating of wings against the bars of a cage. She lifted her gaze and stared boldly into his face. He had very black eyes and it was impossible to read in them whether his words reflected his thoughts.

'Stay,' he said again.

—Stay? If only I had turned tail and run. Now, I would throw this self across the door and bar the way to that self that was once me. But it cannot be done. True, I have power in my hands. With a little incantation of my fingers I can bring you back down the centuries to stand at my side, yet I cannot reach across a few years to warn who I once was.

See how I hesitate on the threshold, rocking on the balls of my feet, sniffing the air, like an animal scenting danger. Danger has an odd smell, wormwood and musk. There are poisons that use these ingredients I know, but few know that they are also constituents of the most powerful love philtres.

O for the chance to edit one's own story. How often do were reread the tragedies of Sophocles, hoping that somehow Deianeira will not send her husband the deadly gift or that this time Antigone will have the courage to resist the lure of the noose? Yes, yes. This is not a play and the past can, of course, be rewritten. —Decades from now a Christian scribe will insert a scene of horror near the end of Herod's narrative so that he might proclaim his prophet king of Jews.

But it is not possible to truly remake the past. Our stories are written with the indelible ink of time in the Book of Life, and not even the Almighty can change the paths we have already walked down. And so there is nothing to be done but watch, with the helplessness of a parent who cannot cry out to warn their child, as I step across the threshold, shutting the door behind me.

33

The beauty of the world is in a touch

12 BCE

AFTERWARDS THEY SAID THAT SHE fainted and that was to be considered a blessing. And Loshema would nod and agree, knowing all the time that it was untrue and that she recalled every bone breaking moment down to the smallest detail.

But nor was it true that she had always been awake. She came back to consciousness on several occasions, and each time was like a first awakening. Confusion then terror. Unable to move, pendulum swings of pain ripping through her belly, her joints cracking and straining, like dry logs set aflame. In the background someone would be screaming over and over again. And with a sickening jolt she would understand where she was. The rack. The rack. Most exquisite of Herod's machines of torture and she was bound to it. She was here because she had been found out, her wickedness uncovered.

Pheroras, my husband. Forgive me. Forgive me. I have sinned against you. Lord! Lord, spare me. Have pity. SHEMA ISRAEL. ADONAI ELOHEINU ADONAI ECHAD. *I confess. I confess. Only let Death release me.* But the screams drowned out her words, and somewhere a part of her would understand that the screams were coming from her own throat, that she was the one screaming. M'SHAOKHD'A, Ă·ZAB·TĀ·NÎ.. *I am alone. I am abandoned.*

Her torturers faces were shadowed and remote, but one spoke with the voice of her mother—

'It is too long.'

And another, unknown—

'Pull. Pull with all your might.'

'It will kill her.'

'No, she is strong. But she is fighting it. Use that bowl to catch the blood.'

No, no. I am not fighting. There is no fight left in me. I confess, tell the king ... I have sinned ... release ... me now... please ... I beg you ... I beg you—

And then came the colours. Oceans of blood, the swelling seas incarnadine. Then a white blaze, burning through the red, like a flame held up behind papyrus. Her heart was a gong struck over and over in a slow deadly rhythm. And the sound made her weightless. The screaming stopped and there was a sense of leaving everything behind.

But in her ear a buzzing. Far away. An irritation. Too persistent to ignore. *Loshemaloshemaloshemaloshema—*

Night fell. The lights went out. And there were dull explosions in the distance. Pitchforks of lightning. Shooting stars. Then pinpricks, wisps, thin feathers that tickled her eye-lashes, and drew her lids up in slow fluttering motions until her focus grew steady and her pupils stilled.

There were three faces looking down at her. Her mother's, Gomer's and a wizened crone, who gave a satisfied nod then addressed Batia. 'Well, it was a close thing. I won't deny I thought we'd lost her. But the Almighty never mistakes a strong one.'

'She doesn't know. She still doesn't realise what has happened.' Gomer cried.

'O my little one.' Batia's face was suddenly so tender that it was possible to glimpse the beautiful woman beneath the veil of wrinkles. 'Don't you know? You have a daughter.' A new face held up. So small, the skin scarlet and puckered, her little fists held up against the intrusion of the world. Fearing she was still dreaming Loshema closed her eyes, but when she opened them again the baby was still there. How was it possible? All those months not knowing yet knowing. Batia placed her on her breast and Gomer began to dab the sweat away from Loshema's brow with a damp cloth.

The weight of the baby released a confusion of feelings in Loshema's throat and she blurted, 'I thought— I thought— '

'Hush.' The crone was gentle, but firm. 'Do not try to speak. Save your words to thank He who has spared you.'

And Gomer chimed in. 'All your learning did not help you.' There was a hint of glee that a woman of 'my education' should show such ignorance with regard to the education of being a woman. 'Your daughter is as stubborn as her mother, and she would not turn her face to the south no matter how much the midwife fought to free her. And you bled and bled until we feared there was more blood on the floor than in your veins.'

Loshema blinked helplessly at her. She could remember the first fiery pains in her belly, the stumbling journey to her chambers then all was darkness and confusion. But now she smelled a thick coppery tang in the air. It made her gag and she began to shiver. Batia was at her side. 'Here, drink this.' A cup was held to her lips and precious water slipped down her throat.

'We must fetch the husband,' the midwife said briskly. She was over in a corner washing her hands in a bowl.

'Yes,' Batia agreed with a smile. 'The poor man has been left to pace outside. He will not have rest until he knows you safe.'

But, at the thought of Pheroras, tears began to leak out of Loshema's eyes and once be-gun they would not stop.

—They think they know why I am weeping.
'It will be a boy next time,' the midwife soothes.
Batia agrees. 'My son-in-law is the kindest man I have ever met. He will not hold a girl against you.'

Everyone knows that there are men who will put aside a woman for failing to produce an heir. But not Pheroras. He will look upon this scrawny piece of flesh upon my breast and his eyes will light up and his voice will tremble a little. 'Our daughter. You have given me a daughter.' No, he will not cast me aside because I am a maker of girls. It is the other thing that I have done.

I see. It is not enough that I should say it, that I should confess my shame before you, you must see it and know it for yourself. Very well then. We must retrace our steps a little. A few months only. Let us go back, say to the month of KISLEV. *We are in the formal gardens on a day that is dull and overcast. Clouds blew in overnight and now stay high and indifferent above the city. There is a breeze that shivers the tops of the palm trees, but down on the ground the air is chill and stagnant. You are looking about. Why here? Why now? Everything seems closed and dark. Patience! You are about to see the world transform. A moment … yes, here I come.—*

To the incurious passerby —a hurrying slave, a Pharisee with business at court— there was nothing particularly remarkable about the woman who entered the courtyard from the east and began making her way towards the tower on the opposite side. Certainly she was well past the first flush of youth, and while not typical of the women of the region, nor was she fantastical in a way that drew the eye. But there was something that only a second glance would reveal about this woman. She glowed with an inner light.

Loshema was aware of the glow, which made everything in the world reveal—even on a dull day such as this— a secret inner radiance. Things were as they had always been yet somehow now they were more. As she walked she was aware of the earth beneath her feet. And a butterfly quivering on the stalk of a lily, far from being dulled by the dreariness of the light, grew in intensity until it glittered, like a tiny living jewel. It was hard to remember not to clap her hands or laugh out loud with delight. Was this how the prophets saw the world, she wondered, full of warmth and promise?

It was hard to believe it of unrelenting Samuel or doom-laden Jeremiah. But perhaps it was true of kindly old Hosea, who could see the divine even in his fickle prostitute wife. And surely what she felt now must be a gift from the Almighty for she had done nothing wrong, nothing truly wrong. For an instant she faltered and the day's colours faded then she brightened again. She could stand up in any court with her head held high. A friendship with her husband's nephew was not against God's laws. It was simply a matter of being hospitable. And besides she was seven years older than him. By the standards of the day she might be considered an aunt.

But a truer part of herself shifted uneasily and asked if it was hospitable to go to sleep with thoughts of a man, who was not her husband, burning behind her lids? Was it friendship that drew her to the library on the thinnest of excuses? A meeting of minds, that was all. After all Plato talked of the 'higher love' that transcends base animal needs, that contemplates with religious awe justice, temperance and holiness.

Yet the thumping in her chest suggested that there were hearts as well as heads somehow in the mix. And with a sinking sensation she knew she must stop what had been going on now for weeks, the looks held just a little too long; her pretence at meekness, staring at the ground with lowered lids then a quick upward glance in the hope of finding his gaze still fixed on her face, the euphoric joy if it was so, angels and symphonies, and oh the plunging black despair if his attention was diverted elsewhere.

His name peppered her speech. Just to say it made the reality of him flare inside her. And when she spoke of Antipater in front of her husband, Pheroras laughed fondly and said, 'You have found your match at last.' It was true. Pheroras had been her teacher, but she had long ago outstripped him in thought and reasoning, her spirit flew in feathers now and she was able to quote whole passages from a single reading, where poor Pheroras had forgotten most of what he had read before he reached the end.

She and Antipater made a sport of it, offering Pheroras opening lines knowing that he could not finish the quotation without unfurling the scroll again. Sometimes they switched scrolls when his attention wandered, watching as he opened the wrong one, staring down at it with a frown creasing his forehead until neither Loshema nor Antipater could contain their laughter. Then Pheroras would stand before them, grinning shyly, like a child joining, without understanding, the humour of adults.

And Antipater's mind was daring. He seemed to care nothing about how shocking an idea was as long as it piqued his interest. He scandalized Nicolaus of Damascus, who revered Herodotus as the father of history, by insisting that there was as much fabrication in his histories as fact. 'Herodotus is a storyteller, aiming to please his audience as much as inform it.'

Nicolaus' already red face turned redder. 'Is it not an obligation of the historian to entertain? To write without reference to literary motif would turn a history into a delivery of facts and figures no better than the household accounts.'

Antipater shrugged. 'At heart I am a follower of Polybius. Truth must take the stage unadorned.'

'And yet you are an allegorizer.' Nicolaus' pale eyes narrowed. 'You do not hold your own mythologies up to the light of truth.'

'On the contrary, allegory is the tool I use to unlock the truth, the very truths, which by nature of their universality, release us from being Jew and pagan, and unite as brothers.'

The colour drained from Nicolaus' red face. Without saying another word he got to his feet and left the room. Antipater settled back in his seat, seeming unperturbed, and bestowed a quick, triumphant grin in Loshema's direction. And Loshema, who had been rapt, despite having heard much the same argument from Pheroras many times, shyly returned it.

Nor was it true that the acid of Antipater's remarks were reserved for pagans. Once, at dinner, he announced, 'There can be nothing above the Law, but in truth I prefer to read Homer.'

Pheroras was scandalized. 'That Homer is an author of astounding talent cannot be denied. But to compare him to the beauty and poetry of our Law— ' He could not go on. Antipater shrugged. 'Yet you, yourself, have said that the universal truths given to us by Moses are to be found in the Greek's works.'

'But— But to claim that it is equal to the Law!'

'There is divinity at the heart of our Law; the rest is commentary.'

Pheroras grew red. 'That is an argument which— Hillel's words do not— Yet you— you— ' Anger was gluing his words together, and Loshema noticed uneasily the cessation in the good natured chatter around the table. The courtiers were listening and frowns were being exchanged especially amongst those who wore priestly garb. Surely this was the moment to back down. Antipater would laugh and make light of it, a theoretical argument only. But it was clear by the glint in Antipater's black eyes that he was far from letting the argument rest.

And, for all his scholarly leanings, Pheroras was no match for the younger man. Antipater's arguments were sparse but viciously pointed, his preference was for the dagger strike —the unexpected source, a logical feint— rather than the crudeness of hammer blow explanations. Loshema had heard it said that he hunted in the same manner, a remoteness about him that some claimed disturbing. Once Loshema had chanced upon the young princes talking.

'The boar was almost upon him.' Aristobolus looked at his elder brother with wide eyes. 'Yet he did not release his arrow until he could near drive the tip through with his hand.'

Alexander raised his arrogant Hasmonaean chin. 'So, he is a killer? That only makes him his father's son.'

A killer? He looked more like a scholar, bending forward meeting Pheroras point for point, the promising disciple of a famous rabbi. And, despite the angry looks of the diners, the argument tickled Loshema, for the truth of it was that she secretly preferred the sweeping drama and vivid descriptions in Homer. If the Law was an endless wall that kept her safe then the *Odyssey* was an architectural wonder full of secret towers and labyrinthine passages. And it thrilled her to know that here, as with so many things, she and Antipater were one. It was all a kind of lightness that Loshema had never experienced before, but there was a kind of darkness there too making it a glorious, deadly game, a game in which she was already making mistakes.

The previous evening the family had been gathered for a small private entertainment arranged by Pallas, Herod's latest wife. A troop of Minoan acrobats were giving a performance and everyone was invited to join the fun. Loshema sat next to Pheroras while the chatter went on about her —Salome was telling an amusing anecdote about a slave who was so stupid that when he was told his master was in his cups he shook all the goblets out onto the floor. It was a well-known theme and there were many variations. When she had finished the company laughed politely, and Loshema stole a glance at the door, willing it to open with an intensity that almost frightened her.

When it finally did open and only a slave, carrying a tray of sweetmeats, entered, she had to fight to hide her disappointment. There was clapping —an impressive leap by one of the acrobats— she forced herself to join in. But her agitation was growing. It was as though earthworms were burrowing into her thighs making sitting still an agony. She tried to concentrate on the acrobats. They were fit young men with shaven heads and long muscled limbs, and the youngest, who was clearly the prize of the group, golden skin and lashes like a girl, made his moves with almost feminine grace. Neither Herod nor Alexander could take their eyes from him. And noticing this held Loshema's attention so that she did not hear when Antipater entered the room.

The acrobats were finishing a set and the sound of applause masked his entry. He bowed to Herod. 'Forgive me, father. I hoped to persuade mother, but she is praying and will not be disturbed.'

Behind him Loshema saw Aristobolus roll his eyes at his older brother. But Herod said merely, 'We will stop for a little refreshment. Come, join us.'

Antipater walked over to the couch where Alexander was sitting, and as he did so Alexander nudged his wife, who swung her legs up, stretching out over the vacant space. Antipater stopped and looked at Alexander. The younger man had a goblet in his hand, and he took a leisurely sip, keeping Antipater waiting as he would have kept a slave waiting, before saying in a flat, insolent voice, 'Forgive me. My wife is with child and needs room to be comfortable.'

Antipater stiffened, and Loshema glanced at the king, but it was not clear if Herod had noticed. Then came Pheroras' voice breaking the tension, 'Nephew, come, there is plenty of room here. My bones are thin enough to permit another.' It was an attempt at humour, but no-one laughed. Antipater gave a final glance at Alexander as if to say, this isn't over. Alexander shrugged his shoulders, while his wife, Glaphyra, smirked behind her fan. Then, his face white, Antipater turned and joined Pheroras, who had positioned himself at the end of the couch. Loshema had not followed him, and so Antipater sat down between them, thanking his uncle for his largesse and according his wife a few formal words of greeting.

Loshema said nothing. She could feel the sudden pressure of his thigh against her own, like an explosion that tore through her breast and made her want to shout or gasp. She swallowed hard, certain that her face betrayed her, but no-one seemed to be paying attention, at least she thought no-one was. Carelessly she let her fingers trail at her side, and when Antipater reached for his cup she reached too so that their hands accidently touched.

'Forgive me.'

'No, the fault was mine.'

She sat back, letting waves of pleasure ripple over her skin. So fleeting but she burned and ached in a way she had never experienced in the marriage bed. He had made no advances towards her, uttered not an inappropriate word, but when he was near it was as if he tore the clothes from her body and all the disguises that went with them, the daughter, the slave, the wife, so that she was left naked before him and could offer him nothing but herself. She stole a glance at his face. He was listening to something Herod was saying, yet she knew he felt her gaze. The muscles of his thigh tightened and his breathing increased, and suddenly her heart burst open and she was full of love, love, love.

And from that moment on the night grew magical around her. The acrobats soared higher than before. The anecdotes shared, especially Antipater's tales, were the most amusing anyone had ever heard. And under it all was a secret language between Antipater and Loshema that allowed them to go on talking without talking, their intimacy undetected, until Glaphyra, Alexander's wife, remarked to Pheroras, 'How charmingly your wife and your nephew get along, uncle.'

Pheroras stared at her in puzzlement then turned to look in Loshema's direction. At once she dropped her eyes to the floor, but not before she had seen Salome's narrowed, knowing look flick towards the King.

In that moment, feeling the strangler's knotted rope about her neck, Loshema made a pact with the Almighty never to court Antipater's company again, and yet the next day she was crossing the courtyard and making her way up the stone steps towards the library.

Antipater had his back to her when she entered. And she stood for a moment on the threshold, drinking him in, telling herself that this would be the last time she spoke with him alone, all in this little space of stolen intimacy until she noticed what he was doing. Upon the desk was a leather satchel and he was taking scrolls from the shelves and stuffing them inside. As she watched he lifted down another, and unfurling it, stood perusing the contents. She was too astonished to speak, but she must have made some small revealing sound because he turned suddenly and, seeing who it was, gave her a bright false smile.

'Have you come to wish me farewell.'

The day drained of colour. Farewell? 'You are leaving?'

'I am being sent to Rome.'

Tears sprang to her eyes. 'But— ' She could get no further.

'It is an honour. My father wishes me to cement our friendship with Augustus.' He gestured at the satchel. 'Your husband has shown me great kindness. He allows me to take books to be my comfort when so far from home.' His voice quavered slightly on the word 'home', but Loshema was barely listening. Almost tearing her skirts with the length of her strides she closed the distance between them so only the desk kept them apart.

'This is their doing.'

Antipater put the scroll down on the desk. 'It does not please my Hasmonaean brothers to see me so close to the king. Alexander thought the throne safely his until I was brought back to muddy the waters. I thought— ' He paused and looked for an instant so woebegone that it wrenched her heart. 'I thought my father had finally come to his senses, that he had seen some ... *quality* in me. But I am a pawn, here to warn my brothers that they are not invincible.'

Loshema was shaking her head without awareness of it.

'Alexander has boasted that he will have my mother spinning with the slaves once he wears the crown.' A look flashed across Loshema's face and Antipater put his hands to his temples. 'Forgive me. There is no shame in being a slave. I meant only— '

But Loshema had moved so that she now stood before him, and before she knew what she was saying, she cried, 'You are Israel's true king.'

Antipater's expression closed, and for an instant she thought he might strike her then he took her by the shoulders and pressed his lips to hers. And she melted, leaning into him, giving herself up, in and of herself, in a way that years of bondage had never managed to extract. Then he was pushing her away, roughly but without cruelty. She stared at him, bewildered.

'I cannot. I would ruin you.'

She took a step towards him. 'I don't care.'

He turned from her, placing his palms on the desk and leaning into them. He was breathing deeply. 'All my life I have tried not to be a Herod.' He turned his head to face her. 'He loved her, you know.' And she understood he was talking of the first Mariamme. 'She died because my father loved her. My mother and I were sent into exile because of love. And Salome murders her husbands, like some modern daughter of Danaus.'

She reached her hand out reassuringly. 'I am married to a Herod.'

But he shook his head. 'I am a Herod in a way that your husband can never be one. I feel it. A worm inside of me, always seeking power. It makes monsters of us, and turns love to poison in our veins.'

She touched his face. 'Then poison me.'

What shall I tell you? Gorgeous fantasies? Lies? Shall I garland the experience with Homeric allusions? —Our bodies ruddy with sun, the pulsing rush of longing, the lover's whisper.— Or is it a more Jewish touch you desire? Shall I speak with Solomon's mouth, offering my breasts as young roes, who feed amongst the lilies; are my lover's kisses sweeter than wine? No. this is not the place for poetry.

Writer that I am I long to retell it all, every detail, but passion's conflagration leaves only fragments. From this distant place I can only conjure splintered moments that no more speak the truth of the whole than a sleeping eye speaks of the waking soul that animates it. Yet I will try, for how can I sit here pen in hand, and not confess that I remember the panting heat, his breath in my ear as he thrust deep into the well of me. —I am yours. I am yours.— Or that I remember the deep responding shudders of my body and the way he pressed my hand to his lips. I remember that in that room I was part of the Almighty's creation and everything was hung about with splendour. I remember that I, who had been lost, now, at last, was found.

34

Letters

11 BCE

To Loshema of the Royal house of Herod from Antipater, Prince of Judea

The world is indeed a very strange place. As a child, I walked the dusty streets of Beersheba wishing only that I might be far away in Rome with all its reputed marvels. I dreamt of making my reputation amongst the greatest minds of the day. Yet here I am, the darling of court, graciously received by Caesar and all I can think about is returning to Jerusalem to be with you.

You fill my thoughts, day and night, the most marvellous sights —the arch of Augustus, the temple of Mars Ultor— fail to arouse my interest, and bread and wine all taste like ashes in my mouth. In truth, my sparse appetites have aroused comment and I am gaining a secret reputation as a stoic or an ascetic of the most exotic kind.

O, Loshema, just to speak your name —which is no name at all— is all I require to sustain me. I have quite lost my heart to you. Please believe me when I say that it was never my intention to dishonour you. Your husband, my uncle, is the kindest man alive. But I had already seen you in the garden in your shift, and I was filled with desire for you before I knew your name. And when I discovered you were to be my 'aunt' if only in title, I was filled with despair.

My pride undid me in the end. I thought myself my mother's child. She is a cold woman, as you have observed, her passions so enslaved to her intellect that she might turn a cool eye towards the king, my father, and his wife, who together represent her greatest love and direst foe. In all the years of my childhood she held duty out to me as both punishment and reward. And by the time my father recalled me to Jerusalem I believed that I was a creature purely of spirit.

If only you had been a stupid woman I might have schooled myself to grow tired of you. But to hear you speak, to listen to the vaulting arcs of your opinions soaring with argument and counterargument, and to hear you voice thoughts I believed the gift of my mind alone was a lesson in humility.

That day in the library, I found my father in me, and my desire for you was overpowering, I took you, and neither your husband nor the king nor the whole Grand Sanhedrin could have prevented it. I love you, Loshema. And if I cannot

252

have you rightfully in the eyes of the Almighty, I will find some other path to make you mine.

Fear not that this letter will fall into the wrong hands. I will give it to my man, Isaac, who is a good loyal servant and may be trusted to be discrete.

To Loshema of the Royal house of Herod from Antipater, Prince of Judea

I greet you and pray for your health. Yet still I possess, not a solitary line penned in your hand. I have bribed a seneschal to bring all news from Judea straight to my apartments, and the poor man must think I am quite frantic to read reports on tax collection or the latest plans to drain a swamp.

Tell me that your silence does not foreshadow regret. I think I could bear any torture other than thinking that you lament our union. My manservant, Isaac, assures me that he delivered the letter to you with great discretion, and that there was no sign of discovery in the days that followed, yet you made no attempt to summon him into your presence or even to deliver a scribbled line of acknowledgement before he was forced to leave. But, then again, if your mind was easily read you would not be the woman I love, and thus I will occupy the sleepless hours of my night telling you of my life, which I pray is still of interest to you.

As I have mentioned previously, my welcome in Rome has been very gracious. I am not a man who makes friends easily, yet the emperor's wife, Livia, has been most accommodating. She is very tall and stately with a wonderful knowledge of herbs and medicinal plants and can quote whole passages from Hippocrates. I think you would like her. She is also a great friend of my aunt, Salome, and speaks so well of us Herods that father would be comforted from his constant fear that we inspire only hatred and envy in those closest to us. Often she refers to us as kindred spirits, and laments that we are Jews for, though she harbours no prejudice, she knows that it disbars us from the highest positions in Roman society.

You would be amused by how much the 'woman' this formidable matron of Rome turns out to be. She is not above gossip. She tells me that the rumour is that your husband is still out of favour for refusing to put you aside to marry the king's daughter. (She had no knowledge, of course, of the pain the tale brought me, but thought it a delightful curio of romantic fiction.)

I must confess that, while I cannot think of my sojourn here as anything less than exile, there are compensations. Rome is a beguiling city, different from Jerusalem in ways I cannot begin to describe. The whole city is a riot of colour, and the impression is of a beautiful woman gaudily painted. But the closer one gets the more powerful becomes the scent of corruption. Bribery is the lubricant that oils every transaction from high to low. No-one is without their price, and I swear even the pauper must be prepared to skim his profits to pay off the militia man who turns a blind eye to his begging. But there are advantages to being in this Babylon of the West. As well you know, Jerusalem is a secretive city, constantly hiding its face from its neighbours, but here, in Rome, secrets flow freely along the gutters with the effluent, and there is little one cannot find out for a price.

I have made a friend of Livia's young maidservant, Acme, a Jew whose welcome to me was nothing short of worshipful. She is a slave, but well thought of, and one would barely know it as she moves about with almost total freedom, and is a valuable source of information. She has confirmed what I suspected, my younger brothers are plotting against me and, worse, their treacheries are also aimed at the king. I have written to my father warning him of my fears for his safety.

I end this letter by entreating you once again to send me some small sign of your affection. I am alone and far from home. Sleep and appetite are denied me, and I lie awake fearing that in my absence your passions have cooled. Have pity on me. I believe that you are the one person in the world who can save me.

To Loshema of the Royal house of Herod from Antipater, Prince of Judea

Are you a witch, a dream? A madman's fevered delusion? All these months and not a word.

My father arrived two days ago with my brothers in tow. I had known of their coming for weeks yet still it was a shock to see them. My father greeted me warmly and told me the circumstances that had brought them here. You will know better than I what has been taking place in Jerusalem, but it appears to me that tensions are beginning to rise to the surface.

Is it true that Salome was so intent on ridding herself of her arrogant nephews that she tricked Pheroras into making false allegations to Alexander, claiming that my father had designs upon his wife? From all accounts the ruse went badly wrong and Salome was uncovered as the perpetrator. From what I hear the court is in a state of paranoia. Salome is in disgrace and my father claims that he does not know who to trust.

Truly, Loshema, you would have pitied him. He sat in my room, his grizzled head in his hands, and wept like a child. He doubted himself, he said. The tales of my brothers' plotting grew by the day, and in any other circumstances he should have executed them on the spot. But his heart was in turmoil and, finding that he could not read even the character of his own sister, he had come to Rome to ask Caesar's advice.

The next day we were summoned into Caesar's presence, and many men of standing were gathered to hear the outcome. Seeing how closely the audience resembled a trial took the shine from my brothers' arrogance. Alexander managed to keep his chin lifted, but Aristobolus grew wide-eyed and lagged behind his brother, as a child hangs back who knows punishment awaits.

My father was eloquent in his arguments. He presented his fears and asked where he had gone wrong? Had he not treated Alexander and Aristobolus only with kindness and respect? There were many men there, who were clearly patriarchs of their families, and they turned to one another and nodded. The atmosphere in the room grew chillier. No-one solicited my opinion, and for that I was grateful as I would not wish to show my hand so openly.

Caesar then turned to the princes and asked them to explain themselves. And, now they knew the game was up. It must have been in their minds that Rome is a harsh place for sons. A man cannot reach financial independence while his father is alive, and the *pater familias* may execute his son on the flimsiest ground without fear of recrimination.

At once Aristobolus burst into tears, and was closely followed by Alexander, who put his arms about his brother and tried his best to console him. In the midst of so many stern faces their vanity collapsed, and it became evident how truly young they are. They were helped, of course, by their beauty. In other circumstances they might have been part of a tableau depicting gorgeous youth, Ganymede and Hyacinthus, *pueri delicati.*

In the face of such pathos father crumbled and wept with them. Soon there was not a dry eye in the house, and even Caesar wiped away a tear. At last judgement was given. Caesar pronounced the boys innocent of the charges, but guilty of not showing sufficient gratitude to their pious parent hence allowing misunderstanding and suspicion to take root. He then took his wife by the hand and opined how the gods had favoured him when it came to family matters.

He left the room shortly thereafter, and the noble company, having had their fill of Jewish drama, followed suit. I was left, facing my father and brothers, who were locked in a familial embrace having forgotten all about me. I turned to go, but my father caught sight of my forlorn exit and called me back. He broke free of my brothers and held me to him, saying that my fears for his safety were well noted and that I was the best of sons, a title I was quick to deny. My modesty earned me more accolades and, as it was clearly expected of me, I turned to offer my congratulations to my brothers. Aristobolus looked at the ground, but Alexander opened his arms and embraced me. Over his shoulder I could see my father's tear-stained face, and in my ear Alexander whispered in a voice of pure hatred. 'There is a child.'

Loshema, what does this mean? Does this explain your silence? The child is mine. I must believe it. And, if it is so, you are in danger. This episode in Rome has only strengthened their resolve against me. Caesar insists that we stay a few more weeks to enjoy the festivities he has planned, but we will leave shortly afterwards. I swear I will be home before the season changes and discover what is what. Have no fear, my love. If my brothers' resolve has strengthened it has only made mine grow tenfold by comparison. They have youth and beauty on their side, but this is not a game for boys, even beautiful ones.

To Antipater, royal prince of Judea from Loshema of the house of Herod

Beloved, I greet you and pray for your good health. If this letter has a chance of reaching you I must write quickly. It has been an agony to receive your letters yet to remain silent as the grave. Salome cast great suspicion upon me and has me watched day and night. Even when I am in the library it is not unusual for her to burst in or to send one of her clerks to suddenly inquire after a scroll, and while I fetch it, his eyes are scouring the desk for tales he can scurry back with to his mistress. It is a wonder that I have managed to keep your letters secret. Be not afraid. I commit them to memory then set them aflame, though it is as if I hold the flame to my heart to watch them burn.

It seems that rumour flies on birds' wings, and you seem very well informed in Rome. Perhaps you already know that your brothers have fallen out of favour. For all Salome has found herself in disgrace the seeds of doubt she planted have taken root.

It came not a moment too soon. Alexander and Aristobolus have ridden high on the wave of discontent and distrust that has split the loyalties of the court in a dozen different directions. They grew bolder, and made full use of their beauty to entice the young men, even their father's eunuchs. And that they thought little of the house of Herod was made clear to all; even I was a victim of their disdain.

I came face to face with them and a group of their favourites on my way to dinner one night. The princes said nothing, but no-one would let me pass, and when they finally grew bored and went on their way one of the band of heroes knocked deliberately against me in a manner that sent me flying, which in my state was a poor deed to say the least. I fell full length, and when I dared look up Alexander was looking down at me with an expression only a slave can understand. It says you are nothing, that you are less than the dirt you lie upon, and if he puffs out his cheeks and blows you will scatter to the four winds.

But I have mentioned my state, and I confess it is not Salome's vigilance alone that has kept me from lifting a pen. I think it will have reached you by now that I have a child, a beautiful daughter. The name chosen for her is Esther, a queen's name. But I will say no more. Only that she exists. You may draw your own conclusions.

I do not know what the outcome will be in Rome. I cannot find it in myself to wish for the princes' death. They are, after all, young and their mother was cruelly taken from them. But something must be done to resolve the situation. I often consider our talks and think of how eloquently you spoke with a wisdom that seemed beyond your years. And I admit that I know you may be a man capable of cruelty. Perhaps it is that iron core inside you that draws me to you. Of course you are right that youth and beauty are blunt weapons in this war. If Alexander and Aristobolus were wise they would remember that such traits did not save their mother.

It comes to me as I write this that perhaps we two have much in common. Our bleak childhoods have shaded our eyes from the glitter of the court, and we can see, as others cannot, the dark belly of the beast. It will take a ruthless man to cut out corruption, but on that score, at least, I have no fear. I beg you to hurry home at the first possible opportunity. Our safety lies in your hands.

35

What is a Jew?

'PLEASE, LOSHEMA. YOU MUST UNDERSTAND.'

Understand? I understand nothing. Pheroras is standing before me, his thin face ashen. He won't look at me.

'I am thinking of your safety. Of the safety of the child.'

Always 'the child' never 'our' never 'my'. Do I imagine it? In all other ways he is a doting father. But there are bigger worries. I get out my chair, begin to pace. 'No, husband. It is not my safety you fear for. It is your own.'

Pheroras presses his fingers to his temples, flashing me a look of such reproach that it is my turn to slide my eyes to the comfort of commonplace things, the worn patch on the couch's headrest where we have lain too often reading; Pheroras' goblet, chipped now, yet too much a favourite to abandon. And here is the nub of the matter. He cannot find it in his heart to cast away a cup yet he is sending his wife and daughter into exile.

'Please!' He keeps saying that, as if it were a balm with magical properties, something purchased from one of the court magicians, spikenard and spells, the spit of a magus. 'Please, Loshema. You know that the court is not what it once was, and the Almighty knows how little trust there was to begin with. But now my reputation is damaged I can no longer protect you.'

At this I turn, ignoring the hangdog looks, the hand held out to me. 'So to protect your precious reputation I am to go. Esther is to go.'

'Loshema— "

'Loshema! Loshema! It is no name and you would make it less than it is.'

'Please— ' That word again. Another man would have sent his slaves to turn me out. Did Herod stoop to plead with Doris? Would I think Pheroras more the man if he suddenly found the Herod in him? What would Antipater have done?

Veins stand out on Pheroras' forehead; his hair is unkempt. 'Times have changed, my love. Herod feels like a blind man in a pit of bears, certain of no-one's loyalty. This is a test, and I have refused his daughter once. I cannot refuse a second time.'

I pause, breathing hard. All my clever words are useless here. Do I imagine I can take on Herod? Then why do I go on fighting, fighting? This is everything I dreamt of, to be free. No more secret trysts. To be with Antipater, knowing I am his and he is mine. And yet it hurts. This is unexpected. Everything I am I owe to Pheroras. It is as if he made me and now can unmake me. Pygmalion turning his true love back into ivory. I am losing something I do not *understand, something I did not know could be lost.*

There are tears in Pheroras' eyes. 'You will have everything. I promise. You will not want.'

'I will not have you.'

Peraea was a country of barren hills and dusty secret wadis that trapped the sun's rays and turned them into burning hellholes so that even the starving goats, who criss crossed the land searching for a blade of grass, avoided them. Loshema's party were forced to ride with their mouths and noses covered, but even then nightfall would see them spitting gritty balls of phlegm onto the cracked earth. And the longer they rode the more Loshema began to see the place as a dog, a stinking yellow dog with its ribs poking through and its shrivelled tongue lolling from its mouth.

Yet their welcome was a warm one. They rode into their destination, a place known as, Beth-aram, a little before sundown, and here at least the thick waters of the river Hieromax could be seen with its ribbon of green to either side. Pheroras had a palace there being tetrarch in the technical sense, and as she was technically still his wife (the divorce not yet formally declared) she was treated with due honours by the steward, Nabal Haresh, who apologised profusely for the rigours of their journey, as though he had somehow been personally remiss in not sweeping the dust from their path.

Loshema, who was covered head to toe in a thin coating of ochre particles, longed only for the chance to bathe, but she recognised kindness in this pot-bellied rather fatherly man, whom she would find out later had no children of his own, and she allowed him to carry Esther as he led the party through to the rooms he had prepared for them.

'Such short notice,' he lamented. 'I barely had time to air them let alone conduct a proper cleaning.'

Loshema looked round the room, which seemed to her so pristine and generally free of dust —nothing short of a miracle in the circumstances— that she felt a pang of guilt assail her for besmirching such tender ministrations with the foulness of her clothes. A bed piled high with soft bolsters and cushions stood in the middle of the room. Portly little Haresh followed her glance and rubbed his hands together in agitation.

'Forgive me, noble lady. I should have sent at once for maids to help you bathe. So noble a person as yourself must be weary after such an arduous journey. I will call for refreshments to be brought up after you have had time to settle in.'

He left, bowing, and Loshema kept her smile to herself until he was out the door. Could she call herself 'noble' now that she was no longer the wife of the tetrarch? Her smile faded.

In the days that followed, Loshema did her best to maintain a measure of dignity. But it was hard. For all Nabal Haresh's kindness she sensed that she was being laughed at by the rest of the household. She thought she caught the gleam of insolence in the smiles and nods, and though her orders were accepted, it seemed a season turned before they were carried out. Once she distinctly heard the words, *Slave wife*, being whispered, but when she turned the maidservants were studiously clearing the table apparently unaware of her scrutiny.

Or was it all in her imagination? Life was so slow in Beth-aram. *Beth-aram*. She ran the words around her mouth, *the High House*. It was the name given to the tetrarch's palace though it was little more than an extended villa, and also the name of the nearby village.

After weeks of boredom she had insisted on walking there unaccompanied, much to the consternation of the dutiful Nabal Haresh, who warned constantly against the dangers of leopards and bandits; there were even rumours apparently of bandits who were suspected of training leopards to carry out attacks on command. But still she had gone, hoping to distance herself from Gomer's constant complaining and to ease the ache in her soul at least for a while.

In her imagination she had seen herself walking along the cool banks of the Hieromax, alone with her thoughts. But when she got there she found the riverbanks overgrown and impassable and the village only a dirt track with a score of hovels crowded along either side. A few sun-blackened goat-herders were going lethargically about their business, their ragged cloaks barely covering their nakedness. They ignored her, as did a woman, who came out to draw water from the well.

She stood, watching until loneliness and the need to belong impelled her steps forwards. Were not the men and women of this village Jews? They believed fiercely in the unity of the deity, the food they deemed unclean, the festivals they attended, all were identical to the practices observed in the capital. Loshema took another step and one of the goat-herders turned to look at her. She met his eyes for a moment and saw something harsh and unforgiving there before he dropped his gaze in deference to her rank.

Then suddenly she was aware of herself, a woman too well dressed to belong to the village, a woman from the city, whose Judaism was peppered with pagan ideas and philosophies. She stood before them, a rejected wife, a scholar, shielded by cool reasoning in a land that produced burning-eyed prophets with the fires of faith oozing from their souls. To these people she was no more a Jew than the animals they herded along the Hieromax. She stood a moment longer, increasingly aware of the lonely sweep of the sky above her head, with neither towers nor temples to interrupt its infinite arc then she turned and walked away.

Nabal Haresh's evident relief at her safe return lifted her heart a little. She agreed to a little breakfast and asked if there had been any letters delivered in her absence, and though she knew the answer, still she felt her stomach plummet when Haresh shook his head. Bereft of her books she wondered what a rejected wife did to fill her days. How had Doris coped through the lonely years— She pulled herself up. It would not come to that.

After a meal of bread and dates, which she found she had almost no appetite for, she called for writing materials to be brought. At least let her thoughts find expression.

> To Antipater, royal prince of Judea, from—her pen hesitated then she added— Loshema, temporary resident of Peraea

My love, you must forgive my writing to you. The situation at home is delicate, I know. I do not mean to trouble you, but I have been here almost a month and received no word. Indeed, I have received no word from anyone. I am blind and deaf to the goings on at court, and this dusty province may as well be my tomb. I fear, if I stay here much longer, I will grow dry and thin, like women of this arid scape, and you will not recognise me.

Life is very slow here. You would laugh to see the way things are done, as though everyone were half sleeping. I swear if the Almighty suddenly decreed that the Jews must clear the Judean desert of sand there would be wailing and gnashing of teeth all over Jerusalem, committees would be formed, engineers from the furthest parts of the empire would be consulted. While here, in Beth-aram, they would shrug their shoulders and begin picking up the grains one by one.

I am glad to hear that you have found favour with your father, and pray that your welcome in Jerusalem was a warm one, and that your brothers' factions have not grown too strong. You are right to fear them, I think. They grew up knowing nothing of mercy, and the Golden Rule of their childhoods must surely be *Strike down your enemy before he is able to strike at you*.

Our own welcome has been a mixed one. Nabal Haresh, the steward here, has been kindness itself, but we are not so well liked by the rest of the household. As my exile continues the servants grow bolder and 'forget' my orders. They carry whispers to the village that the reason my husband set me aside is because the child is not his. I know I have sinned, but it makes me sick to my stomach to hear them take pleasure in it.

Their whispers grew so loud that last night I could not sleep, but crept to Esther's crib and stood trying to determine which Herod my child most resembled. Were those your eyes that stared up at me too sharply, too knowing? Or did she smile with Pheroras' generous mouth? Of myself I could see nothing and I stood in doubt and darkness, the great silence of the place throbbing against my temples.

Forgive me, my love, for pressing my troubles upon you. I only want you to know how precious a single word from you would be. Because, even as they mutter that I will surely face the judgement of the Almighty, I cannot help but think that there must be other ways to see things. Is it not possible that the Almighty in His Wisdom and Mercy has freed me from the ties of marriage? What seems like disgrace may be, after all, His blessing—

Her pen froze. Had Pheroras not taught her that there were dangers in interpreting the Will of the deity? Out of nowhere her nostrils filled with a familiar odour, cedar and lampblack, as though her words had brought the spirit of Pheroras to sudden life in the room. She could picture him shaking his head, his eyes alight with intelligence, saying, *When horror happens we hold up our hands, and claim, 'It is the Will of the Almighty and not to be understood by men.' By what arrogance do we then claim to know His Will when His acts appear in our favour?*

She sat very still until the smell faded then she got to her feet and fetched a lighted taper, which she held to her letter until it dissolved in flame.

Once the letter was gone she felt emptier than before. But it was an emptiness that sat in her belly, like a worm and would not give her peace. She called for her mirror and sat staring into it trying to find the woman whom Antipater claimed he loved, but all she found was a gaunt middle-aged woman, who looked back at her from red-rimmed eyes, the corners of her mouth drawn in two bitter lines. The image frightened her and she set the mirror down, as though it had branded her skin, then she went off to see Esther. After all it was said that women found solace in their children, even children whose presence pierced their hearts with guilt.

Esther was curled on Batia's shoulder. But both baby and grandmother started when Loshema entered the room. Esther began to cry.

'She is hungry. Give her to me.'

Batia looked doubtful. 'The wet-nurse fed her not an hour ago. She is only frightened.'

'I am her mother. I know when she is hungry.'

Batia stared, and Loshema knew that there was a rising, hysterical note in her voice. She moved forward and snatched Esther up. 'There now. There my little one.' The words sounded fraudulent and certainly did not impress Esther, who began to howl in earnest and to push away the proffered nipple.

'She is not hungry,' Batia said again. And something in her comfortable certainty snapped the last of Loshema's composure.

'Best you care for her then as you think me an unfit mother.'

'Loshema— '

But she pushed her daughter into Batia's arms and fled the room before the storm of tears that was rising in her throat could take hold of her.

Later, shame and need made her creep back full of intentions of apology and reconciliation. But, when she pushed the door open, softly this time, Batia and Esther were fast asleep, their heads touching, as though in silent communication. Loshema's lips parted then closed. She shut the door and crept away.

Yet, if she had only understood that life is not to be taken for granted in the young, she would have stayed at that door and barred the way to the Angel of Death with her own body.

Quite when the weather changed Loshema could not have said. And that she did not notice was unremarkable as there were many things these days she did not notice. This morning she had not noticed that her hair was unbrushed when she left her chambers or that she had not eaten breakfast or that the wind was particularly sharp and bitter, billowing out the thin fabric of her dress, like the sails of a ship in flight.

Shunning the courtyard, which was cobbled and treeless, and used mainly for household business, she walked a small distance to a ridge not far from the front of the house and, once there, sat down on the stump of a cedar, which provided a comfortable seat from which to survey the view in summer. But summer had long gone and even autumn was giving way to dark shrill winds from the north that prickled the skin with invisible needles of ice. Loshema noticed nothing of this, sitting straight and still, her eyes fixed, yet unseeing on the bleak mountains in the distance.

And in this state she paid no attention to the elderly man making his way up the winding path that led up to the villa. He was not particularly well dressed; there were thin patches on his clothes and other places where the signs of mending and re-mending were clear. Yet he walked with a certain quiet dignity, and when he saw Loshema he changed direction and stopped a few feet in front of her.

For a while he stood there in clear deference to her rank, but when it became clear that either she had not noticed him or was choosing not to, he bowed, cleared his throat and addressed her directly. 'Noble lady, you must forgive an old man for disturbing your peace. I came to see my brother, who is steward here, which I suppose is not quite the truth of the matter, for my purpose in coming here was to make myself known to you.'

Loshema raised her eyes as far as the blue tassels on the corners of his mantle. 'You are a Pharisee,' she said. But she said it without inflection or tone or interest.

The man before her bowed again. 'You are, of course, correct, noble lady. I am Rabbi Binyamin Haresh, brother to the steward of Beth-aram, but this I have already told you.'

Loshema did not lift her gaze. 'What do you want? If it is payment you seek you must ask your brother to write to my husband.'

'Indeed no, noble lady. Your husband owes me nothing. It is rather, to my way of understanding, that I am the one that owes you.'

'There is nothing that you owe me.'

Rabbi Haresh pulled on his beard, a long beard, greying somewhat. 'Yet it seems I owe you my condolences.'

Loshema lifted her eyes to stare directly at Rabbi Haresh, and they were eyes filled with bitterness and loss and pain. And her pain was of the very worst sort, the kind that howls through the soul on a note too high for the human ear to hear, but perfectly attuned to vibrate and shatter the human heart. Rabbi Haresh gave a small understanding nod. 'To lose a child is a kind of death, I think. It turns the world on its head. And it is little comfort to know that the Lord giveth and the Lord taketh away when the pain of the taking makes us wish that the giving had not occurred in the first place.'

Loshema's eyes, which had wandered back to the distance, suddenly focused. To hear her most secret thoughts coming out of the mouth of this old man sent a jolt through her body. She looked at him suspiciously. 'You are not like the Pharisees in Jerusalem.'

'And what are the Pharisees of Jersualem like?'

'They are— ' She paused. 'They are worldly, but not wise.'

Rabbi Haresh shrugged. 'Am I wise? Let me tell you, a long time ago there was another rabbi, who taught in the village here. Rabbi Gershon was his name. He was old even when I was born, with a long white beard and a bald freckled head.

'No-one could remember when he came to Beth-aram, and there were rumours that he had been one of those who followed Moses across the desert and now lived with us under another name hiding from the angel of Death. And some said he was as old as the hills and the Almighty had created him along with the sky and the earth so that he would always be there to look after us. All nonsense, of course—'

'Rabbi,' Loshema interrupted. 'Even a cast off wife may have a loose-tongued old man whipped from her home.'

'Forgive me. I am an old man and my speech wanders. What I meant to say was that Rabbi Gershon was without doubt the wisest man in the village. And not only the village. Sages from far away would come to seek out his wisdom.

'And being young and full of admiration, I went to him myself one day and said, "Rabbi, how am I to become wise?" Such a question. But he answered me. He had to answer me, you understand. He was my teacher and I had asked a question.

'I thought he would quote scripture at me. But he only looked at me with great sadness and put his hand on my shoulder. "There is only one way to wisdom," he said. "And that is through the gates of pain. The Lord was compassionate indeed when he warned the first amongst us to shun the tree of wisdom, for there is little to be learned that does not first require a sacrifice of suffering." '

Something hardened in Loshema's expression. 'Tell me, rabbi. What has my child's death taught me?'

Rabbi Haresh stroked his beard, considering the matter. 'It has taught you to be a Jew.'

A dry sound from Loshema's throat. Laughter? 'Then it has taught me what I already knew.' She made a movement as if she would rise, but Rabbi Haresh went on hastily, 'Noble lady, before you came here, before the plague took your child, you were a Jew, but you did not know what it was to be one.'

'You speak in riddles old man.'

'Indeed I do. It is a fault of mine. But it occurs to me to put it to you this way, what is a Jew?'

Loshema opened her mouth then closed it again. Every particle of her being was screaming at her to rid herself of this meddlesome old man with the madness to demand of her, *what is a Jew*, while she was grieving for her child, her child, whom she had barely got to know, who had filled her with guilt and shame and something akin to love, and who had slipped away from her in the depths of the night, consumed by a fever that burnt out her soul, leaving her little body limp and lifeless in her mother's arms.

What is a Jew?

Loshema looked at Rabbi Haresh from a place of such darkness that they might have been looking at each other from opposite ends of the universe. He looked abashed. 'Noble lady— '

'There is no nobility about me. I was a born a slave, as well you know.'

'I know only that many men are born slaves who are free in their hearts, and there are other free born men who will forever live in chains.'

'Platitudes.'

Rabbi Haresh sighed and stroked his chin. 'You are right. Of course you are right. Despite the pains I have been through the sum of my wisdom is not sufficient to fill a thimble.' Then, despite herself, Loshema noticed that there was none of the unctuous vanity she had come to associate with holy men in the capital. For his sake, more than her own, she asked, 'Tell me then, what is a Jew?'

Haresh was silent for a while. 'A Jew,' he said slowly, as though the question was still a surprise to him. 'A Jew is many things. When you came here, noble lady, you walked in our village and you looked at the men and women there as if you did not know what kind of creatures you beheld.'

A little colour flushed Loshema's cheeks, but she remained silent. Rabbi Haresh went on. 'Pagans say the word, *Jew*, as though by saying it they have understood it. As though to be a Jew were a simple thing, like a stick or a rock. You scratch a rock you get more rock. What is a Jew? Is he a Sadducee, a Pharisee? Is he the man of wealth, who walks by a beggar or is he the ragged prophet threatening destruction on those who do not follow the Law?

'Or is it because he has suffered he is a Jew? After all, what Jew has not known what it is to be a slave, an exile, an outsider?'

'So I am a Jew because I suffer?'

'Not at all. Suffering is a human, rather than a particularly Jewish condition. By that I mean only to imply that we are practiced at it, though we do not make a fetish out of it, such as the followers of Cybele do. We do not seek suffering, but we learn to live with it. We harness it, even as the king has harnessed the power of the sea in far off Caesarea. We transform it.'

At this Loshema gave a mirthless laugh and a slight shake of her head. Rabbi Haresh dared a step closer. 'Noble lady. You were a slave then a royal wife. When your husband put you aside you were no longer a wife. Did this mean you became a slave again? You were a mother and now you are no longer. Does this make you nothing? You came here and all you saw was the men and women of this place and you despised them. How could these cold, desperate men share the same name as the glittering Jews of Jerusalem? Yet they take this desolate outcrop, where no man has any right to live, and they turn it into their home.

'We are Jews, noble lady, as you are a Jew. Not because we suffer, but because we take our suffering and rebuild the world with it. There are men, who have been slaves or whose grandfathers were slaves, who mourn and beat their breasts and blame the shame of it on their own inadequacies. But our slavery is a thing to be celebrated because we see, without it, we would never have learned to bless freedom.'

Loshema lifted her head suddenly and searched Haresh's face. She did it wildly and furiously, as though she could tear him apart with her gaze. Then the light went out of her and she wrapped her arms about her body and began to rock. Rabbi Haresh stood watching. 'I am an old man,' he said at last. 'I came to give comfort and instead I lectured.' A sharp gust of wind snatched away his words, and sighing, he slipped off his cloak and placed it about Loshema's shoulders. 'Rabbi Gershon I am not.'

Hours later —Loshema knew this because the light had changed— a young boy was sent from the house to fetch her. She looked up, surprised to find Rabbi Haresh had gone; his cloak was still about her shoulders.

'Noble lady, a man has come to see you.'

'A man? What name did he give?'

The boy's mouth hung open. 'A man from J'ruslem,' he offered. Then Loshema wasn't listening any more, but running along the path, heart hammering in her chest. There were no words in her head, no thoughts fully formed. Only a sense that everything would be all right. The past could not be changed. But, with him, there would be a reason for the future.

In the vestibule she flung off her cloak and let her aching, unused limbs carry her to her apartments. The door was open and she rushed in ready to throw herself into Antipater's arms. But it was not Antipater, who turned to greet her, but the last person she expected to see on earth, her husband.

36

In which the young wolf tears at his father's kingdom

9-8 BCE

D URING THE THIRTEEN MONTHS OF Loshema's exile there had been many changes at court. And now that she re-entered this exotic world, seeing it almost as a stranger would see it, she was acutely aware of every alteration even through the fogged lens of her grief. There were new faces. A minister had been changed here, a seneschal there. And, entering the dining hall on the first night, Loshema saw at once that the doddering Nabataean ambassador —famed for his roving eye whenever a pretty youth walked past— had been replaced by a tall handsome man of noble bearing, whom she later found out went by the name of Syllaeus.

And in amongst the new faces were old ones, somewhat altered. Nicolaus of Damascus was in thicker than ever with the king, and followed him around everywhere, like an un-shakable shadow, pen in hand. There was something new, too, about Salome, a lightness —in some women it might have been called softness— that, nonetheless, rolled back the years from her plump, pouched face, and made her trill girlishly, especially when the Nabataean ambassador, Syllaeus, glanced her way.

And the king himself had changed. The grey streaks in his hair and beard were wider now than the dark, and he walked with a slight stoop, his restless eyes never seeming to be at peace. His gaze lit on Loshema in a way that made her blood run cold. And when he beck-oned her forward she walked as the prisoner walks towards his executioner.

'I told my brother to set you aside.' His voice, something cracked about it, an old man's voice. She did not answer, did not raise her eyes.

'I offered my own daughter. For a second time.'

Still she said nothing.

'And yet he chose you. A woman so long past youth's bloom, she could not bear him a healthy child.'

She could not help it. A flash of sheer fury open and unguarded. Men had died for less, but now Herod smiled and leant forward to whisper in her ear,

'There is a devil inside you. I recognize it. The same one is inside me. You imagine it gives you power, that it keeps you safe, but I tell you now, it will destroy you.'

—Ah Herod, if my destruction was the only power that devil possessed I would prostrate myself before it now, like a priestess of Baal. But I don't know what is to happen, and so I

only stand there, stiff and hating, my gaze fixed over his shoulder until Antipater comes into view.—

There had not been a day when Loshema had not thought about him. Yet his memory had become faded and thin until he might have been no more than a character met in a dream. But now he stood not ten feet away, absurdly, shockingly real, and it made her heart, which was a dry shrivelled thing, come to life and squeeze painfully inside her ribcage. He made no sign that he had seen her, his eyes dutifully trained upon the king. But she saw his jaw tighten and his gaze become fixed and false. And she was glad that she could drop her own gaze to the floor.

Every day, every hour, every moment she had spent in exile she had dreamed of seeing his face. Then her child had died, and she had thought she might die too, yet still some part of her had stayed alive, aching for him to come, to tell her that the world still made sense. But he had not come. Instead Pheroras had arrived and, kneeling before her, wept and pleaded for her forgiveness. *Loshema. Loshema, I love you. I thought you would be safe here, that little Esther, may the Almighty keep her soul, would be safe. I was a fool to think that way. A wife is not something to be cast aside, like a piece of soiled linen. It is my wrong that has taken Esther from us. Come with me. Come home. Let me care for you.* And all through this she had sat silently, feeling cold and empty, and noticing that he had grown older during her absence and his hair had receded further from his temples.

In the weeks that followed their return to Jerusalem a kind of twilight settled over her. The world was colourless, a valley of shadows that offered neither hope nor desire. Despite Pheroras' encouragement she did not visit the library. The wisdom there seemed empty, their hours poring over a single passage, teasing allegorical meaning from beneath the words, now seemed ridiculous, a game for indulged children. Besides Antipater would be there.

'I have just come from the library.' Pheroras said. He had returned to their chambers, and found her sitting in the same chair where she had been seated when he left earlier that morning. After a moment he added, 'My nephew sends his greetings.'

She allowed herself a stab of pain. 'Thank him for me.'

'He is anxious to see you return to the library. He asks after your health most attentively.'

She looked up at her husband with an expression of pity and contempt, the man who had left her in plague-ridden Peraea because he was afraid, who now carried her lover's messages without even knowing it. She did not speak, and Pheroras was first to look away.

Loshema let herself sink back into the place where there were no thoughts or desires. She wished Pheroras would go, but he was busying himself about the room, searching for some scroll no doubt that he had misplaced, occasionally glancing hopefully in her direction. Suddenly he brightened.

'Did you not tell me that there was a Pharisee who impressed you with his kindness at Beth-aram?'

Loshema nodded. 'Rabbi Haresh.'

'I too have become impressed with their teachings.' He dropped the scroll in his hand and hurried to her side. 'You recall Hillel, who preached that all that mattered of the Law was that we show each other kindness?'

Another nod. He dropped to a crouch before her. 'In your absence I have grown closer with a number of prominent Pharisees. There are learned men amongst them, men open to new ways, new thinking.'

'Your brother would not like to hear you talk like this.'

'Are the Sadducees his friends?'

'He has gelded the Sanhedrin. They do as he says.'

'But still they judge a man, not by his thoughts or deeds, but by how many generations he can trace his family, and whether he is related to this great house or that. The Pharisees would change all that.'

Loshema felt a flicker of interest, but her face remained rigid. Pheroras leaned closer. 'There are great and learned men amongst them. Some who have the gift of prophecy.' His voice dropped. 'They say that evil times are coming for the Jews.'

'You need not trouble with prophecy to predict that much.'

Pheroras ignored the barb. 'I have invited several members here, to our chambers, to discuss their ideas. I hoped— Where are you going?'

Loshema was on her feet. 'I feel the need for air.'

'Shall I come with you?'

'No need. No need.'

She fled from the room, fleeing the scream that was rising in her throat. *Prophecies; learned men; new ways to think.* All she wanted was to stop thinking. Her child was dead and everything else seemed pointless. At the head of a closed walkway she hesitated then plunged impulsively to her left only to hear a high imperious shriek, and to find herself staggering backwards, clutching her shoulder. Alexander's wife, Glaphyra, was scrambling to her feet, aided by two maids, whom she batted away, as though they were stinging insects. She gathered herself before pointing her peacock fan at Loshema, the tallest feather dangling where it had broken on impact.

'Clumsy fool.'

'Apologies.'

Loshema made as if to move on, but Glaphyra blocked her way. She was plump and fair, and it was said possessed of the same voluptuous charms as her grandmother, a famous beauty who had reputedly seduced Mark Antony before Cleopatra appeared on the scene. She lifted her chin now. 'You speak to a princess.'

Loshema's gaze, which had of late seemed welded to the ground, lifted. 'Then we speak as equals.'

The effect of this was to turn Glaphyra's pretty pink complexion florid. Her eyes flashed, and for a moment she seemed speechless, then her lip curled. 'Any old sow may be dressed in silk. Where I come from they would cut you open for speaking this way to a princess of the blood, and everyone would see that your innards still stink of chicken fat. We are nothing alike. I am descended from the Greek hero, Temenos, and the blood of the gods runs through my veins.'

'That must please your husband greatly. Did his illustrious ancestors not boast that they had swept the Greek and his gods once and for all from Israel's shores? Doubtless a pagan queen would be an asset for a man with ambitions towards the throne.'

The colour left Glaphyra's face and Loshema pushed past, the look in her eyes enough to make the maids drop their heads and step aside.

But as soon as she was out of sight the fire went out of her. For a brief instant the satisfaction of cruelty had pricked at her ailing soul, but alone, once again, she was struck by the shabbiness of the action. Glaphyra was young and afraid. Far from home in a court where power was a game and the rules a kind of madness, little wonder she strutted and postured and shielded herself behind the protection of mythical ancestors. But the burden of more guilt was not to be borne and she ran from it, turning right this time with almost superstitious impulse, only half aware that she was entering the king's private garden.

She was seen by a guard, a great, good-natured fellow, who had once been a slave himself and took a certain personal pride in her promotion, who bowed to her now and let her in without question. A dozen steps then she stopped. She had no business being here and she would have turned and gone back at once, save for the risk of drawing attention to herself.

A fig tree, old and gnarled, but shady. She sank down against its ancient trunk and let the stillness close over her. But it was not a day for remaining within the fragile shelter of her skull. Soon voices intruded, coming from an open window that overlooked the garden, and the voices were familiar. Herod was talking to his sister.

'And I say it will not be done.'

'Am I always to be alone? Since you executed my second husband, I have had no-one.'

'I executed him because you asked it of me.'

'I— I asked?' Salome's voice tinkled with incredulity. 'When have I ever done anything that was not your will?' A wheedling note appeared. 'Herod, brother, Syllaeus is a good man, a powerful man, who one day may be king. Think of the union between our two houses.'

'He is a Nabataean. They worship the earth and the sky. Is that a fit husband for a Jewish princess?'

'And our mother? Do I forget myself or did she not hale from Petra?'

A silence. To mention Herod's mother was a dangerous thing, even for his sister.

'Our mother converted. Tell Syllaeus, if he will convert I will consider the union.'

'He will not. He cannot. Things are different now, and he is a man, a *politikos.* You know very well that to convert now would be to sign his own death warrant.'

'And you know as well as I do, that a young man does not seek love between the thighs of a woman old enough to be his mother without another purpose in mind. I tell you, Salome, he is not to be trusted.'

The sound of things smashing. Footsteps. The slam of a door. Loshema, knowing the danger she had put herself in, got to her feet and hurried from the garden, but not before pausing to give the guard a coin from the purse at her waist.

She walked quickly, her eyes lowered, half wondering why, on this of all days, her slave's trick of invisibility should fail her. And fail her it did, for as soon as she had reached the safety of the common courtyard she spied Antipater standing with Nicolaus of Damascus. They were deep in conversation, but he caught sight of her and broke off. At once she flicked her eyes away and began walking, head down, in the other direction.

But he came after her. She fled through a series of connecting rooms, his footsteps echoing her own. If this had been the old Hasmonaean palace she might have hidden in a thousand places. But Herod's home was not yet three decades old, and it was designed along the clean utilitarian lines of Rome. There were no nooks, no dusty corners where she might take refuge.

The footsteps were closer now. In panic she ran down two flights of stairs, thinking they would lead to the kitchens, and instead found herself in a maze of corridors. With a sense of her own ridiculousness she kept going, searching for another staircase to lead her above ground again. But the corridors grew narrower and grimmer, and the sounds faded, the human sounds that in her anger and guilt she had striven to avoid, so that she walked now in a kind of vacuum, with only her lover as the embodiment of all the fears she was running from.

Indeed, she almost broke into a run as she heard him close the distance between them, but a blank wall brought her up short. For a moment she faced the rough-hewn stones breathing heavily then she turned, 'Antipater— '

But it was not Antipater who stood behind her. For an instant in the dim light she did not understand. This was Corinthus, one of the king's favoured eunuchs. And he was not alone. Behind him, there was a second man, another eunuch appositely nicknamed, Lightfoot. Had Herod sent them to fetch her? Then why not send a slave or a guard? There was no sense in it. They did not speak, but there was nothing humble or self-effacing in their silence. On the contrary they had the look of jackals about them, and to calm her pricking unease she blurted, 'State your business.'

They showed ragged rows of teeth then. And it came to her in a flash that they had been seen much in the company of Alexander. Too late she remembered that there were rumours all about the court that Alexander was taking liberties with his father's eunuchs. How powerful must he have grown to be able to order them after Pheroras' wife? And what had provoked it? Had Glaphyra gone running with tales of slighted pride?

Loshema's childhood flashed before her, the groping hands of men who spotted an easy target, the pagan merchant, who had forced her into the cellar eager to sample what he thought was young, male flesh. Her sex had saved her then. But not here. She understood that as soon as she smelled from Corinthus, a powerful odour of rosewater and lotus petals, womanly scents. He drew closer and her sense of danger increased. Wasn't it said that the eunuchs who were most like women were the most dangerous?

Corinthus reached out a hand and fondled the neck of her robe.

'How dare you!' She slapped him away. Corinthus stepped back, middle finger held to his bottom lip. He cut his eyes towards Lightfoot, who began, as if on cue, to snicker. He was shorter than Corinthus, his eyes outlined with khol, but there was a more powerful set to his body, a latent kind of aggression locked into the thick muscles of his forearms that multiple bangles of gold entirely failed to disguise.

Whether there was a kind of silent communication between eunuchs or the whole thing had been rehearsed, Lightfoot came towards her with that incongruous grace that was the root of his sobriquet. He was smiling. She noticed that just before his fist dove into her stomach and she doubled over and would have fallen, had he not caught her by the hair and dragged her up. Then it was Corinthus' turn. She expected his blow to be lesser, but the impact sent scorching flashes through her body, burning her extremities with lightning currents of pain.

She tried to speak, tried to use her clever brain to talk herself out of the intolerable. But the breath was knocked out of her body. Then she was on the ground, struggling to free her limbs from Lightfoot's iron grasp. Someone was screaming, but she had no time to think who it might be because Corinthus was pulling her legs apart. His manicured hand reached in and groped her intimately then he took hold of the cloth, wound modestly about her loins, and ripped it away.

She felt a rush of air against her spread inner lips and somehow this made her nakedness and shame more vivid. In desperation she tried to close her thighs, but Corinthus was crouching between her legs, splaying her knees, a peculiar, half-mad expression on his face, like a man who longs for something that, at the same time, utterly repels him. Behind her there was a jerk from Lightfoot, as if he gestured towards something.

Corinthus cut his eyes towards his companion then reached inside his robe. He was grinning widely, and Loshema could see the traces of vermillion where he must have previously stained his mouth, a full sensuous mouth, rather moist and loose, and the sight of it brought jumping to her desperately searching mind a line from the poet Propertius to do with 'alluring lips'.

Corinthus' expression hardened. He pulled from his robe an object so alien to Loshema's experience that she struggled for a moment to identify it. It was made of polished wood, about eight inches long and carved in the shape of a phallus, though the tip was fashioned as a wolf's head, gums pulled back towards the nostrils in a vicious snarl. The pupils of her eyes dilated with recognition. A *dilatare*. She knew the term from Antipater.

—*They use them to pleasure each other and sometimes the men who employ them.*

272

—To make up for what they have lost?

—In a manner of speaking. But eunuchs do not wear swords so they are also used as weapons to hurt and humiliate their enemies.

—How?

—Pray you never find out.

Corinthus leaned forward and held the *dilatare* close to her face. She could see the loving craft of the artisan who had carved the wolf's head with such attention to detail it might have been about to tear out her throat. Corinthus began to laugh in a high affected voice. Then he thrust the *dilatare* deeply into her mouth. She gagged and struggled. A tooth cracked. But she hardly noticed as she fought to draw in air. No toy to give pleasure this; they meant to rip her apart.

The world became a dream, a senseless dream in which she did not belong. And she watched and catalogued what was happening with a strange kind of calm, as though she stood quite separately in the room and was appointed narrator of the struggling woman on the floor. It was in this way that she recognised rather than felt the dark stars in her vision, and understood the plea she was directing at Corinthus with her bulging eyes.

He drew back and she was back inside herself once more, trying to sit up and wipe the blood that flowed from her ripped gums. This was no warning. They were going to kill her. And the thought was a crawling horror to her. She could not die, not this obscene filthy death, lower than a slave's death, lower than an animal. The thought of her mother, her husband, her lover coming across her violated remains sent the blood surging through her body and she managed to free herself long enough to aim a kick at Corinthus' belly.

There was not much force in it, but he howled and drew back, clutching himself. And perhaps if he had been acting alone this was the moment she might have escaped. But Lightfoot avenged his brother by dragging her forcibly to the floor. Then he was on top of her, straddling her torso so that she was pinned, breathless, between his muscular thighs.

The sweating reek of him was in her nostrils and his hands were forcing her legs apart. Corinthus was hidden by Lightfoot's bulk, but she knew the *dilatare* was in his hands and that her last moments had come. Death stood watching her from the shadows, blood running from his fangs. And for the second time that day she left her body and stood with him, a dispassionate biographer of her own extinction.

She felt Lightfoot draw in a breath, and saw —though she could not possibly have actually seen— Corinthus ready the *dilatare*, saw the insane joy light his eyes. And equally she spied a third man flying down the corridor, sword drawn. And in the chaos that followed she was neither aloof nor quite part of it.

A struggling limb. Grunts. Shouts. A mouth grown large in a scream. Even a vision of herself curled in a ball. She recorded everything and made sense of none of it. Antipater's face came swimming up out of the confusion. His lips were moving, though the sounds she heard seemed separate and unrelated.

Loshema. Loshema, are you hurt?

At the first touch of his hands on her shoulders she shrank back. But he did not let go, only held her tighter, whispering, *It's over. You're safe now.* Then slowly she began to understand that everything she had thought was happening about her was already in the past, and Antipater was explaining it all to her uncomprehending ears.

She leaned into his shoulder. 'Are they— Did you— '

'No. It would not be wise to openly kill two of my father's eunuchs whatever their crimes. Do not fret. There are other ways.'

Antipater's man ran up. 'They've fled squealing, my lord.'

'Good. Bring wine and warm water and towels. But, for all our sakes, be discreet.'

The man bowed and was gone. Antipater pushed Loshema back a little and studied her closely. 'You are bleeding from the mouth. God's curse on me, I should have sent for a physician.'

'No.' She shook her head weakly. 'It is only a few cuts.' Then anger rose in her and she tried to rise to her feet. 'God's curse on them. Give me a sword and I will finish what was started.' But her legs were trembling and she had to put a hand to the wall to steady herself. Antipater's arm was about her waist.

'They are only symptoms not the cause. They will suffer, but we must act against the one who sent them.'

She raised her eyes and looked deeply into Antipater's. 'Alexander.'

'The young wolf is tearing at the edges of his father's kingdom testing his power. While you were gone he made numerous attempts to ruin me.'

She stiffened. 'And so you thought to visit your child would compromise your position.'

'O Loshema. Is that what you thought of me?' He looked at her sorrowfully and Loshema felt the need to look away.

'You did not come. Nor even send me a line of comfort. Not once. And then she died.'

'And I would tear my heart out rather than do what I have done. I thought you safer for the distance between us. More than once I believed my hour had come, and any association with me was a sentence of death.' He put his hand under her chin and forced her gaze towards his. 'And then you were back and I swore to keep my distance. But when I saw Corinthus following in your wake I knew no good could come of it. Forgive me. Forgive me.' He slipped to his knees and encircled her waist with his hands. But there was nothing of Pheroras in the gesture, nothing pleading. His words were a command and she felt her resistance slipping. Chokingly,

'I thought you had found another.'

'Never.'

'I am so much older— '

'You are young as the morning dew.'

'But I am still bound to my husband.'

Scrambling to his feet he took hold of her so tightly he was hurting her, and she saw that all the gentleness was gone from his face and something dangerous had taken its place, something particularly Herodian in the set of his jaw. 'I will make you mine, Loshema. I swear it.'

37

In which torture reveals many things

8 BCE

*I*have returned to my studies and Pheroras is pleased. Even Nicolaus of Damascus seems happy to see my reappearance. He engages me in conversation, asks my opinions, even consults me on the authenticity of recorded anecdotes.

—Did Salome truly write to Caesar's wife when Herod would not allow her to marry Syllaeus the Arab? Is it true that Alexander's wife, Glaphyra, is hated by all the other royal ladies for her arrogance?—

How flattered I am to answer. I had almost lost my mind to dullness then to grief and to feel my faculties slowly unfurling in the glow of this learned man's attention, and to see Antipater's approving look, is a delight that pierces my frozen heart. See how eagerly I lean forward spilling my thoughts before him as a fool parts with his gold. And not once does it occur to me that this man is an historian, a collector of minutiae and once I part with my insights he will gather them to himself and fit them to his own singular vision of the truth.

But I am only glad to discover that the world still has meaning, and besides Nicolaus tells a good tale himself.

—I was there, you know. When it happened.—

—In Alexandria. At the library?—

—Not the library itself, of course. We were under siege. I was with the children in the royal palace. But I witnessed the moment when Julius Caesar's men set fire to the book repository on the north side. We were on the roof, watching— (He pauses. The memory is painful.)

—You need not go on.— Pheroras says kindly and is ignored.

—It was a strange sight. I hardly know how to tell it. It is the pause I suppose that is oddest.'

—The pause?— (This from Antipater. A quick puzzled glance at me; smiling, and we share the conundrum together.)

(Nicolaus pulls at his beard.) —There was a moment before we saw the flames. But such a moment. It was perhaps as Xeno describes. We waited through an endless series of fractions of that moment, and so, when at last, the first orange flickers appeared it was as though we had waited through all infinity.—

—I cannot imagine it.—

—Dear lady, there are times I cannot imagine it myself. Of course I had read of the Aegyptian belief in a lake of fire which is the final punishment of those who do evil in this

276

life. But to witness the horror of that moment, the pause when surely everything will be well, only to see fire run, like a demon, from floor to floor. All that effort, that wonderful accumulation of human knowledge gutted by pitiless tongues of flame. It is to feel one's own heart consumed.— Nicolaus breaks off. There are tears in his eyes. No-one speaks; his sadness has affected the room. I share a sorrowful exchange with Antipater before guilt makes me remember my husband. I turn to Pheroras, but he has gone. Unnoticed, he has slipped away.

Did I feel a pang to see Pheroras gone? I should make that claim should I not, at least for the sake of appearances? Surely the absence of his sad face brought a well of repentance bubbling to the surface. But this would be to treat myself as I have treated others in this story, to mould reason and motive to my actions so that the threads of the narrative might draw tighter. But it is not a trick I can apply to that self that was once me. Where it feels natural to the storyteller's art to look beneath the surface of the skin of others, there is something fraudulent about filling memory's lacunas with bright false testimonies that comfort rather than reveal.

Let me excuse myself then by saying that in the days to come it is not Antipater's loving looks that fill my imagination, but that image given by Nicolaus when he described watching the Alexandrian book repository begin to smoulder. Because that is what is happening now in this royal court of Herod. Foreign eyes turned towards Jerusalem have long known that fires were burning, yet for the longest time they saw nothing, heard nothing. Caesar's wife, Livia, sends veiled questions to Salome.

—Is your brother well? Does he remain in good cheer? In Rome we hear things that disturb us. Syllaeus, the Nabataean ambassador is here. (I believe he was once dear to you.) But the Judean king he describes, who rules as a despot, who is given over more and more to rages and paranoias is not the Herod we recognise…—

Salome writes at once, ignoring the questions and asking instead if there is no way for Livia to intervene on her behalf. She still loves Syllaeus, and cannot bear the thought of being married off to Herod's friend, Alexas. He is a portly elderly man with nothing to recommend him save for a tongue that always says, yes. She will surely die from grief. What does Livia think when she reads this? Does that austere face draw together in a wry moue? Given Salome's past, if anyone's days are numbered it is surely Alexas'.

And all the time the letters are passing, the tips of the first orange flames are beginning to appear. Alexander's relationship with his father's eunuchs comes to light. And when they drag him off to his prison cell, I cannot help a glance at Antipater and my hand goes to my cheek, which still pains me now and then where the tooth was cracked. And I am not the only one to seek Antipater's attention. Glaphyra turns a deadly look in his direction, even as she sobs and wails behind her husband's disappearing form. Antipater does not acknowledge either of us, but turns to his father, who gives a guarded but approving glance.

The court holds its breath, knowing that the time is ripe for another royal murder. Herod has the eunuchs tortured and their cries can be heard all over the palace. And it is Antipater *that is put in charge of their interrogation.*

'I must see for myself.'

'To what end? Loshema, I gave you my word that they would be punished. Don't you trust me?'

'More than life. But I must see.'

'And if I forbid it?'

'Are you my husband now to hold the Law over my head?'

His hand was around her wrist, hard enough to make her cry out in pain. But she did not; she held his gaze.

'What if I ask it of you?'

'Do not. I must go, and if you will not take me I will find a way.'

'Then go and be damned.'

But in the end he took her, leading her down the very corridor where she had been attacked. One of the storerooms had been hastily converted as there was no ready dungeon in the palace. In happier days the palace had been constructed without consideration for a place of torture. Alexander had been taken to the Antonia fortress, but Herod wanted the interrogation of the eunuchs closer to hand. The aroma of conspiracy was in the air and he desired it to be a dish from which he might take the first bite.

At the threshold Antipater turned to her. 'Do not do this.'

'I have no choice.'

'That is a nonsense. You may choose to do anything you want.'

'But not in this.' Stubbornly.

A flash of anger lit Antipater's face then he closed his eyes and sighed. 'I fear your entering this place.'

She stretched out a reassuring hand. 'Do not be afraid for me.'

He looked at her oddly. 'It is not you that I am afraid for. I am afraid you will see a side of me that will repel you. You will turn from me.'

'Impossible. The stars would fall from the heavens first.'

A frown. 'Why do I love such a stubborn woman?'

'That is easy. What greater love did Narcissus have other than his reflection?'

The guard on the door stepped aside at Antipater's nod. Antipater went through before her. This was not a chivalrous age. And she followed, less certain of herself than she would admit. The room was dim so first came smell, blood and dung and piss and fear. This is a place of death, she thought. And, as if to answer that thought, the shadows drew back and there, at the room's centre, was a figure tied to a contraption that she recognised but could not bring herself to name.

The figure was emitting a series of low groans, more like gasps, and though he was staring directly at Loshema he showed no sign of recognition. Indeed, it took a moment for Loshema to understand that this was Corinthus. There was no sign of Lightfoot, but she could not imagine that his fate was a more comfortable one.

A movement brought the torturer into a small pool of light. He was a thickset, rough looking individual, whose beady eyes sized her up before he offered the customary bow. Loshema did not know him, but that was not surprising. Such monsters, as it was common for the great men of the day to keep, tended to keep low profiles. He addressed Antipater in a rasping growl, like a bear attempting etiquette. 'I bow to you and greet you, great lord. And it is my sincerest hope that the lady has a strong stomach.'

'You are scum, Glaukos. Give me your report. And if you ever mention to a soul that a lady has been in this chamber I will tie you to that rack myself.'

'The great lord shows wisdom as always.'

'The great lord is still waiting.'

Glaukos shrugged a hairy shoulder. He wore only a leather apron, and even in this light it was clear that it was stained with blood. With a meaty paw he scratched the back of his neck, as if to tease memories to the surface. 'This one's the stronger of the two. I'll give him that. Kept insisting that young Alexander was just after pleasures of the flesh.' He glanced at Loshema and coughed. 'We had to stretch him until we heard the cracking. A man can't take much more after that. They'll have to carry him to his execution.'

Antipater glanced at Corinthus' prostrate form then back to Glaukos. 'Did he talk of conspiracy?'

'He talked of many things. He wept a great deal and said that he wished he might have known his mother.'

Antipater took a threatening step towards the torturer. 'The conspiracy?'

And Glaukos not being entirely lacking in wisdom himself answered hastily, 'He told tales of how young Alexander hates the king because he murdered his mother. He said the king had lived too long and it was time to let new blood in. He claimed to have many powerful sympathizers, leading citizens. And he said that they would be ready when he gave the word, and when he should be crowned Corinthus and Lightfoot would have first place in the kingdom as reward for their loyalty.'

Glaukos paused evidently expecting a reaction, but Antipater was silent. Loshema glanced at his face and was shocked to see another man there, a man who was stripped of sympathy, of an essential 'humanness' that she had taken for granted in him, more Herod than Herod. It frightened her in a way that the inert lump of flesh on the rack or the bloody-stained torturer, who shifted uneasily and scratched his hairy neck again, did not. *He is enjoying this,* she thought then pushed the thought to the furthest corner of her brain and locked it in darkness.

Antipater was speaking. 'Bring me a list of all the names this filth has mentioned. I want them all arrested.'

'There are many names, great lord.'

'Miss no-one out.'

Glaukos glanced at Corinthus, who had not said a word despite being the focus of the conversation. 'And the prisoner?'

'Rack him again. We must be certain we have everyone.'

Glaukos' eyes widened. 'Great lord. This man has no more to give. We cracked his bones. Once the bones crack a man will give up his own mother.'

'That may be so. But as you so astutely pointed out this 'man' never knew his mother. Rack him again.'

They went outside, the true outside where the first stars were beginning to show above Jerusalem, into a quiet corner of one of the private gardens. He took her hands in his. 'Do you hate me?'

She shook her head but her eyes were frightened.

'At least say that you trust me.'

A nod.

'You have said it yourself, Loshema. You and I only half belong in this world. We are outcasts waiting to be torn apart by the pack. We cannot afford pity. Our only hope is to seize power when there is a chance. And it must be done at any cost. Do you understand me?'

'At any cost?'

'I have no choice, Loshema. Nor do you. Do you think Pheroras can save you? Alexander and Aristobolus will have him strangled in the courtyard to honour their mother's memory. And you have seen what they have in store for you.'

She shivered at the thought and found she could not stop. He drew her to him. 'Loshema.' He spoke into her hair. 'When I am king you will be safe. I promise you. Only trust me to do what must be done.'

She pulled back then, searching his face for that other face she had seen in the shadows, but it was not there. And when his hands began to move down her body, parting her robe, she took hold of him and drew him towards her. He let out a little gasp of surprise, and his hands tightened on the pale mounds of her buttocks.

Their mouths met then, for an instant, they drew back, staring into each other's eyes, aware that they were on the edge of a precipice, and that this was not the old, innocent love they had shared, but something new and ineffable, a thing that had wound itself about them drawing them together in an act of defiance, something that brought a sense of life and meaning back to the world, but carried, with it, a note of death at its centre. *It is not too late.* Did he say it? Or was it only the rustle of the trees? *Not too late?* No. She closed her eyes and felt herself leap into the unknown.

38

Am I a monster?

8-7 BCE

N O-ONE IS SAFE. HEROD'S FURY *rages about the palace, like the tempestuous north wind. And Antipater rides that wind and drives it, like King David at the head of a hundred chariots.*

Herod, I have known this man all my life. I have seen that there was greatness and madness vying for his soul. In the days of my childhood the madness was a kind of inspiration, the sort prophets embody, a goad to see further and better than other men. But now his frothing jaws are clamped around it, like a bit, and Antipater is controlling the reigns.

Friend is foe and foe is friend. Herod can't tell the difference any more, and as the only thing he trusts is his distrust, he lashes out indiscriminately. See those men there, Andromachus and Gemellus, long-standing friends of Herod's. They have been stripped of their rank, and indeed of their clothes, and are ejected from the palace by the guards with nothing but loincloths to conceal their modesty. And they are considered the lucky ones.

In the years to come there will be much written about the corruption of Herod's court, and not by my pen alone. Men, who were never there, will make extravagant claims on the prurient nature of the place. But I, who have seen it with my own eyes, will testify that it was no better and no worse than the courts of the day, which is to say that it was a wicked place indeed.

If you must picture it, think then of a garden, mirror to that paradise that was the first garden on earth. In this garden the king's madness is like the light from a diseased sun, drawing from the dark netherworld of the earth weeds that are twisted and carnivorous. The strong strangle the weak and are strangled, in turn, by those who are stronger still, all desperately reaching towards that weak and ailing light. For Herod's crumbling mind has only served to fecundate a kind of madness in his courtiers. Far from fearing the wild erratics of the king's caprice, they capitalize on delirium, imagining that they, alone, can prosper in this rotting, tainted soil.

Words are dripped, like poison in the king's ear.

—Yeshua bar Yair's son was told by Alexander that such was Herod's vanity that he was forced to stoop in his father's presence and to deliberately hide his prowess with a bow—

—Did he not notice that the brothers, Yehuda, replaced their cups sooner than anyone when a toast was made to the king's health.—

—Was the king aware that so-in-so of such-in-such had made a jest to the effect, that if

281

Herod wanted to see the face of his greatest enemy all he need do is call for a looking glass.—

Conspiracy is everywhere, and the racked cries of Alexander's friends come up with phantasms to feed the fires of Herod's fears.

—Alexander has written to Caesar claiming that Herod had made an alliance against the Romans with Mithridates, the king of Parthia.—

—Alexander has procured poison in Ascalon so that he might poison his father.—

This last caused a tornado to be unleashed in the palace. See the scene through my eyes. Armed guards storming the apartments, breaking open chests, smashing scent jars, tearing down the hangings from the walls, women wailing, men clubbed to the ground. And the less the drug is found, the more Herod becomes sure it exists. And, in the middle of all this madness, Alexander takes a madder step still.

From his cell he writes a statement in four parts and has it smuggled out and distributed. No further need for arrests and tortures. He freely admits there was a plot and his co-conspirators are Pheroras and Salome. In fact, Salome, whose wickedness tends to the salacious as is natural of her sex, entered his room one night and forced him into an act of intercourse. Who, indeed, does not want Herod's death. A list follows that names every friend left in attendance at the king's court.

My hands are trembling as I put the scroll down. 'And you say this statement has been widely circulated?'

Antipater nods. He looks like a statue carved from obsidian, sharp and hard and twinkling.

'But Pheroras is in terrible danger.'

The strangest look crosses Antipater's face. For a second I glimpse that other face, the otherness of that face. But it is gone and Antipater is shaking his head. 'No. For all my father is a madman, he loves his family, and Pheroras and Salome are all he has left. To lose them would be to lose the last remnants of himself.'

'And I? Am I safe?'

A hand on my cheek. 'You are the safest woman in the world.'

'You think then— You believe— ' I dare not complete the thought.

His lips against the hollow cavern of my ear. 'Soon. I promise you. Soon.'

The Moirai, those Greek goddesses of Fate, are revered the world over as all powerful. Not only mortal men, but even the gods must bow to their decrees. Further, they are said to be possessive of their oracular gift, and likely to throw sand into the eyes of men who boast that they have seen with certainty into their jealously guarded realm. I will think of them in times to come.

Antipater stands in the high audience chamber staring at his father's empty throne. He has his back to me, and though I cannot read his expression, there is something hungry in *the set of his shoulders. If he moves I half expect him to lope towards it. Unaware of me he has stood before that empty symbol of power unmoving, also unblinking I suspect, waiting, waiting …*

But perhaps this is not memory at all. Perhaps it is a dream. Do you see it too? The way corners of this scene are out of sight and ill-defined. Even Antipater's figure has something transparent about it. And where is Herod or his courtiers or seneschals? Not even a slave to scrub the steps. No, this is a false place, an invention to capture that tremulous, underwater moment when we stood on the rim of a new world.

A knock on the door, softly.

—Are you mad? To come directly to my sleeping chamber.—

—I had no choice.—

—Pheroras will be back any moment. I will have to bribe the maids to prevent gossip.—

—There will be gossip enough to distract them. Alexander has been set free.—

—Impossible. How could it be affected? Not a noble in the land would dare.—

—Glaphyra sent pleas to her father. He arrived last night.—

—Herod has no love for Glaphyra. He claims not to know if she prays to the Almighty or one of her exalted ancestors. Why would he listen to the Cappadocian king when he has turned away the counsel of friends?'

A sigh. Antipater has the look of a defeated general about him.

—Glaphyra's father is no fool. Where others claimed Alexander was innocent, he took the opposite tack. He congratulated Herod on his fair-mindedness and promised to dissolve Glaphyra's marriage if she had the faintest knowledge of conspiracy.—

—But surely this did not move him?—

—On the contrary, my father fell to weeping. And slowly the Cappadocian led him round to the view that Alexander was unfairly influenced by forces older, if not wiser.—

—I will not believe it.—

—I wish that luxury was a comfort I could offer you. But the Cappadocian has persuaded him that Pheroras had a hand in it.—

A feeling of falling. An arm around her waist.

—It is not so grim as it seems. Herod called Pheroras to him, and your husband pleaded his case and wept to be called a traitor, while all the time Glaphyra's father pretended to broker a reconciliation between them. I have heard that in his own kingdom he is called, 'the fox', and it is not an ill-judged name. In a single stroke he has freed his son-in-law and weakened my position.—

—He has beaten us. We are finished.—

—Not yet, my love. There is more to come, I am sure of it. Destiny will not overlook me.—

Nor will it. Nor will it!

Glaphyra's father returns to his kingdom satisfied that the world has been set on a true and proper course. The tyrant of the east has proved pliable as a kitten in his hands, and now he can go home. He does not understand, of course, that there are no endings in the tales that make up Herod's life and the narrative can be revisited and rewritten at any time. But for now there is a fragile peace in the kingdom. And besides there are real dangers and betrayals to occupy Herod's restless mind. Syllaeus the Nabataean, who once loved Salome, has begun to wreak his revenge ...

Sleep had been a miser with his gift, and Loshema tossed through the hot still night air, as though needle-sharp seconds were prickling her skin. Beside her Pheroras snored peacefully, his arm trailing on the floor, as though he had forgotten to bring it to bed with him, and the poignant sight of it sent a pang through her, which she told herself was only the irritation of being married to a man who could not even come to bed tidily.

He had watched her ready herself for bed that night, and though she had deliberately dithered about the task, he had still been awake when she climbed in beside him. And now there was something searching about his face. She tried to divert him.

'Sleep well.' She made as if to turn away.

'Loshema.' He took her in his arms and she fought not to stiffen.

'Yes?'

'Only that I love you.'

Her control was pristine. The daughter and sister of whores knew how to fake a smile. But when she opened her mouth to reply he pressed his long fingers against her lips. 'No. It is enough that you share my bed.' Then he rolled over and fell into a dreamless sleep. Yet if he had found peace he had taken hers. There was a hard, knotted lump in her chest, and several times she sat up, clutching at her throat with a feeling that she was suffocating.

Air. She must have air. She slipped from the bed and went to the window, but the night was sultry and choking, a heavy, perfumed blanket against her face. A glance back in the direction of the bed. Pheroras had thrown an arm over the space she had vacated. For an instant the idea of curling up in the safety of that arm appealed, then she dismissed it. There was another arm she wanted.

She slipped down the long passages, through the pools of shadow, with no particular plan in mind, just an urging need to reach Antipater. How she would get there undetected, what she would say once they were face to face seemed unimportant next to her need to find him. Beneath her feet the tiles were still warm and the oppression of the night drew thicker as she moved deeper into the palace.

Approaching footsteps —a guard? A slave on a clandestine mission? A stab of panic made her freeze to the spot with no better plan than to pull her robes about her head, as though, like Hades' helm of darkness, the act would confer invisibility. The footsteps faded and the vast danger of her situation was borne in on her. Retribution was a rippling force under Herod's rule. To condemn herself was to condemn all those she loved. Heart still hammering against her breastbone she lowered her robes and turned back the way she had come.

But entering the main peristyle, she was surprised to see a lamp flickering in the window of the library. Hope leapt inside her, like a flame, and, throwing caution to the winds, she ran like a girl, more amused than amazed that her long limbs still carried her without protest.

Even so she was gasping a little by the time she reached the door to the library, and in her great excitement threw it open with unintended violence. The gasp from within was so bereft of its recognisable shape that it barely sounded human. Loshema jumped back, stifling a cry. And there was a vision trembling before her, Herod, grey streaks showing through the ash-based dye he used to colour his hair and beard, his face greyer still, loose with sleep and wide with blinking terror.

Speechless Loshema fell to her knees, blank with shock, only knowing that she had trespassed in some terrible way. Herod's voice came brokenly across the room. 'I thought— I saw him.'

Unsure if she was expected to answer she glanced up through her lashes and saw that he had slumped down on a bench, his tunic loose over one shoulder, and even in that short glance she saw how the flesh had shrivelled away, an old man's flesh with the bones sticking through. He was speaking again, and despite the danger, she kept her eyes raised.

'I saw him,' he said again in that broken voice. 'Alexander, standing over me with a sword. He wants to kill me.'

Should she answer? Her lips parted but Herod was speaking again. 'And now this.' He lifted a letter from the table and brandished it. 'He has gone to Caesar.'

Alexander?

'Syllaeus, that Nabataean cur. Did I not put down the rebellion he stirred up in Trachonitis? Was it not left to me to roust the rebels and raze the fortress, where he made them welcome, almost without losing a man. And all the while he was seated at Caesar's table spinning a web of lies to ensnare me.'

Herod's face was turned in Loshema's direction but there was an absent quality about it, and she wondered if he were still asleep. Something about the manner of his speech, the closed, occluded face, reminded her of her days as a child, when she wandered freely the warrened streets of Jerusalem, and had witnessed the madmen who stumbled out of the desert, frothing and blithering, oblivious to the audiences which gathered around them.

She dared a glance over her shoulder at the open door, but the movement made him restless and she was forced to continue kneeling in silence.

For a while he did not say anything then he continued on, as though the narrative had been unbroken. 'Wailing and weeping he went to Caesar, vomiting up the stinking bolus of his lies *"Herod has laid waste to Nabataea. Herod has executed thousands of our most promi-*

nent men. He has forgotten his place, has exceeded his authority, has acted as a king!' This last sent a spray of spittle in Loshema's direction.

'And Caesar, the man who called me friend, flew into a rage, refused to allow my representatives to argue their case. And then this— ' The letter crumpled within his fist. His voice shook. 'I have shown arrogance and ingratitude. I have disported myself as though I was a free agent and not the client of Rome. Where I was once treated as Caesar's friend I will now be treated as his subject.' Then out of nowhere. 'Am I a monster?'

Loshema started. And there was a moment when she saw the man peering through the wasted, barnacled surface of the king. And she had a sense of how life grows over us and changes our shape, yet deep inside there is still something left of that unsullied creature that was once our unrealised self. And the knowledge made her heart ache even for this man who was her enemy. The eyes that were looking at her were clear and unblurred, and perhaps very faintly amused.

'Do you think I do not know that they call me Herod the monster, the Lillith who eats up his family and friends? They do not even begin to conceive of the monsters I protect them from.'

But then there were no more words because two slaves of the bedroom arrived, their looks of relief lighting their sweating faces. 'Come to bed,' they implored Herod. 'We have drawn a bath for you, and sprinkled the bed with lavender and hyssop as you like it.'

Herod got up and followed them out of the room meek as a child.

O, don't be fooled. A moment of sympathy does not unmake the heavy layers of murderous intent. The shape of Mariamme's hand still burns in my palm at night. And this was the man who would have had me cast aside from all protection. My head was clear despite the scented strangeness of that encounter. To Herod I was no more than a piece of rag to be used then discarded.

Besides, you waste your pity on the monster. Herod has a trick of surviving. Not long after our encounter Nicolaus is sent to plead Herod's case. He is in luck. In Nabataea the balance of power has changed and Syllaeus is no longer in favour. Besides further reports have reached Rome contradicting his account. It is a foolish, one might say fatal, move to make a fool out of Caesar. In Judea everything is forgiven, everything is forgotten. Or so it appears.

But now Herod is restless. He complains of pains in his stomach, his legs. He has feelings of lethargy, of restlessness; he is troubled by strange forebodings. Evil is in the air, and his nostrils twitch with its cadaverous stench.

His physician gives him liquorice root and extract of Ra for his stomach. Aloe and basil for the pains in his legs. But nothing helps. Something is rotting in Herod's kingdom and he must find it. The vision of his son still jolts him from sleep, and it is the plunge of the dagger that sends him tumbling into wakefulness. He sets a watch on Alexander and his brother. But his instructions are imprecise. It is not clear if the king 'wants' something to be found. And, his courtiers, attuned to giving him what he demands fall over themselves to obey. They run to him with tales real and imagined, and still nothing happens. This is a kingdom of broken glass and everyone walks with extreme care.

For the third time in as many minutes Loshema glanced towards the door then surreptitiously across the table towards the king. The hour was late, but Herod showed no signs of rising. He was sunk deep in his cups, the lids of his eyes so low it even seemed possible he was sleeping. Antipater shot her a brief, sympathetic glance then shook his head slightly; there was nothing he could do.

Not even Salome had managed to stir things up when earlier she had announced, 'How well it is to see our little brother grown so pious these days.'

Herod gave a grunt. 'Pheroras is always the best of us.'

Salome ignored the barb, helping herself to a generous portion of the blood-warm grapes that spilled everywhere from burnished cornucopias strewn about the table. Then she added. 'Certainly the Pharisees think highly of him. I hear they consider our brother quite won over to their cause.'

Loshema did not need to look at Pheroras to know that he had put his cup down and was sitting very still. She, too, was holding her breath. Her gaze slipped to Antipater and she saw that he was sitting back in a relaxed pose, but that his eyes were focused and alert. Salome bit down on a grape and the juice ran down her chin. Someone nearby laughed too loudly and Loshema started at the sound. Herod lifted his eyes from the rim of his cup and looked across the table at her.

'I have made no law that says a man may not explore his religion.'

Salome gave a snort. 'Even if that exploration leads him into dangerous waters, with men who believe that there are laws beyond the written Law.'

But Herod would not be drawn. He shrugged and lifted his cup. 'The *Setinum*.'

One of the favourites bent forward and whispered something in his ear. The king's look darkened. 'Finished? All of it?'

Suddenly everyone was deep in conversation or profoundly interested in the dishes set before them. Over Pheroras' shoulder Loshema noted the Roman proconsul watching carefully.

'Father.' Alexander leaned past Antipater. 'I think I have taken the last of it. Here, take mine.' He lifted his cup, as though he would pour the contents into his father's empty one.

'No!— '

Later Loshema would piece the scene back together, lifting the broken shards with her mind and fitting them to the order in which they occurred. But, in the heat of the moment, there was a sense in which time had ceased to run its usual course and her senses ran contrary to logic, so that the clatter of the metal cup on the cool tiles of the floor echoed in her head even as she saw Herod knock it from his son's hand.

And only then did it seem that the chatter in the room fell into deadly silence and the musicians ceased to play. And Herod was on his feet, staggering back so that his chair fell, an accusing finger pointed at his son's appalled face. And, across the table, she registered Antipater looking at her in shock before she felt the droplets of wine spattering across her face.

It was a turning point. Like a draught of air that fans the flames. It is not long before the news spreads. Alexander and his brother have been arrested.

39

In which the blood of a calf is not considered equal to two lambs

7 BCE

IN SOME WAYS IT IS *all too fast, and in others it is painfully slow. Herod has the madman's need for detail. And so nothing happens, while falsehoods and fabrications are heaped up in place of evidence. An arrested bodyguard gives way under torture, claiming that the princes intend to murder their father during a hunt in the hopes of passing it off as an accident. This is enough to have the huntsmaster dragged to his death.*

Another tortured friend insists that the commander of the Alexandreion fortress is in cahoots with the brothers and intends to provide them with refuge and access to their father's gold. But the commander proves a tougher bird than either the bodyguard or the huntsman. He flatly denies the allegations no matter how much they rack him. Herod is perplexed. Can a man in the throes of agony lie? He has always believed not, but now doubt clouds his mind. He needs a sign. He goes to the Temple, that great symbol of his earthly power, and prays for guidance from that which is un-earthly.

—And it is granted. Come, see!—

They are in the audience chamber, the king, the courtiers, the ambassadors and minor nobles from foreign lands; Herod cannot face his son alone. He has seen the truth of things and must see that others see it too. The courtiers are sombre. Many dress in black. They huddle in groups and talk in subdued tones. But Herod cannot keep still. He is all agitation, jittering with what might be called an old man's haste, tics and tremors. He stoops a little now when he gets up from his throne; his hands tremble, his chin bobs, the fluidity of youth gone.

Alexander's youth has gone too. There is an audible murmur around the chamber when they bring him in. He is still beautiful, but it is a death's mask beauty. Strands of limp hair fall across the jutting angles of the gaunt face and the eyes burn and burn. The king looks at him, but does not quite meet his gaze.

'Do you have something to say to me?'

The young man lifts his wrists, which clink with chains. 'What should I say to you, father?'

'Say to me you are not the author of this!' *Herod brandishes a letter.*

'I have never seen it before.'

'You deny it?'

A nod. The denial only makes Herod angrier. He takes a step towards Alexander then changes his mind. He swings in Antipater's direction. 'Read it.'

Aloud Antipater reads:

When we have accomplished, with the Almighty's help, all that was pro-
posed, we will come to you. Stand by your promise to receive us at the fortress
and to release the gold our father has stored there into our hands.

*There is a pause. Everyone looks at Alexander, whose face is a mask. The mask slowly
cracks and he begins to tremble then he is weeping, huge bitter sobs that shake his thin body
yet seem strangely emotionless. Herod is incredulous.*

'Have you nothing to say? No words to explain— '

*Alexander stops weeping, though his body still shakes. He lifts a manacled wrist and
points towards Antipater.* 'Ask him. He wrote it.'

Antipater's expression is steady. He holds the letter aloft. 'Did I also write it in your
handwriting?'

An intake of breath. Alexander bites down on his lip. 'It— It is a copy. Everyone knows
that Diophantus, the scribe, is your creature, that he can imitate many hands.' *Alexander looks round the room, searching. But suddenly eyes slide away, heads turn.* 'Everyone
knows— ' *he repeats. His voice is small, lost in the vastness of the chamber.* 'Father!' *A
clanking step towards Herod, but the guards restrain him.* 'Father. Can't you see? He has
turned you against me. He is killing everyone that stands between him and the throne. And
when we are all gone, father?' *Alexander's voice drops to a whisper.* 'All he will need to do is
rid himself of you.'

*It is said and cannot be unsaid. Herod turns troubled eyes towards Antipater, who meets
his gaze fearlessly. In his hand the letter rustles just a little and Herod jams his hands over his
ears and moans.* 'Take him away! Take him away!' *Then lower, and to himself.* 'It is to be
expected. His mother was the queen of lies. A rotten fruit from a rotten branch.'

—Please. Let me talk with you.—

—It's not safe. My father is half mad with suspicion. Everyone is watched. Even me.—

—Please I cannot go without knowing. They are saying that a mob rose up in Jericho and
stoned the princes' friends to death. Is it true? Answer me … Answer me!—

—The king rebuilt Jericho after the earthquake. The people remember.—

—But so many … innocent men!—

—Hush. Such talk is deadly. The king deemed those men guilty thus they were guilty.—

—Is this what passes for justice in Judea today?—

—Loshema. Loshema, don't pull away. What do you imagine those tender princes had in
mind for you?—

—They are still young. Aristobolus wrote to his aunt begging her to intervene with the
king.—

—And doubtless received her warmest sympathies in reply.—

—Yes, that's it, jest. Can you not see I am afraid? I don't want their blood on my hands.—

—Nor will it be. Herod will go to Rome seek permission to execute his own flesh and blood and Caesar will never permit it. I, too, will plead for their lives.—

—You will not!—

—Loshema. Listen to me.—

—You're hurting me.—

—Listen! Many things I have heard said against me, here at court or out in the streets. I am cruel. I am a deceiver with all the poison of the Herods distilled in my veins. Yet there is one charge they never leave at my door. No-one has ever claimed that I gave my word and then was false. Have I not made you a vow to make you mine? Do you believe I will keep it?—

—I —

—Do you believe me?—

—Yes. Yes. I believe you.—

—Loshema, forgive me. People fear me because of my father, because I am not of the pure Hasmonaean line. Because I lack the charm to suffer fools gladly. And perhaps they are not entirely wrong to do so. There is too much of my father's unbending nature in me. But I am not a vengeful man. When the time comes I will plead their case. I promise you.—

With the change in the month from Sivan to Tamuz the temperature had been steadily building. And, even in elevated Jerusalem, there were times when the limestone walls of the palace glowed, like the innards of a great brick oven in the yellow light. The heat was hard to escape, and it chased Loshema through the palace towards the solitude of one of the high balconies, in hopes of a breath of air to billow her skirts and lift the hair from her perspiring neck. But passing a chamber where the royal women sometimes gathered to exchange gossip, she heard the muffled, yet definite sound of sobbing. Common sense told her to move on. Yet she walked deliberately to the door and pushed it ajar.

Glaphyra was curled on a window seat, her golden head buried in an embroidered cushion. And the sight of her made, not only common sense, but fear send bells clanging inside her head. She turned to go, but Glaphyra chose that moment to look up. She did not speak but stared at Loshema. And though her round, child-like face was composed, tears continuously welled up and spilled from her eyes, as though she was not a creature of the earth but some watery naiad or nereid.

'I— Forgive me. I did not mean to intrude.' Loshema took a step towards the door. Behind her Glaphyra said,

'They have taken them to Berytus.'

Loshema almost asked who, but catching herself, turned back then nodded. 'I am sorry.'

Glaphyra was staring at her. 'He will have them killed. Their own father will kill them.'

'No. Surely it will not come to that.'

'Yet they are in Berytus.'

Loshema took a step towards the stricken girl then paused. How much did she know? How much was safe to reveal? 'It was Caesar's command that there be a council convened at Berytus.'

'But he did not deny the king's right to ultimate sanction.'

'How could he when it is the right of every Roman patriarch? But did he not also say that, if your claim that they merely sought protection in Cappadocia was upheld, then he should be lenient.' Her fingertips tingled with the desire to reach out and touch the girl, to reassure her that everything was in hand. But that was impossible. Instead she added. 'Your father will speak well of them. And Herod has listened to him before.'

'Herod has refused him leave to attend the council.'

Something plummeted inside Loshema, but she kept her smile fixed. 'Still there are others.'

'Who? Who will speak out for them? They are not even allowed to offer their own defence, but are kept locked away in the village of Platana as though already … already … ' Her voice shrank. There was a silence then Glaphyra's face, which had puckered with the inward turn of her thoughts, smoothed and grew remote again. 'Do you know what the king has done?' she asked coldly.

Loshema stiffened. Glaphyra was no longer speaking softly and the door lay open at her back. 'I fear my sources are less informed than yours.'

'You have heard of old Tiro?'

No … yes? She knew the name. Glaphyra seemed unsurprised by her confusion. 'Why would you? His son was a friend to Alexander. He was known mostly for his prowess as a soldier, a hero of our struggle against the Parthian invaders. The struggle that placed Herod on his throne.' She paused, still holding Loshema's gaze, while the tears continued to roll down her cheeks in two unending streams. Loshema said nothing. Glaphyra's stare —so like the gaze of a wounded child— was sending prickles of unease across her scalp but she kept her composure and waited for the younger woman to go on. Glaphyra pressed her hands against the bench and hunched forward, as though her stomach was hurting her.

'Perhaps because his reputation was spotless he felt he had the right to speak out. He has addressed crowds in the past, and they say his truth was never watered down with flatteries or compromise.'

A tiny light of recognition darted across Loshema's face. Tiro? Yes. She had heard of him. Two noblemen of the Sadducean persuasion mimicking his most famous phrase,

—*A Jew who is afraid of the truth is no Jew at all.*—

—*And a Jew who is not afraid of the truth is no Jew either … Because he is a corpse.*—

Glaphyra noted Loshema's change of expression. She gave a bitter nod. 'O yes. Tiro was a great proponent of the truth. Alexander once told me that to listen to Tiro was more bruising than an hour spent on arms practice— '

'What is your point?' Loshema interrupted. Suddenly she could not stand to be in this room a moment longer with this young woman with her calm, anguished face.

'Do I have a point? This is a tale so commonplace in Judea that you must surely know its ending. What shall I tell you? Seeing the injustices that are perpetrated against my husband and his brother, Tiro went to Herod and demanded a private audience. And once alone, or so he thought, he did not hold back from voicing his opinions. *Have you taken leave of your senses,* he asked. *Where is that extraordinary mind that brought about fulfilment of all your ambitions? Now you find yourself bereft of family and friends, and it seems to me, of that which can be called good counsel.*

'Herod was astonished by this outburst. But he was known to be fond of Tiro —if that creature can truly express feelings which are more the right property of men—. He allowed him to go on, to twist the strangler's knot more tightly about his neck. *Can you not see,* he asked. *Despite their silence, the mass of the people detest your cruelty. And the whole army, with its officers, feels pity for the sufferers and hatred for those responsible. Alexander and Aristobolus are the sons of your queen, the only woman who could rightfully call herself by that name. Will you put them to death and abandon yourself in old age to a son who has ill requited the hope you placed in him?'*

'Be careful, Glaphyra,' Loshema said. 'You tread on dangerous ground.'

'And if I do, it is because your lover has turned the whole of Judea into quicksand. Will you have me arrested as Herod had Tiro arrested, along with his son and the officers and soldiers Tiro named? He even arrested and put to torture Tiro's barber, who, poor fool, went running to the king with tales that Tiro had beseeched him to slit Herod's throat.' Glaphyra suddenly got to her feet and took a step towards Loshema. She was considerably smaller and there was a tightly-drawn look of madness in her upturned face. 'How do you imagine the story ends?'

Hoarsely Loshema answered, 'In death.' Looking down she saw the glint of sharp little teeth as Glaphyra formed a grimacing smile despite the tears, saw the hectic lights that made the eyes too luminous.

'In death, yes. Of course in death. Who does not know that Herod is a word that can mean only *Death!'*

Frightened by the girl's intensity Loshema made a placating gesture. 'Calm yourself. What has happened is unfortunate, but it does not mean— '

Glaphyra slapped the outstretched hand away and drew back, the hard look of madness so strange on her round babyish face.

'They tortured them.' Her voice was featureless, a statue parting its marble lips. 'Old Tiro would not submit though they gave allowance neither for his reputation nor his advanced age. His son was made of similar stuff. But his father's agonies proved too much. He made a pact with his jailor that he would give them whatever confession they demanded if the torture would end and execution follow swiftly.'

There was bile in Loshema's mouth. She wanted to turn and walk away, but a deep-rooted sense of shame held her in place. Glaphyra smiled at her pityingly.

'You have won.'

'I did not wish for this.'

'How could you not wish it? You are Antipater's creature.'

But for this she would not stand. 'You do not understand him as I do. He intends to save them.'

'Then you are more of a fool than his father.'

In the days that followed Loshema tried to forget Glaphyra's words, but they chafed at her conscience and spiked her thoughts with questions she did not want to ask of herself. She would have liked to have discussed things with Pheroras, to hear his quiet thoughtful counsel, even to catch the little partisan hint within his answers, which was the measure of his loyalty to her, always seeking to reassure. But a wife cannot ask her husband for counsel concerning her lover, and so she turned to higher powers and took herself off to the Temple.

From Antipater she knew that they talked the empire over of the great Jewish temple, which lies in the east. Yet her own awe of the place was somewhat tempered with a sense of the familiar and her mixed and unresolved feelings towards the author of its reconstruction. It was a thing of Herod, and so steeped was she in the daily minutiae of the life of the Herodians that she had developed a certain immunity to miracles. Besides she was not naturally pious and attended only those times where her presence would raise fewer eyebrows than her absence.

Her appearance attracted more attention than she had expected. Not that it was unusual for there to be glances in her direction, some veiled, some open and agog —she was, after all, the slave who had defied the odds— but now there was a certain *froideur,* hostile looks, shaken heads. Seeing two men scowl at her then turn their backs, Loshema felt glad to have the company of male body-slaves along with her maids.

At the Hulda gate, she stopped to purchase a sacrificial calf from one of the sellers crowded around the entrance, and was turning to hand it over personally to a Temple Levite, when she was rudely assaulted by a crone, whose eyes were misted white with cataracts. The woman hissed something then spat in Loshema's face. Loshema gasped and her body-slaves moved forward. The act was shocking, against the household of Herod even treasonable. But the crone had melted into the crowd.

'Lady, what did she say?' one of the maids asked, using a corner of her veil to wipe her mistress' face. Loshema shook her head, as though she had not heard. But it was a lie. The words had been clear enough. '*What do you think, slave-wife, that the Almighty laps up calf's blood when you have already offered him the blood of two lambs?*'

She was running by the time she reached their apartments. And, if she had felt strong and alive that morning, she felt her years now as a stitch sank its teeth into her side. Leaning against the doorframe, she called, 'My husband. Where is my husband?'

Pheroras entered from one of the inner chambers. He stopped when he saw her and his hands fell loosely to his sides. And there was no need to ask because his face told all. But it was not all. And the answer to this question only raised the spectre of others. Aware that she was panting, her clothes and hair dishevelled, she mastered herself long enough to demand, 'Where is Antipater?' This was not even diplomatic, and she saw Pheroras stiffen, but there was no time to care.

'He is back; I know it. I must speak with him.'

He was, as Pheroras had said, taking the air. Loshema passed under a low marble arch that led to one of the vast balconies looking eastwards towards the Temple. Clouds had rolled in, and Antipater, his back to her, was silhouetted against the polished mirror of the sky. Hands pressed against the carved balustrade, he was leaning out, almost hovering, as a hawk hovers, above the city and did not notice her arrival.

'Why?'

He turned surprised. She shrank the distance between them with long, unladylike strides. 'You gave your word. You said you would speak for them.'

'Loshema— '

'I listened to you. I believed you.'

He caught her wrists. 'Do you think I did not keep my word?' He was angry now. 'If you were not tied to that … that —he fought for control— that man who is my uncle, I would have brought you to see for yourself. I pleaded with my father. Down on my knees. I warned him that such harshness would reflect badly upon him. You may ask Nicolaus who was with me, and who also tried to persuade him, telling him that, in Rome, they are saying imprisonment is punishment aplenty for their impiety.'

Suddenly he flung away from her. 'I failed. And my punishment is the loss of your love.'

She looked at him, and realised that he did not hover, as a hawk hovers, but rather he was perched alone and forlorn, watching below for the jackals to creep out and begin picking over the carcasses of his deeds, his thoughts, his ambitions. And she felt a deep shame for having seen him only as others saw him, and there was pride in her also at having seen the man that others did not want to see. She went towards him thinking, if he had blood on his hands then mine are no cleaner. Reaching out she laid a hand on his shoulder.

'You have not lost my love. Not that. Never that.'

He turned to her, and so close in height they were that their gaze was almost level, and she felt the warm breath of his mouth upon her face. But he still looked so sad. With the tips of her fingers she traced the crease of his frown.

'We have won.'

'I know.' He caught her hand and pressed it to his lips. 'It is only— '

'Yes?'

'I thought victory would have a sweeter taste.' Behind him the sun broke through the clouds above the Temple, a red sun, the colour of calf's blood.

40

Appearances deceive

6-5 BCE

*H*erod is in a foul mood. He has been away some months overseeing the building of his city in Trachonitis. On the surface at least, he seems to have recovered from the execution of his sons, and has come back expecting a hero's welcome. His family are gathered behind him on the pale steps of the Temple, as he prepares to address the people. But the crowd is thin. Amongst them his quick eye sees dung-collectors, street-sweepers, pedlars, beggars, and immodest women, the dregs of the city. Of the intelligentsia and the nobility there is only a smattering, a group of Pharisees in their fringed shawls, some young lords down from their estates in the north.

There is an uncomfortable silence on the Temple steps. Not even the sound of banging and hammering can be heard for all building activity has been suspended to allow for the king's speech. Herod's family avoid his eye, even Salome. At last the High Priest steps forward. He lifts his arms and offers a blessing, which the crowd ignores; they know he is the father of one of Herod's wives and therefore the king's creature. A corp of Temple guards are sent amongst the crowd, and a few cuffs and blows ensure that they are paying attention when the High Priest announces, 'Your king will address you.'

As is customary Herod begins with a reading from the Torah. This king, who has sacrificed at pagan altars and gifted pagan shrines with his largesse, knows when to play the Jew. He has chosen a passage from Daniel.

And in the days of those kings the God of heaven will set up a kingdom which shall never be destroyed, nor shall its sovereignty be left to another people.

Herod is making an appeal. Do you not see? I have given you a kingdom stronger and safer than any ruled over by Jewish king before, is his message. And it is not too much to say that the crowd thaws a little, most especially when he calls forward the children of Alexander and Aristobolus and embraces them. Their presence seems to touch him deeply. He sinks to his knees; he weeps. And the High Priest intones,

I will wash my hands in innocence: so will I compass thine altar, O LORD.

But when Antipater steps forward it is as if a chill breeze has blown across the crowd. The *cheers die away. They give way to shaken heads, to murmurs and even a sibilant hiss of,* LSHN☒ KWRDY☒ ACHASHDARPENIN. *Slayer of princes.*

The colour drains from Antipater's complexion then rushes back in patches. He looks like a man who has been slapped in the face. He neither addresses the crowd nor moves back, but his hand twitches at the hilt of his sword. And there is no choice. I take Pheroras' hand and step forward. A thin cheer threads through the crowd, led by the Pharisees. Pheroras smiles shyly and a little astonished. And if I could take my eyes from Antipater I might spare a thought to wonder that Pheroras is so eager to accept the appearance of love in love's stead. But all I can think of is Antipater, who, despite the thinness of the crowd, is in a sea of Jews larger than he can hope to meet anywhere else in the world, and can find acceptance on not a single face. To be alone is a terrible thing. To be alone amongst one's own is a kind of death.

—They hate me.—

—They do not understand you as I do. Give them time.—

—I could give them until the sun cools and the stars fall from the sky. I am a Herod with no pure Hasmonaean blood to redeem me. They want the dream of what never was over what might be.—

—All that will change when you are king.—

—You still believe I will be king?—

—Of course. What do you mean?—

—Don't play the woman, Loshema. It does not suit you. You saw my father with his grandchildren. The beast's conscience is pricking him. Soon he will forget that it was I who held the reins of government all the while he was away and it will be, "How has this happened? Who has led me from the path of righteousness and turned me from my sons?"—

—Hush, hush. It need not be so.—

—Nor need it, wife.—

—Pheroras, I- I did not hear you.—

—What do you mean, uncle?—

—Only that my brother is a man who sees what he wants to see.—

I do not like the plan, not one little bit. Not even when it appears to be working. —Look, see for yourself.— Herod has hired an actor, one Metrobius Aesopus, who is all the rage in Rome (if only by naming himself after two of the most respected actors of the century), and we have been invited to hear him declaim passages from **Prometheus Bound**.

We are late, Pheroras and I, picking our way through the couches. Metrobius does not miss a beat, but heads turn in our direction. Antipater flashes a black look as we approach and seems reluctant to offer us space to sit down. His reluctance is rewarded by a lapful of wine knocked from a nearby table as Pheroras attempts the couch.

Antipater springs up, brushing furiously at the stain, which only serves to make it worse.

'Go softly, uncle, lest all your years be in the bitterness of your soul.'

But Pheroras can quote Isaiah too, and counters, 'Is the pot exclaiming, "the potter has no hands?"'

Antipater stops brushing and stares then he stalks from the room, his performance gathering a more attentive audience than Metrobius.

A few weeks later we are in Caesarea at the country estate of one of Herod's noblemen. He has recently taken receipt of a collection of Greek statues and wishes to curry favour by presenting one to Herod. Well he knows that such a gift could never be bestowed in the pious south. But here in Caesarea, with its pagan population and the temple of Zeus-Augustus looming over the town, he bargains on more sophisticated company. And it is true Herod is charmed.

'Well, what have we here?' he says, pointing at a sculpture of Victorious Youth.

What indeed? Herod has one arm around Alexander's young son, Tigranes, playing the scene as the doting grandfather. And who would dare to recall that he has murdered four generations of the child's family.

'Look how the artist has carved the rippling muscles. You might think to see him breathe.'

'Indeed, father. It is a marvellous work,' Antipater chimes in. He turns to me. 'If I am not mistaken this is the work of Herephon of Macedonia.'

This is the moment when I should step closer, wide-eyed and enchanted. Instead I stare at him as though he is dirt beneath my feet then turn on my heel and walk away. I cannot see Herod's face, but I hear him plainly enough.

'Whatever offence you have caused your uncle you must find a way to make amends.' (I see in my mind that he squeezes Tigranes' shoulder.) 'Family is everything.' He sounds pleased. There can be no conspiracies against his person where discord reins elsewhere. But then Salome is saying in a flat, disbelieving voice, 'How mercurial our brother has become. It seems that only the other day Pheroras was singing his nephew's praises. You must tell us, Antipater, how you offended lest we make the same mistake.'

Pheroras' household did not stay at the home of the nobleman, but at the home of a distant relative within town. Pheroras had made the arrangements, and their host greeted them in the fringed shawl of the Pharisees, kissing Pheroras warmly and bowing to Loshema.

'Lady, your name is spoken with affection amongst us for we know that it was you who paid the fine when we refused the oath of loyalty to the king.'

Loshema inclined her head, though, in truth, she had only done what Pheroras had asked of her. *Better for my brother to see it as a woman's foolish act of piety than a deliberate gesture of defiance.*

In the evening Antipater joined them. He seemed in good spirits and sat drinking with Pheroras even after their host had excused himself with many pious quotes concerning intemperance. With their host gone Loshema expected the talk to turn to more serious matters, and watched with a mixture of disbelief and resentment as Antipater reached out yet again to fill Pheroras' cup although it was not yet empty. Lips pursed, Loshema asked, 'Is this wise?'

'The wine must be finished.'

'Not that. Is it wise we should meet like this? If we are caught then all our plotting will come to nothing.'

'If we are caught the failure of our plots will be the least of our worries.'

Loshema began to pace. 'Still. I do not like it. Can you be certain that you were not followed? Salome is not fooled for a moment.'

'It does not matter. She does not have to believe. Only Herod has to believe.'

Pheroras tried to say something, drink and sneeze all at the same time. He made a strange explosive sound and wine came down his nose. The two men began to laugh, and their mirth was only further fuelled by Loshema's scandalized face. Suddenly she could not stomach another moment of their spluttering foolery. She turned angrily, and left the room, expecting Pheroras to follow yet filled with unacknowledged hope that she would hear Antipater coming after her.

Yet, as it turned out, nearly two hours passed before she heard footsteps on the stairs leading up to the roof. She stood there stiffly, with twilight thickening about her.

'There you are. I thought you gone to bed.'

'Is my husband looking for me?'

'Pheroras is asleep on the couch. One of the house slaves is in attendance.' He came closer. 'What are you doing here, all alone?'

'I like to hear the sound of the sea.'

'Ah, I had forgotten you had never seen it.'

'I did not believe such infinities existed.'

'Loshema.' He went to take her hand but she turned away and stood looking towards the sea.

'You are angry with me.'

'Why should I be angry? Is it not entertainment to watch my husband and my lover drinking like fools, while they plot to kill a king?'

He caught her by her shoulder. 'Lower your voice.'

'Why, when all seems a matter of merriment. You enjoyed your father's company today, now my husband's. Perhaps you have decided to make light of everything.'

'Can you think that? It made me sick to see Herod play the doting grandfather with Tigranes today. The poor boy was petrified.'

'Then you should put his mind at rest. Surely Herod has lost his appetite for killing Hasmonaeans by the fifth generation.'

'Loshema, do not talk like this.'

'Why not? I only want to talk as you and my husband talk, as though nothing in the world matters.'

A look of anger flashed across Antipater's face, and she thought suddenly, *he is sober,* and remembered how he had repeatedly filled Pheroras' glass yet never his own. He was looking at her now, as he sometimes looked at her when she had said something that displeased him, as though she was a stranger to him and there was no trust between them.

'If I got your husband drunk tonight,' he said slowly, 'it is because I would know his mind.'

She laughed at this. 'My husband's mind is a limpid pool. All the little fishes of his thoughts swim near the surface.'

But Antipater did not smile. 'What do you know of his plan?'

'As you do. That there are elements amongst the Pharisees, who would move to help us.'

'And you know these Pharisees?'

'Of course.'

'By name?'

'Of c— ' She hesitated. There were familiar faces. Men who were often in her husband's presence, who bowed to her when she entered the room. But did she know them? They were shadowy figures, who did not come to court. They did not join the animated discussions with Nicolaus in the library, and Pheroras often went out alone to dine at their houses. But this was an age where a wife did not expect to accompany her husband, and Loshema had not given much thought to it, until now.

Frowning she said, 'We agreed. It is safer if we know as little as possible, should … should our plans be discovered … '

'But we know nothing and Pheroras knows all.'

In the distance she could hear the drawing in and breathing out of the waves. It was too dark to make out the water, but she remembered suddenly Pheroras telling her how, in the Book of Genesis, there were hints about the old forgotten names of the primal waters which begat Creation, of how the lower waters, *Tehom,* loved the wild upper waters, *Abzu,* and was loved in return. And how the waters wept and lamented when the Almighty tore them apart. She shook her head. 'Pheroras would never betray us.'

'Not you. Never you. But me.' She tried to protest, but he stilled her, his hands gripping her shoulders in that way that caused pain yet brought about a kind of unacknowledged release within her. 'Think, Loshema, how does it look? He has distanced himself from me. I am shunned. And I must play along not knowing where the game is taking me.'

'In public only.'

'Am I better off in private? O, it's all, *welcome nephew* and *together we are the enemy of tyranny,* but still I do not know what is going on. Even tonight, when he has all but drowned in his cups, he will not answer my questions directly, but rubs his nose and looks at me slant.'

Loshema tried to shake her head and found herself gripped more tightly.

'And when was he last in the library? Nicolaus has told me how he shuns his company and will no longer discuss Greek texts, but dismisses them all as *pagan nonsense*. Do you not see what is happening?'

Suddenly Loshema was tired. She twisted free of his grasp and rubbed her shoulders. 'No. I do not see. Must we have conspiracy upon conspiracy? Is it not enough to have one madman in the family without all of us accusing each other?' At another time his shocked pale face would have stopped her, but she went on relentlessly, 'If my husband does not trust you, perhaps it is your reckless nature that gives him cause for concern. You are told to keep your distance yet you follow him about yapping, like a puppy that will not be stilled.' She pushed him in the chest, and he staggered back a pace. 'You say you are not like your father then do not act like him.'

Suddenly she was against the carved balustrade, her stomach against the cool stone. She felt her robe lifted. 'No!'

His voice was a breath in her ear. 'If I am reckless then you have made me so.'

'Not here.' Her arm flailed, but he caught her wrist and pressed it cruelly into the small of her back. She felt him enter her without gentleness and felt herself rise up to meet him.

'Tell me to go.'

'Go.'

His free hand grasped her breast and squeezed it painfully. 'Tell me so that I believe you.'

But she said no more until at last a low growl, something ancient and elemental —a sound pulled out of that chaos which existed before words enslaved meaning to the movement of tongues— escaped her throat and mingled with the sound of the darkly moving waters down below.

—Let me out! Let me out! Are you there? Do you hear me?— My fingernails are bloody. But I must keep trying. —Please. I know you are out there. Please. Listen to me. I must speak with my husband.—

In the silences, when I can find no more breath, I slide to the floor, leaving red trails on the smooth panels of the door; I crouch; I weep. She is listening. Out there. Salome. This is her doing. I am banging on the door again. —This is your doing!—

You cannot live at court without knowing that betrayal comes to everyone, a certainty, like death. But, like death, inconceivable when applied to oneself. And the manner of it is never as we steel ourselves to face. And our reaction never the one we see ourselves giving.

I had always thought to emulate Mariamme's dignity and poise or to echo Alexander's caustic anger, a verbal fist shaken in the face of blind injustice. But it happened in the library, my inky fingers trembling over a line in the Book of Samuel, searching out those regicides amongst us, David, Ehud, Shallum, for the allegorical truth that hides its meaning in the murder of kings, when suddenly the door flew open and there they were, the royal guard.

—What do you want?— That high, false voice. —You are mistaken. Fetch my hus-

band— A crash. My chair falls backwards. And then the dreadful silence when all the noise I have created dies away. A hand on each shoulder and a hand in the small of my back (I won't come easily) and, where I thought myself unrootable, suddenly everything is in motion. The door flies open, the steps descend, and the colonnades, so solid and familiar, now loom then rush past, alive with the ominous vibrations of the air.

They lock me away in a small, bare room somewhere in the viscera of the palace. Windowless, light creeping through in thin tendrils from two small grills set above eye-level. It is not true that the last thing a prisoner hears is the sound of the door shutting behind them. I heard nothing, only silence closing over my head. And by the time I turned, the door was locked and my fists were pounding uselessly on the cedar panels. —Are you there? Do you hear me? Please I must speak with my husband.—

No-one answers, and so long I am left (hours? days?) that I am half dead with thirst and think myself forgotten and then I wish myself so, because when they come, the blank-faced guards, they feed me on a strange diet, the leavings of the kitchen mixed with bitter scraps of knowledge so that I am first nourished then sickened by what I consume.

Salome, her fangs glistening with the most exquisite poison, has gone to Herod with tales of conspiracy. S'NH is our word for it. You can hear the sibilant hiss as she says it. Choking down a dry crust I learn that Herod has begun torturing certain Pharisees in hopes of a confession. The names —familiar names I have heard my husband speak— I wash down my throat with water from a cracked gourd. Then there is only waiting.

Gomer bribes a guard and buys an hour. She brings me wine and figs, but my hands are trembling too much and she puts them on the floor. I am so glad to see her, I want to curl up in her arms, like a child, and bury my head in the secret nook between her breast and shoulder. But we have never been close, my sister and I.

—You look … well.— I am a reflection of horror in her eyes.

—Tell me.—

She winces, but squats down on the floor (as far as possible from my stench) and begins. —They are all dead, Loshema, all the Pharisees betrayed by Salome, every one.—

—Did they confess?— (Foolish question. Better to ask if the sun has changed course.)

—Some showed courage, I heard. They said Rabbi Yakim saw an angel of the Lord, just as Daniel did when trapped in the lair of lions. And his torturers fell silent and Rabbi Yakim blessed them then he died and the angel stood over his body until they took it away.—

Gomer's eyes are bright as she says this, and I cannot tell if she believes the tale or tells it to bring me comfort. Besides, I have seen the eunuch, Corinthus, bloody and stretched on the rack, and it was not angels he was seeing. But Gomer is still speaking,

—He died bravely. But it was not so with others. They told tales. Some so wild I cannot credit that there was truth in them. They said that the Lord, himself, had inspired them with knowledge of the future, and that they had seen the reign of Herod come to an end.

They convinced Herod's young lover, Karos, and that foolish eunuch, Bagoas, that they were to be rewarded in the new kingdom to come, if they would provide details of the king's comings and goings. Bagoas was eager to help for they told him that he would father children.—

Poor Bagoas, so different from the strutting evil of Corinthus and Lightfoot. I see him in my mind's eye, a large fat man, bald in the Aegyptian style, his sad kholed eyes following the fluttering limbs of children as they scampered about the palace. Suddenly there is so much weight upon me I can hardly bear it. With difficulty I lift my eyes to Gomer's. —Gone?—

—And Karos too. And from what I hear Karos had done no more than meet with the Pharisees to hear their proposition. But it did not spare him …—

She breaks off and I know there is more.

—Tell me.—

—Loshema, perhaps …—

—Gomer, please. I sit alone all through the day and night with my thoughts and the Lord does not hear my prayers. Can your truth be worse than my imaginings?—

A frown. A bitten lip then a sigh. —One of the tortured men let slip your husband's name. (Icy talons sinking into my scalp, daggers in my throat.) He claimed that Pheroras knew that his brother's reign was coming to an end, and believed that he would reign in his stead with you at his side as his queen.—

I try to speak, but the words come out in confusion. Gomer is staring at me.

—Surely you knew?—

—No.— Shaking my head and then the impossible. Laughter. Great gurgling monstrosities of sound. I clutch my side as if wounded; I bare my teeth, screaming and howling flatulent mirth into my sister's face, and Gomer sits, ashen, a single red spot in the centre of each cheek, as though we were arguing children again and I have roundly slapped her.

—No … No …— I try to reassure as the mirth runs its course and I am left hollowed out and weeping. —I am not a madwoman … not yet. Only … my husband … a king? Not even Herod can believe in this tale.—

Gomer is angry or frightened or angry because she is frightened.

—It is not for me to say. I only know that they are dead and the king is killing anyone who has offered the Pharisees a kind word.—

—I am sorry.— How weak that sounds.

Gomer gets to her feet. —I must go.—

—You will be back?—

She is avoiding my eye. —I leave tomorrow. —

—Leave? Where are you going?—

—To Galilee.' A blush, a darted look in my direction. —I have accepted an offer of marriage.—

—By whom?— The words come out too sharply. Gomer flashes me an angry look and for an instant I see that young girl, who was once the hope of our family.

—*His name is David bar Yeshua, a cloth merchant.*— Her chin lifts. —*You would not know of him. But he is a good man. A widower with children. He wishes us to join him.*—

—*Us?*—

—*He has offered to take mother. … and I have said yes.*—

—*But Galilee … so far.*—

—*It is for the best. You know how mother is now. She scarcely knows where she is, but she is very taken with the philosophy these Pharisees spout, that patricians are no better than the poor and that slaves are equal to masters. For days she says almost nothing then, when Herod's spies are sniffing about, she can be depended upon to speak longingly of equality on earth for all men.*—

—*No, you are right, Gomer. Best to get her away.*—

There is a silence. I try to stand up, but the hammering of my heart makes it impossible. Gomer frowns and I think she will come to my aid, but she appears paralysed by her own thoughts. For a while she hovers on the verge of saying something then she blurts. —*If I have my freedom to marry a good man, it is your doing … and that is not … it is not … nothing.*—

There is a lump in my throat. So that's it, the summary of my life. It was not nothing.

—*Gomer, tomorrow, before you leave, take that gold necklace with the amethysts from my chest. It is yours now.*—

—*I could not.*—

—*A wedding gift, with my blessing.*—

There is something unsteady about Gomer's mouth. —*Bring it to me yourself.*—

—*Then I shall.*— And, with that lie, we fall into silence again, wondering why there is nothing more to say. And perhaps it is for the best. We have never been close my sister and I. Tomorrow she will begin her life anew and tomorrow I will be dead.

41

In which love reveals itself in surprising ways

5-4 BCE

*T*OMORROW. TOMORROW. AND TOMORROW. WOULD *it be different if we knew the measure of our allotted tomorrows? There I sit in that dark airless cell, suffocating on thoughts of death, not knowing that there are worse fates to be had than mere dying. No, stop, Loshema. Do not cheapen the tragedy of those who are dead with vulgar melodrama. They are gone and I live on if only as a ghost, a reflection, a pupil dilated in the eye of an unknown reader.*

When my tomorrow comes they drag me from my cell, and bring me into the presence of the king dishevelled and stinking. And this is no private meeting. The grim faces of his councillors stand out all around him, Antipater among them, his eyes widening with horror to see this aged woman, whose unbound hair too readily reveals the grey, whose green eyes are hollowed out with weeping. Shamed, I look away, clasping my hands to stop them from shaking. (Did not Mariamme do the same?) He cannot save me. And to try is only to doom himself.

I am friendless here in this room, facing my interrogators. Then suddenly I am not. Large clumsy arms about me and Pheroras clasps me in a manner that tells the world that they will go through him before they will ever reach me. What kind of madness is this?

Herod is so angry he rises from his throne. 'Do you still defy me with this woman? It is she, who has led you against me, she who has insulted my maiden daughters, whom I would freely have given you, she, who has done everything in her power to lead us into unnatural war. Are you not aware that she conspires with those Pharisees, who would see me from my throne?' Something wheedling enters his tone.

'Would it not be better to get rid of this woman, not at my request or out of deference to my judgement, but of your own accord for she will be the cause of war between us. If you claim to be my kinsman, give up your wife now, and you will continue to be my brother and not betray your love for me.' Passion makes him breathless and he clutches his side suddenly, as though it pains him, but he is waiting for an answer. Dear, dear Pheroras. I cannot let him sacrifice himself for me, and gently I start to pull away. But Pheroras will not let me go.

'Brother,' he begins slowly. 'I have been in awe of you all my life, in a way Jonathan to your David, and my love for you is no small thing. Your triumphs have been my triumphs, your enemies my enemies. And, if you had so ordered it, I would even have followed you into battle, though I have no talent for war. But I tell you now, before all these witnesses and before the attestation of the Lord, I would rather die than give up the woman I love. It is not right

306

that you should ask it of me'

A perfect silence follows. The councillors do not dare even to exchange glances. Antipater is so still he might be Nabal the Calebite, whose heart died within him and he became 'still as stone'. And I am a rag kept from falling only by Pheroras' strong arm about my waist. All eyes are upon the king. And Herod is still clutching his side. He puts his free hand out against the throne to steady himself and forces the other hand down, as though he mistrusts it. He looks old, wounded.

'You I exalted.'

He says it so softly, that even in the silence we fail to hear it.

'Sire?' One of his chamberlains steps near. But Herod can see only Pheroras, this brother who stands there openly defying him, full in the knowledge that other men have been strangled to death on a strand of rumour no thicker than a cobweb.

'You I exalted.' He says it louder, and now that the bottle is unstoppered the words gush forth. 'I gave you honours. I raised you up amongst the highest though you had held nothing heavier than a pen in your hand. I offered you my DAUGHTERS! Yet you cleave to that Jezebel and lecture your king about what is RIGHT!'

Flecks of spittle fly from the corners of his mouth and are caught in the brindled shadows of his beard. A thousand deaths stare me in the face. He will have me trampled as Jezebel, my blood spattering upon the walls. Or he will be a Phineas and run us both through the belly with a single spear. I should push Pheroras from me. I should renounce him as he will not renounce me then perhaps he might be spared. But I do not. I am so silent I might be Lot's wife crystallized into her saliferous state.

'Get out. Go!'

Pheroras blinks. He looks like his old self, waking up from a compelling passage in a book. 'Go? Where should I go?'

A vein is throbbing on Herod's forehead. He takes several staggering steps until he is face to face with Pheroras. His hand is clutched to his side again. 'I made you tetrarch of Peraea, did I not? Go there then and be damned.'

—Loshema. Loshema, forgive me.—

—There is nothing to forgive.—

—How can you say that when I sat silent …—

—Did I do better? I should have forced him to leave me. Yet I stood there, struck dumb, for what other course of action can a sane person take before Herod?—

—Then Pheroras is a madman. I never believed he had it in him. Is it true he thought to make himself king?—

—Who can answer that? Yesterday I would have said, no. Today, up is down; darkness illuminates; light obscures.—

—You will go with him then… to Peraea?—

—Have I a choice? A woman must go with her husband.' A painful silence then, —So that is that then. The end of us. My husband has failed to make me his queen. And now I shall never be yours.—

—No. Not that. Never think it.—

—You will go on alone?—

—I will go to Rome. You saw my father today, stumbling, clutching his side. We have but a few months to wait. I am still the heir, and when I am king we will bring about an Israel the like of which has never been seen.—

—And if Pheroras will not give me up?—

A brush of lips upon her forehead. —No power in the world will stop me having you.—

Six months only had passed yet Loshema had a sense that lifetimes had been lived through. It was a source of wonder to her still that she had come to Peraea with such a heavy heart, remembering its dusty hills and its lean, fierce-eyed people, but had, instead, found a Peraea quite unlike the one she recalled. The steward, Nabal Haresh, had greeted her almost as a long-lost daughter, and with Pheroras at her side, the servants were no longer surly, but respectful of her station as the wife of the tetrarch.

Pheroras' presence had been strangely transforming. Peraea's inhabitants had long felt themselves to be the poor country cousins next to Jerusalem's elite, forgotten and neglected, at least until the next taxes were due. But now the king's own brother had come to rule them and they grew in stature and confidence and shed a little of their fierceness.

Loshema went with Pheroras to visit Rabbi Haresh and his wife, and the old man took Loshema's hands in his and there were tears in his eyes.

'The Lord has answered my prayers.' And when Loshema's expression asked, *how so,* he went on brokenly, 'Ever since I came to give you comfort, and instead harangued you with my own point of view, I have had no peace, waking or sleeping. I came the next day to beg your forgiveness, but you had gone. And, having failed to learn my lesson, I have harangued the Almighty —blessed be His name and His mercy— to bring you back so that I might abase myself before you and plead my guilt.'

Loshema found tears forming in her own eyes. 'Rabbi Haresh. You ask for forgiveness where there is nothing to be forgiven. In my darkest hour you reminded me who I was and where I belonged, and if any sin was committed, it was mine for failing to thank you.'

Then Rabbi Haresh's wife spoke up, a small wrinkled, bird-like woman with the same fierce eyes as her countrymen. 'Well, my lady, you are kinder to him than he deserves. Come, let us eat.'

To Loshema's surprise they ate together. She had expected to eat alone with the rabbi's wife, as was the custom outside the Hellenized world of the court, but Rabbi Haresh had insisted. 'Is a wife not her husband's crown?' The dinner was the plain fare of the country, thick vegetable broth and coarse bread, a lamb stew seasoned with dates and rosemary, all served on a simple wooden table, which had been polished by hands and arms passing food back and forth over the years. Neither Rabbi Haresh or his wife seemed embarrassed by their poverty, nor in awe of their esteemed guests. And Loshema found she liked their simplicity and the simple way they expressed their faith without ostentation or false modesty.

At a certain point in the evening Rabbi Haresh grew serious. He ran his finger around the rim of his cup. 'I talk too much,' he said. 'The Almighty knows my good wife has been witness to the follies of my tongue for forty years. But I feel I must say something.' At this his good wife rolled her eyes to the ceiling, but this deterred the Rabbi not in the least. 'We are a people of history, that is to say our history is important to us. Which, of course, is not to imply that the history of other people is an unimportant matter. Only that Jews have come to regard history as a story written by a divine hand, a history like no other history, going back to a time when the only way to retain a history was in the words and the memories of the people, perhaps even to a time when words themselves were new and precious to us.'

Wondering where this was going, Loshema glanced at Pheroras, who was listening with that quietly thoughtful expression that he reserved for everything from the astonishing to the mundane. Rabbi Haresh's wife cleared her throat and her husband looked abashed. 'Yes, yes, of course, you are right, my dear. I can never keep to the path, but must go wandering off into the tangled thickets of my thoughts.'

He frowned to himself and drummed his fingers on the table. 'What I mean to say is that we have perhaps become a little over fond of our history, of where we are from, our lineages, who begat who, and so on. We are guilty of looking at a man, not as the sum of his deeds and achievements, but entirely as a result of where he is from, his blood as we put it. But now I see you here and I remember that the prophet Amos was of humble birth and that king David himself no more than a shepherd among the hills of *Bet Lehem*.' He glanced quickly at his wife. 'Which is to say that I look at you, and I see no great bloodline, but that you are a new light for Israel, a man who cannot bask in the glory of ancestors, but whose justice must speak for itself.'

Frowning at her husband the Rabbi's wife raised her cup and forced a hasty conclusion of his thoughts, and Loshema and Pheroras exchanged amused glances as they joined the toast. But the truth of it was that Loshema understood something of what Rabbi Haresh was trying to say. Here, in Peraea, she had seen Pheroras free of his kinship ties, and how the hidden seed of his nature unfurled in the unexpected light.

Much of his clumsiness vanished and he walked straighter. He was not a warrior king, as his brother was, but suited to ruling in times of peace. It was funny, Loshema thought. Although they were no relation, Pheroras was very like the gentle Hyrcanus, a king quite unlike a king in the manner of those days, whereas Herod craved and demanded love then doubted its sincerity, Pheroras drew the love of the people as naturally and unconsciously as water pouring into a deep accepting well.

As the weeks went by she found herself watching him in quiet moments when he was too occupied to notice, and she would walk away from these moments confused and disquieted, feeling that she had failed to grasp something just beyond her reach.

On the night they visited Rabbi Haresh she got into bed and lay there awake even after Pheroras had joined her. Then, without quite assenting to the action, she rolled towards him and placed her hand on his chest. He stroked her hair.

'Loshema?'

She said nothing, and moved her hand down until she clasped him in the nest of her strong fingers. For an instant he did not respond then suddenly he grew hard and she climbed on top, using her free hand to guide the full shaft of him inside, and she did not release him until his groans led to a shuddering climax of her own.

Afterwards he turned to her with puzzled eyes. 'Why?'

She sat up, gathering the sheets about her and shook her head. 'Because you are a good man and my husband. And because you chose me and that ... that is not ... nothing. And this place. It confuses everything. We live one life in Jerusalem and we come here and we find men live quite differently. And everything is clearer and simpler and yet somehow like a dream.' She turned to him with sudden violence. 'Have you never had a dream that you never wanted to wake up from?'

He took hold of her hands then and rubbed them because they felt like ice. Then he lowered his lips and pressed her fingers to them.

But dreams are dreams and sooner or later the world catches up. There came a day when Loshema sat opposite her husband at breakfast (Pheroras liked to dine simply on dates and bread and a certain wild honey that was a delicacy in the region) and Loshema saw him frown and shake his head over a letter he was reading.

'From your brother?' Herod had sent letters over the months, some disguised, some openly pleading for Pheroras to return. But in this Pheroras had been uncharacteristically obstinate.

'He says he is unwell.' Pheroras held the letter at a distance from him, and Loshema noticed, with a pang, that he could not read it otherwise. 'He wants me to return in order to impart business he trusts to no-one else.'

A strange mixture of dread and elation filled Loshema. 'And will you?'

Pheroras looked at her over the top of the letter. 'There is an afterword by Salome, who tells me that he is not nearly so ill as he imagines.' He laid the letter down. 'I swore a vow never to see him again. No, I will not go. But I will write to Antipater to warn him that rumours of his father's decline are not to be relied upon.' He placed his hands on the table and pushed himself up onto his feet. 'Will you send him a word?'

'I think not this time.' She had spoken too quickly, and to hide her confusion she reached for a slice of that thick Peraean bread and began to spread it with honey, but she felt Pheroras' eyes upon her.

Suddenly Pheroras asked, 'You are happy here, my dear?'

She answered reflexively without meeting his gaze. 'Of course. It has been a happy time for us both.' And only much later, when she remembered these words, did she wonder at her prescience when she chose to speak in the past tense.

Pheroras picked up the letter. 'I have promised to look over plans with Nabal Haresh for the rebuilding of the stables. Do you wish to join me?'

She smiled tightly. 'No, not today.'

'Very well.' He reached over and caressed her hair absently for a moment before leaving the room.

When he was gone Loshema let out a very long breath. Her thoughts were difficult and lacking shape. She felt she ought to write to Antipater yet hesitated. Ever since arriving back at Beth Aram, a strange reticence had overtaken her, and she had lifted a pen but rarely.

Her previous stay had been a chaos of darkness, her letters to Antipater lifelines she had cast out in the hope of rescue. But this time things were different. There was a life here, a simple life made with her husband, where all the complex machinations of the court were meaningless. And she found, to her surprise, that she was tired and craved peace, as though she had always thought herself a fish of the sea, but now, caught upon the shore, had discovered for the first time the joy of sweet, clean air.

As the dream of Peraea solidified around her, Antipater had faded, and with him that need to feel she was spinning her own web in that web of webs. It was good to awaken in the morning without fear, and to know the day was hers to do with as she pleased, and there was a lightness in her bones that she remembered from childhood or in snatched moments of dream where her feet lifted from the ground with the freedom of flight.

But, hearing Antipater's name brought her crashing back to earth. It was as though she had remembered only a reflection of him, a faded distorted thing, but now her mind and body awoke with the shape of his name on her husband's lips, and she was seized with that pull towards a life that held the promise of larger things.

She got to her feet and reached for stylus and tablet. In Beth Haram implements of writing were always to hand, and Nabal Haresh was known to despair of the constant clutter of scrolls and pots of ink and fresh rolls of papyrus that littered every room.

Back at the breakfast table she pushed aside the plates of dates and figs and, instead of the letter she had intended, found herself writing, *I would rather die than give up the woman I love.* And beneath this, she wrote, *I will make you mine, Loshema. I swear it.* But she was not finished and added, *An adulterous wife is bitter as wormwood. Her feet go down to death, Her steps take hold of Sheol.* Then a quote in Greek, ἐπ᾽ εὐτυχίᾳ τῇ μεγίστῃ παρὰ θεῶν ἡ τοιαύτη μανία [sc. ὁ ἔρως] δίδοται. *The madness of love is the greatest of heaven's blessings ...*

The sound of approaching footsteps made her reach for the scraper and quickly erase the dangerous nature of her thoughts. But it was only one of the houseboys, a lad of about twelve, who, being illiterate, posed no threat. Yet, it was not what he read, but what she read from his gaping mouth and round frightened eyes, that had her leaping to her feet. 'What is it? What has happened?'

'The master— ' His unbroken voice, shrill with youth got no further. It was not necessary; Loshema was already running from the room.

She found herself outside, on the terrace that ran along the east side of the palace, without knowing how she got there. Nabal Haresh was coming towards her his arms outstretched, but she pushed him aside and fell to her knees beside Pheroras, who was lying on the ground, a hand clutched to his belly and his face turned into the hasty folds of a cloak that had been placed beneath his head.

'Husband?'

At the sound of her voice he turned his head, and she saw that he was pale and sweating. He smiled weakly at her troubled face. 'A little colic. Perhaps something I have eaten.'

'You have eaten no differently than I.' Then to Nabal Haresh. 'Quickly, help me get your lord to his feet.'

But when they tried, Pheroras clutched his belly tighter and shook his head. In the end it took four of the wiry little Peraean men, shepherds by trade, to carry him to his bed, where he lay his eyes closed, moaning softly.

Loshema called for a physician but this was Peraea, a forgotten backwater where the Almighty's hands alone attended the sick, and there were no physicians to be had. A scrawny weather-beaten man in torn robes presented himself at Beth Haram, calling himself Jehoram Magus. In desperation Loshema let him in. But, after watching him lay his hands, with their dirty fingernails, on Pheroras' forehead, and listening to him claim that this was the Almighty's just punishment on the house of Herod, and that repentance should take the form of a large sum of gold, which he, Jehoram Magus would kindly dispose of, she had Nabal Haresh and three of the sturdiest slaves run him from the estate.

After that Rabbi Haresh came, apologising for having been away when word first reached him.

'How is he, my dear?'

Loshema pushed fingers through her dishevelled hair. 'He knows no rest.'

'Nor you either,' Rabbi Haresh said shrewdly. 'What good is it to your husband if you fall ill?'

'I cannot leave him. You see I have ... I have not ... not always been ...'

Rabbi Haresh put a finger to his lips. 'Peace. The Almighty knows the secrets of your heart. Leave Him to judge. Now tell me what you know.'

'Only what you will have heard yourself. That he fell ill two days ago after the first meal, and that now he complains constantly that his belly is on fire, but retches at more than a single sip of water.'

They went together to view the patient. Pheroras was on his side, the tangle of the bedsheets wound, like a shroud, on the floor. His eyes were closed and he seemed to have found a degree of rest though he moaned softly and constantly. Rabbi Haresh and Loshema spoke in whispers.

'Of course you tried fennel.'

'Yes. And an infusion of elecampane in wine then powdered pomegranate, and even oil of laurel.'

'Without improvement?'

'None. I have sent to Jerusalem. Surely, despite everything, Herod will not ignore it. He will send the best of his physicians.' Her voice grew a little shrill. 'He must.'

'I will pray for him to do so.'

Pheroras suddenly let out a low groan and turned restlessly on his pillow. Loshema looked down at him despairingly. 'Only pray they are not too late.'

Five days later Herod's physician arrived and with him was the king. 'How does my brother?' he demanded. Then, before Loshema could answer he took the stairs, two at a time, as he had done in his youth, and let himself into the main bedroom.

Later, the days that followed were always hard for Loshema to recall. She was numb with tiredness, living through the waking hours (and there were many) on a venomous brew of worry and guilt and fear poisoning her veins, leaving her with a dragging step and a constant dull pain between her temples. She ministered to Pheroras and to Herod too, who rarely left his brother's side except to relieve himself or to berate the physician. Watching the physician's frozen face, Loshema found herself wondering who would choose to be a follower of Hippocrates when credit was given to the Almighty for their victories yet their failures were theirs to carry alone.

But such moments were rare. It was clear that, for all the desperate attention heaped upon Pheroras, nothing was working. Always a thin man, it was a skeleton that lay on the bed now, and Loshema felt the inching creep of the angel of Death. She knelt beside him until her knees were numb, clasping his hand, his hand, whose long fingers had drawn comparisons between Homer's epic and the legendary journey of the Israelites, now icy and inert. He rarely spoke now, and when he did, the effort exhausted him.

Gently releasing him, Loshema started to get to her feet, but he moaned and reached for her.

'Husband?' She pressed her ear near to his lips. His breath was foetid but his voice was stronger than she had heard for days.

'Is he asleep?'

For an instant she did not understand then she glanced over at Herod, who was sitting opposite in a chair brought by Nabal Haresh. His head was nodding, folds of his beard cushioning its fall. 'Shall I wake him?'

'No.'

She waited. Pheroras was silent so long she thought him asleep then she heard him draw in a dry breath. 'Forgive me.'

Tears welled in her eyes. 'There is nothing to forgive.'

'No. Loshema.' His fingers groped for hers and she grasped them and held them against her cheek. They were dry and papery, ancient papyrus about to crumble and blow away. 'You were so young, a child. I should have been a father to you. I took too much.'

She shook her head, not trusting herself to speak. Pheroras was looking at her sadly. 'You are so beautiful. I have never loved as I have loved you. I was wrong to put you aside on my brother's insistence. I am a coward.'

'No!' She said it so vehemently that she feared she had woken Herod, but he slumbered on and she went on gently, desperately, 'You are the best of husbands.'

'I must —he swallowed several times— confess to you.'

She drew back alarmed, that instinctive behaviour learned at court always fearing a trap, then, recalling herself, leaned forward again. 'Confess?'

Pheroras' eyes had grown cloudy, and she felt certain he had forgotten she was there, but he spoke again, weakly. 'The bottle— '

She lifted his cup, held it to his lips, but he choked and pushed it away. 'In the chest.'

She shook her head again.

'My mother's chest.'

And now she understood. It sat in a corner of the room, an ancient cedar chest decorated in the Arabic style, a long ago gift from Cypros, and containing a few remembrances of her never, to Loshema's knowledge, revisited. Pheroras' eyes were closed and reluctantly she whispered, 'The chest, yes?'

His eyes opened. 'Inside a bottle, dark blue, a silver stopper. Destroy it.'

Suddenly her hands were as cold as her husband's. 'What is it? What does it contain?'

He moaned softly and rolled his head from side to side unable to lift his body into a more comfortable position. Without looking at her he answered, 'A love potion that is all. I am so much older. Antipater, he is young. … He sent it to me. His uncle brought it.'

This she remembered. Antipater's maternal uncle, a boorish glut of a man, nodding and winking at her, as though she was a common whore or privy to the lewd secret that was making him shake his belly with vulgar laughter. She forced herself to be calm, forced the slave's training she had received as a child, to wash her expression free of the horror and fear that had seized her, and asked, 'Did you drink it all, this potion Antipater sent you?'

He frowned and his eyes fluttered. 'No. Half. Perhaps a little more. It is thing to be taken a few drops at a time. I thought it a love philtre.'

What have I done? Her mind was racing, chasing itself in terrified circles unable to escape the memory of that last conversation with Antipater.

—*Is it true, Pheroras thought to make himself a king?*—

And the dismissive coolness of her answer. Why hadn't she denied it with all the force in her body? No, not a king. Never a king, with all its monstrous contradictions the loving hate and the hate-filled love, the compromised ideals and the bankrupt dreams.

She closed her eyes praying wildly and hopelessly to the Almighty to break a link in the ineluctable chain of events that brought her to this moment. The touch of Pheroras' fingers on her head made her open them again. He was looking straight at her.

'I wanted to make you my queen.'

'O Pheroras.'

'Antipater will make you a queen.'

'You think I care about that? I don't care about that.' And even as she said it, she marvelled to find it was true. She went on, 'I want to live here with you, in this place, where being a Jew is not something you do with your head, but with your heart and hands, and no-one is more Jew than another.' And her words were a dream not reality, and were woven of possibility and impossibility, built from the shape of something she had not quite grasped but sensed all around since returning to Beth Haram, and had only truly come to appreciate now that it was slipping away. Pheroras' eyes were closing again, and she cried out hopelessly. 'I want to be with you.'

But Pheroras did not respond, and when she looked up the eyes she met were Herod's, awake and watchful, but for how long she had no idea.

42

In which perjury is more easily swallowed than poison

4 BCE

It was strange to be back. Jerusalem, the city of her childhood and the place where she had grown to womanhood, and all around the familiar sounds and sights and smells pierced her heart, finally tearing away the last shreds of the dream she had cradled at Beth Haram.

She had walked at the head of the funerary procession, the widow's place, knowing herself to be a spectacle well-worth seeing, the slave who had ensnared a royal prince. It had a quality of legend, —Esther beguiling Ahasuerus, Rizpah captivating Saul— But, the faces of the crowd, who jostled and elbowed their way forward to get a look at this 'princess of the people', revealed a hint of satisfaction mingled with their sorrow for, if it is good to see the mighty fall, there is an extra thrill in seeing the humble put firmly back in their place. Or perhaps that was only her own fears talking, as she walked before her husband's corpse towards the Temple and an unknown future.

Pheroras had died two days earlier without regaining consciousness. And when it happened Loshema already knew that goodbye had been said, and that the cessation of breathing was simply the body preparing to meet with the angel of Death, simply a ritual to be gone through as she must go through her own rituals, washing him and rubbing myrrh and aloes into his skin and winding him in clean linens. She was surprised to find that she had no desire to cry nor to eat or to sleep, though she dozed from time to time and drank a little wine. The world around her was submerged, peopled by shadows, who spoke in muffled indistinct voices, which, for the most part, she ignored.

It was at Herod's insistence that Pheroras' body was taken back to Jerusalem where he would be given a state funeral, and that the people might see there was at least one saint inside the house of Herod. But, out in front, Loshema heard whispers, and it was the king's name they used most often. *The king does not weep? What kind of man does not weep for his brother? Is he a man at all?* And they made the sign against evil.

But oddly, in this matter Loshema was Herod's ally. She saw how his grief at his brother's death had become a solid, compact thing, not burning or raging, but lying inside him, paining his gut, but without fire, without heat, as though this part of Herod had died alongside Pheroras, and now he carried death with him everywhere inside his belly.

Afterwards when the men had finished their prayers and went off to find Pheroras at the bottom of their wine-cups, and the women had grown tired of wailing and beating their

316

breasts, their conversation turning back to gossip, Loshema left them and climbed the stairs up to the library.

There was no-one inside, but she hesitated in the open doorway aghast to find it just as she remembered. Somehow, in her head, this room had become so identified with Pheroras that she could not imagine that it had not died in some way with him. Now the callous indifference of the scrolls, which had failed to crumble to dust or the row of ink pots that had not thrown themselves, gaderene-like, from the solid surface of the desk, took her breath away.

With a bitter/sweet pang she realised that Pheroras, had he been there, would have brought down all the destruction she could have asked for, with his clumsiness and his habit of getting up too quickly when a thought struck him, scattering pens and papyrus across the floor, or sitting frozen, eyes turned inward on a new idea, while ink dripped from the end of his reed. She went over to the desk and sat down, wondering how it is that pain is so piercing and immediate yet happiness goes by unnoticed until long after it is lost.

In the weeks that followed she spent long hours in the library both comforted and tormented by memories that sprang up, as though every object in the room held some shape of what had gone before, and now was suddenly compelled to release it by that strange incantation which is death.

There was a fresh sheet of papyrus on the desk weighted down with smooth black pebbles. And instantly she was there, with Pheroras, a trip they had taken to the shores of Lake Asphaltitus, the heavy salt atmosphere in her nostrils and every detail of his thin lined face, showing surprise and pleasure, as she presented him with her worthless little gift. She turned her head to banish the image, and here were the shelves, stacked with their books, cylindrical leather containers marking the titles. And how often had she been forced to frantically search them because Pheroras had misplaced a text that was urgently needed. She had grumbled about the task, and now she would never be asked to do it again.

And the bench at her back, where Antipater sat facing her, the morning light, like heaven's sanction on his brow, and his words no more than her words or dreams or thoughts made whole and real, as though there was no beginning between them and no end, but something kin to the great Serpent that the stories of old said encompassed the world, a circle of itself, forever biting its tail.

She beat down the thoughts of Antipater with her fists, beat them down to punish herself, and because she did not trust herself to be able to hold them in her heart and do what had to be done. And when she was done with this, and was wrung out and numb, she glanced quickly towards the door then, drawing a letter from the folds of her robe, spread it out on the table and began to read.

Antipater, crown prince of Judea and the associated territories to Loshema, widow of our dearly beloved uncle, Pheroras

The news has only just reached me here in Rome. I was reading in the emperor's private library, which he has been so good as to give me access, when Acme (a slave of Livia's) rushed in. If you recall, she is a Jew and Aramaic is her home-tongue. Perhaps Livia thought it would soften the blow to allow her to impart the news. If so, I cannot claim it worked; the shock was a most horrible one.

My first thoughts were, of course, for you. Already there are rumours of poison. Can it be? Pheroras was a saint. Who would want to kill a saint? — Loshema read that line again. Was there perhaps just a hint, a reminder that she was complicit?—

How has my father taken the news? The letter I received from the palace was no more than a piece of scribal formality with nothing of the king's mood imparted. I pray that you are in no danger.

Your grief, I am sure, is no small thing, and I daily curse my haste in leaving for Rome, knowing that I am not there to comfort you in your hour of need. But do not fall too deeply into the pit of despair. The workings of the Almighty are mysterious indeed and his ways are infinite and beyond our understanding. Perhaps, if we could see beyond this time of misery, we would rejoice in the knowledge that all our plans have come to fruition and would look back on this tragedy as His Will, a means to an end much as we crush the golden beauty of an ear of corn to make the bread of life.

O, but listen to me. What comfort do my ramblings offer? I curse each cubit which keeps me from you. If I were certain of my safety I would leave tonight and ride an army of horses to death just to be by your side. How I miss those fiery arguments when we knew ourselves alone in the library, the sweetness of your smile just before you scorched my presumptions with the sharpness of your wit and the sun coming up over the Temple mount, if I forget thee O Jerusalem …

Send me a word to tell me how things lie. Is it safe for me to return yet? How does my father's health? Does he look with favour on any of my younger brothers? I hear he still weeps and clutches Alexander's children to his breast, and I fear the time will come when we must act against them in our own interest.

But it may not come to that. Despite your sorrow, try to think of me as a glimmer of light in all that darkness, which surrounds you. You are a free woman now, and I will be with you as soon as you deem it safe for me to return. For now, know that I am with you in spirit, if not body. Pray it will not be too long. And write at once if you can.

She must act. She had known she must act. Yet weeks went by and she did nothing. She would climb the library stairs full of intent, determined to make a decision, but then a great weariness would settle across her shoulders, and, for the first time, she began to notice the weight of her years, how her back hurt when she stood up, and the knotted veins sprouting, like gnarled vine roots, across her hands, which were growing crabbed and stiff with age. Then it was easier to sit in Pheroras' favourite seat by the window, watching the sun spreading its glory across Jerusalem, and feeling its warmth on her face.

And when, finally, she was brought to Herod she went there half asleep. It was a formal gathering. Salome was there and all the high officials, members of the Sanhedrin, the most learned doctors of the Law. But it was the sight of Nicolaus of Damascus, who stood behind the king yet had not come once to the library to offer his condolences, that made her smile beneath the stiff mask of her face and think, *O, Nicolaus, you do not need to give me a lesson in what loyalty means in the court of Herod.* But she said nothing, offering her bow and waiting.

Herod was reclined on his throne beneath a lamb's-wool blanket, his feet propped up on a footstool. He stared at her, like a cobra within its nest, that immobile, inhuman face with only the glittering eyes showing life.

—*There has been a plot.*—

She stood as a stone stands.

—The women of your husband's household have told us everything.—

Doubtless between their screams. But the 'everything' Herod thought he knew may be different to the sum of her knowledge, and so she kept her lips pressed tightly together. Herod watched for a reaction then slumped back on his pillows. He gestured to Nicolaus, as though too weary of it all to continue, and Nicolaus stepped forward and cleared his throat, 'They have said that the poison was procured from an Arab woman —they have skill in such things— and they say it was your mother and sister who met with her.'

A demon of laughter burst from her lungs, startling Nicolaus into silence.

'Did they also procure angels' wings to let them fly from Galilee?' she asked. 'Or perhaps, being Greek, you would prefer that they summoned Pegasus from the clouds and rode upon his back?'

Nicolaus gave a tight smile. 'I am glad that you laugh, lady. But I fear the king does not share your sense of humour. If, as you say, your mother and sister played no part, perhaps you will be so good as to enlighten him with your version of events.'

And now the atmosphere in the room changed. Gone was any pretence that this was anything but a trial. And the questions rained down thick and fast.

—Had she known of a plot?—

—How much had Pheroras taken her into his confidence?—

—Who brought the poison to the house?—

—How much did Nabal Haresh know?—

—Was rebellion widespread in Peraea?—

319

—Was Rabbi Haresh part of a Pharisaic plot to overthrow Herod's rule?—
—Where did the poison come from?—
—Who procured the poison?—
—Who was Pheroras in contact with?—
—Who mentioned poison first?—

Who? Who? Who? She danced about the questions, like a body on the battlefield performing the macabre jig of death while arrows pierce its flesh on every side. But there was no let up. And for all her determination her courage was failing her, and she sensed that the truth was being wrung out between her prevarications and outright lies.

And why should it matter, a voice in her head was asking. Hadn't she chosen to stay when she might have flown, hadn't she waited in the library, with the dust gathering on her head, all those blank days and weeks, knowing the danger of taking tales to Herod. Better to allow him to sniff and worry at his brother's corpse until the stench of betrayal seeped out of the pores of rotting flesh. This was what she had wanted. Her day in court when she would right the wrongs, the dark thread on which her life was strung.

But as she looked from face to face, Salome's narrowed eyes, the hungering look on Herod's as of a man who uses pain as a drug, the blank distant face of Nicolaus, she could not do it. The decision was too terrible. To betray a living man for a dead one or to betray the memory of a good man for the sake of a love that she now doubted ever really to have existed.

She bowed her head, then answering a question that had not been asked, she said, 'I have the poison in my possession, hidden in my apartments. I will fetch it and bring it here.' And, without permission she turned and fled from the room.

But it was not to her apartments she went. As soon as the dust settled Herod would send the guard after her, and she had but a minute's grace when she could still call her life her own. Pulling up her skirts, she took the steps to the library two at a time, throwing herself through the door and across the room. The window was not large, but easily accessible from the window-seat. With the heavy footfall of the guard already at the bottom of the staircase there was no time to think, only to bend her head and narrow her shoulders and squeeze herself out on to the stone ledge.

A rush of air hit her face. And suddenly there was no escape except to take the plunge, which would end the sorrows of this life, once and for all. Yet she balked, even as her toes dangled, unsupported, some thirty feet in the air. The sun was overhead, and below its blind eye were the flat rooftops of Jerusalem, and below them were the streets where men and women in their thousands lived their lives unaware of a single woman shivering above them, like an angel perched on the High Places, *Helel ben Shahar,* about to tumble from the heavens. The awareness of it filled her with the odd sensation that everything around her was real and that she was the dream.

But very soon the sound of axes wakened her from the dream of herself. The sound of splintering wood told her that they were breaking down the door. Time to go. Her right foot edged a little further forward then froze. All her cleverness deserted her, all the wit and sharpness of mind that has always saved her; she could form no thoughts, no plans, and her brain played an endless frightened loop of discovery. Her net was gone.

For the first time since his death she understood how Pheroras had always been her place of safety, and it hit her in the stomach, like a physical blow. All her life, through the haphazard days of childhood, her blossoming womanhood, even her reckless febrile exploits with Antipater, always he had been there, his arms outstretched ready to catch her. No more.

They were in the room now.

— *Lady. Come out! You are wanted by the king.*—

They were blundering about, confused that she was not visible then one cried, —*The window!*—

Her breath was coming in and out in whimpers. She edged her left foot forward then her right.

Behind her a crash. A man's rough voice. —*I have her!*— Fingers fumbling with the neck of her robe. The sound of ripping. And then. And then—

She woke to the sound of voices. They came from far away and she felt no need to open her eyes.

'Never. Not in all my days, majesty. There will be bruising certainly, but nothing is broken.'

The deep rumble of Herod's voice. 'How is this to be explained?'

'I am a physician and a Greek. We would say that the gods were not yet done with her. But your singular god is a mystery beyond my ken.'

'When will she waken?'

'She is already awake, majesty.'

Wine held to her lips. She coughed, sat up, felt it dribble down her chin. Herod was peering into her face.

'I loved my brother,' he said. 'He was weak and unworldly, but I loved him. Do you understand?'

A weak nod.

'Where is the poison?'

Blinking, she sat up. And the pain she felt in her back and legs seemed to fly in the face of the Greek physician's conclusion that nothing was broken. Recognising that she was in her apartments she pointed weakly at a cedar chest. The physician opened it and located the dark blue bottle with the silver stopper. He held it up and Herod stared at it with undisguised fear. 'This poison killed my brother?'

'Yes.'

He turned towards her and she held her breath. But he did not speak for some moments, his jaw working. Then suddenly, 'I believe my physician is correct. No-one could survive such a fall unless they were marked by divinity.' He rubbed his chin. 'So it seems I cannot have you killed.'

Loshema let her breath out slowly, and as she did so, he leaned over her and whispered in her ear. 'But there is nothing to prevent me breaking you with the most exquisite tortures if you fail to tell me the truth.' He waited for her frightened nod then he asked, 'Did my brother mean to kill me?'

Tears welled in her eyes, tears of laughter, of pity, of rage, of hopelessness. Poor, poor Herod. Did he have to drink up every drop of poison himself? She wanted to say, no. Pheroras did not want to kill you. He was angry, but he was no Cain to dream of killing his brother. He died because of me. Because he would have made himself a king so that he might make me a queen. She wanted to say these things, but she mastered herself. After all she had tried to go to her grave with these secrets, but the Almighty had other plans. And so when Herod looked into her face and asked, *Did my brother want to kill me,* she answered, 'Yes. Yes he did.'

There is something terrible about the look of pain on a monster's face. It does not register shock or surprise, like a normal face, only a terrible wretched acceptance that this is how things are. 'Go on.'

'The drug was brought from Aegyptus. Antipater had it prepared to be used against you, and his uncle brought it to our household.' A sharp pain in her ribs made her pause for several heartbeats then she went on in a flat dead voice, 'My husband, you see, he had turned against you.'

Perjury being easier to swallow than poison Herod nodded.

'But when Pheroras … when he fell ill and you came to him and looked after him, he could see the concern you felt for him and was heartbroken. He called for me and said, *Wife, Antipater has played me false. He planned the death of his father —my own brother— and supplied the drug for the purpose. But my brother, I can see now, is as good to me as ever. I cannot hope to live much longer. Destroy the drug that it may not be my brother's ruin.'*

Herod frowned. The bottle was in his hand, a little harmless thing in that great paw. He turned it over. 'Yet you did not destroy it all.'

Loshema did not answer. The room was fading into darkness. A sharp blow to her cheek brought her back and she blinked several times before answering, 'I thought to keep some for myself lest you treat me cruelly.'

A look of dismay. Why are tyrants always surprised when they are called tyrants? He was waiting for more and she went on rather desperately. 'But … the Almighty stayed my hand for I had not yet come to you with the truth.' Her story had the flimsiness of silk. Herod would rip it from her, as his son had once ripped the robe from her shoulders revealing what lay beneath.

Herod sat back, did not speak for several minutes. 'You swear this is the truth.'

'I swear.'

Herod glanced over his shoulder. 'Do you have it all, Nicolaus?'

'I do, majesty.'

And only then did she understand that Herod's biographer had been in the room the whole time, giving her lies the shape they would hold down through the centuries to come.

A sense of what she was doing, of the future distorting under her fingers, like a lump of clay that refuses to hold its shape on the potter's wheel, filled her with blind panic, and she would have called out a retraction of all she had said, but Herod was already getting to his feet. He held an arm out and the physician hurried to his side, tutting.

'Majesty, you have over exerted yourself. The humors of the body do not rest themselves. It is clear that there is now an overabundance of yellow bile in your liver. Come, you must lie down.' Still tutting, he took the king's arm, and Herod allowed himself to be led from the room, like a little child. Nicolaus followed suit.

When they had gone a great weariness, and more than weariness, descended on Loshema. There was darkness at the edge of her vision, but she fought against it, and when a slave entered she called for Diophantus the scribe to be sent to her. He came to her, a narrow-shouldered, beaky man, who by necessity looked down his nose at everyone. She accepted his bow then demanded, 'You have the gift of imitation.'

Diophantus moved uneasily and began to make protestations. But she silenced him. 'Do not lie to me, scribe. Antipater made good use of you. And I will have the same.' And when he rubbed his nose and shook his head, she added. 'Your master's star is falling. Unless you would fall with him, I suggest you do my will.'

He looked at her then. Really looked at her, as though weighing her up and wondering if such a dried up old snake might have enough venom left to strike, then his narrow shoulders rose in a shrug. 'Tell me the handwriting I am to impersonate.'

'Mine.'

Now it was the turn of his eyebrows to rise, but he settled on the floor beside her and arranged his writing implements, while she dictated.

> Loshema, who was once fortunate enough to consider herself a princess of the house of Herod to Antipater, crown prince of Judea
>
> Forgive me for not writing sooner. The loss of my husband has sent me quite out of my mind with grief these last weeks. You were wrong to describe Pheroras as a saint. He was not a saint, only a kind and gentle man, who knew how to love, but not how to hate or plot or scheme. The world is less for his going.
>
> But I detect a well-meaning admonishment in your letter, advising me to move on, and in this you are indisputably right. If there is any justice Pheroras now sits at the Almighty's right hand, but we still living souls must gather our resources and press ahead with those plans and dreams He-Who-Is-Above-All-

Things sees fit to inspire in us.

You ask if it is safe for you to return. I assure you that the king is as anxious to see you as the one who pens this letter. Come home soon, I beg you. Life without you is a wilderness. Waste not another moment in delay lest your continued absence lead to suspicion.

43

In which the time for parting comes

4 BCE

*I*SEE YOU! *Yes, here we are full circle, back where we began in the darkened room, the heavy drapes covering the windows, fumes of incense curling in the air and the monster dying his rotten death on a bed of sweat-soaked silks.*

Of course this is poetics; naturally, we are not back in the exact moment of our first meeting. The days have lengthened since you first ventured here. Herod has rallied then failed, has sought cures and been disappointed, has suffered what would have killed a dozen men and has sent scores of souls ahead of him into the afterlife. And, just in case he has not brought God's curse down upon himself sufficiently, he has imprisoned the great and the good of Israel within the hippodrome, and intends, like a Pharaoh of old, to take them with him when he dies.

Salome is curled at the foot of the bed, wailing. And who can blame her? She's the one who will have blood on her hands when all is said and done. Behind her, the priests swing their thuribles, their eyes closed in prayer, rocking back and forth, shoulders hunched with the effort it must take to beg the Almighty for a miracle to save Herod's rotted soul. The wonder would be if the Almighty could hear Himself think above their endless clamour.

—Come, we can creep closer than this.— Herod's eyes are shut, but along the lids the thin blue veins are throbbing. What are you remembering? Is it the moment when Antipater entered the palace, his head turning as the guards slam the doors and his friends are abandoned outside? But still, the amulet of my letter is in his pocket.

*—***Waste not another moment in delay lest your continued absence lead to suspicion.***—*

He takes a step towards his father, arms outstretched. And, in that instant, time winds itself back and he is only a lost boy yearning for his father's love. But what's this, Herod recoils. And Antipater knows, before there is time to know, that the tide has turned, the wind has changed, the game is up. He gives a strangled gasp, and his gaze darts around the room, searching for a sympathetic face. But not an eye will meet with his. And, when the guards take hold of him, he does the strangest thing; he begins to laugh.

Herod is ashen, but he has to know. 'What is the meaning of this? By God, you'll answer your father.'

Antipater sobers, but when he tries to speak he cannot help himself; he is sobbing with laughter. 'All this time, father. All this time—' He cannot get the words out. Herod shrinks in the face of such madness. 'What is he saying? What does he mean?' But no-one knows what

325

he means. A guard cuffs him on the mouth, and his laughter bubbles with blood. 'Poor, poor father. All your life so afraid. Never trusting a single man, not even your sons. And all along it was her. You should have been watching out for her!' He gestures wildly, trying to pluck me from the crowd. But, of course, I am not there.

Later at his trial they will go after the women. Antipater falls to his knees protesting and arguing, but Nicolaus steps forward brandishing letters intercepted by the king's spies. Do I imagine it or does he favour me with a cold look of complicity? A hammer-blow of fear jolts my dead heart. How much does he know? I see now that Nicolaus is far more than Herod's biographer. That look warned me that he is not merely writing down a story, his responsibilities extend towards creation.

Doris is the first woman to be brought to Herod's attention. She has tried to warn her son not to return to Jerusalem. —**Seek refuge with Caesar. He will protect you from your father's wrath.**— She is turned out of the palace, penniless, the finery she had learned to covet so late in life, stripped from her. Next, is the High Priest's daughter. Is there not correspondence that shows she suspected a plot and did nothing? She too is exiled, and from his exalted position her father tumbles after her.

On and on it goes. Antipater's slaves are tortured, his freed men, his friends, the slaves and freedmen of his friends. Herod is like an overzealous physician, who cuts out the heart of his patient in his eagerness to find the seat of the disease.

Last is poor Acme, slave to Livia, a Jewess by birth, who was in Antipater's thrall. Letters are found, full of helpless devotion and eagerness to please. She has done his bidding. She has forged a seditious letter in Salome's name and forwarded copies to her mistress and Herod. — **When he reads it I am sure he will punish Salome for plotting against him.**—

And she babbles on, condemning them both, quoting the Law as though it was a love letter in Antipater's hand. —**In my anguish I cried to the LORD, and he answered by setting me free. I will walk about in freedom, for I have sought out your precepts.**— Amid the gasps and outrage I hear only the yearning of a young girl, who believes love will lift her from her slavery, and O the dark glass through which I see myself.

It is widely accepted that Acme is the 'woman' singled out by Antipater's outburst. She is condemned in her absence and a letter written to Caesar, in Nicolaus' hand, outlines her complicity and humbly begs advice concerning what is to be done with erring princes. Nicolaus gives me a sidelong glance before he writes the letter. But what can I do? Acme has condemned herself out of her own mouth. She has even mentioned that Caesar's wife has an especial understanding of plants and herbs, and may be used as an unwitting source of knowledge should Antipater find the poison he has procured not to his 'taste'.

Antipater collapses to the floor and lies there prone. But a kick from a guard shows he is conscious and the trial proceeds. The dark blue bottle with the silver stopper is brought in. Antipater refuses to look at it. Even when they bring in a condemned man and force the contents down his throat. The prisoner swallows a dose ten times the few drops Pheroras took, believing it the gateway to love. He is dead within seconds.

And now the last witness has been called, the last charge laid. Nicolaus steps back. There is silence, and into the silence comes Herod's dry, entombed voice, 'My son. Have you no defence to offer me.'

Antipater does not raise his head, but speaks brokenly into the floor. 'I call upon Almighty God to bear witness that I am innocent. If I have plotted against my father let the Lord of All Justice strike me down as He did Er and Onan. Otherwise let His silence be my plea.'

O Antipater, is this all you offer? I would cover my face and weep if I did not feel so many eyes upon me. The age of Miracles, when the Lord's hand was visible on the red earth, is centuries gone. Men, like Herod, believe that they are the Almighty's anointed tools. And to call down the Lord's wrath is only to put the weapon into his outstretched palm.

'Take him out of my sight.' Herod's voice has thunder in it. 'Put him in chains. Lock him away in the deepest dungeon.'

Salome can do nothing with Herod. This brother king, this killer of kin is dying, and she can do nothing to prevent it. Time and again she goes to him, beating her breast and weeping fat tears of self-pity. The question on her lips always the same. 'What will you do with Antipater?'

But Herod does not answer. His legs and belly have swollen. The soft tissues of his bowel are ulcerated and he can neither stand nor rest for the gripe of pain in his guts. Besides he has other matters to attend to. His eagle has been torn down and, savage with hurt, he wants his vengeance. Then he must visit Jericho in hopes of a cure. And time unspools on a dropped spindle until Caesar's envoys return with their answer.

Acme has been put to death. As to the matter of Antipater Herod must do as he sees fit, execute or exile, the choice is his. Salome is eager. 'You see, brother. You see Caesar is on our side. He is too delicate to tell a king what he must do, but he sends his example in Acme.'

And Herod looks up from his bed of broken glass and the question on everyone's lips is, can he do it? Can he kill his firstborn son? Herod sighs. Then Herod surprises his physicians and priests by sitting up on his elbows. 'I am hungry. Salome, fetch me an apple. And a knife, with which I might cut it.' This is a king, who never does what anyone expects. Yet an apple. What does he want with an apple?

—Come! We must hurry. Where now? Why the Antonia Fortress, where the prisoners are kept, of course. Did you understand nothing?

I should have come sooner. I have left it too late. —There is hesitation in your step. You did not think the stench would be a living thing. Did not think that it would thick and filmy, like the cobwebs hanging in corpse-rags from the vaulted ceiling or that your mouth and nostrils would be filled with its foetid hairy breath. Vomit if you must. There are plenty who have done it before you, and the contents of your stomach are not the worst things that have been *spilled across these floors. Only hurry. You are so slow. O, I will go ahead of you.*

The further and deeper Loshema ventured into the bowls of the Antonia fortress the harder it became to navigate the filth-strewn passages. It was clear that the torturers were not particular about where they wrung out their aprons, and she was forced to keep her skirts bunched in one hand as she slipped and slid, the oily yellow light of her lamp no more than a thin halo in the blackness. From time to time she had to stop, to force the muscles of her jaw and stomach to clench against her rising gorge. But a sense that time moved at a different speed beyond these airless tunnels, that everything she did must already be too late, whipped her on.

She had told herself that she knew what lay beneath the airy upper reaches of the Antonia, below those open marble rooms and cool green gardens that made the place more palace than fortress. Still, she believed she knew. After all it was not only Herod's ears that heard the screams in the quiet of the night. But now she was here the atmosphere of despair and desolation was so thick that she was almost choking on its fumes. *You have done this. You have sent him here,* a voice in her head kept repeating. Then when, with recoiling horror, she ignored it and pressed on, it changed its tone, grew thin and heckling, *You will be too late. Too late.*

Up ahead was the final door she must pass through. She pushed it ajar and stepped into the maw of darkness on the other side. There was no-one there, and the sound of the door shutting had such a quality of finality, a sealing of the tomb, that she turned in panic, and was reaching for the handle, when a voice said, 'Who goes there?'

She spun on her heels, and without speaking, lifted the lamp to her face. The halo of light illumined the scarred face of the guard. He blinked at her, confused, a messenger from the underworld surprised to find himself facing the living.

'I bring news.' Her voice was too loud, even though she was whispering. 'The king is dead.'

He stared at her distrustfully. 'I have heard nothing.'

It took all her control not to scream, *Why should you, you dolt. You are the scum of the earth, buried here, like an envoy from Sheol.* Instead she reached inside her robe and brought out a coin. She let it glint in the torchlight the proffered it, saying, 'I need you to tell the prisoner.'

The man took it from her, rubbing it between a grubby thumb and forefinger. 'Tell him the king is dead?'

'Tell him Herod rallied. Tell him he called for an apple and a knife to cut it. But it was a ruse. As soon as he had it his hand he plunged it into his neck. His pain had grown too much.'

The man is goggle-eyed. Herod is a devil, but he is the devil he has known all his life. His voice is querulous. 'What will become of us?'

Desperation throbbing in her temples, Loshema took a step closer to this subterranean creature. 'Listen to me. The news of the king's death is not yet about the palace. Inside one of these stinking cells is the king's son. Think what gratitude he might show the man who set him free.' The guard's pupils dilated with understanding, and he secreted the coin inside his filthy robes. 'You may rely on me.' Without waiting for a reply he disappeared into the darkness.

Knowing her presence was a danger, Loshema wasted no time retracing her steps. And, by the time she emerged in the courtyard there were already cries. *The king is dead. Herod is dead!*

—*Come, join me. We have one last task before we part forever. You are exhausted. This hot desert land has drained you. Men burn here more than you're used to and words can scorch.*

The heat that has followed you, since you first found yourself in the chamber of a dying king, is no less intense. Not even out here in the courtyard. It crouches on the back of your neck and forces your eyes to slits. It's worse for the tinkle of fountains in the garden just beyond the arched walkway. Believe me, if I could offer a better way I would. But this is my punishment. And as my companion, my confidante, my indefinable other, you must share it.

Loshema's appearance in the crowd caused no ripples. With her hair covered she was not particularly remarkable. And even her sea-green eyes were overlooked, set now, as they were, in the lined face of a middle-aged woman. The men and women, packed several deep on every side, had once cheered her; now she was invisible. But of this she cared nothing. She had come to the courtyard in a kind of dream. But no dream that she could possibly hope to awaken from.

Opposite was a raised dais, shaded by a striped awning. Salome was seated at the front next to the Roman governor, her puny husband eclipsed at her side. Despite several well-muscled slaves wielding huge ostrich feather fans, she looked florid and uncomfortable, languidly twitching a small ivory fan of her own. At her back were twelve judges, dressed in black, their flowing beards and robes giving them the appearance of melting wax candles. And to one side sat Nicolaus, his red face gleaming in the sunlight, and for once without his tablet and stylus to hand, the occasion being too serious to record with anything other than eyes. He was gazing in the direction of the prisoner.

But this was unexceptional. Without any sense of observing Loshema was aware that every eye, from the dais to the crowd, was transfixed by the sight of Antipater, who stood, a lonely figure at the centre of the yard, his wrists manacled by a length of chain. His hair had been cut very close to the skull and he was newly shaved, but the purple shadows of bruising were evident along his cheek bones and jaw, and when he moved he limped and jerked, as though the bones of his feet were no longer to be relied upon.

He did not look like a man whose hands were steeped in blood. And it made her heart jerk to see how thin he had become and how he was turning his head, searching for her in the sea of bodies. But, whether the sun was in his eyes or his memory was caught up with his memory of better days, he could not find her in the crowd.

She saw him give up his search and turn to look up at one of the tower rooms, where, until recently, a particular window had been draped and shuttered. Loshema could see that it was open now, and she understood that this was because Herod, who could no longer move or speak, could still hear. And he wanted to hear this.

—What's this? You thought Herod dead. Come, you are cleverer than that. —

'Is it true he's a devil then?' This from a piping page boy near the front.'
'He's a Herod isn't he?'
The pages were shushed by a maid with an anxious eye towards Salome. True there is a distance, but the Herods have a certain reputation. 'Whatever he is, he was caught red-handed trying to bribe his way out of his cell.' This from behind.
'He was a fool to believe rumours that the king was dead.'
'Everyone believed it.'
'Better to have crawled into the darkest corner he could find and stayed there.'
'He nearly made it though. They say the king will be dead by tomorrow.'
'Shut your mouth, imbecile. That wicked old bastard'll outlive us all.'

—A knife. An apple. Symbols of death and life. The rest writes itself. All the story needed was a voice to tell it.—

They were reading out the charges, and Loshema stood stiff and unbending against the roiling motion of the crowd, listening to a description of a man she did not recognise. The Antipater they were portraying was venal, cringing, lacking all subtlety. A child could see through his plotting thus described. Yet, was this not always the way of it? So few could read Antipater's cunning intricate mind. Perhaps only me, Loshema thought. Perhaps not even me.

The charges finished, the court official looked to Salome. But her nod was mere formality. The king's decision was final, and she took her place on the dais only as his mouthpiece. The crowd took her gesture as sanction to give vent to all their pent-up frustrations, and they hissed and jeered with all the childish excitement that their pagan compatriots might have aimed at theatrical fools. A guard stepped forward, and a violent beating of drums began, which Loshema only vaguely recognised as the hammering of her heart. She forced herself to watch as he began unlocking Antipater's chains so that he might walk freely to his death.

The Law stated that he should be buried up to his knees. But the courtyard was cobbled and so they would tie him to a chair instead. Loshema noted that he was walking towards it with that strange careful step of the condemned, which is only a kind of slowness, a kind of bargaining with time. A little more, just a little … and who knows what might just happen. Israel is a land of miracles and the Herods are as entitled as the next man.

At the chair he stopped and looked down at this throne of black iron and rough planks. He seemed lost, as though everything up to this moment had been carefully rehearsed, and only now did he find himself left alone on stage without direction. Off to the side a signal was given that Loshema missed, and the executioners stepped forward.

—Such big, muscled men. How did they remain invisible? But that is the executioners' art. They wouldn't want you to recognise them on the street.—

At the sound of their footsteps Antipater started and turned back to face the crowd. He was trying to speak, but the jeering made it impossible for Loshema to hear. Then he turned and addressed Herod's window and Loshema thought, Not now. He cannot think there is still hope.

The shorter of the two executioners had produced a rope. It was wrapped in soft cloth. But this was no parting kindness, but rather a precaution lest the harsh fibres cut the prisoner's throat and rob the crowd of a spectacle. But, at the sight of the rope, the crowd fell silent, the holiday atmosphere draining away as the same thought crystallized inside each head. Here was a flesh and blood being, exactly like themselves. They had come on the promise that they would see a monster vanquished and it would be a man who died instead.

Loshema felt something fluttering against her arm, and looking down saw that one of the body-slaves had begun to tremble. —If the mighty can fall so far, what hope for the fate of lesser mortals?— And suddenly there was the sound of rustling and scratching, bottom lips tugged, knuckles gnawed, any one of a thousand ways to remind themselves that they were still alive.

Antipater, too, had seen the rope and now something in him seemed to give way. He stopped speaking and stood looking down at his hands. A man alone and aware of his aloneness for the very last time. And, seeing it, tore open all the old wounds in Loshhema's heart and emptied her of her sense of righteousness, leaving only what had been there all along, the deepest and most moving love of her life.

— I feel you grip me. Will I do this? Will I let it happen? But this is then and long ago. What is unfolding before your eyes is not even a memory but something less and something more. And, if there's one thing you've learned from this journey, it's that no-one escapes their fate. Once the piper has been paid the tune must play.—

They pushed him down on to the chair, firmly, but without roughness and then only because he did not respond when they asked him to be seated. Once he was bound, the shorter executioner wound the rope about his neck and handed the other end to his companion.

Both men looked towards the dais.

A pause, into which the minutiae of the world seeps through, a throat being cleared, the whump whump of a fan, the industrious hum of an insect, invisible to the eye. The Roman governor asks Salome a question and she answers. In the front row fat Shlomi the steward, bent with age and almost blind, is pulling at the arm of a slave boy and demanding, 'What's happening now? Tell me. Tell me.'
'Hush. Salome has given the signal.'

The scent of death hovered in the air and the crowd went mad with it. Here was the scapegoat to drive over the cliff's edge. Here was the fallen angel, Azazel, filled with collective sin. In their midst Loshema stood, controlling herself with a kind of savage mastery, knowing that the man dying before her was there because she had sent him there. And the knowing of it was not the same as the feeling of it, and the stony expression of her face masked a terrible battle of failure and loss and justice. Her whole being was concentrated on a single thought, Don't look away.

This was her covenant, the holy price exacted of her so that some part of her might stay whole even and beyond the decisions and the deeds, the lies and the betrayals, the stolen moments and the snatched ecstasies that had led to this day. And she did not break it even when the flesh of his face suddenly jerked and tightened, and the look of fear flared in his eyes. Then the desperate futile struggling. The bulging veins. The vivid rush of blood from his nose. And life fluttering, fluttering, a tamed bird panicking as the door of the cage opens.

Above them the sun beat down, like the wrath of God, the old God of the High Places, the God of Bethel and Horeb, the God of thunder and of the burning Word, whose fury had swept aside men and their cities in oceans of fire and now threw a blanched hectic light across the courtyard that turned everything to shadow. But the crowd had grown still, pulled taut on an ancient memory of when sacrifice had a human shape. And Salome's slaves had ceased their fanning, and the figures seated on the dais were no more than silhouettes hunched forwards, poised on the brink of Antipater's death.

Yet Loshema alone caught the precise moment when it happened —there— a sigh. His head lolling forward, pendulous, broken, emptied of its divine spark.

And that is that. And we are left on opposite sides of now and forever, he rushing ahead while I am standing still, so still. O Antipater. O my love.

You are shaking your head. What made me do it?
It was his punishment.
What made me stay?
That was mine.

The crowd is still watching. They don't understand what has just happened under their noses. Not yet. The executioners will go on a little longer. They must be sure. They have their pride.

Come, time to go. Walk with me before they recognise that the entertainment is over, out into the narrow streets of Jerusalem, where the corn-sellers and the fig-sellers are erecting their stalls. Out where the linen-merchants are displaying purple robes from Sidon and the trinkets on the pedlars' trays gleam gold in the sunlight. Out where the bread-makers are about their business, while the little children go skipping behind them trying to catch the crumbs. On to the dusty streets where a lone woman may not walk unless she is a slave or a widow or a ghost.

I sense you pulling away. You are looking at me strangely.

You thought me your spirit guide, a creature, who fluttered near the ceiling making judgements on the mortal creatures below, and it shocks you to find that I am made of the same dank clay as the rest. A narrator should be above such things. You expected better. But the reflection that we meet in the darkness is seldom wise or beautiful. I warned you at the start. I am no Aeschylus or Ennius writing pious morality plays, and this is no parable to teach men the infinite stretch of God's justice. In this story no-one is innocent; it was simply a question of which of the guilty would be left standing.

You do not know me? It is no surprise. I do not recognise myself. Am I Psyche, who mistook Heaven for the serpent's hiss? Or am I Eve, who took a serpent's bite for Heaven's kiss? Or am I simply a little distilled moment of time, who watched gods topple and empires fall, and a small kingdom rise, like an avarshina, from the ashes, while love grew murderous and murder became an act of love that ended in the death of princes.

Epilogue

Do I regret my choices? Forever until the end of time. But show me a mortal who doesn't. In four days' time Herod will finally die, and, contrary to what he thinks, some will mourn him, those who remember a king who fed his people in times of famine and who built them a temple the like of which the world had never seen.

And Salome, who has never been anyone's fool, will let the great and the good of Israel out of the hippodrome unharmed. One of the younger sons of Herod will inherit, but he won't last long. There will be infighting and betrayals; they're a nasty lot the Herods. And generation after generation they will produce weaker and weaker kings until they vanish completely with Herod Agrippa, the emperor Claudius' fickle friend.

But where does that leave us? All the main characters of this story are gone. And now it is time to part. It will be hard to let go. We've travelled together so long. And we can't pretend the experience has left us unaltered. But you must return to your world of cool rain and clouds. And I?

I fancy I will travel. I have heard in the great Aegyptus there is a group of Jewish women philosophers, who have set themselves up on the shores of lake Mareotis. Or perhaps I will visit the great library in Alexandria. Pheroras told me that once he glimpsed a woman scholar within its hallowed halls. A library where a woman might lose herself in books? I like the sound of that.

Adieu

Author's Note

I have been asked why I chose to ignore the massacre of the innocents in this version of Herod's life. The answer is simply that I based my Herod on the books by the first century historian, Flavius Josephus. There is much debate as to whether there is any historical evidence for the massacre beyond its description in the New Testament gospel of Matthew, and certainly Josephus' writings contain no mention of it.

My interest in Herod was in Herod the man. He has been vilified through the ages yet he was, to all accounts, a good king. Certainly no despot or dictator in the usual sense. He loved his people and put himself at great personal risk to protect them and keep them from starvation.

Living in volatile times, where choosing your friends was more dangerous than facing your enemies, Herod brought great stability to his vulnerable little kingdom. And he went beyond that, to pursue his dream of greatness in vast engineering projects, the remnants of which are still visible to this day.

Herod's weakness was, of course, his paranoia, his feeling that he was never truly loved, a psychosis that grew exponentially after his mother died. As the years passed the light of his humanity grew dimmer beneath the encroaching darkness of his soul. And though he could lash out indiscriminately, his worst nature was reserved for his nearest and dearest, those who should have loved him most. In studying Herod's life, it seems that one conclusion becomes clear, those in most danger of the king's fragmenting mind were those who shared the Herod family name.

Acknowledgements

My grateful thanks to all those who encouraged me to continue writing through a very dark period of my life. Jim Campbell has, as always, remained a true and patient support. His honesty, though sometimes painful, is always welcome. Margaret Morrison-Macleod brought great creative insight into the final look of the book. And finally, my thanks to my mother and Madeleine Jewett for their work in proofing the later manuscripts.

The Promise
When promises can cost lives
L. M. Affrossman

Simon's Wife
A Secret History
L. M. Affrossman

Comics and Columbine
An outcast look at comics, bigotry and school shootings
Tom Campbell

Science for Heretics
Why so much of science is wrong
Barrie Condon

CPSIA information can be obtained
at www.ICGtesting.com
Printed in the USA
LVHW091159210719
624771LV00006B/49/P

9 781916 457232